"A masterful storyteller."
—MARGARET GEORGE

The novels of
KATE QUINN *are...*

"Full of great characters."
—Diana Gabaldon, #1 *New York Times* bestselling author

"Epic, sexy."
—*Publishers Weekly* (starred review)

"Deeply passionate."
—Kate Furnivall, author of *The White Pearl*

"A riveting plunge into an ancient world."
—C. W. Gortner, author of *The Queen's Vow*

continued . . .

PRAISE FOR

Daughters of Rome

"A soap opera of biblical proportions . . . [Quinn] juggles protagonists with ease and nicely traces the evolution of Marcella—her most compelling character—from innocuous historian to manipulator. Readers will become thoroughly immersed in this chaotic period of Roman history."

—*Publishers Weekly*

"A fascinating view of four women during the year of the four emperors . . . Regardless of whether you already have an interest in Roman history, *Daughters of Rome* will fascinate you from beginning to end."

—*Book Loons*

"The two sisters are fascinating protagonists . . . Ancient historical fiction fans will enjoy this intriguing look at the disorderly first year after Nero's death."

—*Midwest Book Review*

"Ancient Rome is wonderfully portrayed in this book, with awesome details of first-century Roman political culture . . . I love a complex plot, however, and this one is layered with great characters, engrossing historical facts, and a little romance."

—PrincetonBookReview.com

Books by Kate Quinn

MISTRESS OF ROME
DAUGHTERS OF ROME
EMPRESS OF THE SEVEN HILLS
THE SERPENT AND THE PEARL

The
SERPENT
and the PEARL

A NOVEL OF THE BORGIAS

Kate Quinn

BERKLEY BOOKS, NEW YORK

THE BERKLEY PUBLISHING GROUP
Published by the Penguin Group
Penguin Group (USA) Inc.
375 Hudson Street, New York, New York 10014, USA

USA I Canada I UK I Ireland I Australia I New Zealand I India I South Africa I China

Penguin Books Ltd., Registered Offices: 80 Strand, London WC2R 0RL, England
For more information about the Penguin Group, visit penguin.com.

This book is an original publication of The Berkley Publishing Group.

PUBLISHING HISTORY
Berkley trade paperback edition / August 2013

Library of Congress Cataloging-in-Publication Data

Quinn, Kate.
The serpent and the pearl : a novel of the Borgias / Kate Quinn.
p. cm.
ISBN 978-0-425-25946-7 (alk. paper)
1. Borgia family—Fiction.   2. Rome (Italy)—History—1420–1798—Fiction.   3. Nobility—
Papal states—Fiction.   4. Political fiction.   I. Title.
PS3617.U578S48 2013
813'.6—dc23
2013004891

PRINTED IN THE UNITED STATES OF AMERICA

10 9 8 7 6 5 4 3 2 1

Cover design by Danielle Abbiate
Book design by Tiffany Estreicher

For my husband's remarkable grandmother,
who served as the inspiration for Carmelina:

Mildred Jackson, née Carmelina Mansueto, a fiery Sicilian cook
who has never (to my knowledge!) cooked for the Pope or
defended her virtue from a Borgia prince, but would absolutely threaten
to fry your ears in a pan if you committed the sacrilege of breaking
the pasta into the pot instead of folding it.

PART ONE

May–August, 1492

CHAPTER ONE

Before all else, be armed.

—MACHIAVELLI

Carmelina

When I first came to Rome, I had nothing to my name but a tattered bundle of recipes and a mummified hand. One was my shame and the other, with a little luck, was my future. "Santa Marta, don't fail me now," I murmured, patting the lumpy little bundle under my skirt, and knocked.

I had to knock four times before the door yanked open, and a serving woman with a face like an angry walnut appeared. "Yes?" she said shortly, looking me up and down. I might be tall, long-faced, and plain at best, and I certainly did not look my best that morning, but she didn't have to make it quite so clear.

I pinned a smile into place. "I seek Maestro Marco Santini. He is *maestro di cucina* here?"

"You're not the only one seeking him. He owe you money? He had to pay the last one in spices, and Madonna Adriana wasn't happy—"

"He's my cousin." All true so far, though anything else I told her would likely be lies.

"Well, he's not here. Madonna Adriana's son is to be married, and Madonna Adriana palmed the feast off on that cardinal cousin of hers. Maestro Santini, he'll be at the Cardinal's *palazzo* now with the other servants, making preparations. *Dio*," the serving woman muttered, "let him be there."

"Where?" I felt my smile slipping. I'd crossed half the city already in too-tight secondhand shoes; my feet hurt and sweat collected between my shoulder blades because a late-May morning in Rome was far hotter than it had any right to be. And if this stupid woman kept blocking my way I'd cut off her thumbs and fry them in good olive oil with a little garlic and make her eat them. "It's very important that I find him, *signora*."

She set me on my way with a grudging set of directions, so I spared her thumbs and plunged back into the chaos that was Rome. At any other time I would have gaped at the noise, the crush, the din, so different from the silent waterways I'd always called home, but life for me had narrowed. Carts rumbled past me on one side, swaggering young bravos in parti-colored doublets shouldered past on the other, sharp-eyed servant girls counted coins to wheedling vendors, and stray dogs sniffed my skirts as I passed—but I saw none of it. I plowed through the crowds as if blind, walking a tunnel of noise and color I'd followed south all the way from Venice to Rome. A terror-laced tunnel with Marco at the end of it: a cousin I hadn't seen in five years who had somehow become my only hope for survival.

Well, my eyes might not have registered much, but my nose did. Even as my heart thudded and my feet ached and my frightened thoughts yammered in my brain telling me I was a fool, my nose was busy parceling out the scents and smells of Rome. You can't turn off a cook's nose: My whole life was fracturing around me like one of those impractical Murano goblets that break the instant you look at them, but my nose was happily telling me *manure, yes, from all the carts; ox blood, my, you don't get that in Venice; let's see, that smell there feels like sun baking on marble, and what's that dusty sweet scent? Incense? Yes, incense, of course, considering there's a church or a shrine in every piazza in this city.* Even with my eyes shut, my ever-busy cook's nose could have told me I was no longer in Venice. Venice was sulfur and brick and the hot, melting-sand smell of sun on glass; rot rising from the canals and salt from the lagoon. Venice was home.

Not anymore, I reminded myself grimly as I passed the Ponte Sant'Angelo where they hung the bodies of those thieves less fortunate than me—those, in other words, unfortunate enough to get caught. I saw one fresh corpse, a thief who had had his hands and ears chopped off and strung about his neck before being hanged. He had a smell too, the rich stink of rot. Beside the thief was a heretic who had been hanged upside down and was now little more than a few picked bones. The crows were busy all over the bridge, pecking and gulping, and I said a quick prayer that they'd never peck and gulp at *my* bones. Which at the moment was far from certain, and for a moment I thought my queasy stomach would heave up what little food I'd been able to afford that morning.

But then I saw my goal: the Cardinal's *palazzo* rising rich and arrogant midway between the Campo dei Fiori and the Ponte Sant'Angelo. "Can't miss it," the sour old walnut in the apron had told me. "Not with that huge shield over the door. Got a bull on it—what kind of crest is that for a man of God?" And even if I'd missed the bull, there was no mistaking the crush of people flowing through the great doors. Ladies in figured velvets and air-light veils; clerics in red and purple robes; young dandies with jewels on their fingers and those huge slashed sleeves—yes, a wedding party awaiting the arrival of the bride.

Those grand double doors weren't for me, not in my too-small shoes and the patched ill-fitting dress I'd gotten used off a vendor who tried to tell me the stains at the hem were embroidery and not old mud. But there's always a separate entrance for servants and deliveries, and soon I was knocking on another door. This time I didn't even have time to pat the little bundle under my skirt and mutter a prayer before the door was wrenched open.

"Thank the Madonna, Maestro, you're—" The young man in the apron broke off, staring at me. "Who are you?"

"Carmelina Mangano." I felt a lock of short black hair spring loose on my forehead, the heat frizzing it out from under the headdress I'd improvised from another length of stained cloth. "My cousin, Maestro Marco Santini—"

"Yes?" the apprentice said eagerly. "You know where he is?"

"I was hoping you could tell me."

"Oh, God in heaven," the boy moaned. "He flitted out to play *zara* this morning—just a round, he said, no more than an hour, just to relax him before the feast. Saints help us, it's been hours now and we're sunk—"

Sounded like Marco was up to his old tricks. "A nose for sauces and a hand for pastry," my father had often complained about my cousin, "and nothing between the ears but cards and dice!" But the apprentice had turned away from the door, yammering and moaning to a cluster of flour-aproned serving girls, and my nose started swooning.

Saffron. Sweet Santa Marta, how long had it been since I smelled *saffron*? Or the sweet sizzle of duck being turned on a spit and sauced with honey and the juice from an orange? A sharper smell, that would be fine vinegar, the good stuff from Modena so tart and yet so mellow on the tongue it could bring tears to the eyes . . .

I'd spent the last weeks breathing fear like air, the sour taste of it and the acrid smell of it—and now I smelled something else, something *good*, and the fear was gone. Without meaning to I'd followed my entranced nose inside the kitchens, past the cluster of agitated apprentices. All around me was a kitchen thronged with people, but I just closed my eyes and sniffed rapturously. *Olive oil.* Good olive oil sizzling in a pan rather than lurking sullen and spoiled in a jar; olive oil so fresh from the pressing it would still be bright green when it was poured . . . the sweet burn of pepper just ground . . . the smoky saltiness of cheese fresh-cut from the wheel—I hadn't smelled good cheese in at least a year. Flour, the fine milled stuff so light it drifted in the air, and something savory baking in a crust . . .

Or *burning* in a crust. My eyes snapped open, and I saw a telltale puff of smoke from the nearest oven. I flew across the kitchen, lifting double handfuls of my stained skirt to seize the hot pan and whisk it out of the heat. The pastry shell bubbled black and scorched, and before I could think twice I was shouting.

"Sweet Santa Marta!" I yelled, and the agitated cluster of white-aproned apprentices and serving girls turned to stare at me. "Letting a *tourte* burn? If you worked for me, I'd dice you all into a pottage!"

"Who are you?" one of the serving girls blinked.

"Who cares who she is?" an apprentice snarled. "Maestro Santini's scarpered off to play *zara* again, and if we can't get that bloody wedding feast ready—"

They began to argue, and I just let my eyes travel the kitchens. What a sight. Small, cramped kitchens, for one thing—the Cardinal with the bull over his door might have spent a fortune on that fine tapestried entrance hall I'd glimpsed as the wedding guests streamed in, but he hadn't spent a ducat on his kitchens. Still, the cramped, smoky fireplace and bowed spit and inconveniently placed trestle tables weren't what made me start cursing. It was the sight of the roast birds *not* being turned and basted on their various spits, the bowls of flour *not* being kneaded into pastry, the eggs *not* being whipped into delicious frothy peaks. The sight of iniquity, immorality, pure evil, and possibly the world's end: a kitchen in disorder.

"If we just send out the roast peacock," one of the undercooks was saying, "do you think they'd miss the veal?" But I cut him off.

"How many wedding guests?"

Blank looks passed between them. I wouldn't need to cook this lot into pottage; it was clearly all they had between the ears. "The menu," I snapped. "Tell me."

"Whole peacock in its plumage—"

"Veal with morello cherries—"

"Bergamot pears with cloves—"

A menu pieced itself together out of the disjointed chorus. A good one, too—Marco was a dice-rolling *pazzo*, but the *pazzo* had trained under my father, and he could cook.

So could I. And there wasn't a recipe here I didn't know as well as my own name.

"Someone get me a small knife." I looked around the kitchens, found a discarded apron, and tied it over my disreputable dress. "And where are the onions? Genovese onions, if you have them."

The pot-boys gazed at me as they perspired in the heat of the banked fireplace; the white-aproned apprentices stood behind the long trestle tables with their haphazard arrangement of pots and bowls and looked at their toes; the serving maids whispered behind their hands before sinks mounded with dishes. "Who are you again?" one of the apprentices said at last, rudely. "We aren't taking no orders from you."

Ah, the sound of an insolent apprentice. How long had it been since I'd put one in his place? Even longer than the last time I'd smelled good cheese.

"I'm Maestro Santini's cousin." I smiled benevolently, finding a small knife and beginning my hunt for Genovese onions. "And who are you?"

"Piero. And just because you say you're his cousin—"

"The wedding guests approach, Piero," I interrupted him, leaching the sweetness out of my voice and letting it sink to a venomous whisper. My father's whisper, the one that could whip round a kitchen shriveling spines as it traveled along. "The wedding party will soon arrive, and the peacock isn't even off the spit yet. The pastry hasn't even been rolled. The one dish I see plated in this ninth ring of hell you call a kitchen is a very nice shad over there. *And the cat is eating it.*"

The maids and scullions just looked at each other and mumbled. The cat hissed at me: an enormous tom with a tattered ear who bent to give a leisurely swipe of his tongue along the length of the fish. Beautiful shad, impeccably braised in what I suspected was the sauce of cinnamon and cloves that my father detailed in the packet of recipes in my pouch (page 386, Chapter: Sauces). Though when I made that sauce I liked to add a dash of salt and vinegar for bite, and just a few threads of saffron to give it color . . .

"Out!" I shooed the cat to the floor, helping it toward the door with my foot. "Out, unless you want to end up on the spit! Now, if you batch of parboiled fools can tell me—"

"Maestro Santini?" A woman's voice sounded behind me. I whirled and then hastily followed the example of the maids and curtsied before the stout gray-haired matron in her elaborate headdress. "Maestro Santini, where—" Her eyes traveled apprehensively around the kitchens, as though she were afraid something would explode all over her maroon silks.

"Madonna Adriana," Piero the sulky apprentice said, and then apparently ran out of inspiration. His eyes hunted desperately around the mess of pots and pans, the piles of flour, and the blackened pastry.

"Madonna Adriana da Mila, I take it?" I swept forward with my most radiant smile, hoping she wouldn't notice my stained dress under the apron. "Maestro Santini has spoken to me often of how honored he is to work in your household." No one had told me anything about her, actually—just her name, the employer in Rome who had been fool enough to hire Marco as her cook. Just an idle line of gossip from my father, but I'd followed the slender thread of that name all the way south to Rome. "I am his cousin Carmelina Mangano, newly come from Venice. Naturally I agreed to assist my cousin for such an illustrious occasion as this."

She reared back. "I agreed to pay for three extra pairs of hands in the kitchens, not four—"

"I work for free, *madonna*." I crossed myself. "As is a girl's most sacred duty."

Madonna Adriana brightened—ah, yes, one of those illustrious silk-clad ladies whose eyes shone not for sweets or jewels or compliments, but for the thought of getting something cheap. Better yet, free.

"Your son's wedding, *madonna*?" I continued in my creamiest tones. It's an art, oiling the patrons—my father had no sweet words for his family but he was a master at oiling up his customers. He could have a cheap old bitch like this one sweetened, spiced, and on the spit before she even knew she'd been skewered. "A happy occasion! All is as it should be here, I assure you."

"I heard, er, shouting." My cousin's employer hunted about the borrowed kitchens with her keen peppercorn eyes. "You're certain all will be ready soon? The wedding procession has crossed the *piazza*—"

"And your son will hardly taste a bite of any dish we make, he'll be so eager to see his bride, but all will be ready anyway." I pinned a smile into place like a capon's little trussed legs, not breathing until Adriana da Mila gave a last dubious look.

"Be careful with that good sugar," she warned over her shoulder. "So expensive!" And then, thanks be to God, she was gone.

"So." I turned on the now-cowed cluster of undercooks and maidservants, foot tapping beneath my aproned skirts. "You know who I am. I am the one who can pull this wedding feast out of thin air." *Can you?* my traitorous thoughts whispered. *You haven't done any real cooking in two years.* But too late to think of that now. "I am the one who is going to save your position in Madonna Adriana's household," I continued in the most confident voice I could muster. Their positions, and Marco's with them. Normally I'd have threatened to cut my cousin's ears off and toast them with basil and pine nuts for abandoning a wedding feast midflow, but now I could kiss him. I hadn't even laid eyes on Marco yet, but already he owed me a favor. Or he would, if I truly managed to deliver this wedding feast.

I'd have to. Because it was quite a favor I needed out of him in return.

My heart began to hammer and I tasted fear again in my mouth, sour and rancid, as I thought of just what I was risking. But I had no time for fear, not now. I was Carmelina Mangano, daughter of a great cook in Venice and cousin to another here in Rome, even if he was a card-playing fool. I was twenty years old and maybe all I had to my name was a mummified hand and a keen nose, but I had a houseful of hungry wedding guests coming and may Santa Marta herself cook me and eat me if I sent them away unfed.

"Everyone listen." I clapped my hands, and when that wasn't enough to stop the apprentices' grumbling, I stamped one foot. "I want to see mouths *shut,* mouths shut and hands moving, because if the wedding procession has turned out into the *piazza,* we've no time to waste. Piero, get that peacock off the spit, brush the breast with honey, and stick it all over with candied pine nuts. You, what's your name? Ottaviano, the bergamot pears; peel them in hot wine and roast them with some ground sugar and whole cloves. Serving girls, the *credenza*. If it's groaning with things to nibble, they won't notice if the first dishes are late. Dried figs, olives and capers, those small Neapolitan limes and pink apples over there, Ligurian cheese if you have it—"

"I don't know where—"

"Start looking." My own fingers were flying over the pot of *zuppa* someone had left over a low fire. I took a sniff, and my ecstatic nose told me *pepper, verjuice, sautéed truffles*—ah, yes, the oyster stew on page 64, Chapter: Soups and Stews. I found a small knife and began shucking oysters into the sizzling mix. Tiny roasted chicks were supposed to go into the pot; had anyone roasted any chicks? All that came to eye was a spit of roasted squab. I tossed the knife down and fished out the packet of papers from my pouch (the other pouch, not the one with the dead hand) and flipped to page 84. *Squab may be used in place of chicks*, my father had written in his tight scrawl. *Add more verjuice and some ground Milanese almonds to thicken the broth.* It was the first time I'd looked at his collection of recipes since the day I'd stuffed the loose-bound ragged-edged pile of handwritten paper into my pouch when his back was turned. For a moment I blinked, looking at the tightly packed lines of text, written in the odd shorthand code he'd employed to keep his secrets from thieving rivals. But not from me—I'd read all his recipes, and now the black penned lines of coded spices and meats was all I'd have of him.

Never mind. We'd never shared much, my father and me, besides recipes. If he could see me now, he'd be the first to drag me back by the hair to face the justice of Venice.

"*Signorina*, the *credenza*—" The harried maids were hovering around me now, too resigned or too desperate to object to taking my orders.

"Put the cheeses out, all of them, and the cold meats." I finished with the oysters and took swift stock of the storerooms, calculating dishes. Salty nibbles to make the guests reach for their wine—once they had enough wine in them they wouldn't notice how late the roast peacock was. "The mortadelle, the sow belly, the salt ox tongues—that prosciutto, slice it very thin first so it looks like marble—*skin* those pears, ox-brain, skin them before you add the sugar!" A steward stumped past, muttering, trailed by a stream of servants with wine flagons. "Keep that wine *pouring*," I called after him.

Was that the clamor of guests upstairs already? I flung another prayer heavenward as I threw myself on an onion and began to chop. "Help me now, Santa Marta. *You* know what it's like to cook for important people." Of course, Santa Marta had cooked for our Lord, but I suspected He would be a lot more patient if His food was late than Adriana da Mila's son and his new bride.

On the other hand, maybe not. Hungry guests are hungry guests, and I very much doubted if the heavenly ones were any more useful than the earthly kind when it came to helping in the kitchen. They say Mary was wiser than Marta, sitting at the feet of Christ and worshipping, but I always had more sympathy for Marta. *Somebody* had to do the dishes while everyone else was worshipping at the feet of Christ. Christ must have thought so too, since He made Marta into a saint, and not just any saint but the patron saint of cooks like me all over the earth. Maybe He was grateful to get a good meal for once, instead of having to do all the work Himself conjuring up fishes and loaves.

We understood each other, Santa Marta and I, long before I'd started carrying her dead withered hand around in a pouch under my skirt.

Despite my flying thoughts, I couldn't help smiling as my fingers sealed a crumble of fresh cheese and sweet olive oil and Genovese onions into a pastry crust. The cramped little kitchens were humming like a beehive, the apprentices were working like hired mules, and I imagined I could hear the murmur of guests upstairs: the whisper of expensive silks, the peal of laughter from a happy bride. The clink of fine glasses, the crunch as salted nuts and honeyed dates and morsels of Ligurian cheese disappeared into the mouths of cardinals and wedding guests and bridegroom alike. The *oohs* and *aahs* that went up as the roast peacock, *my* roast peacock, came swaying in at last on the backs of two serving men, proud and feathered and sweet-cooked and not at all looking like it had been whipped together in a quarter of the time it needed (at least if you didn't look too close).

My heart was hammering, my hair was frizzing out of its scarf again, I had no past and only the barest of futures—a future I was trusting to luck, and to my own rusty skills. If either failed me, I'd probably end up on the Ponte Sant'Angelo hanging next to all the other thieves and renegades whose luck and skill had failed them. Or sent back to Venice where an even more gruesome fate lurked, God help me. But my cheese and onion *tourte* was already bubbling sweet and golden in the oven; I had the smell of olive oil and cinnamon in my nose again; my hands and no doubt my face were covered in flour. I hadn't cooked in two years, but I was cooking now—my old skills were rusty, but not gone. I hadn't lost my touch. And for now, that was enough to call happiness.

Leonello

The man across the table from me was proving a bad loser, but most of my opponents are. Men who play for money do not like to lose, and even less do they like losing to a dwarf.

"*Fluxus*," I said, laying four cards down across the wine-sticky table. "All hearts. The pot is mine."

"Wait now," the heavy fellow on my left protested. "You haven't seen my cards yet!"

"Doesn't matter. You have nothing higher than a *numerus*." I leaned forward and began to scoop coins from the center of the table.

He flung his cards down, swearing. A *numerus*—three diamonds and a spade; a hand that wouldn't win you enough to buy a cup of the rotgut wine they served at this tavern, much less the pot in the middle of the table. I grinned and began counting my winnings. "Another round," I told Anna the tavern maid. "Three of whatever my friends are drinking, and my usual."

Anna winked. My usual was water darkened with just enough wine to make it look like the real thing. With Anna's expert hand mixing my wine, I could keep a clear head all through the night while my partners got drunker and drunker. She was the best thing about the tavern, which otherwise wasn't much but a dim little room, ill-lit from dirty windows, its long tables grimed by smoke and rickety at the legs. Besides myself and the three players I'd just fleeced, a pair of drinkers grumbled and swigged wine and rolled grubby sets of dice, and two boys in black velvet sat by a sullen fire playing *zara* and swearing over the game board. The usual mix for a tavern like this: drunks looking to lose the money they'd earned driving carts or working the docks, and rich boys ducking their tutors in search of whores, wine, and a little low-quarters fun.

The heavyset man on my left was still staring at me, flush mounting in his raddled cheeks. "How did you know what cards I held?"

Dio. I gave him a flat look. No one wants to have lost to a dwarf; therefore the dwarf must have cheated. I could cheat, of course—I could palm cards invisibly from my sleeve to my hand; I could deal games that were all hearts, all jacks, anything I wanted. But I didn't. Tavern cheats are too often beaten to a pulp and tossed out the door, and a beating for a man my size was like to kill me. "I used no tricks, I assure you," I said in a bored voice. "Merely mathematical certitude."

"What's that?" Suspicious. "Magic?"

"It means I count, good sir, when I play *primiera*. I count the cards that are dealt, I count the cards that are played; I calculate the certainty of the cards not shown. Calculation produces mathematical odds, not magic, and thus I knew what cards you held in your hand."

"Big words for a little man," one of the other players guffawed. "You got as many words as you've got magic tricks, little man?"

"Counting must be magic for some." I swept the last coins into my purse. "Do you wish to try it for our next game? I understand you will need to take off your boots when the count passes ten."

I waited patiently while he worked his way through it. My insults are wasted on the drunk. When he figured it out, the flush rose dark to his hairline. "You stunted little piglet!"

Not so stunted as your skill at cards, I could have said. *Or that shriveled prick you keep wheedling Anna to grab.* But I didn't say it. No man likes his uglinesses pointed out; it's a sure way to a bloody mouth or a broken nose. Dwarves don't like it either, but a dwarf's looks belong to everyone. Children, men, women; they're free to point and laugh, to say what they like. I'd known that ever since I was small—or rather, since I was very small and first realized I was never going to grow big.

"Another game?" I said instead, and fanned the deck of cards faultlessly with a flick of my wrist.

The drunk slapped one meaty hand down on the table with a crash of cups, and the *zara* players by the fire glanced up. "You runty little cheat, I'll have your guts round your filthy neck—"

The knife thumping down into the table silenced him. I'd slammed the blade down into the wood precisely between his two first fingers without drawing even a whisper of blood—a pretty trick, if I do say so myself, and one that's bought me many a fast exit. The drunk looked down at the knife in the table, and by the time he realized its point had trapped the wood and not his hand, I'd yanked up my blade and Anna had slipped fast between us.

"Another drink?" she wheedled in that tired sweet voice that was the prettiest thing about her. "The little man already paid, you might as well drink it. Here, our best red—"

He allowed her to pull him away and fold the cup of rotgut wine into his hand, and she allowed him to grope a little at her flat breast while giving me a stern look over his shoulder. I made an apologetic face, sliding a coin across the table in her direction, and turned to my other two partners. "Another game?"

"*Primiera*'s not for me," A big affable fellow, handsome and blackhaired, who had grinned when I slammed the knife into the table. Marco, his name was, and for some reason he always smelled like cinnamon. I'd taken a good deal of coin off him in the past months, but he never seemed to hold it against me. "I'm a man for *zara*, myself," he confided.

Zara is a game for idiots. I never played *zara*, or any game of chance for that matter. Chess was the game I liked best, but chess is for aristocrats. Not many chessboards in the lower kind of Roman taverns, the ones where I made my money. "Fortune be with you," I told Marco, though I knew well enough that he'd lose, and snapped my cards together. Old worn cards by now, frayed about the edges and greasy with thumb marks and wine stains, but I'd made good money from them over the years. I might look like a seedy fellow down on his luck—my leather doublet was battered, my shirt had patches on the threadbare elbows, and the hose stretching over my crooked legs fit very ill—but it didn't do for a dwarf to look prosperous. We're easy enough marks as it is without wearing embroidered sleeves or fine cloaks. Besides, the less coin I spent on clothes, the more I had for books. I fingered the coins in my purse, enough for a good meal tonight and a flask of wine to go with it, and tucked my cards away. "I think I will try my luck elsewhere today," I told Anna as she came back, wiping her hands on her apron. "Your friend is still giving me black looks from the fire."

"You can carry my basket to market for me, that's what you can do," Anna told me, hands on hips. "Least you can do after I sweetened that fellow off the idea of choking you. The *cazzo* had his hand up my skirt like he was fishing for gold."

"The flesh of fair Anna is sweeter far than gold," I said, and offered my arm. Anna laughed as she took it, but not at me. Anna never laughed at me, and that made her a rare girl indeed. Woman, really—she claimed twenty years, but I would have bet twenty-five, and she looked thirty. Life serving drinks in a tavern is quick to put a slump in a woman's shoulders, a sag to her breasts, a net of lines about her eyes. But she still had a sweet dent of a dimple beside her mouth, and it flickered at me as we left the tavern.

"You'll get yourself killed one of these days," she warned as we slid into the crowd. Men and women alike were pressing eagerly along the street, craning their necks toward something I was far too small to see— there must be a dancing bear up ahead, or a cardinal on procession. Maybe a dancing cardinal; I'd pay to see that. "You don't have to twit them after you take their money, Leonello. You'll jape at the wrong person someday, and he'll put a knife in your ear."

"Not before I put one in his." Card play wasn't the only skill I'd picked up over a dubious life of scraping by. Knife play was handy for a little fellow like me who didn't have a prayer in heaven of using a sword or flattening his enemies with a punch. I always kept a knife at my belt, sharpened to a whisper, and two or three more tucked away in places that didn't show.

"There's easier ways to make money than playing drunks for it," Anna argued. She slowed her steps to match mine, something for which I was always grateful. I tried not to scuttle when I walked, striding firmly and keeping my toes straight even though it made my misshapen joints ache, but forever running after longer-legged people made it near impossible not to scuttle like a crab. "The tavernkeeper yesterday," Anna went on, "he was going on how he wants some entertainment in the common room in the evenings. You could juggle walnuts, tell jokes, make people laugh. Maybe even get yourself a suit of motley, be a proper jester. Coins would come rolling in, you'll see. You're funny when you want to be, Leonello."

"Anna," I sighed. "Anna of the amber-bright gaze and kind heart, I esteem you greatly, but I fear you mistake me. I do not juggle. I do not tumble. I do not jest, joke, or jig, and for no price in all God's created world do I wear motley."

"You're a touchy little man, you know that?"

"Just as every rose has its thorns, every dwarf must have some claim to distinction besides his height." I kissed her hand formally as though I were one of the swaggering bravos in slashed doublets and curled hair roistering and laughing in the crowd ahead. *Tall* swaggering bravos. "Perhaps you would care to share my meal tonight? The pleasure of your company would be most welcome, at table and bed."

"A fishmonger already asked me," she said, regretful. "I'd rather it was you—you don't smell like fish and sweat between the sheets."

"Another time, perhaps." Anna made a pleasant bedmate every now and then, when I was in the mood for company more lively than my books. She was affable rather than passionate, but a dwarf learned not to expect passion in the women he bought. Affable was good enough, and she would even take a half hour afterward to massage my stunted legs until the crooked muscles loosened. "I can't go giving it to you for free," she'd said the first time I took her to my bed. "I may not be pretty, but even a plain girl like me can't go giving it away, not if she wants to get by in this world."

"Give it away?" I'd snorted. "You're the first woman in years who hasn't wanted double payment to make up for my deformities."

"You're a little man, true enough," she'd said, taking my chin and turning it toward the light. "But *deformed* don't say it right. You'd be handsome, Leonello, if you didn't scowl so much."

And she'd be pretty if she had the coin for a silk dress and a pair of velvet slippers, but she didn't. I didn't say it, though. I had a viper tongue that enjoyed spitting cruel words, but not to the one friend I had in all Rome.

Anna was craning her neck at the crowd lining the street. "I hear music—do you think it's a wedding procession?"

"You're the tall one, sweet lady. You tell me."

She pressed her way into the crowd, me sliding after her among all the legs like a fish negotiating the currents of the Tiber. "The bride, the bride," someone whispered over my head. "I can see her horse!"

"It *is* a wedding procession," Anna said down to me, delighted.

"Pity. I was hoping for a dancing cardinal."

"I don't understand half the things you say." Anna tucked a limp strand of hair back behind one ear. "You think she'll be pretty? The bride, I mean."

"It's some rich boy's new wife," the man behind me disagreed before I could reply. "Five *scudi* says she'll be pockmarked and plain."

I wriggled my way past Anna to the front, with half an eye to following the bride and her retinue from her father's house to her new husband's. Wealthy brides toss coins into the crowds along the way, if they aren't too shy, and I wasn't too proud to pick a coin off the ground. Close to the ground as I was, I could get the lion's share—a lion's share for Leonello the little lion.

Liveried servants were trotting along in columns now, forcing back the crowds on either side of the street as the procession began in earnest. A troop of pages with chests of the bride's belongings—a critical buzz went up at the sight of the elaborately painted wedding chest, wide as a coffin, elaborately gilded and painted with saints. Yes, this was a wealthy bride. Grinning boys tossed flowers into the streets, musicians thrummed lutes not quite in tune with each other . . .

"There she is!" Anna breathed. "Blessed Virgin, will you look at that?"

A white mare wreathed in lilies and roses clopped along impassively under the most glorious of Madonnas.

"Holy Mother," a voice behind me whistled to the man who had bet the bride would be plain. "You lost your five *scudi*!"

A cat may look at a king, they say—and a dwarf may look at a beautiful woman. Most men will be reprimanded for staring at a beauty, warned off by menacing looks from her husband, or a brother's hand clapped on a dagger, or a cold glance from the beauty herself. A man's stare means desire, and the good women of Rome must be safeguarded from the desires of men. But dwarves have no desires, not when it comes to beautiful women, so no one minds if a dwarf gawps. Besides, a beautiful woman's nose rides the air so high she is not likely to look down far enough to see me. Caps were doffed across the street, men bowed outlandishly in hopes of catching the bride's eye, and I just crossed my short arms across my chest and stared coolly.

Dio, but she was a beauty. Perhaps seventeen or eighteen years old, laced into a rosy silk gown draped over her mare's white flanks in such abundant pleats that I could list at least three broken sumptuary laws. Breasts like white peaches, a pale column of a neck, a little face all rosy with happiness—and hair. Such hair, glinting gold in the sunlight, twined with pearls and tucked with cream-colored roses.

Most brides look shy, flustered, bemused. Some cry, some titter nervously, some sit stiff as jeweled saints in a niche. This one laughed like a pealing church bell and kissed her hands to the crowds as she bounced in her velvet saddle with sheer pleasure. She was having far too much fun to cast her eyes down in a crowd like a girl of good birth should, too much fun drinking in everything the world had to offer. Perhaps that was why her dark eyes traveled far enough to see me, looking back at her instead of doffing my hat.

She grinned at me—no other word for it. Grinned and blew me a kiss as if I'd been a tall and handsome man, and then the mare swept her past in a billow of silk and rosewater. I wondered what her new husband was paying for her. Likely he'd decide she was worth it.

"I wouldn't be stuck pouring drinks in a tavern if I looked like that," Anna said wistfully. "I'd be dressed in silk and dining with cardinals, and they'd be pouring drinks for me."

"That's Madonna Giulia Farnese, I heard." The man who'd lost his bet whistled as the last of the liveried servants hurried past, and the crowd began to disperse back to its usual business of shopping, thieving, and gossiping. "She's for one of the Orsini. A dowry of three thousand florins!"

"I heard it was five thousand," someone else disagreed. "And the Orsini are the ones who paid it—"

"Cheap at the price," the first man said lustfully, nodding after the white mare. I could still see a glint of gold where the bride's head bobbed above the crowds.

"Cheap at the price," I agreed, and escorted Anna to market. She chattered on about the pearls in the bride's hair, and the cost of the rose-colored gown, and wouldn't she look pretty in rose-colored silk too if she could ever afford it.

"Not as pretty as the bride did, though," she conceded, and I couldn't help but agree with her. Not many women could match Giulia Farnese, later known to all Rome as La Bella. They should have called her La Bellissima, because from that day to this I've never seen a woman lovelier.

Giulia

I n all the world, there was surely no girl as happy as me: Giulia Farnese, eighteen years old and married at last!

Mind you, weddings aren't always such occasions for bliss. Isotta Colonna cried all the way through her wedding last year, and I'd have cried too if I'd been standing next to a man so fat he was practically a sphere. Lucia Piccolomini cried even harder; *her* husband was a pimply boy of twelve. And my sister, Gerolama, looked sour as a prune when she said her vows, but then Gerolama usually looked sour, and at least she was a good match for her wizened raisin of a husband. "She's lucky to get him," my brother Alessandro had told me privately at the wedding banquet. "A razor tongue and a nose like a blade—we haven't got enough ducats to dower her past all that." He'd pinched my chin judiciously. "You'll do better, I think."

And I had! It had taken time, of course—I'd have been married at fifteen or sixteen like some of my friends, but my father's death (God rest his soul) had put a halt to all the various negotiations, and then my brothers had spent another two years scraping together a better dowry for me. "And wasn't it worth the wait?" Sandro asked, gleeful. "Not just another provincial merchant for my little sister, but one of the Orsini. We're lucky for this match, *sorellina*—you'll live in Rome now, and better than a duchess."

Orsino Orsini: my new husband. I had to wonder what his family had been thinking, naming him that, but he was *young*! Just a year older than me, and not a sphere either, thank you. My new husband was lean as a rapier, fair-haired, with eyes like . . . well, I hadn't gotten close enough to see what color his eyes were, truth be told. We met at the exchange of rings, and his gaze had been downcast the whole time as he fumbled the ring onto my finger and murmured the vows. He took one shy glance at me as I recited the words that made me his wife, and he blushed pretty as a rose.

He was blushing now, stealing shy glances at me from across the splendid *sala*. Oh, why couldn't we sit together at our own wedding feast? We'd be sharing a bed in a few hours; why not a table now? But Orsino in his slashed blue doublet with green-embroidered sleeves sat at one long table with the rest of the men, swamped by a lot of cardinals like fat scarlet flowerpots, while I was immured across the room with the other women, wedged between my stout mother-in-law in her maroon silks and my sister, Gerolama, who sat finding fault with everything. "I've never seen such display. There must be ten different kinds of wine at least; I only had three at my wedding!" I ignored her, smiling across the room at my new husband and boldly raising my glass to him, but he just blinked nervously.

"Did you notice the glass, Giulia?" Madonna Adriana whispered. "All the way from Murano, diamond-point engraving—from my cousin the Cardinal, as a wedding gift to you. You would not believe the expense!"

Judging by the *sala* of his *palazzo*, he could well afford it. The ceiling was high-arched and gorgeously painted; my slippers rested on a wonderfully woven carpet instead of plain flagstones; the long tables were covered in blue velvet and set with gold and silver plate. I tried not to stare, tried to look as if I were used to such careless luxury—after all, the Farnese are a family of noble birth in Capodimonte; I'd been raised in a *castello* overlooking Lake Bolsena in surroundings of great comfort, if not precisely this level of pomp and glitter. But I lost all ability to look blasé when the stream of dishes began appearing, carried in by sumptuously liveried serving men and wafting such tantalizing smells that I had to stop myself from gobbling like a pig at a trough. Yes, my mother-in-law's cardinal cousin was a man of God, but he certainly believed in his luxuries. He had bowed and kissed my hand when my procession arrived in his courtyard, but I couldn't remember which one he was—all cardinals look the same in those red robes, don't they? Fortunately you don't really have to remember their names since they're all "Your Eminence" this and "Your Eminence" that. I flashed my dimples across the room at the whole flock of them, a gesture of coquettish thanks I'd practiced before a mirror as a little girl. At least until my brother Sandro had told me to stop fluttering my lashes because I looked like a drunken hummingbird.

"I didn't get any Murano glass at my wedding," Gerolama was grumbling.

"So kind of His Eminence," I whispered to Madonna Adriana. I was already determined to get on with her—Orsino and I would be sharing the spacious quarters in her family's *palazzo*, at least to start, and I was going to have my widowed mother-in-law eating out of my hand if it killed me. Fortunately, she didn't seem hard to please: just commiserate with her now and then about the rising cost of everything, and she purred like a cat in the cream. Later I supposed Orsino and I would have our own home, but I was in no hurry. Madonna Adriana could bustle with the keys and the account books all she liked; I had no interest at all in fighting her for control of the household. I was going to spend the rest of my days with my feet up in the loggia and my hair spread out in the sun, eating candied figs and playing with my beautiful fat babies. And the rest of my nights in bed with my handsome young husband, making more babies and committing plenty of carnal sins to tell the priest at confession.

"The first of the sweets, *sorellina*." Sandro crossed the room with a flourish of a bow, presenting a dish for me. "Peaches in grappa—your favorite."

"You'll make me fat, brother," I complained.

"Oh well, I'll eat them then." He popped a soft spiced peach into his mouth. "Delicious. Madonna Adriana, your cook has outdone himself."

"Give me those!" I snatched the plate, smiling at my elder brother. He was six years older than I, and we shared two other brothers as well as sour Gerolama, but Sandro and I had always been each other's favorites. We had the same dark eyes that snapped laughter even when we were trying to be serious, and we'd grown up making faces at each other during Mass and getting smacked by our harried mother whenever we smuggled a grass snake into the priest's shoe. It had been Sandro who held me when our mother died giving birth to a baby that didn't live. Two years ago when my father joined her in heaven, my older brothers had been the ones to assume the mantle of family authority, but it had been Sandro who stroked my hair and vowed that he'd look after me now. I'd missed my brother terribly when he went to the university at Pisa to begin his career as a cleric, but now he had come back to Rome to start work on the lowest ecclesiastical rung as a notary. He wasn't a very good notary, and I didn't imagine he'd be a very good cleric either— Sandro adored chasing girls too much to ever abide by any vow of chastity, and he had a theatrical streak better suited to a jester. But even if he was the worst churchman on earth, there was no better company to be had at the evening *cena* table.

"So tell me, Sandro—" I lowered my voice as Madonna Adriana began telling Gerolama how terribly expensive the roast peacock had been. "Why isn't my husband getting up from his chair to give me peaches in grappa?"

"Have some pity for the poor lad! Married at nineteen, and not to some cross-eyed convent girl he can intimidate, but to a nymph, a Helen, a Venus!" Sandro thumped a fist to his heart, a dagger from the heavens. "As Actaeon was struck down for daring to gaze upon Diana in her glory, so young Orsino fears to gaze upon his bride in all her glory—"

"Shut up, Sandro. Everyone's looking."

"You like everyone looking." Sandro grinned, coming back down to earth. "My little sister is the vainest creature in all God's creation."

"You sound like Mother." God rest her soul, she had always been scolding me for vanity—"You think the Holy Virgin worries how she looks, Giulia *mia*?" But from what I could see, the Holy Virgin didn't need to worry how she looked because she was always beautiful, in every painting I'd ever seen of her; beautiful and serene in some becoming blue gown-and-veil combination that had probably been sewn by angels. We earthly girls had to put a bit more thought into our appearance if we wanted to look half so fine, so I just said an extra Paternoster every morning in repentance for the sin of vanity as I plucked my eyebrows.

"Never mind," Sandro was saying. "Young Orsino will get up his courage soon enough after another dance or two."

"So let's encourage him." I gave the dish of peaches a regretful look, sucking the sweet grappa off one fingertip, but really I'd already eaten heartily as a peasant tonight (oh, that roast peacock, and there was some kind of delicious pastry thing with sweet cheese and onions!). "Dance with me, Sandro."

"Does a priest dance?" Sandro rolled his eyes up to the heavens with great piety. "You offend my clerical dignity, not to mention my vows."

"Your vows weren't too offended when you were flirting with Bianca Bonadeo earlier. During *my* vows, mind you."

"Then a *basse-danse* at once."

"The *basse-danse* is boring!" Orsino and I had already opened the floor with a *basse-danse* earlier in the evening. All that decorous gliding around palm to palm, and he hadn't quite had the courage to look me in the eye. I preferred something livelier from the viols; a tune that got my blood running, and maybe gave me a chance to show a flash of ankle in the turns. "Let's dance *la volta*."

"You're the bride, *sorellina*." A word to the musicians, and a smattering of applause rose as my brother led me out to the floor. I gave a graceful half spin, flaring my airy rose-colored skirts to acknowledge the applause before the lively beat of the viols began, and I seized Sandro's hand. A beat or two as we pirouetted through the first steps, and then Sandro put his hands to my waist and tossed me into the air in the first lift. I knew how to land so my skirts belled, throwing my head back and laughing, and I dipped my bare shoulders into the candlelight in the direction of my new husband. *Look at me, Orsino,* I begged silently. *Look at me, dance with me, love me!*

G erolama tried her best to get me good and scared before the bedding. "The duties of marriage are heavy," she whispered as she helped Madonna Adriana and the other laughing women unlace my rose-colored dress. "Very heavy indeed."

"Only as heavy as the man," I giggled, and she limited herself to martyred glances after that. I felt giddy, high-sailing as a full moon in the sky, flushes coming so hot to my cheeks that I pressed my hands to my face to cool it.

"You're far too excited, child," Madonna Adriana clucked at me as she unlaced my sleeves. "Try not to expect too much."

Expect too much? I was about to be a woman at last! I'd heard dark whispers of how much it hurt, of course, but I didn't believe a word.

Mares didn't shriek pain when they were ridden, and I didn't think I would either.

Oooof, what a relief to get out of that tightly laced dress. I really had eaten too much, but those little marzipan *tourtes* that had circulated at the end of the night on brightly colored majolica plates really had been too delicious to resist. Besides, I always eat when I'm happy. Orsino had summoned the courage by then to offer me the dish himself. "You're beautiful, my lady," he'd said shyly.

"Your lady wife," I'd corrected, and saw with delight that he had blue eyes.

"Into bed with you now." Gerolama had tied my shift up tight around my neck again, and she held the weight of my hair out of the way as I dived between the sheets. Silk sheets, not linen—I was hard-pressed not to gape again at the sheer openhanded richness of everything around me. Was Madonna Adriana's household as sumptuous as this? I wriggled my toes against the soft silk and dearly hoped so. I'd been raised in simpler surroundings—the trees and lakes of Capodimonte instead of the basilicas and loggias of Rome; provincial simplicity instead of urban luxury. I *longed* for urban luxury.

"Such hair you have," one of the other women admired as Gerolama piled my hair into the bed beside me. "So long!"

"You wouldn't believe how much trouble it is to comb," I confided, but I did adore my hair. Dark blond, the color of crystallized honey, but I sunned it every day in the garden over the brim of an enormous straw hat, and the sun shot streaks of yellow-gold and apricot-gold and white-gold through the mass of it till it looked (a certain besotted page boy had told me once) like it had been mined out of the earth instead of grown on my head. And it was long hair, too—when I shook it out loose as I did now, it covered me in great slow ripples all the way to my feet. "Only because you're so short," Gerolama told me, but it wasn't my fault I got the blond waves and she got the meager tufts. I'd spent hours when I was little massaging her scalp with chamomile paste so her hair would grow in faster, and what had I gotten for my pains? Slapped hands when it didn't work. I ask you.

Surely Orsino would like my hair. I wished I could strip off this filmy shift and greet him in nothing but my hair, but I didn't quite have the courage. "Tomorrow night," I promised myself, and settled for tugging my shift off my shoulders again as soon as Gerolama and the other women left. What was the use of having nice firm white breasts like mine if no one saw them? Besides, they were Orsino's breasts now just as much as they were mine.

My bed had a striped cover of black and white velvet, and the sheets were damp with crushed rose petals. The tapers threw flickering golden shadows around the chamber, striking glints off my hair, and I experimented with various poses. Reclining or sitting up? Hands folded, or arranged beneath my cheek? Hair pulled forward over one shoulder, or both? Oh, Holy Virgin, would he just *get* here? I'd had quite a lot of wine at the wedding feast, and if Orsino dawdled too long I'd be fast asleep.

I yawned. The candles had burned down halfway.

In the end, he caught me dozing. The creak of the door brought me bolt upright in bed, wiping frantically at the corners of my mouth (*Holy Virgin, please don't let my husband catch me drooling!*) and biting my lips to give them color. Just think, tomorrow I'd be a married woman in her own right, and allowed to wear lip color if I wanted, instead of bite-bite-bite till my mouth was chapped.

He entered the room tentatively, the candle in his hand casting wavery shadows. His neck looked skinny above his fine nightshirt, and his fair hair was mussed. He was chewing the inside of his cheek nervously, until he caught sight of me sitting in the big bed with my hair all around me, and then he just stared. He had a slight squint, I saw, but hardly noticeable when he dropped his eyes and blushed as he was doing now.

I brushed my hair back away from my bare shoulders and smiled at him. "Orsino," I started, and didn't really know what to say next, so I just laughed softly. Look at the pair of us—I think he was more nervous than I was.

Never mind. We'd figure it out together.

I lifted my hand with a smile and held it out to him. "Come to bed, husband."

He stared at me a long moment. Just stared, and then he gave a resigned little sigh. "Excuse me," he mumbled. "I wish—I'm very sorry, believe me, but I'm not allowed." And he turned away with his candle and rushed out of the room. The click of the door closing seemed very loud.

I gazed at the door, stupefied.

Don't expect too much, Madonna Adriana had told me.

Whatever I'd expected of my wedding night, it certainly wasn't this.

CHAPTER TWO

—✦—

For those destined to dominate others,
the rules of life are turned upside down.

—RODRIGO BORGIA

Carmelina

It's a bit tricky, knowing what to send up to the bride's chamber the morning after her wedding. If you don't know the bride (and as busy as I'd been yesterday, I hadn't gotten one glimpse of Madonna Giulia Farnese), then your best course is to deputize a maid to tiptoe up to the chamber door and have a nice long listen through the lock. If you hear weeping, then prepare a nice bracing hot posset with red wine and strong spices, something her mother-in-law can carry in to her along with a lot of soothing words about how marriage isn't really so bad. If you hear giggling and whispering through the door, then you send up something light that can be eaten by two, preferably fed to each other with the fingers while making a great deal of mess that can be kissed away with more giggles. A hot sop with morello cherries works well—strips of butter-fried bread and a dipping sauce of cherries and sugared wine always goes down a treat with hungry young lovers, and the small joke of cherries plucked and eaten is sure to make them giggle.

But I hadn't even collared a maidservant yet to send up to the bride's door when the bride herself came padding into the kitchens. The maid-servants were all still asleep in the black hour just before dawn, as was the rest of the household. Except, apparently, for me and the bride.

"Excuse me," a voice said behind me, and I nearly jumped out of my skin. I'd been far too nervous and jittery to sleep after the wedding festivities; I'd spent the night in the empty kitchens restlessly poking at the banked fires, snatching up a broom to sweep the flagstones one more time, or flipping through my father's collection of recipes and hearing his hectoring voice in my head. Hastily I dropped the cloth I'd been using to wipe down the tables, and offered a curtsy to the small silk-clad figure now hovering in the doorway.

"Madonna Giulia?" I hazarded. I hadn't had even a glimpse of the bride in all the frantic wedding preparations yesterday, but the carvers and maidservants who carried my dishes out to the guests had been all abuzz about the bride's hair, which supposedly came all the way to the floor when loosed—and the girl now standing in the kitchen doorway had hair that cascaded all the way to the floor in a lustrous honey-blond curtain. I couldn't say I envied it—if I had hair down to my feet it would just pick up all the stray chicken bones and dustings of sugar that seem to accumulate on every kitchen floor no matter how busy you've kept the scullions with their brooms. But it certainly looked lovely on her. "What can I do for you, Madonna Giulia?"

"I don't know." Her eyes barely fastened on me; she stood in her blue silk wrapper in the dawn chill, tracing one bare toe over a crack in the stone floor. "Do you have any more of those little marzipan things?"

"I do, *madonna*." I rummaged among the neatly covered dishes where I had stored the leftovers of the wedding feast, trying not to stare at her. Adriana da Mila's son had bagged himself a beauty for a bride: small and voluptuous and juicy as a roast duckling just off the spit—but her little oval face was morose. "So you liked my marzipan *tourtes?*" I couldn't help but ask.

"They turned out to be the best part of the night," she said with a gusty sigh. "So I thought I might as well come down and eat a lot more."

I offered her the dish, pleased. I *am* very good with marzipan—it takes a certain touch, a sort of delicate firmness. "I'd thought to come up in another hour and offer you a hot posset, *madonna*, or maybe some of these leftover baked apples—"

"I'll take the apples too." She took the dish out of my hand, turning in a swirl of silk wrapper and hair. "Thank you."

"I wish you every happiness in your marriage, *madonna*," I called after her with another curtsy. "Enjoy the marzipan."

"There's not much else to enjoy," she said, exiting with another sigh. I stared after her for a moment before shrugging and sinking down at the table I'd just wiped down. I was too tired to worry about moody brides. She'd liked my food—that was all the cook ever needed to know.

Sweet Santa Marta, but I was tired. Even after the last of the guests had wobbled home, tipsy but replete—even after the last table had been cleared in the *sala*, the last dish covered and stored, the last scraping swept up in the kitchens—even after I'd sent the maidservants and apprentices to their beds, I hadn't been able to rest. They trailed off far too tired to question my orders anymore, yawning and giddy from hard work (and the gulps of wine they'd been able to steal from the flagons before they went out to the guests). I was far too exhausted and nervous even to doze in a chair by the kitchen fire—and besides, Marco might come home at any moment, and if someone spoke to him before I did, then this frail concoction of a plan I'd constructed like a soap bubble in a sink might go *pop*.

In the end, I might as well have gotten a good night's sleep. The household rose before dawn, servants and pot-boys first, and now they were starting to look at me oddly again and wonder why I'd appeared from nowhere and why they were following my orders at all. So I didn't give them time to think. "*Basta*," I called, stamping my foot on the flagstones to get their attention. "We're to pack all Madonna Adriana's supplies into the wagons by dawn, down to the last kitchen pot and sack of sugar. She'll want everything back at the Palazzo Montegiordano by the time it comes to eat in her own *sala* tonight, and I've only met the woman once but I know she'll count every last spoon and dock it from your wages if it's missing."

That started a grudging ripple of laughter. "So start carting everything out into the courtyard," I called over the ripple. "The mouths are shut and the hands are moving; that's how it works in my kitchens. And if so much as one packet of saffron goes missing from what I spent all night counting . . ."

Soon I was directing the flow of work as the undercooks packed up the dishes they had brought for the wedding feast's preparation. No hot flood of excitement and wonderful smells this time to keep me whirling through the hours, just sheer exhausted discipline. But being a cook isn't all wafts of warmed honey, and pastry rolling out sweet and flaky under your hands. It's shouting and sweeping and scouring and scrubbing as well, and I'd been raised to know it. I had Madonna Adriana's every last spoon and servant packed into the wagons by the time the sun rose—and it was when I ran back to the Cardinal's dark cramped kitchens to take a last look around that my wayward cousin returned.

"Sweet God in heaven," I heard a man breathe behind me.

I turned, fists on hips, and looked at my cousin leaning in the doorway between the kitchens and the courtyard. All six and a half slightly ashamed feet of him. "Hello, Marco."

His eyes traveled over me, puzzled at first. He hadn't seen me for at least five years, after all, and even when we'd shared the same kitchen under my father's tutelage, Marco hadn't paid me any attention. Why would he? A favored apprentice with his eye on a master cook's status had no time for his skinny broom-handle of a distant cousin, even if she was always underfoot with her loud opinions about what should go in the sauce. "Carmelina?" he said at last.

"The very same," I said, and marched past him to yell into the courtyard for the wagons to proceed on to the Palazzo Montegiordano without me. "Sit down, Marco. We have a lot to discuss."

In the end I didn't see any point in tact. I told him everything (or almost everything), and by the time I was done he was pale and shaking.

"Oh, sweet Jesu," my cousin groaned. "Sweet Jesu, Holy Mother, and Santa Marta, help us."

I could have told him Santa Marta had already helped me considerably, but matters were dicey enough without bringing a mummified hand into the mix. I patted the little bundle under my skirt. "Marco—"

"What have you *done*?" He stared at me across the trestle table where we'd both collapsed. The cramped little kitchens were sunny, scrubbed, and eerily quiet after yesterday's bustle—Madonna Adriana's staff had risen early to pack and go home, but the rest of the Cardinal's household was bound to be sleeping late after the festivities. I reckoned we had a good hour of solitude here before we'd have to be gone.

"I don't know what I'm doing," I said honestly. "But I won't go back there."

"You have to go back! You know what will happen to you if you don't? To *me* if I help you?"

I looked at my cousin, sitting there with his big hands lying helpless on the scrubbed trestle table. I'd been in love with him when I was twelve, and who wouldn't be? Tall, broad-shouldered, arms corded with muscle from hours of whipping eggs and shouldering huge joints of meat onto spits; springing black curls and an easy smile; and if that weren't enough, real talent in the kitchen. Marco's big hands could whip up the most delicate of pastry shells, the airiest of sugar confections, the subtlest of sauces, and I'd loved him for that as much as his broad shoulders and his white gleam of a smile. But I hadn't hankered after him long before realizing that for all his other gifts, Marco Santini had not one drop of common sense.

"No one's going to catch me," I said in as soothing a tone as I could muster. "Who looks for a runaway Venetian girl clear down in Rome?"

"How *did* you get so far south on your own?" His eyes ran over my cropped head. I'd finally stripped off the flour-and-egg-smeared rag I'd kept tied about my head, and my chopped hair had no doubt fluffed up in hundreds of frizzy little unbecoming black curls.

"I traveled as a boy," I confessed, running a hand over my mangled head. "I bought a doublet and hose secondhand in Venice, and a mask.

It was Carnival, so everyone was in masks." Not much of a disguise, really, but I was tall and skinny enough to pass for a lanky boy, and the mask had helped. Half the revelers on the road those long weeks had been japed up in hilarious disguise and outlandish beaked masks for the pre-Lenten revelries. What a nightmare of a journey it had been. Sleeping in inns where the rats ran squeaking and scampering over my legs at night; choking down the stale bread and rock-hard meat that were all I could afford; the achingly slow boats that stopped at every village port and turned a journey of weeks into more than a month.

"Where'd you get the money for travel?" Marco was demanding. "I know you didn't have any coin!"

"I got my hands on enough to get here," I hedged. Never mind how; that was none of Marco's business. Besides, if he knew I had any left over, he'd just want to borrow it for a sure bet on a cockfight. Marco always had a sure bet on a cockfight.

"Well, I don't know why you came to me, but I can't help you." He slumped in his chair, running a hand through his curly hair. "I don't even have a post anymore. Madonna Adriana, if she hasn't dismissed me already—"

"Yes, your post. Tell me, Marco, where *were* you yesterday? When you should have been applying yourself to Madonna Giulia Farnese's wedding banquet?"

His eyes shifted sideways. I reached for the jug of wine I'd corked and set aside earlier, pouring out two cups and watering them well. "*Zara* this time?" I asked, noncommittal. "Or the dogfights?"

"Both," he muttered. "Lost a hand or two at cards, so I thought I'd change my game. Just a match or two, I couldn't leave yet—my luck was just about to turn! I never meant—"

"You never do," I said, but without heat. This wasn't the time to be angering my cousin. I pushed the wine into his hand, watching as he took a doleful sip. Wine had never been Marco's vice; only gaming. My father had finally sacked him for it, distant cousin or no.

"You still have your post with Madonna Adriana," I said as he folded his big hands around the cup. "I covered for you."

"You?" His head jerked up. "How?"

I shrugged, taking a sip from my own cup to hide my smile. Really, I'd have felt quite smug if I hadn't been so tired and scared. Two years out of a kitchen, at least for any serious cooking, and I'd pulled off a wedding feast for near on a hundred guests. With a strange kitchen, strange cooks, *and* no warning to speak of, thank you. "My father trained me too, Marco," I said instead. "Madonna Adriana never knew you were gone."

"My thanks—" he began, and stopped. "Oh, Jesu, I see what you're doing. You want—"

"Let's not talk about what I want. Just what I'm owed." I kept my voice mild. "You owe me, and you know it."

His big shoulders slumped even further.

I traced a circle on the table's scrubbed surface. "I can be an asset, you know. Help you in Madonna Adriana's kitchens. Help manage your apprentices—that Piero is trouble; you should sack him and take on someone who doesn't steal wine from the *credenza* and grope the maidservants. I'll help with the big banquets too, fill in when you have to hire extra hands—"

"And what do I do?" His head jerked up, anger coloring his cheeks. "What do I do for you, *cousin*?"

"Just take me in." A little meekness wouldn't go amiss, I judged, and though my father had been fond of pointing out that I didn't have a meek bone in my body, I knew well enough how to fake it. "A place to sleep, Marco. My meals. That's all."

"That's *all*? I'm off to the cells if anyone finds out I helped you. Or worse." He bolted another mouthful of his wine. "Why can't you just go home, little cousin? Your father, he might shout and roar, but surely he wouldn't—"

"He'll never take me back now, not the way I've disgraced the family." I gave a chop of my hand, cutting off that line of action like a cleaver. My family in Venice—my father, my mother, my younger sister—they might as well be dead to me now, because I was certainly dead to them. "You see, there's this."

I reached under my apron and tossed the folded packet of pages across the table at Marco.

He knew that packet almost as well as I did. "Where did you—" He lunged for it, thumbing rapidly through the pages, pausing at the stain at the corner of page 112 where a thumbprint of egg white and nutmeg showed in a familiar yellow smear. "Your father's *original* recipes?"

"Every last one he's ever collected over forty years of cooking."

Marco's face had lit up, but now it fell again. "But they're in code— they always were, he never taught anyone the code—"

"I know it. I can teach you. Then you'll have all his recipes." Except for the one ingredient or two that my father always left out of the written recipe and left to memory, just in case someone stole his code. May God forgive me for saying my father was a suspicious bastard, but most cooks are. Of course, I knew all the omitted ingredients, too.

Marco's dark eyes lifted, regarding me keenly across the table. "How did you get your hands on this? He's always kept them closer than a church keeps its relics."

I couldn't help but wince at the word *relic*. Yes, good thing I hadn't brought up the mummified hand. No need for my skittish cousin to find out he was sheltering a thief of far worse things than recipes. "He sometimes takes his recipes to show prospective customers," I said instead. "It impresses them—the codes, the secrecy. He'd angle visitors anywhere he could find them; get them talking about the wedding feast they were planning for their niece or the farewell *cena* they were hosting when their son left for university. Then he'd whip out his recipes and show how he could do it better than whoever they'd hired. He got quite a number of new patrons that way." My father would be angling for clients at my funeral Mass, of that I had no doubt. "The last time he visited me, I—well, I waited till his back was turned, just before he left, and snatched them out of his pack." I'd already had the half-formed plan of fleeing. Once I had that packet of recipes in my hand, the plan had crystallized from yearning into action. That was when the fear had started, too—what my father would do to me if I was caught, what the laws of Venice would do to me—but it hadn't been enough to stop me.

"Your father will kill you," Marco groaned. "He'll kill *me*, if he catches us—"

Probably. "Marco, do you really have nothing but ricotta between the ears?" I put just a hint of tartness into my voice, like the last squeeze of lemon juice going into a sweet sauce to give it bite. "Forget my father and look at what I'm giving you. Your post with Madonna Adriana, safe and sound—and with my father's recipes you can be the best cook in Rome just as he's the best cook in Venice. In return, all I ask is shelter. A place in the world for your newly orphaned cousin Carmelina, come to live with her cousin and of course devote her labors to his kitchens."

He chewed his lip.

"Madonna Adriana won't fuss," I wheedled. "Not when I work free. And her new daughter-in-law can't stop raving about my marzipan *tourtes.*"

Marco looked at me, then down at his wine. I drained mine, not taking my eyes off him though I heard movement in the next room. The Cardinal's household, stirring at last. Servants would be bustling into the kitchens at any moment.

"So—" I raised my eyebrows. "Do we have a bargain?"

Giulia

A good dose of sugar does wonders for one's state of mind. After devouring all the marzipan and half the baked apples at the crack of dawn (I always eat when I'm upset), I had a cautious flash of insight: Maybe my husband hadn't come to my bed last night because he was drunk and felt he might prove incapable? Even virgin girls like me knew what could happen to a man after too much wine. Perhaps he'd had one cup too many last night, so his mother scolded him and told him to wait until he was sober. Could that be why he'd said he wasn't *allowed*?

Surely Orsino would come to me today. Perhaps even this morning: a passionate young man kicking down my door, impatient to possess his beloved. It was just like the fantasies I'd dreamed up as I read Petrarch's sonnets, imagining what would happen if Petrarch had ever summoned the courage to simply sweep golden-haired Laura into his arms rather than moon about kissing her discarded gloves and writing her some admittedly excellent poetry. Surely Orsino had more courage than Petrarch—at least I was his wife, unlike Laura, who had been somebody else's wife—and Orsino had a perfect right to sweep into my chamber if he liked. So I stuffed the crumb-scattered plates under the cushions on the wall chests, rinsed my mouth with rosewater from the ewer until my breath was sweet, pinched my cheeks to make them glow, and crawled right back into bed with my hair freshly combed about my shoulders. And once again, waited.

But the only person to come through my door without a knock was my mother-in-law, which was not what I had in mind at all.

"Ah, you're awake," she said, with no surprise on her face at all to find me alone. "I'd thought to let you sleep, after such a long night."

Did she know exactly how I'd spent that night? I looked at Madonna Adriana da Mila, square as the bed in a gown of violet velvet with embroidered golden-brown sleeves, her face placid under the fringe of darkened curls escaping her matron's headdress.

"Up, up, now," she said with a brisk clap of her hands. "We must get you dressed at once. There is someone who wishes to speak with you."

"Orsino?" I tossed the sheet aside. Oh, did I have questions for my new husband, and whether or not a wife was supposed to present herself in modesty and silence, I intended to ask them.

"No, my son left early this morning. We have an estate at Bassanello, you know—his attentions were urgently required."

"So soon?" All my sugar-induced hopefulness drained away. "I assume I will be traveling to join him."

"Perhaps," she said brightly, and patted my cheek. "Now, I think the white and gold brocade—I saw it in your wedding chest yesterday, it will be just the thing with all that splendid hair of yours."

Maids came bustling in then, giggling and whispering and whisking me out of bed before I could protest any further. I was briskly laced into the white and gold brocade dress, and Madonna Adriana herself spent a great deal of time pulling puffs of gold-embroidered shift through the slashes of my sleeves. "Spanish brocade, so expensive, but *what* quality. Your brothers certainly spoil you!" A skinny cheerful-looking girl introduced as Pantisilea—"your personal maid from now on, my dear"—looped my hair in a lot of elaborate coils on the back of my head and covered it with a filmy veil, and I stood in the middle of all the bustle and wondered what in the name of the Holy Virgin was happening. I wanted my own chamber back, even if it was half the size of this one and not nearly as luxurious; I wanted sour Gerolama with her suspicious eyes ferreting everything out in a heartbeat; most of all I wanted Sandro, who might have a theatrical streak to suit a traveling player, but who for all his jokes and japes wouldn't let anything happen to his *sorellina*. But I wasn't under Sandro's protection anymore, or my family's. Just my young husband, who suddenly wasn't anywhere to be found.

"My, aren't you a vision," Madonna Adriana beamed. "No necklace, dear, you'll soon see why—yes, I think you can go. Down to the courtyard, now, and don't dawdle."

I looked at her bland broad face again for a moment. "Very well."

If you don't know what lies ahead, make a good dramatic entrance and hope for the best. I swept down a series of steps with my chin high, through one vaulted chamber and then another, into the framing arches of the loggia lining the courtyard. I stopped there for a moment, blinded by the sudden glare of sunlight from the open sky above after the dimness of the *palazzo*, and when I blinked and shaded my eyes, I saw before me a man's hand.

"Come," said a man's deep voice.

I'd prepared a pretty little speech of inquiry on my way down the stairs, meaning to ferret out my husband's absence at once, but instead I found my hand resting on the broad ringed one before me. The hand of Madonna Adriana's august cousin the Cardinal, who had so generously hosted my wedding feast. What was his name? I'd been introduced to him half a dozen times, but all cardinals looked alike to me: just a flock of unctuous scarlet bats.

"Your Eminence," I managed, and sank into a curtsy on the marble step.

"No, no." He raised me up. "Age must bow before beauty, and I see here a man thoroughly old and a girl thoroughly beautiful."

He made a graceful bow, more suited to a man in doublet and hose than one in clerical robes. When he straightened I saw he was taller than I, even though I stood two steps above him. To match that majestic height he was built like the bull on the emblem above his door, a bull with an eagle's nose and dark eyes that gleamed with some inward amusement. His words had a Spanish burr.

"Come," he said again, and drew me down into the mossy space of garden. "I suppose you wonder why Madonna Adriana sent you to me?"

"To thank you for hosting my wedding feast," I hazarded. He was leading me on a deliberate promenade, through banks of May-blooming flowers and marble statues in niches twined with vines. A fountain splashed in the garden's center, a stone nymph pirouetting through the splash of water. "It was a beautiful banquet, Your Eminence," I said truthfully enough. It was only what came after that had been so utterly unsatisfactory. Orsino and I should have been parading around this fountain right now, laughing a little, and I would have plucked one of the spicy gillyflowers growing from that marble urn and tucked it behind his ear, and if he'd had a drop of gallantry in his soul he'd have kissed it and given it back to me . . .

"I am glad you enjoyed yourself." The Cardinal's voice was deep, sonorous, made to reverberate around dimly lit cathedral vaults. No wonder he had gone into the Church. "I confess I had another motive for hosting your wedding banquet."

"Do you know why my husband is gone so suddenly?" I couldn't help asking.

"To that I also confess."

"What?" I stopped, hand still resting on his. "*You* sent him away?"

"I did," the Cardinal said frankly.

I opened my mouth to say—well, Holy Virgin knew what. But—

"Is this her?" a boy's voice said behind me. I turned to see a tall auburn-haired youth only a year or two younger than me, his loose shirt and hose wrinkled as if he'd slept in them. One of my younger guests last night, I vaguely remembered, though I hadn't been paying attention to callow boys now that I had a husband of my own.

"Juan," the Cardinal said mildly. "Go away."

"What? I just wanted to see the new concubine." Juan looked me up and down with a leer fit for a lecher of fifty. "You can come whore for me if you don't want His Eminence my father," he told me with another smirk.

"Juan," the Cardinal said much less mildly, and the boy straightened.

"Just wanted a look! I could have a concubine too, you know. I'm old enough!"

"You are sixteen, and a nuisance. Leave us." The Cardinal turned back to me, nonchalant, as the boy mumbled something that might have been an apology and beat a hasty retreat. "I hope you will pardon my son, *madonna*. He is young, and inclined to be rude in the face of beauty. A form of awe you must be well acquainted with."

I barely heard him—the bottom had just dropped out of my stomach. "Forgive my slowness, Eminence," I said at last. "I'm just a stupid girl, so I didn't realize—you sent my husband away so you could have me yourself."

"Yes," the Cardinal said cheerfully.

The bottom fell out of my stomach, and a great tremble went through me. Astonishment, disbelief—but mostly rage, and without stopping to think, I slapped him. A good hard slap, too—I could snap a man's head around like a whip with one of those.

The Cardinal was rocked clear back onto his heels. He looked at me, lifting a hand to his face—I saw just how dark and glittering his eyes were, and all my rage turned to horror. Oh, Holy Virgin, I'd just struck a man of God—a *cardinal,* no less—

Then he threw his head back and laughed.

"Stop laughing!" I stamped my foot on the garden path, and then wished I hadn't because I felt like a child. "Nobody should be laughing after I hit them! I have three brothers and a sister who hates me; I *know* how to slap!" A red mark was already rising very nicely on his cheek.

"Indeed you do," the Cardinal choked, still laughing. "But dear God in heaven, I haven't been slapped by a pretty girl in decades, and I didn't realize how I'd missed it. Almost enough to make me feel young again. I'm sixty-one," he added, "if you're wondering."

"I'm not wondering anything except how to get out of this—this den of vice!" I was trembling head to toe, under my heavy white and gold skirts. "Did my husband know about this arrangement, or did you cook up some crisis to take him away?"

"Of course he knew. He was well paid, too. Though he probably regretted the bargain, once he saw what he was giving up."

"Bargain—when did you *make* this bargain? I've only met you yesterday!"

"On the contrary; we've met half a dozen times. Clerics all look the same to girls with their eyes on the young gallants." He ran a hand over his dark hair with its bare dent of a tonsure, rueful. "You came to Rome last winter, when your brother Angelo was looking for a wife. Probably he was hoping to show you off as well; get the bidding started. I saw you at Mass, oh, at least a dozen times. Shall we say that you stood out? I once lost an entire sermon contemplating your profile."

I narrowed my eyes at him. My insides churned in fright, but I was not going to let him see that. "And you thought, just by watching me a few times in church, that I would be willing to be your—plaything?"

"Watch ten girls of marriageable age at Mass," he said, and his ringed hands sketched the scene in a few eloquent gestures. "Two will listen with great attention—genuinely pious." He tilted his head down; suddenly the picture of a demure young girl. "Five more will listen with false attention, because their mothers told them a show of their devout and hopefully pretty profile is the best way to get a husband." He gazed ahead, a rapt acolyte with just a dart of the eye looking for watchful suitors. "Two more will listen with no attention, because their mothers aren't watching them closely enough." A hand raised to the mouth, a whisper and a titter. "And one girl out of ten will make no pretense of listening no matter what her mother says, merely sit with her eyes sparkling and her thoughts turned in on some tremendously entertaining secret. That is the girl who will leave the church in uncontrollable fits of laughter when a priest with a cold sneezes on the Host before elevating it." He straightened, looking at me. "That is the only girl worth watching."

"What a talent for mime," I said rudely. "You should have been a mountebank instead of a cardinal. One of those charlatans who uses stage tricks to sell quack potions."

"In many ways a churchman is a mountebank," he said, unruffled. "You know how many stage tricks we use at Mass? Don't go crossing yourself; I suspect a girl who can laugh at the elevation of the Host without fearing for her immortal soul already has a fine appreciation for theatre."

He touched a curl by my cheek with one fingertip. I scowled, lifting a hand in warning, and he shook his head at me benignly. "You get one slap for free, my dear, but not two."

I lowered my hand, swallowing around the thickness in my throat. "So you saw me, you wanted me, you decided to have me? It's so simple as that, Your Eminence?"

"Desire is the simplest thing on earth," he returned. "Every man in the church wanted you after you ran out on that sneezing priest. I was the only one bold enough to try."

"Oh?" I gave him my sister Gerolama's superb sneer. "And how did you do that?"

"You have a mouth like a pearl, did you know that? Small, but perfect. I made inquiries with my good cousin, Adriana da Mila, and she found your brothers were searching about for a husband for you. One meeting was enough for Adriana to tell me you had a sweet nature to match that sweet face—"

"You had her vet my *temperament*?" I couldn't help exploding. "Like a *horse*? 'She has pretty gaits but does she kick when she's put to the saddle—' "

"Of course I had your temperament vetted! You know how many

beautiful faces hide foul tempers? But Adriana assured me it was quite the opposite with you, and accordingly, her son Orsino was supplied to your family as a prospective husband. And as for Orsino," the Cardinal added, "if you're wondering, he agreed to the proposition. He understood my patronage would bring him considerable compensation. Favors, posts, commissions, and so forth. Well worth the loan of a wife."

"He couldn't have agreed to that." I sat down very suddenly on a marble bench beside the fountain. The stone nymph gamboled in the water, laughing at me. "He wouldn't have."

"It's a common enough arrangement." Amusement still laced the Cardinal's deep voice, but he sounded gentler, as though no longer smiling. I didn't know; I couldn't bear to look at him. "My last mistress had three husbands in succession, each more compliant than the last. They profited from my patronage, she had respectability—and the children she bore me had protection."

"Children?" My voice was a stupid echo; I gazed at the arch where the rude boy Juan had disappeared. Of course. A cardinal who didn't blink at propositioning a wife of one day certainly wouldn't balk at producing bastards.

"Five children living." He sat down on the rim of the fountain opposite me, not too close. "Four here in Rome, three boys and a girl. A daughter in Spain whom I rarely see, now that she's grown and married."

And older than me, no doubt. Not that there was anything so shocking about that; Isotta Colonna, who had cried all through her wedding, had been standing next to a human sphere of sixty-four. Three quarters of the girls I'd giggled with at Mass were wed to husbands twenty years at least their senior.

Nineteen-year-old Orsino with his blushes and his blue eyes. I'd thought I was so lucky.

I looked the Cardinal square in the eye. "If you wanted me so badly, why didn't you take me last night?" I made myself ask. "It's your *palazzo*—no one would have come to my aid. You could have done whatever you wanted with me."

"My dear girl." The amusement was back, laced through his voice like a thread of honey through cake. "I've never in my life had a woman by force, and I don't intend to begin now."

I jumped to my feet. "Then let me go home!"

"Certainly," he said. "Your new home is at the Palazzo Montegiordano, with your mother-in-law Adriana da Mila. She runs a comfortable household there—my daughter stays with her; I do hope you and Lucrezia will be friends. She's a delight, and too often lacks the company of other young girls. Your husband will stay in the country at Bassanello, though I wouldn't be surprised if he comes to bleat apologies at you for being the cowardly sprig that he is. I will come too, from time to time, to pay you court."

I lowered my lids in scorn. "And if I say no?" *Could* I say no? Or would I go to hell for defying a cardinal? Oh, Holy Virgin, who ever would have thought getting married would make everything so *complicated*?

"Say no, and you will be none the worse off." The Cardinal rose in a rustle of scarlet silks, his majestic height dwarfing me again. "In fact, you will be considerably the richer. You'll have a pliant young husband— he's a spineless little coward, but he's still a better prospect than most of those withered gray specimens who manage to wed girls like you. You'll have enjoyed the pleasant sensation of being courted for yourself rather than your dowry, which all women should experience at least once in their lives." A glance at the braided hair beneath my veil. "Before their bloom fades, that is."

I threw my head back and gave him a slow arrogant smile.

His mouth curved, and he clapped a hand to his heart as though my smile had pierced it like an arrow. "And," he concluded cheerfully, "you'll have a casket full of sparkly things—gifts from me. I'm rather good at presents, as any of my former mistresses can tell you."

"I don't want your gifts."

"Then throw them away," he said carelessly, and took possession of my hand again. "All I want is to give them to you. It's called being besotted, my dear. You should try it sometime."

He turned my hand over and brushed his lips across the inside of my wrist. Or would have, if I hadn't yanked my hand away. "Don't touch me," I warned. Ever since I was twelve and first starting to bud from girl to woman, I'd been pinched and squeezed and eyed by men. Page boys and manservants and bravos swaggering in the street; the tutors who were supposed to teach me dancing and Dante; strange men who made a point of brushing too close when I made my way through a crowded church after Mass; the priests who heard my confession. Every man thought he could get away with a stroke and a pat, and an unmarried girl doesn't have much choice about it all except to sidle away as fast as possible before she's accused of leading him on. But I was a married woman now, and I didn't have to pretend I didn't feel the gropes and the pinches anymore. "Don't touch me," I warned again, a little shakily. *Who tells a cardinal no?* a small voice whispered in my head.

"Never fear," he chuckled, not at all offended, and made another of his elegant bows. "I won't touch you till you ask me to."

"I assure you that will never happen."

"We'll meet again soon," he promised, ignoring my protest, and strode off with the vigorous steps of a much younger man. He left me so quickly, he'd disappeared up the steps into the loggia out of earshot before I realized he'd left something in my hand.

I opened my fingers and couldn't help a gasp. A rope of pearls sat in my palm, elegantly coiled, with a single pear-drop pearl larger than any I'd ever seen in my life.

No necklace, dear, Madonna Adriana had twinkled as she helped dress me. *You'll soon see why.*

That old hag. My procuress of a mother-in-law had *known*. She'd sent her own son out of the way to the country and then dressed his new wife to go whoring.

I clenched a fist around the necklace and stormed back to my chamber. I wished Madonna Adriana had still been there, with her creamy satisfied smile—I'd have flung that pretty pearl in her face. As it was, there was only my new maid Pantisilea, going through my boxes and chests.

"Are you *spying* on me?" I shouted.

"Madonna Adriana's orders." My maid looked apologetic. "Did you meet the Cardinal, Madonna Giulia? Is he handsome? I haven't seen him up close—"

"Get out!" I shouted. "Get out and stay out!"

Her eyes fastened on the necklace looped through my fingers. "Oooh, that's *pretty*! I like a bit of jewelry myself; it shows a man has serious intentions—"

"Out!"

"I'm going, Madonna Giulia, I'm going."

She gave me a curtsy and a comradely giggle as she scampered out, which I resolutely refused to return in kind. "Your name is *ridiculous*!" I yelled after her instead, slamming the door. Pantisilea, indeed. That nosy piece of string was no Amazon warrior queen; she wasn't even a maid—she was a common spy. A spy of my very own, to keep my mother-in-law informed of all my actions, all my doings, all my secrets. I had no one to trust here at all.

I upended the table beside the bed, taking a small mean comfort in the crash of a vase, a goblet, and a prayer book. I flung the pearl necklace down on my wedding chest and eyed it as though it were a snake. I would *not* try it on.

Not for another hour, anyway.

I held out that long.

My Cardinal had good taste in jewels, I'd say that for him. I'd still throw his pearls at his feet if he dared call on me again. "Take that, Cardinal Borgia," I said aloud, tugging the rope of pearls over my head.

Rodrigo Borgia. I'd finally remembered his name.

When a man gives you jewels, even if you're planning to throw them back in his face, you should remember his name.

CHAPTER THREE

※

*Saturn has impressed the seal of melancholy
on me from the beginning.*

—FICINO

Leonello

Hector, son of Priam, fierce as flame. I declaimed the words silently, reading from the book in my hand as I strolled across the piazza. *Thrice-noble Hector, seizing from behind, sought by the feet to drag away the dead, cheering his friends—*

A properly gloved and veiled housewife on her way back from confession gave me a dubious glance. My lips must be moving along with my thoughts, like a mumbling madman. I made her an impeccable bow and said gravely, " '*Thrice, clad in warlike might, the two Ajaxes drove him from his prey.*' Did you know that, good *signora*?" I showed her the book. "Thrice!"

She crossed herself and hurried away. A blind beggar raised his sham of an eye bandage to give me an incredulous glance before remembering to drool and stare vacantly again.

*Yet, fearless in his strength, now rushing on—*I went back to declaiming in my head, swaggering as much as any mighty Ajax.

Two butcher boys paused to guffaw at the dwarf striding along with his nose buried in a book and his hand clapped to his dagger hilt as though it were a hero's sword, but for once their snickers slid off me without pricking. I was a man grown, thirty in a year or two, but the tale of Troy converted me every time back into the giddy schoolboy I'd been when I first read it. And thanks to a lucky *chorus* hand in a game of *primiera* last night, I'd finally had the coin to buy a certain battered book I'd been eyeing for a month—not just the simplified *Ilias Latina* I'd read as a boy, but Homer's own version, the Greek translated into Italian. Only a woodblock print, to be sure; Priam's plea to Achilles was lamentably smudged, and water stains all but obscured Hector's duel with Ajax. But a book nonetheless, a new book for my modest private library.

Then up rose Achilles, dear to Jove—I whistled through my teeth, resuming my stroll toward the tavern where Anna worked. I'd need to play a game or two more at the tables if I wanted any food this evening, since I'd spent all the coin I had on the book. Then I could go home, back to my tiny rented room above the print shop in the Borgo, and pass the rest of the evening sprawled on the cot, mug of wine in my hand, reading by the clear light of the beeswax taper I brought from its box only when I had a new book to read . . .

But when Achilles' voice of brass they heard, they quailed in spirit . . . "Anna?" I called as I came into the tavern, tucking the worn volume back into my doublet just before the death of Patroclus. "Anna, my good lady, have you any easy marks for me tonight? Let me—"

That was when I saw the tables empty of customers; heard the odd and eerie silence, except for the muffled wailing of the tavern maids weeping into each other's shoulders.

"What?" I looked at the maidservants, from face to tear-blotched face. "What's happened? Where is Anna?"

"In—in there," one of them quavered. I flung open the door to the kitchen, and my buoyant book-fueled happiness popped like a bubble.

A nna had died fighting. There was that, at least.
    "When did you find her?" I asked the tavernkeeper around lips gone numb.

"Early this morning," the man complained. "One of the maids, she comes to light the fires and set the pots boiling at dawn, and what do I hear upstairs? A great wail, and by the time I'm down to take a look, the stupid girl's gone and emptied her stomach all over the floor!"

Enough to make anyone lose her stomach, I thought. Anna lay on the long trestle table of the kitchens, head tipped back, skirts mussed about her bare legs. Her hands had been spread wide like the figure of Christ on a crucifix, spread wide and staked down to the table with kitchen knives through the palms. She'd still managed to tear one hand free, making a desperate lunging attack. I picked up her free-dangling hand, stiff and cold, and saw blood congealed in dark crescents under her nails. She'd raked her attacker hard.

Good girl.

"This'll put business off for weeks," the tavernkeeper grumbled. "Who wants to drink their wine and throw their dice at a tavern where a dead girl's been staked, answer me that?"

Though maybe if she hadn't scratched her attacker, he might not have cut her throat. It wasn't the knives through her hands that had killed my friend—it was the messy slash across her neck, amid half a dozen shallow panicked ones as if the murderer had never cut a throat in his life.

I could have taught you better, I thought. One hand to grasp the forehead, pull the head straight back, and drag the knife across the throat in one straight deep stroke. Dragging it *across* the throat, that was key—drag it around, and the cut wouldn't score deep enough. *You found that out, didn't you, whoever you were? Took you four tries before she died.*

"Who did this?" I asked quietly.

"What's it to you? It don't matter, no one'll catch him."

No, probably not. A common girl found in a tavern with her throat slashed—the Tiber filled up nightly with bodies like that. Mostly they were raked up, carted off, and dumped unclaimed into anonymous graves. Who cared? Not the priests, who wouldn't say a Mass for the dead unless they were paid by some member of the living first. Not the constables, those corrupt swaggerers more interested in loot and bribes than in finding murderers. No one would bother calling a priest or a constable in, not for someone like Anna.

I reached out and closed her eyes, half-open and staring at the knotted rafters. "Who did this?" I asked again.

"How should I know?" The tavernkeeper shrugged heavy shoulders, eyeing the blood that had run from the table to pool and dry on the floor. Behind the kitchen door at his back, I could hear the other maidservants twittering and wailing. "One of the other girls said there were three men in for a bit of fun late last night—throwing dice, spreading money around, eyeing the girls. Maybe Anna stayed to wait on them."

"You were here?"

"I went to midnight Mass," the tavernkeeper said virtuously.

"You went to fuck that carter's wife you like to visit when her husband leaves Rome with his mules, but no matter. These three boys—did your girls say anything else about them?"

"Well dressed. Anna could have turned a pretty profit, pulling up her skirts for something better than dwarves and fishmongers. Things got out of hand, I imagine."

"No, she wasn't raped." I tugged her rumpled skirts down to cover her ankles. She had no blood under her skirts or bruises on her thighs. Bruises on her knees, as though someone had tried to force them apart, but Anna must have fought too hard. The knives through her hands, I guessed, had been to hold her still . . .

"Who's going to take care of this mess, I'd like to know?" The tavernkeeper went back to his complaining. "I'll have to pay double to those maids, just to get them in here to clean that floor! And they won't go touching that body, not a whore who's died unshriven."

"I'll tend the body." I crossed the kitchen, climbing up on a chair to reach the box where the tapers were kept. I took a handful and hopped down from the chair. "I'll pay," I said, forestalling the tavernkeeper's sputtering, and began setting the tapers about Anna's still body. Cheap tapers, made of rancid-smelling tallow. She deserved beeswax for her death vigil. Of course, Anna had deserved a great many things. A silk

dress, like that lovely young bride we'd watched in her wedding procession a fortnight ago. A caring husband, a loyal family. A kind death in
a soft bed at sixty, not a horror of a death staked to a kitchen table at
twenty-five.

"Close the tavern today," I told the tavernkeeper, who had started
to fuss again. "I'll stand vigil for her tonight, and see her buried on the
morrow."

"I believe the dwarf's in love!" The man raised an eyebrow, starting
to grin.

"Keep that filthy tongue in your head before I saw it off," I said
evenly. "She has no family to bury her, so I will."

"Well, it's your money."

"Money won at a very lucky hand of *primiera*," I told Anna's still
body when the tavernkeeper had tramped heavily out. "A *chorus*, four
cards of the same kind! A rare hand, that one. I bought a book with it,
but I'll take it back. Should be enough to see you properly buried in a
churchyard. Maybe even a Mass or two for your soul . . ."

Anna lay still. A thick drop of congealing blood collected at the tip
of her finger. *Just an ordinary tavern maid*, I thought. Plain-faced, limp
hair a little grimy; illiterate, hard-used, and old at twenty-five. A hundred like her in every *piazza* in Rome. Nothing to set her apart from
any of the others—except maybe that sweet dent of a dimple at the
corner of her mouth when she gave her kind smile.

"'*Around him stood his comrades mourning.*'" I quoted Achilles's
lines of grief when he lost his friend Patroclus at Troy. "'*With them,
Peleus's son, shedding hot tears as on his friend he gazed—*'" Yanking the
remaining knife out of Anna's still-staked hand. "'*Laid on the bier, and
pierced with deadly wounds . . .*'"

"Who're you talking to?"

I turned to see two of the maidservants standing in the doorway,
peering with nervous swollen eyes. "She's not talkin' back, is she? They
say ghosts hover around the bodies of them who died violent—"

"Just saying a prayer for her." I saw their eyes dart away from Anna's,
which had reflexively slid open again to stare glassily at the ceiling. I

smoothed down her eyelids, weighting them closed this time with the last two *scudi* from my purse.

"God rest her soul," one of the maidservants quavered, crossing herself. A girl not so different from Anna, but lacking that dimple and the streak of kindness that had gone with it. This girl been known to bump me with her hip as she passed, just to see if she could knock the cards out of my hand, but now her eyes were bloodshot and her chin quavered. "God rot those who did this to her!"

"The tavernkeeper says you two saw them." Casually I straightened the folds of Anna's skirts. "Three men, wasn't it? What did they look like?"

"What do any of them look like?" the other maidservant shrugged. An older woman, harder of face and tight about the mouth. "Men out for a good time, that's what they looked like."

"One had a *mask*." The first girl gave a watery snort. "You know how these young bravos are. It's all so terribly entertaining to dress up like it's Carnival and go to the slums!"

"So he was young." I took some care smoothing the hair back from Anna's blood-mottled cheeks. "How young? A boy, or a young man?"

"Who can tell behind a mask? He was young, that's all, and he had money. Splashing coin all about while he played *zara*."

"The other two?"

"Just men," the older woman said, impatient. "What's it to you?"

"Better if we know what they look like. What if they come back?" I gave a dark look at Anna's corpse, so still on the table between us. "What if it's one of you lovely girls next time they feel like a bit of fun?"

"Not likely." The first girl made a face, dingy light from the windows cutting sharp shadows over her nose, which had been broken at least once by some drunken sailor or laborer. "One was right ugly—in livery, you know. Some lug of a guardsman. I wouldn't service a man like that for a bag of ducats."

"You'd service the Devil himself for a single ducat," her friend told her. "Much less a bag of them!"

"What kind of livery did this guardsman wear?" I cut in before the first girl could bristle.

"I don't know, he had a cloak on. Had a horse embroidered on his chest, though."

"It wasn't a horse," the other girl contradicted. "It was a bull. All embroidered in red."

"No, it was a horse . . ."

"The third man?" I said, crossing Anna's hands over her flat breast. "What did he look like?"

Blank looks and shrugs among them. "Just a man," the older woman said finally. "Sounded like a Spaniard. Or maybe he was Venetian." A sniff. "Who can tell with these foreigners?"

Dio. "What about him, this Spaniard or Venetian?"

"He came later, after the other two. Pinched my bottom, and didn't even offer a coin. Said they should all go back to the Inn of the Fig, because there were prettier girls there."

I felt a sudden savage wish that they *had* gone back to the Inn of the Fig, and killed some prettier girl than Anna. A pretty girl with a black heart and a greedy hand; someone who had abandoned a baby on a hillside or given customers over to be robbed and killed by bravos—some girl with sins on her head that merited such a death.

Such a death. Staked to a table, and for what? Had Anna fought too hard, and they'd panicked and cut her throat to silence her? Even in a tavern as seedy as this one, shrieks of murder and blood coming from the night might have roused a response from one of the cramped little wine shops or rented rooms across the narrow street.

I wondered how many noble families in Rome liveried their guards in a red bull or horse.

I wondered if it was the guard who wore the marks of Anna's nails on his face—or the Spaniard-Venetian, or the boy in the mask.

I wondered if any of them went to Inn of the Fig regularly.

The two maidservants wandered away, unnerved by my sudden lapse into silence, and I was just as glad they were gone. I lit the tapers around Anna's body and settled back onto my stool for her death vigil. I felt the volume of the *Iliad* in the inside of my doublet and pulled it out.

"'The Greeks all night with tears and groans bewailed Patroclus,'" I read. "'On his comrade's breast, Achilles laid his murder-dealing hands, and led with bitter groans the loud lament.'"

No loud lament here. No one to care Anna was dead but me. Not like Patroclus, who at least had all the heroes of Greece to mourn him." "'They washed the corpse, with lissome oils anointing, and the wounds with fragrant ointments filled . . .' No oils and ointments for you, my good lady," I broke away from Homer to tell my friend. "I'll be lucky if I can buy a Mass for your soul."

The coins on her eyes gleamed at me. "'All night around Achilles swift of foot, the Myrmidons with tears Patroclus mourned.'"

I broke off, closing the little book. "At least Achilles knew who killed his friend."

Anna was silent. I looked at her.

"Who killed you, my girl?" I asked her. "Answer me that, eh?"

No reply.

Giulia

S o you are confessing to the sin of fornication outside the vows of your marriage? A grave offense, *madonna*."

"No," I said, exasperated. "That's not what I said at all. I said *he's* trying to tempt *me* to the sin of fornication outside my marriage vows. He started trying the day after my wedding, two weeks ago. I ask you!"

"So you desire a man besides your husband, and that man a most holy cardinal?"

I glowered in the direction of the confessional grille. The dark little space was stuffy and smelled of stale incense, the wooden shelf was hard under my knees, and through the ornately carved wood of the grille I could see only flashes of the priest's vestments. His disembodied voice was pinched and disapproving. I hadn't really expected a priest to take my side on this, especially not over that of a cardinal, but—well, I'd been raised to take my troubles to the confessional, and habit died hard.

"No," I tried again. "Cardinal Borgia is the one doing the desiring, not me. He thinks by waving a pretty necklace or two under my nose—"

"You are guilty, then, of tempting a man of the Church to break his vows of celibacy?"

"Considering his five bastards, I think he's broken them before," I pointed out.

"It is not your place to reprove a man of God." The priest certainly had no trouble reproving *me.* The voice pinging at me through the grille was icy. "The Cardinal's fleshly sins are a matter for his own conscience. You must not add to his burden."

"His burden?" I sputtered. "What about mine? A wife with no husband, abandoned in a—a den of sin!" Surely that would move him? Priests were always going on about dens of sin.

"Even through this screen, I can see you have the curse of beauty," the priest continued, clicking his tongue. "Beautiful women are traps laid by the devil to snare the vows of men. Sheathe yourself in modesty and self-effacement, *madonna*, and do not add to the burden of this man of God by tempting him with your body."

"I don't want to tempt him with my body!"

"All women are thirsty for admiration. Has this man of God laid a finger upon you?"

"No," I admitted. "But he wants to." He'd visited once more, just a week ago, and I'd refused to say a word to him—I told the priest as much. "I sat there with my hands folded in my lap. I didn't give him *any* encouragement."

But it hadn't really made the impression I'd hoped. "Ah," Cardinal Borgia had said, amusement lacing his deep voice. "Disdainful silence. Well, if you're content with wordlessness, I shall be as well. Who needs conversation, with something as lovely as you to gaze at?" And he'd put his chin into his hand and gazed at me with slow-burning appreciation for a solid hour.

"I was twitching by the end," I told the priest. "You know what it's like to just sit in silence being stared at? You wouldn't believe how my nose itched, and all he says through the whole hour is 'Would you mind sulking with your head turned the other way? I would be grateful for the chance to admire that perfect profile.' What do you do with a man like that? No matter what I say, he just doesn't *get* offended."

"Then his will is stronger than your vanity. Three Acts of Contrition—"

The priest rattled off a list of penitential prayers that would have me on my knees until Candlemas, but I closed my ears, mutinous. These priests, they always stuck to their own kind. Everybody was at fault but them. When I was twelve and just starting to strain the lacing of my bodices, my confessor was a friar who breathed communion wine on my neck and whispered that he'd absolve me of the sin if I would just let him get a look at my ripening apples. That was the word he used, "apples." I told his superior everything, and somehow it had all ended up being *my* fault: the budding little temptress swishing about, unsettling the poor men of God. I'd never really trusted priests since. And I'm not very fond of apples, either.

"*Ego te absolvo*," the priest on the other side of the confessional grille finally said, and rattled off the rest of my absolution. I crossed myself resentfully and left the confessional box before I could choke on either the incense or the hypocrisy. *Men*, I thought as I made my way past the line of penitents waiting for the priest, and looked about for an altar where I could light a candle. I missed the old cross-eyed Madonna at the church in Capodimonte where I'd said all my confessions growing up. Here at the Santa Maria Maggiore everything was far grander: the huge columns were all Athenian marble, the arch and the apse had been inlaid with splendid mosaics of the Virgin, and all the saints in their niches looked snobbish. I finally paused before the altar of Santa Anna— she had a kinder face in her elaborate fresco than the censorious Madonna, and she also had very fashionable slashed-velvet sleeves. "Men are all the same," I told her, lighting my candle. "Doesn't matter if they're doubleted or cassocked, does it?"

"*Sorellina!*"

I turned to see my brother Sandro, waving his hat overhead in a flourish as he caught sight of me through the church's throng.

"A far cry from Capodimonte, isn't it?" he continued as he made his way to my side before Santa Anna's candles. He looked out over the high-vaulted transept, the richly gilded saints, the inlaid floors of the basilica. "But you're moving in grand circles these days." Sandro's dark eyes crinkled approvingly at my green velvet gown, my billowing embroidered sleeves, the silvery net into which I'd packed my hair. Finer than he was used to seeing me dressed—the way we'd been raised, silks and velvets had been saved strictly for holy days and celebrations, but for the Borgia and the Orsini, brocade and pearls were for every day. "I imagine the priest clucked at you for vanity," Sandro continued, "but how many other sins can you have committed in just a fortnight or two of marriage? For myself, I've got the usual batch of carnal offenses to work off. It does seem unfair that a little flutter with a pretty girl gets me twice the penance a student or a soldier would get. There are distinct disadvantages to the clerical life, at least on the lower rungs. One isn't really able to get away with serious sinning until one is at least a cardinal. I suppose that should motivate me to climb the ladder; how do you fancy me as 'Cardinal Farnese'—"

I hadn't seen my favorite brother since the wedding. He said some business had taken him from the city for a few weeks—"One does have to put in the occasional hour or two of work as a notary, unfortunately." I suspected it was a girl who had taken him away from the city, not notary business, and I scowled at him because it had been a pair of weeks when I really could have used some brotherly assistance.

"What, no fond greeting?" He mimicked my glare. "Marriage isn't sweetening you as much as I'd thought it would, *sorellina*."

"Not much of a marriage thus far," I said, still glowering. "Orsino has gone to the country, and Cardinal Borgia is trying to seduce me."

Sandro hooted. "Oh yes! The aging Cardinal, a squid in red robes, winds his caressing tentacles about the trembling figure of the maiden fair—"

"Sandro, be serious!"

"—she twists, she turns, where shall she go? Andromeda chained upon the rock for Neptune's monster of the deep, a melting beauty shrinking in terror as powerful arms pull her toward her doom—"

"Shouldn't the future Cardinal Farnese be reading Scripture rather than Greek myths?"

"—with all her strength she fights her fate, this virgin sacrifice to the lusts of a primal god—"

I stood there simmering while my brother doubled over with laughter. People were starting to stare, but that never bothered Sandro. I took him by the sleeve and pulled him away from Santa Anna, between a marble column and the line of penitents filing one by one into the confessional. "Sandro, stop chortling! It's not funny."

"Of course it's funny." Sandro swallowed his last chuckles, dark eyes dancing. "Borgia's a mitered old goat, *sorellina*; all Rome knows that. Don't tell me *you* don't know how to handle a randy cleric! Just level him with that icy stare you've perfected, the one that turns men into worms. And if that fails, deal out one of your slaps that could drop an ox—"

"I already did," I confessed, and my sore heart eased a little as Sandro tweaked my cheek just the way he always had since we'd been children. Maybe his japes drove me to distraction sometimes, but he was still my big brother, and a girl with a proper big brother is never alone. Rodrigo Borgia would do well to remember that, and so would my husband.

"Don't get your feathers ruffled, Giulia; you're a married woman now, not some Turkish concubine at a slave market. You think some swaggering priest can just sweep you off and put you in a gilded cage?" Sandro hooted laughter again at the thought.

Actually, that's exactly what he has in mind. But suddenly I hesitated to say it. I'd wanted nothing more than to spill my troubles to my brother as soon as he returned to Rome, but now I felt a pang of caution ripple through me. Maybe my husband didn't care about defending my honor with a rapier, but Sandro certainly would. My brother generally favored the world's sins with an amused and lenient eye, but his leniency would end when it came to the protection of his favorite little sister. I *wanted* his protection, of course—but not if I got my brother cut to ribbons. "What do you know about Cardinal Borgia, Sandro?" I asked instead.

"Gossip, of course." Sandro tucked my hand into his elbow, turning away from the confessional line. "And my venial sins can always wait their turn for a good gossip. Let me escort you home."

I put up my sunshade as we came out of the church into the *piazza*, and my guards straightened hastily from where they had been lounging on the sunny steps. When I was an unmarried girl I'd only ever been trailed by an eagle-eyed mother or maidservant when I went out, someone to make sure my eyes stayed on the ground and not on the men. (As if that ever stopped me from peeking.) These days I had a whole retinue: a quartet of armed guards in the yellow and mulberry Borgia livery with the bull embroidered on their chests; a page to carry my train; Pantisilea, my cheerful maid, to hold my sunshade and gloves; and every last one of them was paid to spy on me. Toadies.

"So—" I gestured them all back a few steps as we set off across the *piazza*, lifting my velvet hem as I skirted a puddle. Pigeons flapped and squawked across the stones of the *piazza*; vendors hawked bits of wood or rag as fragments of the True Cross or the Shroud of Turin; beggars squatted with bowls outstretched toward the veiled women hurrying in and out of the church. "Tell me about Cardinal Borgia."

"Got under your skin, has he?"

"I'm serious, Sandro!" What kind of man *was* my suitor? What could he do to my brother, if Sandro came to his door steaming with fury on my account? More importantly, what *would* he do? I didn't know anything about Rodrigo Borgia, really. Madonna Adriana did nothing but sing his praises dawn to dusk: his learning, his wit, his taste in all things artistic, the influence he wielded in the College of Cardinals, but I didn't know if I could believe any of it. May the Holy Virgin herself consign me straight to hell before I'd give the Cardinal himself the satisfaction of *asking*. I didn't have anyone to consult but my brother, who might be only a notary but always knew all the gossip in Rome.

"He's Cardinal-Bishop of Porto e Santa Rufina," Sandro began, ticking the titles off. "Administrator of Valencia, and spent some years there—he is a Spaniard, you know; *Borgia* used to be *Borja*. There's some who said the Borja used to be Moors or Spanish Jews, but I wouldn't put much stock in that. Dean of the College of Cardinals, which means he'll summon the Conclave when it comes time to elect a new pope—"

"All these titles and elections," I said, impatient. "Tell me the interesting parts!"

"Rich," Sandro said. We had left the *piazza* now, plunging into the maze of narrow winding streets that coil and twist back on each other in such a vast citywide knot that any non-Roman is instantly lost. As none of them will hesitate to tell you, as soon as they sense you had the temerity *not* to be born in the Eternal City. "You saw his house—he's one of the richest cardinals in Rome, I daresay."

I thought of the huge pearl, currently lying on my windowsill where the sun could strike velvet gleams out of it. I'd flung it down there instead of locking it away in one of my chests, determined to let one of the servants steal it, and *that* would teach His Eminence a lesson when he learned I'd lost his precious present and didn't even care . . . but none of the servants would touch it, too afraid of getting their hands chopped off as thieves, I suppose, and it really looked so pretty lying there in the sun gleaming and singing at me. I didn't know what to do with it, only that I was *not* going to wear it.

At least not where anyone could see me.

"—bastards, of course," my brother was continuing in his cheerful recitation of my suitor's vices. "Seven or eight by various mothers, in Spain *and* Rome—"

"Five living, he told me." I made a face. "I've met one—Juan; he's sixteen. He's forever dropping in to smirk at me and make rude remarks. There's another son, supposedly; he's only just returned from the university in Pisa; and a younger boy and girl who still live with Madonna Adriana, but they're all visiting their mother now and I've not met any of them. If they're anything like Juan, they'll be a sorry batch."

"All provided for, though," Sandro allowed. "The daughter's been dowered to the skies; Juan Borgia is Duke of Gandia in Spain—"

"I know. He's forever underfoot. Duke or not, he's still a witless, lecherous idiot."

"—and the elder boy in Pisa was made Bishop of Pamplona by fifteen." Sandro gave an envious shake of his head. "Oh, for a doting and all-powerful father. How am I ever supposed to be a bishop or a cardinal someday without one? I'm far too lazy to *earn* it."

All-powerful. I kicked at a stone, wobbling for a moment on the tall wooden stilt clogs I wore to elevate my slippers out of the mud. Comfortable tooled-leather slippers; an old pair. In my chamber I had a prettier set, gold-buckled and brand-new, made of supple diamond-patterned snakeskin. Yet another gift that had appeared anonymously at my bedside one afternoon, all tied up with a silk ribbon the color of a cardinal's robes. *Not just any cardinal, but one of the richest and most powerful of cardinals.*

Too powerful for a humble notary of twenty-four to challenge, even over such a serious matter as a sister's virtue.

"Why the sad face, *sorellina*?" My brother stopped in the street, his smile disappearing from his lean handsome face. Thanks to the stilt clogs my head reached his shoulder instead of the middle of his chest, and he didn't have to look down so far. Cardinal Borgia was tall too—I was forever craning my head up at the men in my life. "The Cardinal hasn't been pressing you in earnest, has he?" Sandro continued. "Flirting is one thing, but if he thinks he can turn one of the Farnese into a common courtesan—" Sandro looked ominous, but he still couldn't resist striking a pose: the noble Galahad, hand on imaginary sword. "That Borgia bull is a powerful man in Rome, but that doesn't mean I won't take a rapier to him! Chase him through the streets at swordpoint—"

"Oh, be sensible!" I snapped. "A notary from the provinces, taking on a cardinal of Rome? He could swat you like a fly." That now seemed perfectly clear.

"Maybe." Sandro dropped his theatrics. "Doesn't mean a brother isn't obligated to try, if someone threatens his sister's honor."

That's what Orsino should have done, I couldn't help thinking. *That's what husbands* always *do, brothers and fathers too.* I'd grown up listening to wives whisper, complaining of strict husbands and the jealous guard they kept on their wife's virtue—but how queerly flattening to have a husband who wasn't jealous at all. Of course Orsino Orsini didn't love me; I was resigned to that. We didn't even know each other, after all. But he married me with the intention of giving me to someone else, and that I wasn't resigned to at all.

I'd tried sending him a letter, telling him so. Telling him to come for me, telling him what the Cardinal said to me, telling him—oh, Holy Virgin knew what. But my maid Pantisilea said apologetically that she'd just have to hand the letter over to my mother-in-law. "I'm sorry, Madonna Giulia. She's a right interferer, Madonna Adriana is, but all the servants have got their orders." I'd yanked my letter back and burned it myself rather than give my mother-in-law the satisfaction.

"Giulia?"

"Don't worry, Sandro." I aimed my brightest smile up at my brother, who still looked worried. "I shouldn't have troubled you. It's just an old man with a wandering eye, after all—you think I can't defend my own honor against that? In truth I'm flattered! It's much more entertaining to be a wife than an unmarried girl, I can tell you. Come, we're almost back to the *palazzo*, I'll show you my new quarters. I live better than a princess now—I know you said the Orsini were rich when Orsino began inquiring for me, but you have no *idea*. Embroidered Spanish velvet for my bed hangings, and such a carpet . . ."

Carmelina

The room I was allotted in the servant quarters of the Palazzo Montegiordano was tiny. Just enough for a pallet and a small chest that doubled as both chair and storage for my clothes. I could touch all four walls without moving from the spot.

Santa Marta save me, it was paradise.

Madonna Adriana da Mila had started to fuss when Marco presented his newly orphaned cousin from Venice. "Cousin?" she said dubiously, looking from Marco to me, and I suppose she thought he was just trying to bring his whore into the household for easier access.

"Cousin," I said firmly, and cast my eyes down and let Marco do the arguing as a good girl should when accompanied by the man, be he father, husband, brother, or cousin who owns her life.

Madonna Adriana brightened when Marco mentioned my skills as a cook: "The marzipan *tourtes*, those were her own contribution to the wedding feast, *madonna*. I believe the bride spoke highly of them? Carmelina's skill with sweets is surpassed only by my own—"

I took a moment to huff quietly through my nostrils at that, but I kept my eyes lowered and let Marco take the credit. Maybe he was getting the credit for my wedding feast, but I was getting something in return, so all in all you couldn't say I hadn't been paid a fair wage for my work.

Madonna Adriana brightened even further when I murmured that of *course* I would be adding my hands to the kitchen at no extra cost to Marco's wages. "I can't give you a room, now," she warned. "Perhaps a pallet in one of the storerooms . . ."

In the end I had my little cubby, which had once been a spare storage space for oil jars. I didn't mind; the whole little space had the tang of good olive oil, and when I stretched out in my little bed at night I breathed it in rapturously as I slid into sleep. The first sleep I'd had in months that hadn't been broken by fearful dreams.

Not that there was much time for sleep. Adriana da Mila had a constant stream of guests: innumerable Orsini cousins who expected equally innumerable trays of nibbles and wine; matrons who called to inspect the new golden-haired daughter-in-law; and of course Cardinal Borgia, who everyone said was laying siege to that same golden-haired daughter-in-law. Except for that one surprise visit to the kitchens the morning after her wedding, I still hadn't seen much of Madonna Giulia except for the occasional glint of bright hair as she drifted past in some distant upstairs loggia, but she did keep a steady stream of servants running upstairs with plates of my baked *crostate* of quinces and apples, and my white peaches in grappa, and my *offelle* thick with sweetened French cream. The girl did love her sweets, or rather, she loved *my* sweets, and if Marco was freshly annoyed every time he saw me and was reminded of how neatly I'd angled my way into his life, well, he did like having an extra pair of hands in his kitchen. Particularly if those hands were mine, and particularly on days like today, when a page boy brought the order down from Madonna Giulia for a plate of stuffed figs with cinnamon, sugar, and chopped almonds, right in the middle of the midday rush.

"Carmelina!" Marco didn't even glance at me, his hands flying as he stuffed a roast suckling pig.

"Yes, *maestro*." My own hands were already reaching for the figs, the sugar, the almonds, and a knife to chop them fine. "Piero, the cinnamon."

"It's over there." He tilted a brusque shoulder in some vague direction.

"And I want it over here, apprentice." The steel in my voice got him moving, but he slouched his way across the kitchens with deliberate slowness, took his time selecting among the spices, and tossed it down before me so it spattered my workspace.

"Now you can get me a cloth to wipe that up," I ordered, and he looked at me resentfully. Half the apprentices already loathed me, and the maidservants only grudgingly followed my orders. I had saved Madonna Giulia's wedding banquet, and perhaps their positions along with it, but what did that matter? Kitchens have a hierarchy as rigid as any royal court, after all, and I was an interloper: not quite cook, not quite scullion, not quite servant. Someone Marco had brought in personally but clearly disapproved of; someone who gave orders but took them too; someone trusted with the delicate pastries for the daughter of the house, but who also pitched in with the scouring and cleaning fit only for the lowest pot-boys. I was an unknown quantity, and no kitchen likes an unknown quantity of anything, be it spices or servants. Marco really would have to make my place clear if he wanted peace in his kitchens, but for the time being he preferred not to look at me, and I'd have to carve out whatever authority for myself that I could.

"Piero?" I said, making my voice a whip. "A cloth."

"Yes, *signorina*," he said, insolently polite, and took his time with that too.

"Thank you," I told him, aware the others were listening, and turned back to my work. Only to see the cat wandering across the table, tracking his paws through my neat spread of flour.

"Out!" I brandished the cloth at him, but the lazy bastard just hissed at me. As far as I was concerned, a cat who didn't earn his keep by mousing might as well be drowned under the cistern. "One of these days I will turn you into sausage," I warned. "With a little garlic and fennel and splodges of pork fat, and then I'll eat you with a smile, just you wait."

The cat *miaowed* at me insolently and managed to knock over a jug of cream I was saving for whipping as he jumped to the floor. The cream went all over my skirt, and I could hear the maids giggling as I rushed back into my little chamber for a fresh apron.

I stopped there, closing the door behind me and folding my floured arms across my breasts. "I thought I'd left *you* well hidden," I said finally.

A withered and mummified hand lay half exposed in the nest of my clothes inside my small chest. I suppose I'd uncovered it in the dawn darkness this morning when I'd been hurriedly rummaging for a clean shift.

Why did it look different, sitting on a heap of clothes, than it had in the reliquary? I'd seen it so many times when I was a girl: the blessed and sacred hand of Santa Marta, carefully preserved and displayed in the convent of the same name in Venice. Not the largest and most illustrious of Venice's many convents, not by any means—but one where my father said most of his infrequent prayers. It made sense to a thrifty soul like his that Santa Marta was the one to intercede if you wanted to cook for the Doge at Carnival or were hoping to be hired for the wedding banquet of the latest Foscari heiress. What does the Holy Virgin know about the desperate prayers that come from a kitchen, after all? No one ever saw the Holy Virgin cooking. So when my father felt the need of a little divine assistance in his work he would take us—my mother, my sister, and me—to the Convent of Santa Marta, to pray at the altar of their church. And on that altar you could very clearly see the severed and preserved hand of the patron saint of cooks herself.

Of course, I never laid much faith that it *was* the saint's true hand. There's nothing more practical than an order of nuns with choir stalls to repair, and with so many convents in Venice competing for well-dowered novices, an abbess needs a little something extra to bring the wealthy families flocking to her doors. San Zaccaria had countless relics; Santa Chiara had one of the nails that had pierced the hands of Christ; and they had rich young girls lining up to join. So, some long-ago abbess of the Convent of Santa Marta might well have shrugged her worldly shoulders and made a discreet perusal among those purveyors of relics who can get you anything from a fragment of the True Cross to a lock of Mary Magdalene's hair as long as you're not too fussy. And lo and behold, the Convent of Santa Marta had a relic of its own to display: the hand of its patron saint, which was said to come to life and make the sign of the cross whenever it granted the prayers of the faithful. Not a famous relic; I doubted anyone had heard of it outside Venice. But it brought a cluster of novices with hefty dowries, and the hand soon had a beautiful new reliquary of silver and ivory, studded with garnets and pearls along its sides and set with a rock crystal viewing window through which the worshippers could see the hand itself: a little withered, a little dark and dried, but still boasting a carved gold ring on one small curled-in finger.

I shivered, looking at the hand now in the heap of my clothes. Maybe it looked different now because I'd stolen it.

So help me, I didn't mean to. I only wanted the reliquary. I was desperate to get out of Venice, desperate to get to Rome, but not so desperate that I would have stolen a sacred relic (or even a not-so-sacred one). I'd needed money, and I reckoned the reliquary would be worth a good three hundred ducats after I broke it down to its anonymous components of cabochon jewels and carved silver panels. I should have had three hundred ducats as a dowry from my father—three hundred ducats he'd given to the convent of Santa Marta instead as an offering, once it was clear I'd never marry. That convent *owed* me. And what with one bit of bad luck after another, it was really the only place I could go for quick money after I'd stolen my father's recipes and bolted. The only place with anything valuable at all, anything that might stake me enough for my journey south.

So I took the reliquary, but I'd never have taken the hand. I broke the rock crystal viewing window with the heavy base of an altar candlestick, looking desperately about the empty church as I shook out the shards. I couldn't bring myself to reach inside and touch the relic itself, so I just muttered an incoherent prayer of "Santa Marta, please forgive me" as I shook her hand out of the reliquary. I meant to wrap it respectfully in the embroidered altar cloth, but I heard a noise from the nave and panicked. I'd managed to distract the nuns, get in alone, but I'd known I'd only have moments, if not seconds. I just snatched the reliquary box and ran.

The box was empty when I took it. I'd have sworn an oath on that. But the hand's dried palm must have caught on the broken edges of the viewing window as I bundled everything up, because later I found the dark curled thing tangled in my cloak at the bottom of my pack, after I'd sold the pieces of the reliquary for far less than they were worth. I'd stared at it in horror, but what was I supposed to do then? I'd already taken ship, the cheapest passage I could find from Venice to Ferrara. Even if the boat had turned around on the spot, I couldn't have taken the relic back—I'd have been arrested for desecration of a church.

I'd meant what I told Marco that first morning, sitting in those cramped little kitchens. *I can't go back.* If I'd just stolen from my father— well, I'd likely be returned for whatever punishment he deemed fit. But a desecrator of church altars wouldn't be forgiven. I didn't know what punishment they had in Rome for desecrators, but I'd heard how other thieves of God had been treated. I could be strung upside down from a public gallows, hanging there while the crowds threw rocks and rotten vegetables at me, until the blood burst inside my head.

And if they found out just who I was—what I had been in Venice— well, I'd be shipped back there, to La Serenissima and the hands of my enemies. And I'd face a far worse punishment than hanging upsidedown on a public gallows.

I shivered at the thought, tasting the sour tang of terror in my mouth again, and crossed myself as I looked at the dark shriveled thing in the nest of clothes. I certainly couldn't throw it away like trash, but what *did* I do with it? I'd thought of leaving it at a shrine or an altar somewhere—but relics in the Holy City are a hundred to a *scudo;* likely the hand would just have been tossed away as rubbish. I couldn't send it back to the Convent of Santa Marta in Venice, either; not without giving myself away.

I didn't have the faintest idea what to do with the thing.

I had to steel myself to touch it with my bare hand. I could cut a lamb's throat for the kitchen spit as briskly and unsentimentally as any man; I could plunge my hand into a mass of still-steaming pig guts and empty them out for sausage casings; but I flinched as I picked up the withered hand and laid it on my bed. It felt dry and wrinkled to the touch, like a raisin.

I hesitated, then dropped to my knees beside it. It might not be my patron saint's true hand, but it had still been sacred to her, a relic of her church. If I gave my prayers to it, she would hear me. Only, what *was* the proper prayer to a saint whom you have robbed and desecrated?

"Santa Marta," I said finally, "don't be angry with me. You know I couldn't—you know I had to leave." I was glad I didn't have to get into that part of my story—the small matter of who I was. Being sanctified, Santa Marta would just *know* that without me having to go through all the sordid details. "I'm sorry I had to steal from you, I didn't mean—"

I stopped. This wasn't going well at all.

"Santa Marta," I began again. "Help me to stay hidden here, and I dedicate all the dishes these hands of mine will ever make to you. The roasts, the fowl, the sauces, the sweets—all to your name. My hands and all their works, from this day, if you will forgive me my sins against you."

I looked down at my hands. Scarred with old knife nicks, the faded burn on my wrist where a too-hot sauce had once splashed, the calluses from wrestling with spits and jerking feathers from dead pheasants. What saint besides the patron of cooks would want hands like that?

For the first time, I really looked at the curled-up hand now lying on my bed. A small hand like mine; useful for stuffing the cavities of small birds. Narrow fingers, one still wearing a filigreed gold band, the sort of ring a cook would choose because it wasn't too elaborate to wear while kneading bread dough. The withered palm was broad—and was that the remnant of a callus at the base of the forefinger, in the same place where I had one after years of pressure from the handle of a knife?

I smiled for what felt like the first time in months. Maybe this wasn't the true hand of my patron saint, but it *had* been the hand of a cook.

Maybe we still understood each other, Santa Marta and I. Maybe she wasn't so angry with me after all. She had been at my side for Madonna Giulia's wedding feast, after all—even if Marco did get the credit for it, the good saint and I both knew who had really pulled it off.

"It *was* a good feast, wasn't it?" I asked the hand, and was rather disappointed when it didn't move. If it had made the sign of the cross at me, I'd have known my vow had been heard.

Or maybe I'd have just fainted dead away.

"*Carmelina!*" Marco's bellow from the kitchens. "Why are you dawdling, little cousin? Those figs won't stuff themselves!"

"Coming, *maestro*," I called, and hastily found my spare apron to replace the soiled one. The hand I carefully wrapped in my finest linen kerchief and stored at the bottom of my chest. "Not as good as a silver and rock crystal reliquary," I said aloud, rising. "But you'll never be more needed than you are with me."

I made the sign of the cross and whisked out of my little room that smelled like olive oil. I was a thief and a desecrator, and I was probably bound for hell one day, but Marco was right. Madonna Giulia's figs were not going to stuff themselves.

CHAPTER FOUR

※

The sword of the Lord will descend swiftly, and soon.

—FRA SAVONAROLA

Leonello

The Inn of the Fig was a step or two grander than the kind of establishment where I normally made my living. The maidservants wore neat gowns and clean aprons and for the most part looked indignant if you thumped them on the hip after they brought your drinks. The wine was subtler, the tapers beeswax instead of smoky tallow, the trestle tables clean-scrubbed rather than sticky with wine, and the crowd of dusty traveling pilgrims and habitual gamblers had a greater sprinkling of velvet-clad boys escaping their tutors for a little noisy fun among the cards and commoners. Accordingly I bought a new shirt and polished my boots, brought a seldom-worn cap of faded velvet from the chest at the foot of my bed, as well as a few rings for my stubby fingers that weren't silver but looked real enough, and for three weeks came nightly to the Inn of the Fig to play dice, *zara*, and all the other games of chance that I normally scorned. I ordered wine that I pretended to drink and ordered rounds that my fellow players drank to the dregs, and through it all I kept my ears open.

A tricky business, asking questions over a hand of cards. One had to time the questions after wine had begun to loosen tongues, but before it had addled wits; after the game's cards had been dealt, but before the tensity of the final hands set in. Men flushed with victory and money were quickest to talk, and I spent three weeks losing coin and gritting my teeth as my opponents made jests about little men who were short in luck as well as stature.

My heart thumped the first night I saw a man with a bull on his livery, and an uproarious game of *zara* got me the information that he worked in the household of Cardinal Borgia. But in came three more guardsmen bearing the Borgia bull, and over that night and the next I learned that they were all far too newly arrived in Rome to be the men I sought: hired just this past week from the country, to guard the Cardinal's *palazzo* and the Palazzo Montegiordano, where he kept his not-so-secret cache of bastard children. All over Rome churchmen and noblemen alike were hiring more guards. Pope Innocent was sinking fast; every rumor reported him nearer death's door, and everyone knew the city would erupt in chaos the moment he died. Rome always did at the death of her Holy Father.

Still—"That's what I saw the guardsman wearing," the hard-faced maidservant had nodded when I showed her a sketch of the Borgia livery with its red bull. "What kind of emblem is that for a man of God, I ask you? He won't be Pope next, not with a sigil like that. Cardinal Piccolomini, he's the one leading the odds now. Or Cardinal Sforza . . ."

I cared not two *scudi* who would wear the papal tiara after poor wheezing Pope Innocent breathed his last, but I oiled up to a good many Borgia guardsmen at the Inn of the Fig in the days following. "Give us a hint, you must know who the Cardinal will vote for, a big man like you working in his household!" And out the cards would come, and the coins, and the questions.

In three weeks, I had him. A big fellow with a cheerful ugly face, shirt half unlaced against the raging heat that refused to cool even in the night, sweat beading on his temples. I'd been steadily losing to him all night, enough that he looked at me with a benevolent gleam of friendliness, and when yet another round went against me, he shook his head and offered to buy me a tankard of wine.

"I always thought little men like you would be luckier than the rest of us," he said, waving the maidservant over. "A full-size man's supply of luck for a dwarf; that should make you a natural at *primiera*."

I shook my head ruefully, sweeping away my winning hand that would have taken the pot had I bothered to play it correctly. "I've never been lucky, my friend."

"Niccolo," he said. "I've taken enough out of your purse, you might as well have my name in return. And a drink."

An irritable-looking tavern maid slapped down my tankard, scowling as I blew her a kiss in thanks. "There's a face that would sour vinegar," I whistled as she turned away. "There was another one last night, dark-haired, pretty as a new day. I'd hoped to see her tonight." Dropping a wink. "She liked me."

"Good thing she isn't here then, my friend." Niccolo the guardsman leaned back in his chair, giving a proud slap to the Borgia bull on his doublet. "Every girl likes a man in a uniform best."

"Don't underestimate a woman's curiosity." I made a gesture from my prominent forehead to my broad chest to my short legs that didn't reach the floor. "A girl sees this, and she wants to see more. You know how many I've had that way? I could cross Rome without putting foot to floor, hopping between the beds I've visited."

"Get on with you," Niccolo scoffed, but he looked interested. Most men are—base curiosity isn't just a female vice. Men look at me and wonder secretly how a man of my size can perform a man's most basic function. In the lowest quarters of Rome you can find shows where dwarves tup each other before an audience that has paid good coin to watch.

"Of course, when a woman's had a dwarf, there's no telling what else she wants." I took another swallow of wine, letting it slosh on the table. "There was one woman . . ."

I told one of the dirtier stories in my arsenal, never mind that it came from a Venetian sailor with a gutter for a mouth, and not from my own memory. Niccolo the guardsman guffawed, topping me with a story of his own that I found just as improbable, and we ordered another tankard of wine and the room grew smokier and noisier as the night grew darker outside, and our voices dropped to a confidential pitch.

"—and there was the girl who liked a rope," I confided in a slushy whisper. I was emptying a third of my cup on the floor for the inn's dogs every time Niccolo went for a piss, but I knew how to play the part of a drunk. "She liked tying down, she did; arms staked out wide like Christ on the cross. She said it reminded her of His infinite sufferings." I demonstrated, holding my arms out not just in imitation of God's only Son, but of Anna on her table . . . and Niccolo's cup halted on its way to his mouth.

"*Dio.*" I shook my head, reminiscent. "That girl, I used to think she was a runaway nun. She used to weep after I was done, beg me to cut her throat and take her away from her sins. I always thought someday some bastard might take her up on it. Leave her with her throat opened and her arms still spread like a crucifix."

Niccolo's cup thudded back down to the table, untouched, and I felt a small savage thrill bloom in my chest. *Yes*, I thought, *yes, yes . . .*

"Holy Mother," he said, trying to laugh. "That's a girl worth staying clear of, little man. Things go wrong with girls like that, you know?"

"Maybe." I gave a careless shrug, but the bloom in my chest was spreading. It takes a very cold man indeed to listen untouched when he hears some vivid reminder of his last crime—and Niccolo, I judged, was anything but a cold man. His mouth was plastered wide in a grin, but the grin twitched at the corners and his eyes had stretched to show the white all around.

Better yet, he was more than halfway to drunk. And drink combined with guilt is a powerful loosener of tongues.

"You have your pleasure with the girl first," I said, "and who cares what happens after? Not your fault if something goes wrong."

"Sometimes it is," he said. "Sometimes things go bad, and they go bad so fast—"

A bead of sweat rolled down the side of his neck. I watched it slide below his collar. "What went bad?" I murmured.

"He just wanted a girl, you know? A common girl—common girls do things the courtesans won't unless you pay double." Niccolo's words were pottage in his mouth. Next sentence he'd be weeping; soon after that he'd be snoring on the table. I'd have to work fast.

"What then?" I encouraged, soft as a priest in a confessional.

Niccolo blinked hard, blinked again. "So we took him out."

I traced a circle around the top of my tankard. "'We'?"

Niccolo's unfocused eyes no longer saw me. He stared over the table, and whatever he saw was horror. "Me and Luis, he's the Cardinal's man from Valencia, one of the stewards, he—I used to like him."

"Don't you anymore?" *Spaniard.* Not a Venetian; a Spaniard after all.

A shudder. "Not after what he— God save me." Niccolo made a bleary sign of the cross. "God save *her.* The poor girl. I paid, I had a Mass said for her soul—"

"Did you, now?" I said softly. The bloom in my chest rose toward my mouth: a bitter flood of triumph. "Did you indeed, my friend?"

But he didn't hear me. His head rested on his folded arms; he mumbled something incoherent and a moment later began to snuffle and snore.

I didn't bring my cards when I came to the Inn of the Fig the following night. I brought a book instead—a tattered volume of Cicero's letters that I knew mostly by heart. I'd had to sell the *Iliad* to pay for Anna's burial. A sad, shabby little burial presided over by a priest who didn't even bother to hide the fact that he was drunk; attended only by me and a few of the maidservants at the tavern. No family, of course— girls with loving families do not end their days staked by the hands to tavern tables.

I was reading through Cicero's *Consolatio* again, boots propped on the table, when Niccolo ducked into the inn's common room. It was not far from midnight, but he hailed me when he saw me, and I let him wheedle me into a game of dice. He seemed to remember nothing of the previous evening's slurred secrets, though he made rueful jests about guards who couldn't hold their wine well enough to at least stay awake. I assured him I'd fallen asleep long before he did, and proceeded to lose another purse. He was just beginning to loosen from wine and winning when a thin, irritable-looking man in a sober gray doublet came and seized him by the shoulder.

"Getting drunk again?" he demanded shortly. "You know His Eminence wants his guards sharp; we don't know when we'll be called to the Vatican. The captain will have your ears on a string if you aren't at your place for the dawn shift! Up with you, up—" And he dragged at Niccolo's big arm.

"Luis?" I said.

His eyes slid coldly over me. "Yes?" he said, and I heard the Spanish tang to his voice. A short man with clean hands and neatly trimmed nails. A tidy shirt and unspotted hose, a pen case at his belt instead of a knife. Just the sort of man to accompany a headstrong boy on a slum-hunt for cheap whores; keep him in line and clear up any resulting messes.

He dismissed me with a flick of his hand, chivvying again at Niccolo, who sheepishly got to his feet and gave me a nod of farewell. The Spaniard hurried him along, and for a moment the man's shirt collar pulled away from his neck.

Barely visible at the base of his throat, I saw the beginning of three scratch marks. As if a woman had raked him with her nails, and very hard.

The Spaniard gave his collar an irritable tug and vanished into the crowd with Niccolo. I folded Cicero back into my doublet and rose. I'd have no more need for books tonight.

I stayed well back from them, tracking the sound of Don Luis's high, irritated voice. I'd marked the area around the Inn of the Fig well during the daylight, and now I moved silently in the dark. The dangerous part of night: when the earliest risers have yet to venture out, when the last drunks are staggering home, when the lurkers hope to bag one more purse or one more kill before slinking home with the dawn. There is no time so good as the hour before dawn to commit murder.

I looped ahead of my prey, doubling through the dark almost under their noses, but they were too busy scouting the shadowed corners to search the ground almost under their feet. I slipped into the deep shadow thrown by a vast *palazzo* and waited for the two figures to cross the *piazza*. I should have waited further until they separated, until I could take them alone—but I didn't want to wait. There were two of them, and both larger than me, but one was drunk and neither knew I was there. And it was dark, so very dark. Even a dwarf may seem a giant in the dark.

I took a deep breath and flung my voice into the night so it boomed. "Don Luis!"

They halted, twisting their heads in the blackness. Clouds had slid over the moon; the night air was summer warm and acrid-smelling. I smelled mud, horse manure; heard a dog whine and what sounded like a beggar's mindless weeping from an alley. Niccolo the guardsman was just a big shadow beside a shorter one, but I saw him cross himself.

"*Don Luis!*" I shouted again. "Why did you stake her hands to the table?"

The Spaniard's head whipped toward the sound of my voice, seeking me out, the breath huffing short and angry through his nostrils. It was Niccolo, wine-stupid and darkness-blind, who mumbled, "She wouldn't stay still."

"Quiet!" the Spaniard hissed.

"She wouldn't stay still," Niccolo repeated, near tears, "and Luis said the boy would have better luck fucking her if she was still. And he took his knife—"

"*I said quiet!*" Don Luis shouted, and he obeyed his own words. He never spoke again.

I whispered no prayer as the knife left my hand. Santo Giuliano the Hospitaller is said to watch over the souls of murderers, but only peni-tent murderers, and I had never felt less penitent for any act in my sorry little life. I just murmured, "Anna," and her name winged the blade from my hand straight as a spear. I saw the bare glint of metal in the dim moonlight fading through the clouds, heard the gurgle of blood trapped in the Spaniard's throat, and knew I'd thrown true.

He pitched over onto the mud-fouled stones of the *piazza*, the apple of his throat cored by my knife. Niccolo the guardsman gaped for a moment, still peering through the darkness for a glimpse of me. Then he gave a wail and fled.

I had already slipped a second knife from my cuff, at the ready, but he stumbled as I made my throw. The blade sank deep into his hip rather than his back, and he gave a howl that set dogs to barking clear across the vast expanse of *piazza*. I cursed silently and flung a third blade through the dark, but that one missed altogether, clattering on the stones as Niccolo picked himself up and hobbled on.

My legs were far too short to achieve more than a spraddle-footed jog, an effort I'd pay for later when my bowed leg bones protested having to carry me so fast. I'd never be a match for any full-sized man in a footrace, or any able-bodied child for that matter. But for a wounded man with a knife in his hip, and a leg now bleeding and buckling beneath him? My scuttle was quick enough.

I tracked Niccolo across the *piazza* and into the maze of dark twisting streets beyond. *Idiot*, I told myself harshly, *you'll be robbed and murdered yourself in streets like these.* Foolhardy for any man to set foot in Rome's lawless alleys once dark fell; sheer insanity for a dwarf who was anybody's prey even in daylight. But I heard Niccolo panting before me, moaning whenever he had to lean his full weight on that weakening side; I smelled his blood rank and metallic against the night smells of tallow smoke and sewage, and another finger knife had already somehow found its way from the tiny sheath inside my belt seam to my hand. *You could let him go*, a voice in my head suggested, maybe even the voice of Santo Giuliano, who would like me to repent for my taking of life. The man who had staked Anna's hands with knives was dead, after all, and Don Luis had likely been the one to cut her throat. But Niccolo must have held her down, too. He'd protested, perhaps; winced from the pangs of guilt; even bought Masses for her soul—but he had held her down, all the same, and I felt not one drop of mercy.

Ahead of me, my quarry was slowing. I heard whimpers in his gasps, and the scent of blood came even more sharply to my nose. He must have tugged my knife out of his hip; the wound would be running freely now. I hesitated when he turned limping and panting over the Ponte Sant'Angelo—it provided a long straightaway, and I could have flung my finger knife at the shadowy shape scurrying away across the bridge. But it was my last knife, and if I missed I'd be weaponless, and if there was one bitter lesson I'd learned it was never to be without a weapon. I'd have to take Niccolo up close, and I quickened my screaming legs to a splay-footed sprint. Pilgrims crossed the Ponte Sant'Angelo for a look at the Basilica San Pietro, but I didn't think that was Niccolo's goal.

I trapped him within sight of the Palazzo Montegiordano's vast façade. He was stumbling and whimpering ahead of me, looking back over his shoulder in frantic terror to see what thing was chasing him through the shadows. Maybe he thought it was Anna, come from the grave to wrap her butchered hands about his throat. I veered to scrabble a stone out of the gutter, slimy with sewage water and rat droppings, and sent it thudding into the small of his back. He let out a scream and went down, and before he could clamber to his feet I was squatting over his back like an incubus. I grabbed a handful of his sweat-slick hair, yanking his head up and setting the knife point at his throat.

"Niccolo," I purred into his ear. "Tell me who the boy was."

"What boy?" He was weeping now. "What boy? I don't—"

"The boy in the mask. The one you took out for a night in the slums, and somehow cards and wine led to staking a girl on a table. I know you remember who *she* was." I spared a glance for the imposing facade of the Palazzo Montegiordano. There were more guards in the Borgia bull, standing watch under the torches—any instant now they'd notice the little struggle in the street just outside their circle of torchlight. I tightened my grip on Niccolo and lowered my voice. "The boy in the mask—who was he?" Another young guard in the Palazzo Montegiordano, perhaps, someone Niccolo had taken under his wing? A page? Someone richer; maybe a cousin of Don Luis or some young bravo who was a guest at one of the Cardinal's banquets? "*Tell me his name.*"

Niccolo thrashed, gibbering in terror, but I sank all my weight into his shoulder blades and he couldn't dislodge me. I might have a child's legs and arms, but I had the torso of a man, and I was heavier than I looked for a man just a hand-span taller than four feet. I had him pinned like a dog, and he froze when the point of my knife drew blood at his throat.

"Who—who are you? The whore's brother?"

"Anna," I whispered into Niccolo's ear in a venomous hiss. *"Her name was Anna."*

And a stunning blow took me across the back of the head.

I caught a bare glimpse of a guardsman with a red bull on his chest, gazing down at me as I toppled from my perch on Niccolo's shoulders. The guard reversed the pike he'd used to club the back of my head and drove the butt into my wrist, and through a blaze of pain I could feel the knife slipping from my fingers. *No,* I thought, *no, a dwarf can never go without a weapon.* But my weapon was gone, and I blinked to see the sickly gray of dawn lightening the sky as boots thudded past me, thudded toward me, thudded all around me.

"Your Excellency?" A voice floated somewhere overhead. "Look what we've found!"

"Sharp eyes," replied a young man's voice, and a booted foot kicked me over onto my back. I blinked at the yellow glare from the torches that now surrounded me like a witch hunt. "And what have we here?"

In the jagged shadows of dawn and torchlight I saw a boy's narrow amused face. A handsome face, with auburn hair and a pair of black bottomless eyes. The eyes were the last thing I saw before the dark swallowed me.

Giulia

I'm a lazy creature, God knows, but I wasn't used to such idleness as this. As an unmarried girl in my father's house, there had always been some duty at hand: handwriting exercises to copy out for my tutor, an altar cloth to be embroidered under my mother's exacting eye, the turns of the *basse-danse* to practice with my sister for a partner, songs by Machaut to finger on the lute. When I wasn't occupied by tutors, my mother believed in making me useful: setting me to help the maids with the household mending, or taking me with her to dispense alms to beggars.

And now? I had nothing to fill my days at all. The vast *palazzo* ran smoothly, servants whisking through their tasks and making their reports to Madonna Adriana, who sat in the middle of the busy web like a most competent spider. I had no tutors now to make me memorize verses of Dante, and the daily mending was done with no assistance from me. I could still embroider altar cloths, I suppose, but I hated embroidery. I could go to church, but I had only so many sins to confess. I was surrounded by more luxury than I'd ever dreamed of; I slept on silk and wore French brocades; I could eat roast peacock and strawberries for every meal if I wanted—the richness that lapped all around still took my breath away, and I won't say I didn't appreciate it. But I had nothing to *do*.

"Tend your beauty," Madonna Adriana said, patting my arm. "Hair like that needs daily sunning, you know. And if you don't mind my saying so, you are putting on just a tiny bit of weight, so perhaps fewer candied cherries and some daily rides. We shall have to see about getting you a horse . . . Yes, do go brush that hair. Beauty like yours is a gift! God knows it won't last forever, so you should get whatever you can from it while it's in full bloom."

But there were only so many hours I could spend buffing my nails and brushing my hair and massaging rose-petal creams into my neck to keep it white and soft. I twanged flatly on my lute for a while, flipped through a book of verse Cardinal Borgia had sent me—but finally gave in to the temptation of the summer heat outside. I laced myself into a peach linen overdress embroidered about the bodice in spring flowers, and trailed in my bare feet down the shallow flights of marble steps leading from my chamber to one of the enclosed gardens within the Palazzo Montegiordano. Only to be accosted by a cherub in pale blue silk who flew across the garden staring at me as though I were a unicorn.

"Is this her?" the cherub breathed, bobbing up and down like a puppy. "This is La Bella? Oh, Madonna Adriana, she's *beautiful*! You said she was beautiful, but I didn't know *this* beautiful!" And she flung her arms around my waist.

"Ooof!" The child nearly took me off my feet. Righting her, I saw she was no child but a girl a year or two from betrothal age: eleven or twelve with a lively little face, pale blue eyes, and a cloud of curling blond hair just a shade darker than mine.

"Lucrezia," my mother-in-law chided, gliding down into the garden like a well-oared galleon. She had a boy by the hand, a few years younger than the girl, wide-eyed and curly-haired in a miniature doublet of slashed velvet.

"I'm sorry, Madonna Giulia," the girl said, and withdrew to make a beautiful little curtsy before me. "I am Lucrezia Borgia, daughter of His Eminence Cardinal Borgia, who said I was to make you love me if at all possible. And I very much want to make my father happy, so can you love me at once, please?"

"Your father is very cunning," I told her, but couldn't help the laugh that burst out of me at her earnest expression.

Madonna Adriana beamed. "This is Joffre, His Eminence's youngest son," she said, indicating the boy she held firmly by his plump ten-year-old hand. "They have been visiting their mother this past month or two, but they have finally returned home. Lucrezia has been bouncing since dawn to meet you."

"I have heard *so* much from my father," the girl in blue confided. "He did not exaggerate at all. Do you really have hair down to your feet? Can I see it? Do you use a bleaching paste or just the sun? I would use a bleaching paste on my hair, but Madonna Adriana won't let me—"

I wanted to make my polite excuses and return to my chamber—refuse to be charmed by anything connected with Cardinal Borgia—but somehow I found myself dragged farther into the garden by my would-be lover's bastard daughter as Madonna Adriana disappeared back into the *sala* with little Joffre. Lucrezia went on chattering even on the in-breath, and I should have enjoined her to be silent and godly as befitted a girl on the brink of womanhood. But I remembered being twelve and bursting with words no one wanted to hear, so rather than reprove her I smiled and unnetted my hair and shook it down around my feet.

"My father said you had beautiful hair!" She clapped her hands in admiration. "He calls you Giulia la Bella."

"Does he?" I hesitated, but I couldn't resist adding, "What else does he say about me?" Not that I was *interested,* of course. But I had to talk about something, didn't I?

"My father says he loves you," little Lucrezia said, matter-of-factly. "I want hair like yours. How do you make it grow so long?"

"Massage your scalp every night when you comb your hair out," I found myself telling her. "Until your head tingles, like this—" And somehow we were both sitting in the grass under the sun, Lucrezia sitting with her back to me.

"Ouch!"

"It's good if it hurts; that means it's growing." I rubbed her scalp until she yowled some more. "For beauty, you have to suffer a little."

Lucrezia tilted her little chin over one shoulder to look at me. "Is it worth it?"

"Very much. Don't let the priests tell you differently." I produced the little silver comb that I always tucked into my sleeve and began stroking it through her untidy curls. "So your father talks about me?"

"Yes, he wants to have you painted for his study! With a blue dress and a dove in your lap, as the Virgin."

Apt, I thought a touch sourly.

"I'm to have my portrait painted soon too," Lucrezia confided. "For my betrothed. He wants a look at me, and I have to look pretty, I *have* to. If I don't he'll marry someone else, and my heart will break!"

"And who is your betrothed?" Gently I teased a knot out of a curl behind her ear.

"Don Gaspare Aversa, Count of Procida." She pronounced the name with satisfaction. "A very noble gentleman in Spain."

"A good match. Have you met him?"

"No, but my father says he's young and handsome. I'm only to have the best." Lucrezia gave a wriggle of satisfaction. "Father loves me."

"Sit still," I told her. "You've got tangles."

"I always do." She heaved a gusty sigh. "I wish I didn't have curls."

"Yes, you do. Because you won't need a hot poker to make ringlets, the way I do."

She gave a little bounce of satisfaction at that, then sat still as I worked the comb. I found I was humming and felt a twinge that I realized was contentment. I hadn't had a companion since I came to this *palazzo*, not really—not someone with whom I could sit and giggle, someone who wanted nothing more out of me than a few words of gossip and my hands combing her hair. Just Madonna Adriana and her coin counting, or the innumerable Orsini cousins who came to inspect me over plates of honeyed *mostaccioli* and make equally honeyed inquiries about why I hadn't accompanied my husband to the country. I ask you!

"Since when has my cousin's house been taken over by Greek goddesses?" A deep voice sounded behind me, a voice I knew well with its thread of amusement and its Spanish burr. "Demeter and Persephone, in the flesh."

Lucrezia scrambled to her feet, performed another exquisite curtsy in the grass, and flung herself at her father. I expected him to reprove her—my own long-dead father certainly would have set me on my feet with a stern little lecture on the tenets of womanly dignity—but Cardinal Borgia hugged his daughter tight, lifting her in the air so her blue skirts belled.

"No, no," he interrupted her as she began rattling off some question in Spanish. "Madonna Giulia doesn't speak our Catalan, remember?"

Lucrezia dropped easily out of Spanish. "Can I be painted as Persephone for my portrait for Don Gaspare? I'll hold a pomegranate and wear flowers in my hair—"

"Only if Madonna Giulia will consent to be painted as Demeter." The Cardinal's dark eyes moved to me. "As she sits now, with her hair around her and corn in her lap. What do you think, Lucrezia *mia*?"

"I think she needs flowers for her hair too," Lucrezia decided, and dashed at once to the rosebushes lining the rosy stone walls of the garden courtyard.

"Clever, Your Eminence." I threw my comb at Cardinal Borgia as he settled into the grass beside me and tossed his square cardinal's hat carelessly beside the fountain. "Sending your daughter to help seduce me!"

"Is it working?" He gave a lazy blink, leaning on one elbow like a Roman emperor.

I smiled involuntarily, watching Lucrezia gather rosebuds into her skirt, her hair a bright aureole in the sun. "She is very charming."

"She is that." He watched his daughter with undisguised fondness. "I breed beautiful daughters, Madonna Giulia. Would you like one?"

"I want sons, thank you," I said with a sniff worthy of my straitlaced sister. "Sons from my husband, not from you."

"Don't parrot your *duenna*," the Cardinal said amiably. "Women say they want sons, because they know their husbands want them. But beautiful women always want daughters."

I blinked. All right, so perhaps I'd dreamed of a daughter once I was married. A little girl with my fair hair and dark eyes, and Sandro's outrageously long lashes which I somehow hadn't inherited along with the eyes (which was injustice on a grand scale, but hopefully my daughter would be luckier). A little girl I could sit with in the sun, just as I had been sitting with little Lucrezia Borgia.

Cardinal Borgia lay watching me. "She'd have my name," he said, "if that daughter you bore was mine. And a nobleman for a husband, just as Lucrezia will."

"While I'm reviled as a whore and an adulteress, and my daughter is raised by Madonna Adriana instead of me?" I jerked my chin up. "Just like Lucrezia and her brothers? Little Joffre, who I just met, and Juan the young lecher, and that other one who just returned from the university in Pisa. Where is *their* mother now?"

"Happy proprietress of three prosperous Roman inns and a slew of property along the Tiber," the Cardinal said promptly. "All gifts from me. Vannozza has no cause to complain. We had ten years and four children together, she and I, and remain good friends. Her latest husband did not care for a slew of Borgia bastards in his home, so—" A Spanish shrug at the rosy walls of Madonna Adriana's garden, followed by a chuckle. "And I can tell you Vannozza is not reviled by anybody, as an adulteress or anything else. They wouldn't dare."

"Even though her children are all bastards?"

"My dear girl, no one cares for such things! This isn't France, you know, or England, where everyone is either straight-laced or provincial. Our lords here, the Duke of Milan, the Duke of Ferrara, the King of Naples; they raise all their children together in luxury, and no one cares which child came from which womb! They're men of the world, and so am I."

"You put yourself equal with the King of Naples and the Duke of Milan, then?"

"I put myself equal with any man living."

"Madonna Giulia, look!" Lucrezia ran up happily, spilling a skirtful of roses into my lap. "All red; they'll be beautiful in your hair. May I?"

"If you like." I lifted my mass of hair from its pile on the grass and began to bundle it back into its net, but the Cardinal's hand stopped me.

"Leave it." Was his voice a trifle hoarse? "I've not seen it loose before."

I pulled my hand away from his but let my hair drop around my shoulders again. Lucrezia whirled around me, a blue butterfly tucking a rose here, a bud there, exclaiming in delight as her father looked at me—and looked—and looked—

I flushed. Most men have the good grace to drop their eyes when you catch them gaping, or at least feign interest in the Pinturicchio altarpiece or flowing fountain or dogfight or anything that they can find to look at just past your shoulder. "Don't you know it's rude to stare, Eminence?" I said tartly.

"Yes." But he went on looking, and his eyes were black and full of fires.

"There!" Lucrezia stood back, satisfied. "Now you look *exactly* like Demeter, all peach and gold and red."

"Gather some more flowers, then." I smiled up at her. "And I'll weave them into a crown for you, Persephone."

"Blue flowers," she decided. "To go with my dress—" And she skipped off in search of violets and hyacinths among the roses.

"I'll hate to lose her to a husband," Cardinal Borgia said as naturally as if he had not been gazing at me a moment ago with his heart in his eyes. "She's my comfort. Sons are always trouble—"

I thought of leering sixteen-year-old Juan, and agreed.

"—but daughters are a man's delight." He watched Lucrezia gathering flowers, and shook his head. "Sometimes I wonder why I chose the Church, Giulia. Scheming and whispering and plotting, and that College of Cardinals like a nest of chattering red hens ... when I could have this." He gestured around him. "Sunlight. Flowers. Children. You."

"You can't have me," I told him. "And I don't believe you at all, Eminence. You like scheming and whispering and plotting. Don't try to tell me otherwise just to tug on my heart."

He grinned, and it surprised me. His eagle's nose and watchful black eyes took on a different cast above that youthful white grin in the swarthy face. "I do have *some* regrets. You, for example."

I raised skeptical brows. "I suppose if you weren't a cardinal you would have married me?"

"No, I'd probably have some rich wife as square as a four-poster bed," he said candidly. "But I'd have the time to devote a week to seducing you properly. Thanks to the College of Cardinals and their dithering about the Pope dying, I've hardly been able to devote any time to you at all."

"A week?" I batted a rose out of my eye that had come loose from Lucrezia's twining. "Is that how long it usually takes you to seduce a woman? What a sorry opinion you must have of female virtue."

"On the contrary. What I have is a high opinion of my own skills. But even I need *time*," he complained. "Normally one begins with a necklace, then there is a banquet with the right kind of music and light conversation. Then perhaps a trip to the countryside where I could show how magnificently I sit a horse. A few more gifts—perhaps a perfume that I had mixed for you specially; I have a very good nose for a woman's scent. What's that you're wearing now, honeysuckle and gillyflower? I thought so. Then a more intimate *cena*, on a pleasure boat along the Tiber, if one can find a place where the mud doesn't stink to the heavens and ruin the mood ... yes, usually it takes a week."

He sighed. "And yet here we are, nearly two months later: you still laced into that dress when you should be naked in the grass right now with a golden-haired little girl already growing in your belly, and I have the College of Cardinals to thank for it." Rodrigo Borgia cocked an eyebrow at me. "One thing to be thankful for if the Pope hurries up and dies. I'll finally have time to devote to you."

My face flamed the same color as the roses in my hair. I didn't know where to put my eyes, or my hands, and I didn't have the faintest idea what to say. All I could think was that I'd had plenty of men *look* at me as though they wished they could see me naked, but this was the first time I'd had one *tell* me so. It wasn't poetic, not at all. Did Petrarch ever say a word about Laura lying naked in the grass? No, because it wasn't poetic, and it wasn't romantic, and it certainly wasn't seemly either, so why did my skin feel warm all over? I fumbled for words, any words, around a tongue gone suddenly thick. Oh, Holy Virgin, my mother's instructions on the art of polite discourse had never prepared me for a conversation like this! "So the Pope is dying?" I finally managed to say, inanely.

"Yes, quite soon. Of course he's been dying for years, so who knows if he means it this time."

The Cardinal turned on his back in the grass, putting his dark head into my lap.

I leaned over him, glaring. "Did I say you could do that?"

"No."

"Move at once!"

"No."

"Now, really, Eminence—"

"Spill me out by all means." His eyes sparkled. "Lucrezia's feelings will be hurt, of course—she is very protective of me, especially when I'm tired."

I studied his face upside down, the dark eyes sunken and the swarthy skin grained under them. "You do look tired," I admitted, grudgingly.

"Dying popes mean more work for everyone else. And since it's me who will call the Conclave once he's gone, well, the bribes begin to fly. Do you fancy an emerald bracelet? Cardinal Piccolomini slipped it under my plate just yesterday. He wants my vote to make him Pope, of course. They all do. Cardinal della Rovere is ready to stab me on sight just for the way I've been nodding when Cardinal Carafa whispers in my ear. I nod as much as possible. Irritating della Rovere is one of my chief pleasures in life."

"Don't *you* want to be Pope? I looked down at him. "I thought all cardinals did."

"Not me," he said airily. "A pope who adores his bastard children, who seduces beautiful golden-haired brides? Perish the thought."

"Popes can have bastards, just like all those great lords you were speaking of. Pope Innocent has two." I knew all the gossip.

"Actually he has sixteen."

Apparently not *all* the gossip. "He doesn't have a mistress, though," I countered. "Not after he was elected, Sandro told me. A pope must keep up appearances."

"See? Why would anyone want to be Pope?" Cardinal Borgia yawned. "Certainly not me."

"Liar. You *do* want to be Pope, of course you do, so why pursue me at all? You'd have to give me up, and then where would I be?" I knew exactly what my mother would say, not to mention my confessor. "If I give my virtue to you, I go to hell for it."

"My dear girl, of course you wouldn't. What do you think confession is for? Humor me," he added as I looked skeptical.

I sighed. "We confess sins so we may repent them, of course."

"Yes." He crossed himself, still lying down. "But one needn't really worry about the fires of hell just for a few carnal sins, Giulia Farnese."

"That's not what I was taught!"

"If God truly objected to my batch of beautiful children and my devastating passion for you"—reaching up from my lap to run a finger down the side of my face—"would He have elevated me as one of his most holy cardinals? No. He would simply smite me dead with a bolt from heaven, or at least a timely plague. Our Heavenly Father says as much through his inactions as his actions, after all. If He does not act, then He approves."

I scowled, moving away from the hand at my cheek. "You're twisting things about."

"Not at all. Merely pointing out that the fires of hell are not *quite* so inevitable, when it comes to fleshly sins, as mothers like to tell their daughters." He sat up lazily. "Allow me to educate you."

"Can you do that while keeping your hands to yourself?" I swatted him away as he plucked a rosebud from my hair.

He ignored me. "It's not the sin that matters, dear girl, it's the repentance afterward. I could take you to my bed and keep you there all day—this afternoon, perhaps? No? Ah, well—and before I left I could grant you absolution for everything. All you would have to do is say a few prayers in penance."

"A few Misereres don't make up for fornication." My confessor would have been quite adamant about *that*.

"Why not?" Cardinal Borgia inhaled my rose deeply. "I have God's authority to state that they do."

"And what about *your* repentance? You don't seem particularly sorry about any of this!"

"Of course I am." His voice was serious. "I am deeply penitent that I cannot enjoy your favors as your wedded husband. And to expiate those sins—lust, envy, hopefully fornication—I would give an Act of Contrition and a donation to the poor-box for every kiss you gave me." He picked up my hand and kissed it swiftly. "You see? I have had my kiss, my soul is washed clean, and the poor are enriched."

"That is *not* true repentance."

"Of course it is. God made us imperfect, dear girl. Thus He also made loopholes, so He has an excuse to forgive us."

I was hunting for the flaw in that when Lucrezia ran up with a skirtful of violets and daisies. "Madonna Giulia, can I have a crown?"

"Certainly." I took a handful of violets, grateful for the distraction, and began threading the flower stems together into a chain. I didn't want to talk anymore about dubious loopholes in God's forgiveness, and Cardinal Borgia didn't pursue it either. He just looked amused, and he lazily beckoned his daughter with one finger so he could whisper something in Catalan. She giggled and dashed off, and he put his head back into my lap.

"Stop that," I said.

"At once," he said, reaching up to wind a lock of my hair around his fingers. His own hair was very black, untouched by gray.

Lucrezia came back with another giggle, pressing something into her father's hand that he concealed in his sleeve. "Is my crown ready, Madonna Giulia?" she entreated me with a whirl of pale blue skirts.

"There you go." I draped the chain of daisies and violets over her hair, smiling as she pirouetted over to the fountain.

"Madonna Adriana says I can sun my hair this afternoon, after I'm done with my Latin exercises and my dancing practice." She stood on tiptoe over the water, craning to see her reflection. "You will sit with me, won't you?"

"Yes," I found myself saying. "All afternoon, if you like."

"I wish I could sit with you." The Cardinal rose from the grass, dusting off his scarlet robes. "But I fear I am expected at the Pope's bedside. He gets fretful if he doesn't have company with his afternoon cup of blood."

"*Blood?*" I couldn't help saying.

"Yes, he drinks a dram of blood every day. Drawn from the veins of virgin boys—some charlatan of a doctor told him it had restorative powers. Personally, I would just make my peace with God and die." Cardinal Borgia leaned down and placed a kiss on his daughter's blond head. "Off with you, little one. Your dancing hardly needs improvement, but the Latin verbs most decidedly do. If you can translate a page of Cicero's letters for me by tomorrow, and recite it with a good accent, I'll see you have a new dress for your portrait to Don Gaspare."

Lucrezia dropped another curtsy and flew away to her tutors. I rose to follow her, but the Cardinal put two fingers to my wrist and stopped me. "I should like to have you painted as well, Giulia."

"As the Virgin?" I raised my eyebrows. "And when did I give you permission to call me by name?"

"Not as the Virgin," he said as if I hadn't spoken, and his fingers slowly circled my wrist. "Nor as Demeter. I think perhaps you will make a better Persephone than my daughter."

"Do you, indeed?" My education had been limited to the usual subjects: embroidery, dancing, beautiful handwriting, enough arithmetic to keep a household's books, and enough Dante to provide me with witty quotations. No one had ever demanded that I translate Cicero; I was taught only enough Latin to say my prayers—but Sandro and my other brothers had learned their Latin and Greek from a balding heron of a classics tutor, and my mother had allowed me to sit in on the lessons while I embroidered, since it kept me out of trouble. Mostly I'd sat making faces at Sandro and tying my embroidery into hopeless knots, but I picked up a few other things. The Greek verbs and Latin declensions went in one ear and out the other, but I liked the stories of the ancient gods and their innumerable love affairs. "If I'm Persephone," I went on, "then what does that make you, Your Eminence? The lord of the underworld who kidnapped me and kept me against my will? Can I eat the pomegranates, or will the seeds doom me to stay here forever like Persephone?"

"I always wonder if Persephone didn't eat her pomegranate seeds willingly." Slowly Cardinal Borgia's hard thumb rubbed back and forth across the inside of my wrist. "If she didn't decide she wanted to stay with her dark lord after all."

"Who would want to be queen of the underworld?" He had drawn me closer, my hand still trapped in his. If he tried to kiss me, he'd get another good hard slap.

"Perhaps the underworld wasn't so bad." His thumb passed over my knuckles now, very lightly, back and forth. "Dark, maybe. But a great many good things can happen in the dark." Back and forth. "I think Persephone knew that, when she swallowed those seeds."

I had nothing to say to that. I could feel the heat that had spread down my neck, but I refused to look away from him, refused to blink and blush and giggle like a flustered convent girl. The silence enveloped us. His stroking thumb passed my knuckles, down the length of my fingers.

"Until next time," he said.

"When?" The word came out before I realized it. Oh, Holy Virgin, I'd been telling myself I wouldn't ask!

He smiled faintly. "Who knows? It all depends on the Pope's health."

"You want to be Pope next," I said. It was not a question. "Don't you."

"No." His thumb skimmed back and forth along my fingertips, the barest of touches. "I want to be with you. In the dark."

He stepped away, releasing my hand. His scarlet shape had disappeared up the stairs and into the *palazzo* before I realized that once again he'd left something in my hand. Something he'd sent Lucrezia to fetch, and hidden in his sleeve.

Not a necklace this time. No rubies or pearls; no gilt-buckled snakeskin slippers or enameled hand mirrors or silver nets for my hair: the gifts that had been turning up in my chamber nearly every day, wrapped in cardinal-scarlet ribbons.

A pomegranate.

Carmelina

M y cousin surprised me that Sunday by looking me in the eye as he reached for his hat and cloak. "Er—" he began, and stopped. He cleared his throat. We had the kitchens to ourselves for once—most of the cooks and maidservants had already gone to Mass. The flagstones gleamed, the trestle tables were scrubbed white, sun poured through the small leaded windowpanes, and I'd been looking forward to a little quiet. I had a *crostata* of summer peaches to make, and I was itching to try a new idea I'd had for the crust: a sort of ribboned twist of flaky pastry layered about the top in a spiral. But Marco still lingered, twisting his cap between his hands and looking more than a bit shamefaced. He'd be late to Mass. "Um," he said at last. "Many thanks, Carmelina. For, er, yesterday."

"I'm the one who owes you thanks, Marco." It wouldn't hurt to remind him of his generosity in sheltering me here. I looked down again at the bowl of peaches I was sorting for the *crostata*, separating the ripe from the bruised. "I'm glad to help any way I can."

Marco hadn't lost himself at the gaming tables *quite* as thoroughly as he had the day of Madonna Giulia's wedding . . . but I'd still had to cover for him when the hour for *cena* approached and he hadn't returned in time to begin preparations. I'd taken charge: supervising the rack of ribs onto its spit for the Borgia children, checking the *tourtes* as the apprentices filled the crusts, seasoning the salads before the maids carried them out, overseeing the decanting of the wine. Marco had returned, flushed with embarrassment, sometime after the rack of ribs had come back from the *sala* as a pile of picked bones.

"I couldn't leave," he insisted to me now, as though I'd argued with him. I remembered him saying just the same thing to my father, in the same tone of voice. "My luck was just starting to turn—one more hand and I'd have made it all back!"

"Yes, Marco," I sighed into the bowl of peaches. As master cook to a cardinal's cousin and his treasured bastards, my cousin brought home twenty-five ducats a year—and how much of it went to dice, to cards and bull-baitings and bets on when the Pope would die and who would be Pope next? I'd seen Marco lay a week's wages on whether one roach would cross a floor faster than another.

"I won't do it again," Marco said confidently. He'd said that to my father, too. And still at least twice a week he'd make some excuse and slip out for a few hours between noon and the preparation of the evening meal, excitement burning in two bright spots along his handsome cheeks and his eyes gleaming fever-bright. "I won't forget you covering for me. You're a savior, little cousin."

He reached out, giving my chin a tweak of thanks. He had a fondness in his eye that surprised me—normally he regarded me with irritation, as if he still didn't quite believe how I'd finagled my way into his kitchens.

"I am thankful, Carmelina," he said now, and there was no resentment in his voice. "I may shout at you sometimes—and you know I don't approve of what you've done, not at all. But I'm glad to have you here."

"Thank you, Marco." I couldn't help being touched. He *was* my distant cousin, after all—the last family I had, really. I liked it much better when he didn't resent me. "Though you shouldn't apologize for shouting, you know," I added. "All cooks shout."

"Dear God in heaven, your father did." Marco shook his head, reminiscent. "Then he'd lay across the side of my head with a ladle if I still wasn't moving fast enough to suit him. And now I do the same to Piero and the other apprentices."

"Fire Piero," I advised, tossing a peach aside as I felt a rotten spot under my thumb. "The boy's insolent, and he's no good with pastry."

"I hate getting rid of people. You fire him when he comes back from Mass."

"Gladly." That would raise my status among the apprentices, and no mistake. Respect had to be earned in a kitchen—if I fired Piero, and the *maestro di cucina* backed my decision, they'd all look at me differently. Hopefully with fear. Apprentices work better when motivated by a little terror.

Marco lounged against the doorjamb, cloak slung over his arm. "Pity you weren't born a boy, little cousin. You'd have made a better cook than me."

"I *am* a better cook than you," I told him. "Remember when you were sixteen, and you ruined that beef loin stew because you were busy getting odds on the Palio? Who do you think saved that stew? Who threw in raisins and rose vinegar and Greek wine until it was edible, *and* got it off the fire all by herself when her father's back was turned? Me, that's who, and me no more than twelve."

"That was you?" Marco whistled. "I owe you, then. Or at least the skin on my back does. Aren't you coming to Mass?"

"No church would have me." Not with the sins I had on my soul, and I didn't see how could I ever confess those sins to a priest without giving myself up to the justice of the Church. Early this morning I'd taken the withered hand of Santa Marta from the little hanging pouch I generally carried under my overskirt, and just said my prayers to her instead. It would have to be enough. Besides, I really was itching to try that new crust. If I could roll the dough out in a spiral twist without toughening the texture . . .

"Can you keep an eye on the maids when they get back from church, then? There's, er, a shrine I want to visit across the Borgo after Mass—"

There was a *primiera* game he wanted to visit across the Borgo after Mass, or perhaps a cockfight.

"Enjoy your shrine," I said, raising my eyebrows just a touch, and Marco gave me a little-boy grin and was gone in a whirl of hope. Today, *today*, was the day his luck would turn, after all. If not today, then certainly tomorrow.

Always tomorrow.

The maidservants were already starting to trickle back, those who hadn't bothered to go confess their sins after Mass, and I quickly set them to work polishing silver and taking inventory in the storerooms. At least these were proper kitchens—really, I savored the chance to have them all to myself. The chief kitchen with its ovens and eternally revolving spit, separated as it should be from the scullery where the flagstones were silvery with fish scales and the pot-boys scrubbed an eternal procession of dirty dishes . . . the cold room after that, where cream tops could be whipped up in peace and the game stored away from the heat of the ovens . . . the courtyard where wagons arrived at all times of night and day with wood for the ovens and game for the spits and fish still flopping-fresh from the river.

In an ordinary kitchen I'd have to spend my free hours frantically catching up on those tasks that always seemed to pile up in a busy household: the wood ash to be removed from the ovens, the game to be vigilantly checked for the first faint signs of rot, the floors to be swept and swept and swept again. But here everything was cool and organized: the game didn't go bad because there was room to store it properly; there was an endless succession of scullions and pot-boys to empty the ovens and keep the floors swept; loads of kindling and barrels of wine were delivered by the cartload and I never had to think about my fires dying or my household going thirsty or capons going unflavored.

Yes, I could get used to cooking in a household like this. The kind of household where I could get the occasional hour of peace and quiet—put my peach *crostata* in the ovens and take time to update my father's recipes, if that was what I felt like doing. And I rather did, this afternoon. Once I'd regarded my father's recipes as just as sacred and unchangeable as the stone tablets handed down to Moses—but now I was starting to make a few changes of my own. A pinch of saffron to bring color and warmth to a sauce; a dash of salt for bite in a sweet *tourte* . . . what *did* my father have to say about a peach *crostata*, anyway? I turned the worn pages to page 261, Chapter: Pastry, savoring my own uninterrupted thoughts in the silence, but I should have known no cook ever gets an uninterrupted hour to do anything. Even in a household as luxurious and well appointed as this one.

"Oh, ho!" I heard a boy's voice behind me. "I thought I knew all Madonna Adriana's servant girls, but you're new."

"Out," I said without turning. I had no intention of being interrupted by some page boy or manservant with fancies of kitchen girls brought to bloom too early by the heat of the kettle steam; girls with half-unlaced bodices sucking honey from the tip of one finger and just aching to be bent over a trestle table and rubbed with olive oil like a fresh-plucked duck. Santa Marta save me from the overheated male imagination! "Out of my kitchens at once," I repeated, and turned a page.

"They aren't your kitchens, my lovely. They're Maestro Mantini's, or whatever his name is."

I turned and glowered, but my glower faded fast as I took in the auburn hair, the long lean body lounging against the door frame, the patchy wisps of reddish beard and the fine doublet carelessly unlaced over hose and fashionable shoes of tooled Spanish leather. Not a page boy or manservant, but Juan Borgia: second son of Cardinal Borgia, a boy of sixteen who was already Duke of Gandia and had his own household in the city but still spent a good deal of time at the Palazzo Montegiordano visiting his little sister, Lucrezia, and younger brother, Joffre. I had seen Juan Borgia from a distance now and then, swaggering with his friends or mussing his sister's hair or ogling Madonna Giulia—and I had overheard quite a bit more about him from the maidservants.

Who had all, I noticed, abandoned their inventorying and silver polishing to disappear speedily into the storerooms the instant he appeared.

"Your lordship." I rose, bobbing just enough of a curtsy for respect while keeping my voice firm. "I do apologize most humbly, but I am the cousin of Maestro Marco Santini, and he has left his kitchens in my trust. He is most particular about those he allows near his fires and ovens."

"They aren't his fires and ovens, they're mine." The Duke of Gandia caressed the hilt of the rapier at his waist, grinning. "And so are you, my pretty."

Apparently he hadn't noticed that I wasn't pretty at all. I suppose anything female is pretty to a boy of sixteen, even something long and plain as a stalk of asparagus and wrapped in a cinnamon-stained apron.

"I work for Madonna Adriana, your lordship," I corrected, eyes down, "and with respect, these kitchens are hers."

"Who do you think pays for it? She lets me do what I like, Adriana does. My father, my sister, my brothers—the old bitch knows who keeps her bread buttered." He moved into the kitchen with a swagger. Or as much of a swagger as he could manage in such fashionably pointed shoes. "So, are you Maestro Santini's whore?"

I felt my cheeks heat, but kept my gaze on the floor. "I am his cousin. Recently orphaned—"

"Cousin and whore, then." The Duke of Gandia waved a careless hand, looking me up and down. "I've never had a kitchen whore before. What's the difference from the ordinary kind?" He leaned close and took a sniff, his downy cheek pressing against mine. "You smell better, that's certain."

I jerked my head away, edging around to put the table between us. "Your lordship—"

"Come on, then!" He grinned, grabbing me around the waist. "Let's baste you with honey and give you a good hard spin on my spit."

As if I'd never heard that before. *Santa Marta,* I asked my patron saint silently, or at least her hand, *did the apostles of our Lord hang about your kitchen asking if you wanted a spin on their spit?*

"Pardon me, your lordship," I said brightly. "Just let me put away my recipes here; Maestro Santini will flay me if I leave them out—"

"Recipes, eh?" He grabbed a page, squinting at it upside down. "Looks like rubbish, all that coded stuff. Is it spells and magic? Did

Maestro Santini find himself a whore, a cook, and a witch all in one? Maybe you can cast a spell for me. Get that pretty blond piece Giulia Farnese wet for me instead of His Eminence my father; she's too ripe for an old man . . ."

"No magic here!" I trilled a little laugh. "Just a recipe for bull's testicles. Does your lordship know how to cook testicles?"

"Testicles?" His grip loosened a little on my waist. "Er—"

"They have to be fresh, of course." I whipped a white peach from the bowl on the trestle table, so ripe my fingers sank into the soft flesh. "Ideally, just snipped off the bull and still dripping blood. Then you skewer them on a spit—" I rammed a skewer through the peach with more force than strictly necessary. "Or you can serve them in slices." Sliding the fruit off the skewer, I took the biggest knife Marco had, a monster of a thing like a battle-ax mated with a cleaver, and halved the peach with one vicious *whack*. Juan Borgia winced, and I thought I heard a suppressed giggle from the storerooms where the maids were still hiding. "Fry in a pan with spring onions"—another *whack*; the peach fell into quarters—"and prosciutto." *Whack*. Eighths. I stabbed a chunk of peach flesh on the tip of the massive knife and held it out toward the Cardinal's son, reddish peach juice dripping off the blade like blood. "Hungry, your lordship?"

Definitely a splutter of muffled laughter from the storerooms, but the Duke of Gandia didn't hear it. He looked at me, enthusiasm definitely waned. I gave a quick glance at the front of his hose and saw that his spit wasn't up for skewering anything at the moment. "Never mind, you're an ugly wench anyway," he scowled. "The cook can have you."

He stalked off, and I swept a deep curtsy, careful not to smile until he was safely gone.

The storeroom doors creaked open, and I looked over as half a dozen giggling maidservants tiptoed back into the kitchen. "You lot weren't very helpful!"

"Sorry, *signorina*," they chorused, curtsying. "Looked like you had him well under control." They collapsed into shrieks of laughter again.

"'Spin on my spit'?" one of the girls choked. "Oh, *honestly*!"

I looked between them. "You've heard that before, have you?"

"Who hasn't!"

I joined the laughter, giving my big knife an expert flip in honor of the Duke's deflated face and even more deflated codpiece.

"Can you teach me to handle a knife like that, *signorina*?" a pockmarked maid asked. She'd never given me anything but scowls before—most of the maidservants had resented the kitchens' invasion by an assistant cook, a woman no less, who was suddenly giving them their orders. But now they all stood grinning at me, fists on hips. "I could stand to learn a few things," the maid went on, giving my knife a nod. "Useful, having a blade on hand next time *il Duche* comes prancing round with his codpiece flapping open!"

"If it was his big brother Cesare, now," another maid whistled, "I wouldn't be needing any knife!"

"Or Maestro Santini," the first maid giggled, lowering her head confidentially. "You're his cousin, Carmelina—does he have a woman? Do tell, do tell!"

"The only woman Marco keeps is Lady Fortuna," I dismissed, "and he only wants her when he's playing *zara*."

I couldn't help but be pleased, though—the first time the maids had even unbent enough to call me by name.

"So Maestro Santini's a fool," the pockmarked maid shrugged. "He's still a handsome one."

Nods all around, and I couldn't help but shrug in agreement. Handsome my cousin mostly certainly was, and one of the few men I could look *up* at; so pleasant for a girl like me who had grown long as a kitchen spit by the time she was fourteen. "How about that inventory, now?" I said briskly to the maids. "*And* the silver. You know what I always say: mouths shut—"

"'—and hands moving,'" they chorused.

"Exactly. And afterward, maybe I can show you all a few tricks with a knife that might help fend off *il Duche* in future."

They went back to their work with good-humored complaints. I smiled, going back to my recipes. Perhaps I'd found a foothold in Marco's kitchens after all—my own place in the hierarchy of the kitchens.

The peach still sat on the trestle table where I'd quartered it, oozing juice, and I popped a chunk into my mouth. "Add cherries to the peach *crostata*," I mused. "In a lemon pastry shell brushed with a little sugar and rosewater, and that spiral twist on top . . ." I looked around to be sure the maids had retreated out of earshot, and brought out the little bundle of Santa Marta's hand, opening the bag's drawstrings.

"What do you think?" I asked it. "Peaches and cherries? Or peaches and blueberries?"

The hand remained still. Of course it did; it was a dead hand. It didn't *move*, no matter what greedy nuns said. I shrugged, tucking the bundle back inside my overskirt. "Cherries," I decided, and popped another slice of peach into my mouth. But I couldn't help wondering, as I cleaned the knife on my apron, if I'd need it again to deal with Juan Borgia.

CHAPTER FIVE

❖

Benefits should be conferred gradually;
that way they will taste better.

—MACHIAVELLI

Giulia

The mare had cardinal-red ribbons braided in her silvery mane, and a placard round her neck. She was waiting for me in the stable yard when Madonna Adriana sent me down.

"Oh—" I picked my way across the straw-scattered cobbles in my tall stilt clogs, as grinning stable boys and guardsmen fell back before me. The dapple-gray mare pawed the ground, and I bent forward to read the placard hung about her slender neck.

To carry my Persephone out of the underworld if she chooses. The words were written in the bold slashing hand I was coming to know very well. *Or for a pleasure ride beside her lord of the underworld, should she choose to stay.*

No signature; just a big *R* with a trailing loop. I touched it. "Rodrigo," I said aloud, experimentally. Hard to think of a cardinal as anything but *Your Eminence.* Hard to think that just a few months ago I hadn't given any thought to Rodrigo Borgia except as just another flapping scarlet bat in a flock of red-robed churchmen at my wedding. And now, well, I hardly knew what I thought about him—except that I was spending far more time than was good for me remembering the way his thumb had flicked along the very tips of my fingers. It wasn't a sin, strictly speaking. A man could touch a married woman's hand in greeting with perfect propriety. But it was one of those not-sins that I'd decided not to take to my confessor. Somehow it *would* turn out to be a sin, then, and my fault to boot, and I'd be on my knees the next two weeks in penitential prayer for something that wasn't my fault at all. And not telling my confessor about that touch on my fingertips seemed to make it more important than it should have been . . .

The mare lipped gently at my sleeve, ribbons fluttering in her mane. "I should give you back," I told her, scratching the velvety nose, "but you're a love, aren't you?" She was beautiful: small and fine-boned, perfectly suited to a short rider like me, her dapple-gray coat brushed to a satin gleam and a lady's hunting saddle of dark polished leather and wine-red velvet fitted to her back. I had no doubt that the stirrups were perfectly fitted to my height.

"Let's find her a stall," I told the grooms, who had gathered in a semicircle of admiring silence around the mare. They began dashing into the stable with rakes and armloads of hay, while I took hold of the mare's red leather reins and led her after them. "Persephone," I said. "Should I call you that? I don't suppose you eat pomegranates, do you? Not good for horses." I still had the pomegranate in my room, not knowing quite what to do with it. I hadn't laid eyes on Cardinal Borgia since the day he pressed it into my hand—he was busy at the Vatican, Madonna Adriana said, since there didn't seem to be any doubt now that the Pope had finally made up his mind to die. "You'll not see my cousin for a few weeks, I imagine," she told me this morning. Lucrezia had already flitted off to her lessons—language tutors that morning, to improve her French, and a music tutor to teach her the lute—but little Joffre still dawdled and yawned over his morning cup of sweetened lemon water, and Madonna Adriana ruffled his hair affectionately. "The children will miss their father, won't you, my love? And perhaps you will miss him too, Giulia dear."

I'd given her a long look. A stout woman, perhaps, but well preserved for forty-six years; her bosom still high and handsome, her perpetually smiling face unlined; well-suited to her maroon and violet velvets and elaborate headdresses and heavy gold rings. "How can you do this?" I asked her at last. "Act the pander for your own son's wife? How *can* you?"

She hesitated, and her smile faded to something kinder than I was used to seeing. Something more than her usual professional charm. "It's a hard world for women, Giulia." She spoke as baldly as I. "I wasn't born with your beauty, but I still had to make my way somehow. And if the world's hard for young women, just wait and see how cruel it can be to widows and orphans. My husband was a good-for-nothing, and Orsino—well, he's a great comfort and the light of my eye, but he's no firebrand to make a swath in the world." Her eyes rested on little Joffre. "My boy will need help if he's to get on as he should."

"This is your way of *helping* him?"

"He has just received administration of the city of Carbognano," returned Madonna Adriana. "A pretty little place, and prosperous too. Later perhaps he will embark on a military career. It could be the making of him. And all of it is due to my cousin Rodrigo. If not for him, I would have lost everything after my husband died—my brothers-in-law would have stripped Orsinio's inheritance away, left us with nothing. So in return for all the protection and kindness I look after Rodrigo." My mother-in-law smiled, taking her arm from around Joffre's shoulders and reaching up to give my chin an affectionate little chuck. "Now, why don't you go down to the stables, my dear? Rodrigo sent something over for you. I think perhaps you do miss him, just a little?"

Yes. Her sympathy so startled me that I almost gave myself away. Yes, I almost missed the Cardinal. I found him unsettling, unnerving, overcharming, and overbold—but rooms after he left them seemed flat, somehow.

Madonna Adriana had smiled at my silence. "Down to the stables, dear." I found her kindness more disquieting than her early smugness. How was I supposed to be rude to her when she was kind?

"Ho there!" A young man's voice sounded from the stable yard in frank admiration, bringing me out of my unsettling thoughts. "That's a beauty!"

Go away, Juan, I thought. The Cardinal's second son had been making a pest of himself lately, hanging about to ogle me and move his eyebrows in what he clearly thought were seductive expressions. But when I peeked around my new mare's nose, I saw that the young man peering into the stable was admiring my horse, not me. I also saw that he wasn't Juan.

"So you like my horse?" I stepped out from her other side into view. "Better than you like me, I think."

My husband, Orsino Orsini, straightened from his assessment of my mare's slim hocks, gaping at me. He wore riding leathers and boots spattered with white summer dust from the dry roads; his fair hair was mussed, his sleeves rolled up to show arms still bony from youth. He held his cap in one hand and the reins of his gelding in the other, the horse every bit as dusty and travel-weary as his master.

"You've come from Carbognano?" My voice came out calm and even, I was pleased to hear.

"Yes, well—yes."

"I hear Carbognano's pretty." I stroked the mare's gray velvet nose. "Not that I've seen it yet."

He flushed. "Yes, it's very pretty."

"A long ride for the hottest part of summer." The sun had slammed down like a hammer on Rome with the advent of July, sending long shimmering bars of summer light cutting palpably across the streets, making the gutters steam. Everyone sensible stayed inside under the shaded loggia with cups of chilled wine or lemon water. "What brings you here?" I asked. "Husband?"

He looked down at the straw, twisting his horse's reins between his fingers. "My mother sent for me. She thinks with the Pope to die so soon, I should be here—important things happening, it could be very advantageous for me—"

I felt a wave of hot rage at that. His *mother* summoned him, did she?

A letter from Mamma had him hop-hop-hopping all the way from Carbognano? I stroked my mare's sleek shoulder, blindly, realizing that all the stable boys were eavesdropping by now. Of course they were—the exiled husband come face to face with his straying wife; that was entertainment on a level with any bearbaiting or bullfight. Who wouldn't eavesdrop?

I tilted my head at the boy raking the same pile of straw over and over by the hayloft, the two grooms who had decided the stall right next to Orsino needed immediate cleaning, the four other grooms fiddling with needless bits of harness or bags of grain. "Leave us."

They filed out with evident disappointment.

"They all think I'm Cardinal Borgia's mistress." I met my husband's eyes. "Of course, everyone in Rome is starting to think that by now. People stare when they see me at Mass; you know that? They snicker behind their prayer books and they think I can't hear them. Thank the Holy Virgin my brother Sandro is off in Perugia again this past month, or he'd be coming to the door with a rapier in hand. Like a brother should."

Orsino avoided my gaze, leading his tired gelding past me into one of the empty stalls.

"Of course, I'd have thought my husband would be the one coming to the door with a rapier," I continued, "when it comes to defending my honor."

He began unfastening his horse's girth. "I'm not supposed to see you," he mumbled, concentrating on the buckles. "Mother said I'm not to stay here—just stable my horse, and then I'm off to stay with some cousins, so I don't—"

"So you don't even lay eyes on me?" I led my mare into the stall beside Orsino. "I'm your wife."

"Not really. Not the way it was arranged, it was very—" His eyes flicked up at me over his gelding's back. He had beautiful eyes, really— I'd been so pleased at our wedding when I saw what a clear blue they were, with that slight natural squint that gave him such a look of shyness. "It was different, once I saw you. I wouldn't have—"

"Sold me?" I didn't try to keep the bitterness out of my voice.

He hauled the saddle down from his horse's back. "No."

"So change your mind!" I didn't know how to deal with my new horse's girths and straps; I'd never unsaddled a horse in my life, so I tied her reins to the rail where they wouldn't tangle. "I'm still your wife; we can—"

"You don't understand," he blurted out. "I made a bargain with Cardinal Borgia, and he's not one to cross on a bargain. He's a powerful man. He could squash me like— He's not *good*, you know, for all he's a man of God. He always gets what he wants. And he doesn't care how he gets it. He's not kind."

"He's been kind to me." I came out of the stall, dropping the latch behind me. "Kinder than you've been, husband."

"Of course you'd think that." Orsino gave a defeated shrug of his bony young shoulders, dragging the bridle over the gelding's ears. "I hear he's very generous to his concubines."

"I am *not* his concubine."

"Juan Borgia says—I met him on the way to the *palazzo* here, he wouldn't stop twitting me—"

"That lecherous little nit couldn't be trusted if he told you the sun would rise tomorrow morning," I snapped. "I am not his father's mistress, or concubine, or whatever other choice word he or you have for it!"

"The Cardinal gave you that mare, didn't he?" Orsino nodded bitterly at my new horse where she stood lipping hay in her new stall. "Pearls and jewels too, Juan told me."

"I've not given him anything in return." I met my husband's eyes as squarely as I could. "I will swear by any saint you like, Orsino. I swear by the Virgin—which I still *am*."

He averted his eyes, scuffing his feet a little as he shuffled out of the gelding's stall.

"You want proof?" Outrage seized me in a red rush. I'd never touched my husband before, except the gliding of our palms in the grave measures of the *basse-danse* at our wedding, but now I took him by the sleeve and dragged him away from the row of stalls, back to a darker alcove out of sight of all but an inquisitive old mare at the end of the row. I could still feel the tingle along my fingers where Cardinal Borgia had stroked them, and I scrubbed my hand along my skirt to banish it. I was Orsino's wife, and I had no business thinking of such things. I faced my husband resolutely, taking a deep breath as I took his hand and hooked it through the laces of my bodice. "I am as much a virgin now as I was on our wedding night," I said. "And if you like, I will prove it to you."

His head jerked up, and that blue gaze held mine. "Prove—"

"You're my husband," I said. "Even if you haven't taken me yet, you have the right. I'm yours. Or at least, I'm supposed to be."

Hesitantly his fingers touched my bodice ribbons. "You're so beautiful," he breathed. "I couldn't believe my eyes, looking at you across that banquet table—"

It took a real effort to leach the exasperation thoroughly from my voice. "Then *do* something about it! *Be* my husband, in more than just name!"

"You want me?" His eyes pleaded with me. "You really do?"

No, I thought. *Not at all.* But what did wanting matter, or love either? Girls like me took the husbands chosen for us; we went to their beds and bore their children and managed their households and did it with good cheer, too. It was what I'd been taught all my life; what I'd been bred and raised for. What did it matter if the wedding vows had been a lie from the start? I'd said them in good faith; made a vow to God as well as Orsino, and wasn't that more important than what I *wanted*?

I looked at Orsino's narrow, handsome face, his blue eyes and his fair hair still speckled with dust, and I felt no desire at all. But I did feel sorry for him, sorry and guilt-sick that I'd even been tempted to throw my holy vows aside all because a man with a voice like a roll of thunder told me he wanted me naked in the grass.

Besides, another voice whispered in my mind, *give yourself to Orsino, and Cardinal Borgia won't want you anymore.* And that would be one way to solve this whole guilt-laced mess. "You're my husband," I repeated firmly, making myself put my arms around Orsino's neck. "And I keep my vows."

Oh, Holy Virgin, surely it wasn't supposed to be this awkward! I stepped out of my tall stilt clogs, but the difference in our heights proved too unwieldy, so I stepped back into them and stood there tottering while Orsino murmured into my neck and tried to unlace my bodice. I tightened my arms around him, tried to tug him down into the straw, but he gasped something about the stable boys catching us. We stood pressed together against the wall of the stable, grappling not at each other but at the layers of clothing between us. He couldn't get my bodice ribbons unknotted, and I hardly had better luck with the ties of his hose. It seemed an age before we finally fit ourselves together. He was so hesitant he hardly hurt me at all, but my wince at the brief stab of pain nearly paralyzed him. "I'm sorry, I didn't mean—"

"No, no!" I had to put my arms around his neck again, smile reassuringly as he began to move in such anxious little jerks that I could hardly feel him at all through the grappling of limbs around my tangled skirts and his bunched hose. He covered my mouth with his, less a kiss than a place to muffle his groans, and I couldn't help opening my eyes to stare past his cheekbone at the old mare gazing mournfully at me over her stall door.

Is it like this for you? I thought. *Surely not. I've seen horses mate.* And from what I now knew about how people mated, I thought the horses had the better idea.

It seemed an endless agony of awkwardness, but it was all over in the time it took to say an Act of Contrition.

"Giulia," Orsino gasped again into my neck. "Giulia—"

"Shh." I smiled, stroking his cheek. At least there hadn't been much pain to speak of—one heard such horror stories from nurses and maidservants. Generally the more elderly and devout the source, the more ghoulish the story.

"I shouldn't have doubted you." Orsino looked down, fumbling us apart again. I hadn't bled very much, but it was there, a spot or two on his hose. "I should have known you wouldn't lie."

"Now you know." He'd addressed me by name, at least—surely it was a start? And it would be better next time, in a proper bed like our wedding night was supposed to be. I settled my skirts, reached down into the straw, and found his cap for him as he did up his hose.

"I'm not supposed to leave Carbognano." He fidgeted with the cap. "But I could come back to Rome in secret now and then, if we planned it right. Or you could come to me; tell Mother and the Cardinal you were off to visit your sister . . ."

He trailed off as I looked at him. "I thought I'd be coming to Carbognano with you," I said at last. Pretty Carbognano, Madonna Adriana had called it. Pretty and prosperous. I had imagined a place for gardens and outdoor fetes; for hunting and riding and learning to love the husband I'd been given, and not having to think anymore about deep Spanish voices that had no business reverberating around in my stomach the way they did. A place for raising that golden-haired little girl I'd set my heart on. "I think Cardinal Borgia would let me go," I continued when Orsino didn't answer. "He doesn't want me unwilling, you see. And now that you and I . . ." Men prized virginity so highly—surely the Cardinal would want nothing more to do with me now. I had a pang at that thought, and swiftly banished it. Orsino was looking at me guiltily, and dread clenched in my chest. "Why won't you be taking me to Carbognano, Orsino?"

"I don't dare risk it." My husband's voice was miserable. "The Cardinal gave me Carbognano. If I took you away he'd want it back, and my mother—"

"So what do I do now?" I tidied my bodice ribbons, tugging the trailing ends until they were exactly, perfectly even. "What do you want me to do, husband? Live with Cardinal Borgia like he's my husband, and visit my real husband behind his back?"

"We could manage that," my husband said eagerly. "If we were careful . . ."

"You know, it's odd." I tucked a stray lock of hair back into its net. "All these weeks, Cardinal Borgia has been offering to make me his whore. And the only time I've *felt* like a whore is here and now."

"Giulia—"

"Don't touch me." I recoiled from his hand as though it were a viper and glided away with all the icy grace I could summon.

Hard to summon any kind of grace with a trickle of blood running down my thighs. Along with what remained of my pride, and my dignity, and my hopes.

"Madonna Giulia!" Little Lucrezia flew to greet me as I reentered from the stable yard. "Did you see the mare? My father chose her just for you, even though he's been so busy with the College of Cardinals this week. Can I see her, now that I'm done with my French lesson? Please say I can ride her someday—"

"Ride her whenever you like." I kissed the top of Lucrezia's blond head and moved past her to the stairs before she could see my haze of tears.

Carmelina

Gathering herbs is generally work for menials or for apprentices who need punishing. Up at dawn to fill a basket in the garden, then the washing, the chopping, the drying. No one wants to do it, so I bought myself a little goodwill among the still-sulky apprentices by volunteering for the task. I liked gathering herbs. Moving through the pots and plants with my skirt hem slapping against my ankles all damp from the dew, sniffing the sharp clean scent of fresh rosemary and mint and thyme, savoring the moist cool part of the morning before the summer heat set in. At that hour just after dawn, I could see the day spread out in front of me smooth and perfect as a just-risen pan of cream: no stews spilled yet, no pots dropped, no burns on fingertips from too-hot skillets or rude scullions to be put in their place. Cool, herb-scented, solitary perfection.

Except this morning I had company among the hedges of rosemary. "Madonna Giulia?" I said in astonishment.

My mistress turned, still wrapped in an embroidered robe over her night shift, the pink dawn light gleaming off her hair. "I'm sorry, I didn't see you behind those hedges."

I rarely saw her before noon, and hardly at all in the past week. Madonna Giulia's husband had come to the *palazzo*; the whole household was talking of it, and he hadn't been supposed to see his bride at all, but the grooms were full of highly embroidered stories of the things husband and wife had supposedly been shouting at each other in the stable yard. I didn't put much faith in gossip, but Madonna Giulia *had* stayed largely in her chamber ever since. When she did appear, her face was somber, even when she was tucking into a plate of my honeyed baked pears or strumming discordantly on a lute so Lucrezia could practice her dancing with earnest little Joffre for a partner.

Though Madonna Giulia *had* had enough energy to tell Juan Borgia to "go sit on a pin, you despicable little boy" when he came wheedling through her door. The maids all enjoyed quite a giggle over that, especially when we saw him stamp off red-faced and muttering curses.

My mistress looked grave now, though, running her fingertips over the waving spears of fresh chives. "May I assist you, Madonna Giulia?" I ventured. "I can make you a posset if you want something to help you sleep . . ."

"Possets won't help. I haven't slept all week." Hollow blue-smudged eyes looked far better on her than they did on most women. "I was looking for gillyflowers, gillyflowers and honeysuckle? My mother used to make a perfume out of the flowers for me, back in Capodimonte. Now I've got all these expensive scents tied up in ribbons next to my cosmetics, but I just want to smell like honeysuckle and gillyflowers again."

She looked sad, and it didn't suit her. Her small face was meant for laughing, that cherry mouth for smiling and those dark eyes for sparkling. Standing among the chives and wild mint, with her eyes lowered and her bare golden head tilted to one side, she looked as small and firm-fleshed and perfect as a capon, all ready to be sautéed in white wine and garlic and coriander (or at least that was how I liked to sauté a capon, though my father had some interesting ideas involving cinnamon and must syrup; page 187, Chapter: Game). Madonna Giulia had the kind of beauty to make most girls scratch and spit, but I just found myself admiring it. I'd always been plain as a kitchen ladle, and it was no use envying those born luckier. Besides, I wasn't sure I'd trade my cook's nose or the skill in my hands for any amount of golden hair. A talent for sauces and pastry lasted longer than any youthful bloom of skin or perfect white bosom—and it didn't come with the attentions of powerful, middle-aged, morally dubious churchmen.

"You'll find gillyflowers in that small garden by the south loggia, Madonna Giulia," I said, taking pity on her. "This is the kitchen garden, so it's mostly herbs. But there's a honeysuckle vine here—" and I cut a branch for her with the small kitchen knife I took out every morning with my basket.

She brightened as though I'd offered her pearls, taking a deep sniff of the blossoms. "Smells like Capodimonte," she said, and, plucking a blossom, she sucked the nectar out of the base. "Would you like one?" She offered me a flower with as much graceful courtesy as though it were a cup of fine wine.

I wrinkled my nose. "Not after making sweets every day, Madonna."

"You're the one who makes them? Those heavenly strawberry things and the marzipan *tourtes*, and the little sugared fruits?" Her eyebrows were darker than her hair; they flew away at a wide angle of surprise, and she smiled. "You've got a gift! I've never tasted anything better."

"The marzipan, the sugared fruits, or the strawberry *crostate*?" I couldn't help asking. "Or the honeysuckle?"

"All of them. What's your name?"

"Carmelina Mangano, *madonna*. I'm cousin to Maestro Marco Santini in the kitchens—I just arrived from Venice in May." I wondered if I had to stand still while she spoke to me, out of respect, or if she'd mind if I kept on with my work. Madonna Adriana liked all activity to halt the moment she addressed a servant, but Madonna Giulia looked a deal more informal. Or maybe *lonely* was the better word. There was no one of her own age in the *palazzo* besides the maids, after all. Perhaps even my conversation was better than Madonna Adriana's coin counting or little Lucrezia's prattle.

"I eat far too many of your *tourtes*, you know," she was confiding now. "But I'm sad, and I always eat when I'm sad." She looked about her for a seat, but this was no pleasure garden with benches and fountains; just a businesslike square of well-ordered shrubs and hedges and pots sheltered from the winds by high stone walls, so with a little shrug my mistress sat herself down on the grass between the sage and the chervil.

"Madonna Giulia, your robe—" I began to say, looking at all those delicate embroidered hems, but she waved a hand in unconcern.

"Bother the robe. My mother used to have me on my knees in the kitchen garden every week, picking feverfew for headache remedies and valerian for sleep draughts. Of course I was more interested in how to make skin creams and scent"—sniffing at the branch of honeysuckle in her lap again—"but I never minded the dirt much. What brings you all the way from Venice, Carmelina?"

I shifted my basket to the other arm, pinching a sprig of rosemary between my fingers to get the scent. Perfect for the roast shoulder of pork we'd be putting on the spit for *pranzo* in a few hours—I began clipping sprigs as I gave her the short, careful, mostly fictitious account of how and why I'd left Venice. She listened with apparently rapt attention, fingers knitted beneath her perfect chin. "Are you truly interested, *madonna*?" I couldn't help but ask. "It's not an interesting story." Not with all the shocking bits like theft and altar desecration left out. And besides, well-born girls like her did not find anything about girls like me interesting. We existed only to serve girls like her: serve them, groom them, and feed them, not talk to them.

She must be lonelier than anyone thought, if she was so pleased at the conversation of someone like me.

"It's all interesting." She smiled up at me, and a dimple appeared in her rosy cheek. "I've never worn a mask for Carnival, after all, or ridden in a gondola, or traveled outside Capodimonte. Well, except when I came to Rome, of course. Are you sorry to leave Venice?"

I suppressed a shudder. "No, Madonna Giulia."

"Oh, don't bother calling me *Madonna* anything. I keep looking about for my mother when I hear that."

"Begging your pardon, but I can't." Firmly. "Madonna Adriana would have the skin off my back."

"I suppose she would, wouldn't she?" A snort. "Is she a good mistress to serve?"

I stripped a cluster of roses, tossing the petals into my basket for jellies. "She is a great lady of admirable thriftiness."

"Yes, isn't she dreadful? She's an old pander, and she's cheaper than a vendor hawking secondhand clothes." Sigh. "If you're hoping to find a husband here in Rome, Carmelina, my advice is to find one *without* a mother."

"I won't be looking for a husband, Madonna Giulia." I moved on from the rosemary to the sweet marjoram, clipping a handful. Excellent for flavoring pork liver *tommacelle.* "I've no dowry for marrying."

"You've got a dowry in those hands." Giulia sucked the nectar out of another honeysuckle blossom. "Any man would count himself lucky to get a wife who could cook like you."

"That's not how it works," I found myself telling her as I pinched a few brown-edged leaves off the marjoram sprigs. Apprentices always skimped on this part, but I wanted only the best and freshest leaves for *my* dishes. "It takes money to marry, especially if you haven't got family or at least a beautiful face. My father could only afford to get one of his daughters married properly. My younger sister was the pretty one"—not to mention the one who had kept her virtue instead of surrendering it to a good-looking apprentice—"so she got the dowry."

Maddalena had a baby now. I'd found that out just a week ago. After much wrestling with myself, I'd sent a short letter to my sister in Venice, asking after the family. Sent more than a month back, by way of Bologna so they'd never know I was hiding in Rome . . . she'd finally scribbled a few lines back, begging me not to write again. *Father is still so furious I didn't dare tell him about your letter,* Maddalena had written, with that pious little sniff of hers I could almost hear on the page. *He'll never forgive you, you know, and I don't see why he should!*

But she had told me about the baby. A boy. *You'll never have any of your own, so pray for mine.*

Madonna Giulia was looking at me with a penitent expression, as though my lack of husband and dowry were her fault. "Did you ever want to marry?"

"Most girls dream of marriage," I shrugged. "But I've seen enough of the world to know it's not like the songs and poems, even for the pretty girls with bags of ducats to bring their husbands. I reckon kitchen work suits me better than a husband and children."

"My brothers scraped together three thousand florins for my dowry," Madonna Giulia said. "Sandro said being pretty would count for something, too—like your sister. But it didn't, not really. None of it mattered. I still didn't end up with much of a husband."

She looked sad again, and I wondered about those highly colored rumors from the grooms. The argument between Orsino Orsini and his bride. "Signore Orsini is very handsome," I murmured to be diplomatic, as I moved on to yank up a good stalk of nightshade. No good for cooking, nightshade, but it's excellent for poisoning rats.

"Yes," Madonna Giulia said in a flat voice. "My husband is very handsome."

Another little silence. The sun was rising higher now, already drying the dew on the frilly parsley leaves I was tossing into my basket by the handful for *vivarole zuppa*. A clear blue sky—in another hour it would be hot, the sun laying in a haze over the garden, the smell of the herbs drowned out by the stench of the narrow crooked Roman alleys rising up outside in a waft of sulfur and baked rot with a whiff of dead fish from the river.

"My mother used to say that a woman has three choices." Madonna Giulia bent her head to the honeysuckle branch again. "Wife, nun—or whore. And once you've chosen, there's no changing it."

I could hear her thoughts continue on silently. She certainly wasn't a nun, and she wasn't really a wife either—not with a husband she wasn't allowed to see. And Cardinal Borgia pressing to make her his whore . . .

"My mother said the same thing to me," I said. "But she was wrong."

Madonna Giulia's head rose. "Why?"

"Because things never turn out as neat and final as that." I gathered a handful of fresh rocket for the green sauce I was planning to make later, flicking a spider out of the basket. "Nuns become whores, whores become wives, wives become nuns." I shrugged. "And some are a combination of two or three. Whichever we are, we all get by."

Madonna Giulia looked startled at that thought. Startled, and thoughtful. She twirled a honeysuckle blossom between her fingers, silent, and I finished filling my basket with the herbs Marco and his other cooks would need that day. Borage flowers, blue and fresh, for adding color to a salad . . . fresh chard, for a Bolognese *tourte* I meant to crisp up this morning on a sheet of copper . . . handfuls of spring onions to be simmered with the drippings of a spit-roasted haunch of mutton. And one last thing—I left my basket for a moment with a brief curtsy, vanished from the herb garden, and came back with an apron full of blossoms.

"Gillyflowers," I said, presenting them to Madonna Giulia in a waft of their clean spicy fragrance. "If it pleases you, I'll take them to the kitchens with your honeysuckle there and simmer them in good clean water to make scent."

"Would you have any of those little honeyed strawberry things?" She brightened again. "To eat while we're waiting for the scent to boil? I always eat when I'm waiting."

"I believe I would," I said, and decided I liked my new mistress.

Giulia

I thought I'd go for a ride," I announced when Madonna Adriana looked up at me. My mother-in-law sat drinking a cup of warm spiced *hippocras* and gossiping with her steward, the only member of the household required to sit and nod as long as she felt like talking about the rising cost of everything. "Have the grooms saddle my new mare for me?"

"Rather a hot day for a ride, my dear."

"I don't believe I asked your opinion," I said evenly.

Madonna Adriana only smiled. "At least take a proper retinue with you; the streets are seething." She crossed herself. "It will be even worse when the Pope dies, God bless his soul."

My finest dress wasn't suited for the heat—mirage pools gleamed in every *piazza*, and even the pigeons seemed too listless to fly upward when the church bells tolled. The scarlet figured silk with the gold-embroidered bodice wasn't suited for riding either, but I badly needed the invisible armor that always sheathed me when I knew I was looking my best, so I threw my fine skirts across the saddle any which way and turned my mare out of the stable yard. I wasn't much of a rider—I grew up in Capodimonte where trees and hills and lakeside paths crowded the eye instead of city alleys, but my mother disapproved of women who followed the hunt and had ensured that my riding lessons had been mostly concerned with keeping my skirts draped and my back straight while sitting pillion. But my new mare had gaits as smooth as milk and turned at the lightest touch of the rein. My guards clopped behind me, impassive in their livery with the Borgia bull, and I could see a pair of women whispering behind their hands and market baskets as my little party trotted past. *The old bull's new heifer*, I imagined them saying. *Her husband doesn't even care, isn't she lucky? My husband would cut the heart out of any man who tried to make me his whore, man of God or no!*

I eased the mare to a stop when we reached our destination and slid down from my tooled saddle. "You're an angel," I whispered, feeding her a bit of that so-expensive sugar I'd snitched from Madonna Adriana's table. I dropped a kiss on her nose and turned to my guards. "Remain here," I said, and passed through the wide *palazzo* doors.

The elaborate *sala* where I'd danced at my wedding feast had been dismantled. The long tables had been cleared of their fine cloths and upended; the tapestries were being stripped off the walls and rolled up by busy manservants; maids trundled out the delicately carved footstools one by one. The daybed with its crimson satin cover was gone, and I saw a steward hand-packing a crate with the Murano glass goblets in which a company of guests had raised a toast to my marriage. The room was half sacked, half furnished, draped with dropcloths, bustling with activity around a man it took me a moment to recognize because for once he was not in scarlet robes.

"Madonna Giulia," Rodrigo Borgia said, turning from the lists he was scanning with his steward, and making me his fluid courtier's bow. "How fortuitous. Here I've been locked away with a cluster of fretting cardinals for a week, and the moment I step out for a private task, you appear: water in the desert! Just stand there for a moment, and allow me to drink in the sight of you. What luck that you happened to call when I was for once at home."

"Not luck at all," I said, moving out of the way as a pair of maids scurried out with a carved wall bench. "I suborned Lucrezia. She always seems to know your doings; I suspect she charms it out of your guards and servants. She told me this morning you'd come back here to do"—I looked around the chaos—"what, exactly?"

"I thought it prudent to pack away the more precious of my belongings, now that the Pope is so close to the end." He waved a ringed hand at the footmen trotting off with shoulder loads of rolled tapestries, the gold and silver plate being carefully packed into straw-bedded crates by maids with gentle hands. "The Pope finally *is* dying, by the way. One assumes his daily dram of human blood proved ineffective."

I didn't care if the Pope was dying or living, or if he had drunk human blood or angels' milk to preserve his health. I studied my Cardinal, so different in shirt and breeches and hose rather than his scarlet finery. Not a handsome man, not with that eagle's beak of a nose and heavy chin and full amused mouth. Not a young man either; he had lines about his eyes and I saw graying hair curling crisply at his burly chest above the lacing of his shirt and on his broad forearms below the rolled-up sleeves. Weight had begun to settle in that big frame, making his shoulders heavier and his belly broader than it must have been when he was young—but he was tall enough to carry it. A bull of a man, indeed.

"How old were you when we last had a papal Conclave?" he continued, that deep bass voice rolling about the painted vaults of the *sala*. "Perhaps you don't remember that charming custom the mob has of sacking the old residence of the new Pope? One can track the rise and fall of the votes by counting what looters come to which doors . . . not that I have any likelihood of donning the papal tiara, of course, but sometimes the sacking begins before the vote is strictly over, and encompasses the losers as well as the winners." He gestured around the rapidly emptying room. "Should any looters come to my *palazzo*, they will find it empty of anything worth stealing."

"Almost." I threw back the cloak I'd worn in the summer heat to cover my rich dress on the seething streets. His necklace looped my throat, the huge teardrop pearl almost disappearing between my breasts. He stopped in his tracks, his eyes fastening on it.

Wife, nun, or whore, my mother's voice whispered in my ear. *Once you've chosen, there's no changing it.* I'd become a wife, and I'd assumed my life complete: fulfilled, finished, tied up with a ribbon. Things hadn't quite turned out that way, had they?

My Cardinal stood gazing at me. I reached into my sleeve, taking something out and holding it in both hands, and his breath caught as he saw his pomegranate. The fruit's rosy skin split easily, even though my hands were trembling, and I heard Carmelina the cook's crisp Venetian voice in my ear now. *Nuns become whores, whores become wives, wives become nuns. And some are a combination of two or three.* Words that had echoed strangely through my head all week. Was I here because of them?

No matter. I was here. And I never looked away from my Cardinal's dark gaze as I dug half a dozen jewel-like seeds from the pomegranate and swallowed them.

He crossed the floor in three violent strides and seized my hand, bringing it up to his face. I felt the roughness of beard stubble as he pressed each of my pink-stained fingers one by one against his mouth. His arm circled my waist like a chain, and his thumb had slipped from the nape of my neck down inside the edge of my shift, caressing slowly back and forth between the twin points of my shoulder blades. The pomegranate fell from my hand, rolling on the stripped floor, and I twined my fingers through his black hair as I pulled him hard against me. "Out," he said to the servants as he set his lips between my breasts just below the pearl, and as he trailed kisses upward toward my throat I heard rather than saw them fleeing with nervous stifled titters. Then I felt a hard mouth on mine, kissing me as luxuriantly as if we had all day, as if there weren't a dying Pope and an imminent papal Conclave to take precedence, as if nothing at all could take precedence over this.

"Bed," my Cardinal whispered, lifting me up as if I weighed no more than his cardinal's hat and carrying me back through the empty echoing rooms. "Fortunately there are still one or two not yet packed away—"

"Wait," I managed to murmur against his mouth. "Wait—" And I squirmed free of his arms.

"What?" He cupped my face in his big hands. "What, Giulia?"

I was breathing as hard as though I had run a race, and my mouth felt swollen from kissing. My heart hammered. I felt more naked under his eyes than I had ever felt in my bath. "You should know something." I felt a scarlet blush mounting up toward my face, but I held his gaze steadily. "I've been— Orsino bedded with me—"

I saw the snap of some emotion in my Cardinal's eyes—anger? Outrage?—and rushed to finish. "You mustn't punish Orsino. He's my husband, it was his right—and it was only once. And he doesn't—he won't—he's gone back to Carbognano now. He doesn't want me. Not enough." I lifted my chin. "But I'm no virgin anymore, and if that means you don't want me either—"

I stopped. Every inch of my skin was vibrating to be held, to be lifted and kissed and comforted, but I refused to look away from the big swarthy man standing so close to me. I hadn't solved the guilt-laced mess that my marriage had become by bedding my husband—and maybe that one act had doomed anything with my Cardinal. But if I was going to break my vows, I wouldn't do it by lying to him. If he didn't want me now, I didn't want him. I'd go home and cry alone.

He considered me a long moment. Then he walked around me,

leisurely, and the skin of my neck prickled where I could feel his warm breath. "My dear girl," he said, and his fingers at my back began slowly unlacing my gown. "I don't care in the slightest."

My voice came out in a squeak. "You—you don't?"

"Virginity is a vastly overrated thing." My bodice loosened, he began on my sleeves. "It's pleasure I want to give you"—one sleeve slid off my arm to the floor—"and most virgins get precious little of that." The other sleeve joined it. He put his hands to my shoulders and slid my red dress away, down to the floor in a ripple of scarlet silk. His hands glided back up my arms, the backs of his fingers barely brushing my skin through the thin shift, and I forgot how to breathe.

"So to answer your question," he said conversationally, easing the shift off my naked shoulders, "yes, I still want you. I want you more than any woman I have ever met in my life, Giulia Farnese. I want you more than the Pope's throne."

He set his lips against my bare shoulder for a long moment, and then he turned me so we stood face-to-face again. I stood naked and quivering, but he didn't look at my body; he looked into my eyes. "Do you believe me?"

For answer, I yanked the pearled net from the nape of my neck and shook my hair down around me in a billow of gold. I'd wanted to give myself to Orsino like this on our wedding night but I'd been bundled into a sheeted bed in a dark chamber instead, and hadn't had the courage to get out of it because a wife above all things must be modest. But modesty wasn't required in a mistress, so I faced my lover in nothing but a cloak of loose hair and a pearl.

His eyes were full of me. He held out a hand and said something in Spanish I didn't understand.

I reached out, linking my fingers with his. "What does that mean?"

His free hand slid around the smooth skin of my waist, up to my breast. "'*Come to me*,'" he whispered, and he lifted me up and carried me back through the empty, echoing rooms. I was too breathless to reply, but not too breathless to look around as he laid me down on a carved bed with a striped cover of black and white velvet. The same bed I'd lain in alone on my wedding night, now moved out of its chamber for dismantling, and I had a fleeting moment of wonder. Just what had I done?

Then he was kissing me again, mixing Italian and Spanish with every other word as he pulled me to the velvet bed beneath him.

"Rodrigo," I whispered. And let it happen.

Leonello

I passed my imprisonment calculating the mathematical odds of imminent death. Frankly, my gift for analysis was proving not at all helpful. The odds of survival were decidedly against me.

Murder is a small enough sin, providing the victim is no one of great value. No one had fussed about searching for Anna's killers, after all. Who cared for the death of one common tavern maid? A cardinal's steward, that was a more serious matter, but not insurmountable. In the end, most courts of law prefer money to blood. Had I been a rich man, I would have laid a judicious bet that my punishment for knifing a man through the throat would be a hefty fine and a sentence of banishment from Rome. One could live with such a punishment; there were other cities besides Rome to make a living, and they all had drunken men waiting to be relieved of their money by a man who knew what to do with a deck of cards.

But I had no money for such a bribe, no assets worth seizing. And a dwarf could hardly be sentenced to the galleys to pull an oar or exiled to some ragtag army to fight Turks. Besides, if there was anything a court of law liked better than coin, it was a spectacle of public punishment to give the mob. The hanging of a dwarf, now that was an event to draw a crowd. Better than a play any day.

I looked around my dank little cell. Not much bigger than the room I rented in the Borgo. The difference was all in the details. My rented room was meticulously clean, the floor swept and polished instead of riddled with rat droppings; the bed an impeccable square of clean linens instead of this pallet of moldy straw. My room had a window with a tiny sliver of a view out onto the domes and spires of the Vatican, a bracket for tapers that gave cheerful yellow light when I stayed up too late reading as I always did. My room had a modest chest of clothes and my even more precious cache of books, mostly purchased from the printing shop downstairs. That printing shop survived chiefly on cheap smeary broadsides and scurrilous pamphlets, but over the years I'd culled a fair collection out of their shelves: Marcus Aurelius, even though I thought him a poxy bore; some plays by Sophocles; Dante and Boccaccio and Ovid. My books. For my days I had cards, but at night I had books. And now I was stuck in a cell darkened to perpetual twilight, and I doubted I would ever read a book again.

My eyes stung.

I didn't even know how long I had been held here, wherever *here* was. A few days? Maybe I'd be saved until after the Pope died, whenever that was. Rome always erupts into violence when a pope dies—what better way to keep the mob calm than to give them a dwarf's bloody execution?

Perhaps I had another week. Or perhaps only a few days. However long poor old Innocent could hang on.

I almost wished he'd hurry up and die. There were only so many hours I could pass massaging the cruel aches of my shackled legs and running mental odds on my method of execution. My battered deck of cards and the worn volume of Cicero's letters had been taken from my doublet when the guards searched me. Providing the boredom didn't kill me first, I'd soon be marched out through a jeering crowd, up a crude flight of steps to a gallows, and feel a rope snugged about my neck. Or perhaps I'd be lucky. Perhaps they'd let me go after lopping off my hands, or my nose, or my ears. Cut out my viper tongue; gouge out my eyes. Then let me go, as an example of Christian mercy.

Dio. Sometimes I wish I were a stupider man. A clever imagination is no blessing in a cell.

So I was almost glad when a guard with the Borgia bull on his chest came and took me away.

I could barely walk after being kept shackled so long. The third time

I tripped, doubled over with knifelike pains down my exercise-starved legs, the guardsman simply hauled me up by one elbow and dragged me along so my toes trailed the floor. I was content to be dragged, bumping up a series of stone staircases, through a long passage and then a richer series of anterooms. Elaborate carpets, gorgeously dyed tapestries, gold and silver plate proudly displayed to gleam on an intricately carved *credenza* . . . Where *was* I?

"Your Excellency," the guard grunted as I was hauled through yet another set of wide doors. "The dwarf you wanted to see."

"Put him down, Michelotto."

I was dumped onto another very fine carpet and had to bite back a scream as my legs protested. The guardsman faded back against the wall, and I gave him a cordial nod before turning my attention to the figure slouching behind the desk. "You will pardon me, Your Excellency," I managed to say politely. "I fear I must remain seated for a moment, or else fall over when I try to rise."

He looked at me with a thoughtful gaze as I began to rub my knotted thigh muscles. The same boy I remembered from just before my fall into unconsciousness: a lean amused face, auburn hair, a pair of black and penetrating eyes. Up close I could see he was perhaps seventeen, but he lounged back in his carved chair like a man grown—like a man who was master of all before him.

He continued to inspect me, top to toe, like a spavined horse he was nevertheless considering for purchase. "Fascinating," he said at last. "How in the name of God the Father did someone such as yourself manage to murder one man, wound another, and then chase him halfway across the city?"

"Did you see the men afterward, Your Excellency? The man I killed, and the man I tracked?" No point in denying it; I'd been squarely caught.

"I saw them," he returned.

"Then surely you know how I did it."

"I wish you to tell me, which is entirely different."

My turn to inspect him top to toe. He gazed back as calm as a leopard, not offended at all by my scrutiny. He wore an ornate silver cross over a bishop's purple robes, but I saw nothing of God about him other than his clothes.

"I killed the first man by a knife through the throat," I said at last.

"You are not tall enough to reach his throat."

"I threw the knife."

"From a distance, in the dark? Impressive."

"Yes," I said. It *was* impressive. Even the guardsman against the wall, a colorless sort of fellow with eyes like wet slate, had pursed his lips in a silent whistle. "The second man I hit in the hip, when he turned and stumbled," I said. "It slowed him enough that I could pursue him."

The young Bishop steepled his fingertips. "And what did you mean to do when you caught him?"

"Ask him a few questions. Then cut his throat."

"Even if he gave you the answers you wished?"

"Yes."

"What questions did you want answered so badly?"

I remained silent. He grinned, a flash of white teeth in a swarthy face.

"It was about money, or a woman. It always is."

"A woman," I said.

"He stole her from you, I suppose."

"No. She was just a common tavern maid. But three men decided to kill her, including Don Luis and Niccolo the good guardsman, so I decided to kill them."

"Why?"

Why, indeed? Murder, imprisonment, the gallows: so much trouble for a woman I didn't even love. It would make a better tale if I had loved her—songs of brokenhearted men and the revenge they wreak for lost love are always popular in taverns. But I hadn't loved Anna, or she me—in another year, I doubted I'd remember what her face looked like. There were so many faces like hers, overtired and ill-used and quickly forgotten.

"Why?" the young Bishop asked again.

"Because she mattered," I said. "Tell me, what has happened to the guardsman? Niccolo."

"The wound in his hip was very deep. It suppurated, despite the surgeon's best efforts. He is raving now, and sinking fast. Did you poison the blade?"

"No." Sometimes even a dwarf could simply come up lucky. I smiled.

"So, you bagged two of three killers." The Bishop noted my smile. "Is that worth your current imprisonment?"

"Had I managed to kill all three, yes." I saw no point in lying to him. My end on the gallows would come regardless of whether I groveled or swaggered, whether I spat rude words or fawned at his feet. I managed to rise, wincing as my tingling legs protested, and rubbed my chafed wrists together inside their rope.

The Bishop continued to watch me thoughtfully. "These men weren't your first," he said at last. "You're accustomed to killing. I know the look."

"From your own mirror, Your Excellency?"

He laughed. "You have a viper's tongue. I'm surprised no one's cut it out before now."

"I'm surprised myself."

"How many have you killed?"

"Four or five."

"For money? Or on behalf of some other tavern maid?"

"For protection. Men who sought to rob me and thought they could kick a dwarf about in safety."

"Most men think that. You killed them for it?"

"Men of normal size don't have to kill when they are attacked by drunks or thieves." I felt very numb but oddly pleased at how conversationally my words were coming out. "They use their fists; they make a few lunges with a dagger; they kick and wrestle. That can make an attacker think twice and maybe retreat with a few bruises." I gestured down at myself. "I can put a knife through a man's eye at a distance, but once he closes the gap I am helpless. I cannot hit him, punch him, wrestle him, bruise him, or in any way stop him from doing what he wishes. A man moves to attack me, and I must make the decision to kill him at once or let him do whatever he likes to me."

"You could wound rather than kill."

"Ineffective," I said. "Wound a man, and he'll be so angered at being bested by a dwarf that he'll report the attack, either to the constables or to his friends. I have a distinctive appearance. I'm not likely to remain unfound if someone unfriendly is looking for me."

The young Bishop regarded me another moment. "If you still had your freedom, little man, what would you do? What is it you most wish for?"

Books, I thought. *To be tall. To* matter. "I'll settle for the woman's third killer," I said.

"To put a knife through his throat, as you did with poor Don Luis?" The Bishop leaned forward between two elaborate branches of beeswax tapers, taking a dagger from his belt and laying it down on the desk with its hilt toward me. "Perhaps you would favor me with a demonstration."

"No," I said.

"I don't like being refused." His tone was mild, but his brows met over the bridge of an eagle nose.

"And I don't like demonstrating my skills with an inferior blade."

"It's Toledo steel."

"It's a dagger. Fine for a street fight, but not for throwing." I was starting to feel lightheaded. Hunger, fear, or danger? I wasn't sure. "Give me my own knives."

He looked at me for another moment, then tilted his head at the expressionless guard still standing before the wall. The man fished in his doublet and handed over my set of slim finger knives. "These?"

"Those." Only two of the four, but I suppose two had been lost in the nighttime chase. I held up my bound hands. "Well?"

"You are a rude little man." But the young Bishop nodded, and his guard cut my hands free. I took my time flexing my fingers, working the blood back into my tingling palms and massaging my aching wrist where the colorless guardsman had struck me with the pikestaff. The Bishop looked impatient.

"I'm a busy man," he began.

"And I'm a dead one," I told him. "Of the two of us, I think my time is the more valuable." With that I picked up the first of my knives and whipped it past his ear close enough to stir his auburn hair. It bedded itself in the tapestry behind him with a soft *thrum*.

He never moved. I sent the second knife whizzing after the first, burying it deep in the wall. He turned to look and saw that I'd thrown them so close together that he couldn't have passed a sheet of vellum between the two blades.

"Impressive," he said. "Where did you learn your skills?"

"As a child, from a mountebank's show," I said. "They wanted me to tumble and juggle. I joined the knife-throwing act instead."

"More dangerous than juggling."

"But less humiliating."

He picked up something from his inlaid desk, and I saw my weathered volume of Cicero. "Unusual for a man of letters to work a mountebank's show. You read Latin?"

"Poorly."

"You did not pick up that from a knife-throwing act."

"No, from school. My father wanted more for me than a mountebank's show; he thought book learning might get me a post someday as a secretary or a tutor. Pity he was wrong. Why all the questions, Your Excellency? No matter where I learned my skills, flight is not among them, and so I am still bound for the gallows."

"Maybe not." He rose and began tugging the knives free from the wall, and my pulse leaped in sudden violent hope. "Do you know who I am, little man?"

"No."

"I am Cesare Borgia, Bishop of Pamplona. My father is Rodrigo, Cardinal Borgia."

"Father?" I raised my eyebrows. "Isn't it traditional to pretend he's your uncle?"

"I never pretend anything," said Cesare Borgia. "And my father will be Pope after Innocent dies, and can do what he likes."

"Last I heard, he was running a distant third in the pools." If the young Bishop wished to banter, by all means, let us banter. For a chance at life, I'd talk papal gossip till the sun rose. "Behind Cardinal Sforza and Cardinal della Rovere, I believe."

"My father has already bribed Sforza," the young Bishop said. "Four mules loaded with silver."

"Christendom comes cheaper than I thought."

"Fortunately for my father. I've come from Pisa to aid His Eminence in angling for the votes he needs while he attends the Pope's deathbed. He had time today, before returning to the papal chamber, to give me a few instructions. He wants me to hire someone."

I laughed. "Surely not me!"

"I am to use my discretion. My father has enemies. They will not be able to reach him once the Conclave begins, but they might try to reach his family instead. My brother Juan and I can look after ourselves, but we have another brother not eleven years old." His face softened briefly. "And a sister."

"*Dio*," I said, "His Eminence your father has been busy."

"My family is vulnerable. We have guards, but visitors ushered past guards can turn out to be assassins in disguise. My father wishes a bodyguard who will stay close to the family, as a last defense. Someone easily overlooked."

"You might want to choose a taller man than me."

"I would," Cesare Borgia said coolly. Outside the leaded windows, I heard the distant pealing of a bell. "But my father also wants his mistress protected. He's making a fool of himself over a girl of eighteen, and he doesn't want a strapping young guardsman trailing her footsteps day and night. A stunted little man like you will suit him far better where she is concerned. And your skill with knives"—tossing my blades to the desk with a clatter—"will suit me very well. No one who comes looking for my sister or my father's mistress will look twice at you, not as anything more than the jester who makes Lucrezia laugh or the attendant who carries Giulia Farnese's train. They'll think it until the moment they have a blade in their throat."

"Well, well." I found my mouth suddenly dry. The tolling of bells was louder now, as though another bell tower had joined in. "This task you offer me—will it save me from the gallows?"

"If you perform it satisfactorily. There may even be lasting employment for you, past the election of the new Pope. I have no objection to hiring murderers, and neither does His Eminence my father." Cesare Borgia scooped my knives up in one hand, careful of the sharp edges. "Useful souls."

"We are." The nicely calculated set of odds I'd constructed around the likelihood of my death went tumbling down. Outside, the clamor of bells had risen to a storm, but nothing could match the storm of emotion raging inside me. Who knew hope could be such a violent thing when it surged in the chest like this? "Oh, we are."

"What is your name, little man? You would not tell my guards. Even Michelotto, and he has a frightening way about him."

"I am Leonello, and no one frightens me. What in the name of God are those bells pealing for?"

"Those?" Casually, Cesare Borgia crossed the room and flung open the leaded windows. The mad cacophony rushed in, assailing my ears. Surely every bell in Rome was ringing. "I imagine the Pope is dead, God be praised. Which means my father has a funeral to attend, and I have a Conclave to bribe." Turning to face me in a swirl of purple cassock, he proffered my knives back to me in a hilt-first steel nosegay. "What do you say to my offer, Leonello?"

"I have a condition."

His brows drew together. "You are hardly in a position to name conditions."

"This house you speak of, for your sister and the mistress," I said, ignoring him. "Does it have a library? And can I use it?"

He laughed. "Yes. And yes."

"Then, Your Excellency"—I gave my most elaborate courtier's bow, taking my knives back from his hands—"I am your man."

CHAPTER SIX

———— ✦ ————

Carmelina

R oast peacock," Marco told me dreamily. "With a flaming beak
and a gilded breast. And a sugar subtlety for a sweet afterward,
molded in the shape of a bull—the Borgia bull, you understand?—dyed
red . . ."

"No, no, and no," I said firmly. "Cardinal Borgia doesn't care for
elaborate meals at the best of times, and this is hardly the best of times.
You're cooking for a Conclave, not a wedding!"

But Marco was full of dreams, not listening to me at all. Cardinal
Borgia, in the insane rush of preparing for Pope Innocent's massive
funeral and the papal Conclave to follow, had suddenly found himself
in need of a cook to provide his meals during the protracted voting. And
having far too much caution to hire a strange cook when his own grew
ill, he had asked his cousin Madonna Adriana if he could borrow her
cook: Maestro Marco Santini.

"Think of it!" Marco was striding up and down the kitchens, waving
his arms. "Cooking for the College of Cardinals!"

"Just *one* cardinal. Everyone else in the College will rely on his own cook too, to guard against poison." Except for those cardinals who announced their faith in God, prayer, and the integrity of his fellow churchmen, and trustingly ate the food that came from the papal kitchens. In other words, those cardinals who had no chance of being elected Pope and were thus in no danger of being poisoned by anybody.

"—dining with Cardinal Borgia after the votes are cast every evening, everyone admiring my roast peacock—"

"All of them far too busy scheming and dealing to pay any attention to your roast peacock."

"—noticing how delicious my hot sops are—"

"I wouldn't count on your sops being very hot, considering they'll have to be passed through who knows how many sets of gates and servants and tasters. Cold meats, Marco, chilled salads, and sauces that won't form a skin when they cool!"

"And afterward if just one remembers my name and the food I served . . ." Marco's eyes glowed as he punched a big fist into his other palm. He could see it now, I knew: cook not only to a cardinal's cousin but to a cardinal himself. Maybe even the future Pope, whoever that would be. The Conclave, locked together for a day or a week or a month or however long it took to form a majority, would decide. I put my chin on my hand, looking at my cousin ruefully.

"Stuffed croquettes with sturgeon." Marco snapped his fingers. "Carmelina, the recipe, let me see it. Is it mint, sweet marjoram, and burnet in the filling?"

"I like to add a little wild thyme too." I flipped to the folded page in my father's collection, deciphering the coded lines (page 227, Chapter: Pastry). "And be sure to roll them up like wafer cornets, see here . . . Sturgeon croquettes, though, far too rich. I'd just serve a good roast fowl."

Marco was dreaming far too large to hear me, though, and I couldn't help but catch his enthusiasm as we spent the night poring over my father's recipes and packing the requisite dishes, supplies, spices, and utensils he'd be able to take along in Cardinal Borgia's entourage. The Conclave would not convene for another ten days at least, not until after the mourning period for Pope Innocent was traditionally concluded, but Marco was to join Cardinal Borgia's household now. "You'll look after the kitchens for me here, won't you?" Marco asked me as an afterthought. "Keep the apprentices in order? It will just be Madonna Adriana, Madonna Giulia, and the children to cook for . . ."

"I think I can feed four in your absence."

"That you can." Marco laughed. "Good thing you're not a man, little cousin, or I'd be worried you'd steal my place here."

"If I were a man, I would," I told him. I could tease him now without seeing resentment flare in his eyes. Marco might not have liked the way I'd thrust myself into his life, but in the end he was far too good-natured to hold a grudge for long. "You really should go now, Marco. Cardinal Borgia has the funeral rites to get through before he even starts thinking about the Conclave, and he'll want a hot meal tonight."

Marco rose, stretching. "Remember," he said, taking my face between his hands and giving it a playful shake for emphasis. "Count all the spices twice or Madonna Adriana will dock your pay."

"I don't *get* paid."

"She'll dock mine, then." He stood, still holding my face between his hands. "You know, Carmelina, I'm glad you're not a man. I like you better this way. I should have paid more attention to you when you were running about underfoot in your father's kitchens. Skinny little thing you were."

"Still am," I pointed out. "My sister used to say I looked like a basting needle."

Marco wasn't listening. "I should have . . ."

What? I thought. Married me when he was an apprentice; taken my skillful hands for a dowry? If he had, we might still be standing here in these kitchens—but we'd have babies, and I'd be so busy looking after the babies that I'd have no opportunity to cover for him when *zara* games lured him away from the banquets he was supposed to be preparing. No, it was better this way.

"Time to go," I said again, and made a show of dusting off the table so I could turn away from his touch. Hopefully before he could feel my cheeks heat against his palms. My cousin was a fool, but he was a handsome one with his black hair lapping over his eyes. And I wasn't immune to the touch of a handsome man—even if it was far more a sin for me to enjoy that kind of touch now than it had ever been when I was a girl, given what I had become.

No use dwelling on what I had become after girlhood.

"Shall I place a bet for you on the new Pope?" Marco was asking me as he shouldered into his doublet. "They're running odds on Cardinal Sforza at three to one!"

The soft look in his eye, I saw with some amusement, had already gone.

Marco was gone too, at dawn the following morning, as Pope Innocent's funeral rites began and the cramped wooden voting cubicles were erected in the Sistine Chapel for the coming Conclave. I found the silence in the kitchens unnerving. After all the tumult of the Pope's long-awaited death, now there was nothing to do but wait. Half my apprentices—that is, Marco's apprentices—did not even come to the kitchens, and I dismissed the rest after the midday meal was done. They scampered off to watch Pope Innocent's funeral cortege, and to gossip about who the Conclave would elect to succeed him.

Though how long that would take, even Santa Marta herself probably didn't know. I'd heard of one Conclave that went on for literally years, but we lived in more practical times. If the voting dragged on too long, Marco's meals would no longer be needed: the cardinals would be restricted to bread, water, and wine until they chose a new pope.

Still, I couldn't help but design a menu as I started preparing the midday *pranzo* for Madonna Adriana and her clutch of Borgia wards. "What would you serve to a group of power-mad churchmen in the grip of voting fever and indigestion?" I asked Santa Marta, whose hand I'd placed in a nice decorative box on the spice rack. Altogether it seemed a more respectful place for her than forever being squirreled away under my apron. And if anyone saw her, well, half the servants in the household carried some kind of relic for good luck. No one would have any reason to guess that mine had been acquired a trifle more illicitly than most.

"Clear broths, you think?" I went on. "Something very light and soothing on an uneasy stomach and an even uneasier conscience . . ."

"Whoever are you talking to?"

I turned from my trestle table to see Madonna Giulia in the doorway to the kitchens, one hand on the jamb and her blond head cocked inquisitively. I curtsied, but she waved me up as she always did.

"Don't let me interrupt, Carmelina. I'm just down for something sweet to nibble. I rang for a page, but he never answered—must be off clustered in the *piazza* with everyone else, waiting for the white smoke. So I thought I might as well come down myself." She threw an envious look in the direction of the *piazza*. "I wish I could be out there, too."

"Can't you, Madonna Giulia?" I moved to the larder, rummaging for sweets. I'd run out of her favorite marzipan, but I had half a cold strawberry *tourte* I'd made with a chilled summery sauce of honey, mead, and lemon.

"I promised I wouldn't leave the *palazzo*." She made a face. "Lucrezia and Madonna Adriana and I are to stay inside until the funeral *and* the Conclave are done. We're not even to go to confession. Rodrigo says it won't be safe."

She said the all-powerful Cardinal Borgia's name quite unselfconsciously, I noticed. The servants were running a collection on how long it would take Madonna Adriana's daughter-in-law to succumb to him— Marco had lost a week's salary when a month passed and she still hadn't (to anyone's knowledge) given in. Maybe I should put a bet in myself that the *castello* Farnese had fallen at last . . .

Madonna Giulia picked a strawberry out of the flaky *tourte* crust to pop into her mouth whole. "What's that you're making there?"

"Part of your midday meal, *madonna*." I added a few pinches of sugar and began cracking eggs into the mix. "Elderflower *frittelle*."

"I don't see any elderflowers. Just cheese."

"The elderflowers are soaking in cold milk. I'll add them with a little saffron, then roll the dough out into balls and fry them in butter. Right now it needs more sugar."

"How do you know? You didn't even taste it."

"I just know." Adding a pinch more.

"Don't you even have to measure it?"

"It only needed a pinch."

"And that's something else you just know?"

"Yes, *madonna.*"

"Can you show me how to do that? When Rodrigo comes back I can give him a plate of *frittelle* I made with my own hands. He'd like that, I think."

"His Eminence doesn't care for delicacies. Very plain tastes in food, he has." Perhaps the only thing he liked plain—his taste in wine, decor, and mistresses was certainly luxurious enough.

"Teach me?" She made a tragic face. "Please?"

I relented, and my mistress soon stood before me giggling and ready to work, her silks wrapped with one of my aprons. What a strange household I had landed in, where the mistress of the house presented herself not only to a possible pope as bedmate, but to her own cook as apprentice. "Combine those two creamy cheeses there into the mortar," I instructed, and began showing her how to knead them together.

"I'm not getting in the way, am I?" She already had a dribble of cheese down her apron. "I'd hate to put you behind on your work . . ."

"No work to do, not with such a reduced household. More of a kneading motion, Madonna Giulia, you're just poking at that cheese—" I reached for a crock of grated bread. "I've been sitting about all morning planning what I'd serve the cardinals if I were summoned to cook for the Conclave instead of my cousin. It's a dicey business, dishing up *cena* for a college of nervous old men plotting the day round."

"Cardinal Borgia's not so old as that." Madonna Giulia gave a blush at what looked like some reasonably blissful memory. "What would you serve a Conclave?"

"Nothing elaborate—add a pinch of grated bread now, and we'll measure in the elderflowers." She got bread crumbs all over everything and upset the bowl of milk. After I'd strained the flowers out of it, fortunately. "First I'd serve a simple thick rice *zuppa* with almond milk, I think. Very bland, very soothing—half that flock of cardinals will have stomach sores by the time the voting's done. Now, give that *frittella* mixture another good hard knead, and turn it out on the table—too fast, too fast!" I rescued it before it went to the floor after the milk. "After the *zuppa*, a spit-roasted capon with just a squeeze of juice from a lime, nothing more—poisons can hide out too easily in a spicy sauce."

"And the Cardinal says the cavities of birds are excellent for passing bribe offers back and forth to other cardinals." Giulia fetched a crock of flour at my direction, dipping her pink fingers in and sprinkling flour far too lavishly over the table, the floor, and her own skirts. "They're supposed to inspect all the birds, but he says you can always hide a slip of parchment under a wing."

"An unstuffed capon, then." I took the flour away from her before she had us wading in it. "Roll out the dough on the surface, now—not too hard—just patch that hole there where it stretched too thin—" I rolled a handful of dough into a neat little ball. "Like this. Unstuffed capon, a plain salad of lettuce and borage flowers—borage makes you brave, and they'll need that for the vote. And simple sugared *biscotti* for a sweet, since sugar aids the digestion."

"I suppose it's all very stressful," Giulia said a bit wistfully. Misshapen little balls of dough were piling up under her soft hands. "As soon as the Pope died, well, Cardinal Borgia vanished like he'd been magicked. I suppose he'll have time for me afterward, however it turns out."

She gave a little sigh, and I wondered if her Cardinal stood a chance of being elected Pope. And if he was, where did that leave a mistress, even one as beautiful as this? Popes had to keep up *some* appearance of virtue. Children born on the wrong side of the blanket could at least be passed off vaguely as nieces and nephews, but how did one hide a mistress? Giulia Farnese couldn't exactly be concealed as any kind of niece.

I didn't dare ask, though. "Very good," I said instead for her lopsided little pile of elderflower *frittelle*, and began mentally flipping through other possible dishes for *pranzo* if they came out as ghastly as they looked.

A deep voice sounded from the doorway. "You must be the concubine."

Giulia and I both turned our heads. Leaning against the doorjamb, arms folded across his chest, was a very small man. He wore a battered doublet and disreputable boots, and a dusty bundle sat at his feet as though he had just walked in from the streets. He had hazel eyes, deep-set under a prominent forehead, and they were fixed coolly on Giulia.

"I am Giulia Farnese," she said, cocking her head in puzzlement and wiping flour off on her borrowed apron.

"The Cardinal's concubine," he said. "Yes, I know who you are. I am Leonello." He made a surprisingly agile bow. "Your new bodyguard."

I couldn't help but eye him dubiously, and I saw Giulia doing the same. A dwarf for a bodyguard?

"Say it if you like." He looked amused. "I'm a trifle short for the job."

"Well, *I* wasn't going to say it." Giulia bent down and lifted up the one-eared cat, who had turned up to rub adoringly along her skirts. "It didn't seem polite. Not that it was very polite of you to call me a concubine, Messer Leonello."

"Just Leonello." He picked up his bundle and moved into my kitchen, swinging himself up nimbly onto a chair. His feet dangled above the floor like a child's. "And you *are* a concubine. Just as I, you can plainly see, am a dwarf. A dwarf, however, with a certain skill in knife play. No attacker will notice I'm here, until they pay for it with their lives."

"You've killed before?" I couldn't help asking.

"Yes," he said casually, and helped himself unasked to an apple from a bowl I'd set aside to make a *crostata*. That was when I started to dislike him.

Giulia, however, had bent her friendly smile on him as she scratched under the tomcat's chin. He purred and arched for her just like her Cardinal. "Did Cardinal Borgia hire you to protect me?"

"Yes, you and his daughter as well. I've not met the daughter yet." He took a finger knife from his cuff and cored the apple neatly. His fingers were stubby, but deft; he flipped the knife without even glancing at it as he looked Giulia over from top to slippered toe.

"It's not polite to stare," I told him tartly, whisking Giulia's *frittelle* aside and trying a little quick repair while she wasn't looking.

"I've seen you before," he told Giulia as though I were not there, crunching into his apple. "I watched your wedding procession in May— it took me a moment or two to place your face. I admit, at the procession I wasn't looking at your face."

I bristled at his cool rudeness, but Giulia just laughed, unoffended. "At least you admit it! Juan Borgia just lurks and licks his lips when he thinks I'm not looking."

"I've yet to meet him, but I suspect I will not enjoy the experience. Have you met his elder brother?"

"Cesare Borgia? No, but I heard he's come back from Pisa. Lucrezia adores him. What's he like?"

"Not a lip-licking lurker, that's certain." Leonello crunched on the last section of apple, eyes turning from Giulia to me. "And who are you, my very tall lady, besides the cook?"

"Just the cook." I began melting butter in a skillet, pushing the lump over the heat as it sizzled. "Not even the cook. The cook's cousin."

"Carmelina Mangano," Giulia said warmly. "The best cook in Rome. Try some of this strawberry *tourte*, if you don't believe me."

"No, thank you." His eyes traveled over me, speculative. "You're a long way from home. Venice?"

"How did you—"

"The accent. I've played cards with far too many Venetian sailors." He reached for the bowl of apples again.

"Stop that," I snapped. "Those are for apple and quince *crostate*."

"My apologies." He tossed the apple back. "So, a Venetian. But *Mangano*, that's surely not a Venetian name?"

"Sicilian," I said brusquely, and tossed the first batch of *frittelle* into the hot butter. "My father was born in Palermo. But he made his career in Venice."

"Another cook, no doubt." Leonello's eyes drifted to my kitchen-scarred hands, then back up. "Did he cut your hair just to keep it out of the skillets?"

I raised a hand to my head. I kept my short hair covered whenever Marco and the scullions were underfoot, but with the kitchens to myself I'd left off my usual scarf. My chopped black curls stood out every which way.

"I like it." Giulia noticed my awkward silence and jumped in. "Much more practical in a kitchen, surely. And I'll wager it doesn't take hours and hours to dry like mine. Can I fry the next batch of *frittelle*?"

"With hair like that you're either a cook, a nun, or a recent invalid," the little dwarf continued, grinning at me as I ceded the skillet to my mistress. "Or you have a taste for dressing up like a man during Carnival. One hears things about Venetian women . . ."

Unease bloomed inside my chest. He sensed it, I swear, because he cocked his head as though he were trying to read my thoughts. Or my secrets.

"I had to travel alone when I left Venice," I said at last, averting my eyes to Giulia's skillet. She had tossed in far too many *frittelle*, and they were smoking in a way they shouldn't. "I thought it safer to travel as a man. Give them a stir, Madonna Giulia—"

"To be sure," the dwarf agreed, tipping his chair back on two legs. He was almost handsome, despite his stunted height and oversized head. His hazel eyes made a striking contrast to his dark hair, and his features despite the prominent brow were bold and regular. But he sat there at my table, twirling a slim knife between his oddly double-jointed fingers, and my unease swelled to fear. I didn't like him. I didn't like his face, I didn't like the way he was playing with that knife, I didn't like the way his gaze fixed me—idle, curious, as though I were some anomaly to be solved. Santa Marta save me, but I could not afford to be solved. I could not afford curiosity. I could not afford to be discovered as anything other than a cook.

"I burned the *frittelle*," Giulia said mournfully, oblivious to the looks passing between us. She gave a poke to the little scorched lumps in the pan. "Maybe we can scrape off the blackened bits . . . Here, let me try another batch."

"Next time, Madonna Giulia!" I said brightly before she had the whole kitchen up in flames. How had she gotten those little lumps both scorched *and* raw? "Don't you wish to introduce Messer Leonello to Madonna Lucrezia?"

"Yes, I suppose we should. She's upstairs with Joffre and the tutor; they're translating Homer . . ." Giulia stripped off her apron and put her arm companionably through that of her diminutive new bodyguard, leading him away. Leonello looked back over his shoulder at me, lazy as the lion he was named for.

Leave me alone, I almost cried out. *Just leave me alone!*

But I did not think this oddly dangerous little man would do anything of the kind.

Giulia

I see it, I see it!" Little Lucrezia's voice rose into a squeal, and she flapped her hand at me. "White smoke!"

"Where?" I rose so fast I spilled my embroidery to the ground, whirling to the edge of the balcony where Lucrezia stood leaning out so far that I put a hasty hand on the sleeve of her nightdress.

"There, just above the *Piazza* San Pietro—"

"White smoke?" Madonna Adriana began to rise from the table where she was playing a halfhearted game of chess with little Joffre, but a bored voice interrupted us all midmotion.

"It's a cloud."

I turned back to my new bodyguard. "How can you tell, with your nose buried in that book?"

"Because even if there's been an election, they won't release the white smoke until dawn." Leonello turned a page in the book he'd borrowed without permission from Madonna Adriana's library. "You can't see white smoke until it's light, so what's the point of lighting the fire until the crowd down there will be able to see it?"

"Stop making sense," I told him, and flopped back into my chair. Lucrezia blew out her breath, settling back into her perch. Madonna

Adriana went back to her chess game, her curl knots bobbing, and little Joffre yawned hugely. The sky was still quite black, but between the sweltering heat of the summer night and the tension of the past week, not one of us in the household had been able to sleep. I was the first to leave my bed, throw a pale green silk robe over my night shift, and creep up to the loggia at the very top of the *palazzo*. But Lucrezia was soon creeping up after me, her hair still bound in its plait for sleeping, tugging sleepy little Joffre behind her, and Madonna Adriana in her billowing shift wasn't far behind.

"You children should be in bed," she reproved, but soon enough she was ordering tapers and wine and plates of soft-roasted chestnuts to keep us in comfort as we kept vigil over the view toward the Basilica San Pietro. I winced as the tray of chestnuts arrived, thinking of poor Carmelina the cook rousted from her bed downstairs just to feed us, but perhaps she was awake too. These past six days, with the Sistine Chapel and a college of twenty-three cardinals locked inside it in Conclave, the servants had been every bit as prone as I to hanging out the nearest window in search of that plume of white smoke. Three days in a row it had been black smoke, and a disappointed shout had gone up each time at the sign that yet another round of votes had been burned with no majority to show for it. White smoke, now—that meant we had a new pope.

More than ever, I worried just who that pope would be.

"Six days," I fretted. "Is that usual, for a Conclave?" It had been eight years since the last papal election, and frankly I remembered nothing about it. What was a pope to a girl of ten growing up in sleepy little Capodimonte?

"The last Conclave took only four days." My little bodyguard turned another page of his book. "And of course there was one that took two years, but that was seen as a trifle leisurely. The cardinals were finally locked in and the roof taken off the voting room, and they were told they would sit there in the open weather until they'd picked a pope. A few showers of rain concentrated their attention wonderfully."

I could never tell when Leonello was joking. His educated monotone never varied no matter what he was saying. Only a certain gleam in his deep-set hazel eyes indicated when he was laughing on the inside. After six days of his company, I must admit, he mostly laughed at me, but I liked my new bodyguard too much to mind. He sat now with his feet propped on a small table, short fingers flicking through the pages of a volume of verse by the light of a branch of tapers. Someone had found him a clean shirt and a secondhand doublet with the Borgia bull, both hastily altered to fit his small body, but his boots were still disreputable.

"This Conclave had better not take two years." I picked up the embroidery I was far too nervous to work on. "I can't stand much more of this suspense."

Leonello looked up at me over the edge of his book. "Do you want Cardinal Borgia to win?"

"Don't we all?" I said lightly. Madonna Adriana did; she could hardly concentrate on her chess game what with all her glances at the black sky over the basilica. Lucrezia and her brothers certainly did; they could do nothing but whisper about how their papa would soon be *Il Papa*. Even now Lucrezia was hanging over the rail of the loggia again, scanning the sky.

"I doubt you want him to win," said the dwarf. "Popes don't have mistresses, do they?"

"They can have children!" I put my chin up. "Pope Innocent had sixteen."

"Oh, youthful indiscretions are one thing. A young man is expected to keep a mistress or two when he's first starting his way up the ladder. And further up the rungs, well, a cardinal can get away with keeping a seraglio like this." Leonello waved a hand at the bower of women and children. "Installing that same seraglio in the Vatican, however . . ."

Rodrigo won't give me up. Not after those hours we'd spent in his emptied *palazzo* on the black and white daybed . . . and on the floor beside it . . . and in the summer-warmed grass of the garden with bees stumbling drunkenly between blowsy heat-fried roses. Not after the way he'd coiled my hair around his hand and murmured to me in

Spanish, telling me I was beautiful. How he'd made me *feel* beautiful, when his leisurely hands skimmed my naked shoulders or took their time exploring the tender skin on the very inside of my elbow.

But I hadn't seen him since that day, when he put me on my new horse and kissed my hand and sent me back to the Palazzo Montegiordano. The Pope had died just a few days later, and my Cardinal had disappeared into the Vatican for the papal funeral rites, and then into the Conclave. All I'd had was one brief note: *Don't leave the* palazzo *until the funeral and the voting are both done*, he'd written in curt haste. *The streets are dangerous, and I won't have you or the children harmed. I'll send a bodyguard.* Surely that meant he wouldn't give me up, even if he became Pope? *"I want you more than the Pope's throne."* Those had been his own words.

What do you know about men? a cruel little voice said in my head. *The last man you staked your future on was Orsino Orsini, and he sold you for advancement. Who's to say Rodrigo will do any differently?* A pope's throne was the greatest prize in Christendom, after all. Surely worth one ordinary golden-haired girl, no matter what promises were made in the heat of passion.

Maybe I'd be left with nothing but Orsino after all. Orsino and his clumsy hands and squinting gaze and weak voice . . . Only now, everyone in Rome would know I'd given myself first to the man who became Pope.

"Is it true, *sorellina*?" Sandro had roared at me just yesterday afternoon. I'd had a vain hope that maybe he wouldn't hear the gossip about his little sister when he returned to Rome, but that hope had died a quiet death in my breast the instant I saw Sandro storming into the garden of the Palazzo Montegiordano where I sat sunning my hair. "Cardinal *Borgia*? He forced you, didn't he? You never would have given in to that old whoreson. If he forced you, I'll have his head! I'll plant it in a pot of basil like Isabella and Lorenzo—"

"Sandro, stop shouting. This is no time for your dramatics." I'd taken a deep breath to calm the flutter in my stomach and launched into my well-prepared explanation, but my brother continued to pace and glower and interrupt me with curses: "I never thought you were fool enough to break your marriage vows! And with a man who's had more mistresses than *Zeus*!"

"What marriage vows?" I'd said bitterly, and Orsino's part in everything had come out then, and my brother's anger had (mostly) shifted off my shoulders. "That Spanish whoremonger is lucky he's locked in the Sistine Chapel right now," my brother had said darkly as a parting shot. "Or I'd track him down and geld him like Abelard. And that goes double for your spineless little snip of a husband."

"You will not do anything of the kind and you know it! The Orsini and the Borgia are powerful families—"

"And if they want to collude in despoiling *my* sister, they'll find there's a price!"

All I could do was gulp and mutter a prayer for Sandro's safety. Daggers drawn over a woman's honor; it all sounds very well in the songs, but in real life I found myself sick with fear when I imagined my big brother lying dead in the street for beginning a feud with one of the most powerful cardinals in Rome.

In any event, rapiers and daggers would have to wait until after the vote. *It all comes down to that blasted vote*, I thought, and rummaged for more of the sweet roasted chestnuts. I always eat when I'm nervous.

Leonello was still looking at me, one dark brow raised as if he were reading my head clear as the words in his book. "Stop reading my mind," I told him.

"All dwarves are mind readers. Didn't you know that, Madonna Giulia?"

I threw the last roasted chestnut at him.

"Dio." He caught it neatly. "What are you, a child? The concubine of a possible pope should conduct herself with more gravity, as befits her lover's station if not her own."

Madonna Adriana gave a *tsk* at his rudeness, but I was already used to it. The first afternoon he'd spent in my company I'd been twanging at my lute, trying to memorize the fingering of a new song. Leonello had listened for an hour, trying to read, and finally put the book down and his thumbs in his ears. "You sound like you're strangling a cat," he said frankly. "But I must admit you look very fetching strumming away like that."

I'd giggled, stilling my fingers on the strings. "I am terrible, aren't I?"

"Torquemada would condemn what you are inflicting on that poor instrument," Leonello told me, and I liked him for it. I had spent more than a fortnight in his company, and after all the silent obsequious servants his tartness refreshed me, like a tangy draft of lemon water on a hot day.

"You think His Eminence will give me up?" I found myself asking my bodyguard now, voice low as I fiddled with my embroidery.

"I wouldn't." Leonello had already gone back to his book. "But no one's offering to make me Pope."

I winced at that, then swore as I ran the embroidery needle into my thumb. "Oh, Holy Virgin, I give up. Lucrezia, come here." I tossed the embroidery aside. "Let me brush your hair out. That braid is coming unraveled."

She curled up on a stool before me. "Maybe Leonello can juggle for us!"

He kept reading. "No."

"Not all dwarves juggle," I told her as I loosened her plait. "Just like not all cardinals have beautiful blond daughters."

"No, only the best ones do." She gave a little bounce on her stool. "Oh, I wish Cesare and Juan would come tell us what's happening! Cesare always knows everything."

Frankly, I was glad neither of Rodrigo's elder sons were underfoot. I'd finally met Juan's elder brother when he came to visit his sister just after Pope Innocent died: Cesare Borgia, auburn-haired like Juan, but taller and more self-possessed. He'd looked me over once and dismissed me from mind. *Just another of my father's whores*, he might as well have said, before disappearing with Juan on some mysterious business of Rodrigo's. The Pope hadn't been dead even a day before Juan was bragging of the urgent services he would be performing for his father during the Conclave, but Cesare told him to hold his tongue and dragged him out on some doubtless-illicit errand.

The night dragged on. I sat working my silver comb through Lucrezia's curls, Adriana began to doze in her chair, and Joffre had fallen asleep entirely with his head on the chessboard. Leonello examined the game around the boy's head and moved one or two pieces—"twelve moves to the win, starting with the knight to *here*"—and Lucrezia chattered to me with all her breathless unconcern.

"My father says that when he's Pope I'll have *princes* begging for my hand in marriage! Don Gaspare won't be good enough for me then, my father says, though I don't know if I want to break the betrothal. I've had one broken betrothal already, last year to Juan de Centenelles—"

When her father was Pope. *When*, not *if*. I sighed, stroking the comb through Lucrezia's hair.

"More chestnuts, Madonna Giulia?" A voice sounded from the door to the loggia, and I twisted my head to see Carmelina the cook standing with a plate in hand. She wore a robe over her night shift, like me.

"We did get you out of bed," I said ruefully. "Go back to sleep after this! We can fetch our own wine and sweets if we want more."

"Nonsense, I'm always up before dawn." She came forward and set down the plate beside the chessboard, her Venetian accents as crystal-sharp as the glass they produced. "If you'll just— Oh, Santa Marta save me!"

I heard a mournful *baaaa*, and looked to see a baby goat come pushing its way around Carmelina's skirt. Huge-eared, woolly-white, he looked around him and gave a pitiful bleat that woke Madonna Adriana with a snort.

"What's that?" she demanded as I giggled.

"Dinner." Carmelina regarded the goat grimly. "It's been escaping the kitchen ever since last night, trailing after whoever it could find. You'd think it would be smart enough to know it's going to end up spitted and stuffed, but I suppose goats aren't known for their brains." Her tone turned musing. "The brains can be very tasty too—chopped up small with sweet marjoram and parsley..."

"You can't kill him," I protested. "Look at that face!"

The goat kid gave another pathetic *baaaaa*. Carmelina looked down at him, fists on hips. "Looks like dinner to me, Madonna Giulia."

"Well, he's not." I scooped the goat up into my lap. Lucrezia giggled as he began to nibble on a corner of her sleeve, and I stroked the floppy white ears. "I'm granting him a reprieve from execution."

"Where were you when I was arrested?" Leonello murmured, or I thought he murmured, but he had retreated back behind his book again.

"What else can I make for evening *cena*?" Carmelina was demanding. "We don't have roast kid, we'll be reduced to pottage and hot sops."

"I don't mind pottage and hot sops," I wheedled, cuddling the goat. "Do you, Lucrezia?"

"No, no, *please* don't kill him!"

Carmelina gave a dour look at the goat. "You got lucky," she told it, and turned to go.

"Who do you favor for Pope, *Signorina Cuoca*?" Leonello looked up at her from his book. "Our Cardinal Borgia? Or one of your fellow Venetians, Cardinal Girardo or Zeno or Michiel?"

"It's none of my business," she said curtly.

"If we only concerned ourselves with our own business, life would be very dull." Leonello's smile was lazy. "I find *your* business, for example, very interesting indeed."

Carmelina gave a scowl and vanished. My favorite cook had *not* taken to my new bodyguard. Every time he addressed her, she looked as if she wanted to scratch and spit.

"You shouldn't needle her," I told him as the door slammed behind her. "It doesn't do to offend the cook—you'll eat nothing but burned stews."

"I can't help it." He looked at the door where Carmelina had vanished. "That's a woman with secrets if I ever saw one."

"We all have secrets. Don't you?"

"Oh, many."

"Tell me one. More than a fortnight you've been my shadow, and I don't know anything about you."

"Are you sure you weren't switched at birth with a peasant baby, Madonna Giulia? Girls of your birth and rearing do not care to know about the lives of their servants."

"All right, keep your secrets." I stroked the goat in my lap, distracting him from nibbling on my sleeve. "At least tell me what you're reading."

"Homeric hymns." Leonello ran an appreciative hand over the finely tooled leather binding. "If I stay in this household much longer, I will be very spoiled for books."

"I like poetry. Petrarch especially. In some moods anyway."

"I'm never in the mood for Petrarch."

"What's wrong with Petrarch?"

"Inchoate longings in saccharine verse for a blond bore."

"You do not have a poetic soul," I started to say, but a cry came from Lucrezia, who had risen from crooning over the goat in my lap and flown back to the balcony.

"White smoke! It *is* white smoke this time, I see it!"

Madonna Adriana flew out of her chair so fast the chessboard overturned. Little Joffre woke with a start and tumbled to join his sister, tripping over a scatter of black and white pawns. Leonello looked up from his book and I hoisted my new pet under one arm and rushed to the rail, craning my neck toward the vast shadowy shape of the basilica.

The sky had gone from black to gray, the faintest line of pink showing in the east. Just enough light to see the plume of white smoke venting upward from the basilica.

Habemus Papam. We had a new pope.

"*Deo gratias,*" said Leonello. He sounded amused.

"Leonello." Madonna Adriana's voice was sick with tension. "Go to the guards and have them send someone to the square immediately."

No one had to ask what for. As we spoke, the new Pope was being robed in the prepared papal vestments, readying himself for his first appearance at the window where he would give his first papal blessing.

What pope? The words pounded in my ears as I followed a squealing Lucrezia and a bouncing Joffre down the stairs toward the entrance hall to wait. *What pope?*

I had no idea what to hope for.

In the end, Rodrigo returned before Madonna Adriana's messenger could fight his way back through the jubilant thousands who had flooded the streets of Rome. We waited in the anteroom, all of us. Joffre bounced so incessantly that Adriana slapped him; Lucrezia was alternately praying and bubbling. Leonello stood throwing his knives over and over into a wall, making star patterns and circle patterns and crucifix patterns with the blades. I put on my pearl and the scarlet gown I'd worn when I went to Rodrigo's bed, and I paced nervously before the windows looking at that plume of white smoke. The goat trailed after me nibbling at my hem, and the servants clustered whispering, not even pretending to work.

A thunder of noise and people crashed through the double doors of the anteroom. A flood of pages and guards and stewards and churchmen suddenly filled the *palazzo*, all jabbering and gesticulating at once. A pair of handsome young men, both proud and auburn-haired, one in a bishop's gown and the other in a soldier's half-armor, stood flanking an imposing broad-shouldered figure in sweeping layers of gold-embroidered white.

Cesare Borgia lifted his hand as Juan grinned, and tossed a flutter of handwritten paper scraps into the air. They had drifted down from the window into the crowd when the Holy Father gave his first blessing:

"We have for Pope, Alexander VI, Rodrigo Borgia of Valencia."

"I am Pope!" my former Cardinal shouted, his deep voice a bull's roar of triumph. *"I am POPE!"*

He started forward with that swift stride of his, embroidered cope fluttering behind him like a conqueror's banner. Servants, churchmen, relatives, children all converged, but he bulled through them and came to me. I sent my little goat slithering to the floor and rose, mouth dry.

"*I am Pope*," he repeated, and grabbed me up in such an exuberant embrace that my feet left the floor and flew out of my slippers. He laughed, a sound like warm bubbling wine, and I laughed with him, lowering my head to kiss him before God and congregation and hangers-on and all. I heard whispers begin to ripple around the anteroom, but why should I care for that? Rodrigo didn't care, and his opinion was now the only one that mattered.

I pressed my lips against my lover's ear in the middle of all the tumult. "Your Holiness," I whispered, and bent my head to kiss his ring.

PART TWO

June 1493–November 1494

CHAPTER SEVEN

❖

*The dishes should be tasty and pleasant to the palate,
as well as delightful to the eye.*

—BARTOLOMEO SCAPPI, MASTER COOK

Carmelina

Signorina Carmelina!" The assistant steward's voice bored into my
ears, high-pitched and aggrieved. I didn't answer. I was making a
tourte of caravella pears, which I normally could have made in my sleep,
but this time I was making a miniature version hardly bigger than my
thumb, and it required very close concentration. I'd already grated the
pears and cooked them slowly in butter . . . added the almond paste, the
candied citron . . .

"*Signorina?*"

A spoon of filling, just a spoon into a shell of very thin pastry . . . I
rubbed my hands briskly up and down my apron. Pastry required steady
hands, and I'd need very tiny strips like shutters to seal the *tourte* up.
Then glaze the top with sugar and rosewater . . .

"*Signorina!*" An insistent finger poked my arm just as I was arranging the last little louvered flap of pastry. The little *tourte* fell apart in my
hand, and I seized a wooden ladle from the nearest bowl and swung it
in a short arc as I whirled.

"Santa Marta!" I yelled. "Sneak up on me again, and I'll braise your liver in white wine and serve *that* to the Pope and his guests!"

The steward ducked my ladle, surprisingly agile for such a bulky little man. The red-haired pot-boy squeezing past us with a load of pans wasn't so wasn't so lucky; the ladle fetched him a good whack across the ear, and he yelped.

"What?" I snarled, scraping my ruined *tourte* into the waste. It had been a long series of days, and the horrid news I'd just heard from the market about that poor fruit seller who got herself so gruesomely murdered had hardly helped my peace of mind—and now I was so close to getting the recipe right!

"It's Maestro Santini again." The steward sounded ominous. "And he's in a bad way."

I muttered a prayer and sent it skyward as I dropped my ladle and flew into the courtyard. But my prayer died in vain: Marco was in no condition to cook. He leaned against the wall that shielded the carcasses and barrels of the kitchens from the street outside, and he stank of wine. A very bad Lagrima vintage, from the smell.

"Little cousin," he wheedled, one eye peering at me through a fall of black hair. "My sweet Carmelina—"

"Never mind your fancy words." I flew under one of his arms, hoisting him up before his knees could buckle. "How much did you lose?"

He squinted at me. "Who says I lost anything?"

"Because you only drink when you lose. And you only drink this much when you lose badly." I grabbed a handful of his hair, hauling his head up before it could loll against my neck. "How much?"

"Hardly anything." He swayed again, and the wine fumes could have suffocated an ox. "Just ten ducats . . ."

"Marco!" Near half a year's salary.

"It was just one time, one little game . . ." He looked around at the ring of apprentices and stewards and manservants, noting the significant glances and rolled eyes for the first time. They all knew Marco's tricks as well as I did, but somehow he seemed to think they all believed him when he said *it was just one time.* "What?"

"The sweetmeats," I shouted. "The three hundred pounds of sweets we're to deliver for Madonna Lucrezia's wedding!"

He shuffled his boots, abashed. "Oh . . ." I wondered what it was about my cousin and weddings. One hint of nuptials in the air, and his sense of responsibility went straight to the Devil. On the other hand, maybe all men were like that. Marco looked shamefaced, swaying against me.

"Never mind." I knew well enough how to carry on without my cousin. "Just sleep it off, and then— Oh, sweet Santa Marta, catch him!" Marco's hard-muscled arm began to slide heavily off my shoulder.

The apprentices just gaped. Useless, the lot of them. Piero and a few other bad apples from my first days in Marco's kitchens had long since been weeded out, but I wasn't impressed with the new batch: brains no bigger than capers, one and all. Madonna Adriana was cousin to the Pope, and now installed in an even more luxurious *palazzo* with the Pope's daughter and mistress—but she still liked to hire on the cheap. Why pay for experienced servants when raw green apprentices and untrained youngsters could be had for half the price? *She* didn't have to train all those young lummoxes, after all. I did. And they all just stood there slack-jawed as Marco nearly slithered to the ground and took me with him.

The only one to move was the red-haired pot-boy, the one I'd accidentally whacked with a ladle. He made a lunge and caught my cousin under the arm before he hit the floor like six and a half feet of drunken ox. "What's your name again, boy?" I barked. One of the new boys; scullions came and went like stray cats.

"Bartolomeo, *signorina*." He looked about fourteen, thin as a spit but tall for his age, with wide bony shoulders. A wooden crucifix showed through the lacing of his flour-sprinkled shirt.

"What are you doing up in the kitchens anyway?" I demanded. "I set all pot-boys to work in the scullery; there are more pots to scrub than fleas on a dog."

He looked shame-faced, hitching a skinny shoulder under Marco's limp arm. "I followed the smells." A long rapturous sniff. "What *is* that, *signorina*?"

"That's a decent start on three hundred pounds of wedding sweetmeats, that's what *that* is." Madonna Lucrezia Borgia would become the Countess of Pesaro and wife to Lord Sforza in just two days' time, and the wedding celebrations at the Vatican would be like nothing Rome had ever seen. The papal kitchens would of course feed the vast crowd of wedding guests following the ceremony, and provide the private evening *cena* the Pope intended to give for his daughter and her new husband . . . but Giulia Farnese, may God bless her generous flighty heart, had batted her great dark eyes at the Pope and begged my services and mine alone to provide the sweets that would circulate among the guests after the ceremony. And since, after a year of passion, the Pope was still purring and arching for his mistress like a boy of sixteen, he'd granted her wish in a heartbeat.

If it had been Marco in charge, he would have just flipped to the back of my father's recipe collection (page 428, Chapter: *Dolci*) and churned off a list of the usual favorites at such banquets: sugared pears, candied cherries, sweet *biscotti*. Easy enough . . . but I didn't want to settle for *easy*. I stayed up late in the kitchens, sprinkled with sugar and sticky-fingered with honey, experimenting with one idea after another in a fever of excitement. Miniature *tourtes* of caravella pears and sweet summer strawberries sliced thin as a holy wafer; blood orange segments layered and honeyed in pastry stars; violets and apple blossoms encased in shells of crystallized sugar; pale candied almonds feathered and slivered and layered together into little pastry swans; insubstantial crisps of burnt sugar that melted on the tongue; and Giulia Farnese's favorite marzipan rolled out into fanciful shapes and dyed in the Borgia colors of mulberry and yellow. Tiny, beautiful, delicate, mouthwatering; everything a bride in the full bloom of youth was supposed to be. My wedding gift to the young Lucrezia Borgia, even if she never knew it.

Three hundred pounds of refreshments called for a great deal of sugar; the kitchens were now a rolling boil of luscious smells. After so many hours of nighttime experimentation I hardly smelled it anymore, but young Bartolomeo looked as if he were about to faint on the wave of sweetness. "What *is* that?" he breathed again.

"Sugar, cinnamon, candied pine nuts, rosewater, saffron, cloves, almond paste, and pepper," I said briskly. "Among many other things."

"You can't put pepper on sweet things," he objected.

"You most certainly can," I sniffed. "Ground fresh over seared baby peaches with a dollop of rosewater-whipped cream—" Another of my late-night inventions.

He looked interested. "Can I try one, *signorina*?"

"Certainly not. See Maestro Santini safe to his bed, and then get back to your pots." I turned back to the chattering scullions and under-cooks with a clap of my hands. "I want to see mouths shut and hands moving! We're running behind, you clods, and it's not just Madonna Lucrezia who will be eating these sweets, it's ambassadors from Milan and Mantua and Ferrara and who knows where else. Back to work!"

They all scattered, used to obeying me by now. The red-haired pot-boy was already shouldering Marco past the wine cellars, and I couldn't help shaking my head in grudging affection as my cousin was hauled off with his curly head lolling. Normally it did no good for a kitchen's state of mind, seeing their leader drunk and incapable. But there was something so endearing about Marco's little-boy guilt when he lost his money, and his naked joy when he won it—there wasn't a maid in my kitchens who could hold his lapses against him, or resist covering for his absences.

Well, I wouldn't need to do much covering today. As long as I delivered Madonna Lucrezia's sweetmeats for her wedding guests, after all, no one inside this insulated billow of kitchen steam would get in any trouble on account of Marco's lapse. And if the maids and pot-boys no longer grumbled at my orders, well, they knew after a year of working side by side that if there was anyone who could roll out that endless line of wedding sweets in time, it was me. I smiled, giving an automatic pat to the little bundle of Santa Marta's hand under my skirt, and reached for the bowl of caravella pears to try my miniature *tourte* again. Marco had objected, saying you could never make a *tourte* so small it could be eaten in one bite; the crust would surely blacken in the oven before the filling cooked.

My nose and I, we knew better.

Leonello

Well?" my mistress said anxiously. "What do you think?"
She turned a circle before me, skirts flaring, and I looked
up from the finger knife I was sharpening and scrutinized her top to
toe: Giulia Farnese, now known to all Rome as Giulia la Bella, the Venus
of the Vatican, the Pope's beloved. Her famous hair had been twined at
the back of her head into a complicated mass of gold plaits; she wore
green and gold Spanish brocade with full flounced sleeves; her gold-
embroidered slippers peeped out of her fringed hem. "Beautiful, of
course," I shrugged. "No different than the previous six dresses."

"Don't I look sallow in green?" Giulia gave another turn before me.
"Please tell me I look sallow."

"Why on earth do you want to look sallow, Madonna Giulia?" I
slipped the finger knife back into its hidden sheath at my wrist.

"This is Lucrezia's wedding day! Everyone has to look at her, not me
or that primping girl who's to carry her train, or anyone else. I need to
look *plain* by comparison." Giulia flew back behind her dressing screen
again. "Very plain," her voice floated out.

"Then put a sack over your head and be done with it," I said, returning to my book.

Maids descended on La Bella behind the screen with more armloads
of brocade—"*Madonna*, have you considered the gray velvet with the
gold embroidery?"—and I sat back more comfortably against the tapestried wall, feet dangling far above the floor, Giulia's gold head bobbing
above the edge of the screen in my peripheral vision. Her chamber
looked as though a rainbow had exploded inside it: silk gowns and velvet
gowns and brocade gowns lay strewn across the huge curtained bed;
pairs of sleeves hung like dismembered arms over the cushioned footstools; the wall benches were six inches deep in tasseled gloves and
embroidered caps and beaded veils. Madonna Giulia's pet goat, now
grown to full slothful maturity and forever paroled from the possibility
of ending up in a *crostata*, lay curled in a corner placidly eating a velvet

slipper. Maids bustled back and forth: linen maids, cosmetics maids, seamstresses, robe makers, the two maids assigned to keep La Bella's skin white, the three maids whose sole job it was to tend her hair—all of them pink-faced with excitement. Lucrezia Borgia was to become the wife of Lord Giovanni Sforza, today, and none other than Giulia Farnese would lead her to the altar.

At which decision I had to wonder if the Pope had taken leave of his usually shrewd senses. Lucrezia at thirteen was a fetching little thing: blond, sweet-faced, tall enough to resemble a woman; conscious enough of her dignity to glide rather than bounce. But standing beside La Bella, she would be nothing but an afterthought.

"Not that one," I heard my mistress say as the maids whisked her green and gold gown away and began holding up alternatives behind the dressing screen. Considering she was now the most notorious woman in Rome, Giulia Farnese was surprisingly modest—much to the great disappointment of all the male servants, there was no half-dressed parading about the *palazzo* for the Pope's concubine. "No, not that dress either—or that—"

"The yellow-green dress," I called out from behind my book. "It's the color of cat vomit. You still won't look ugly, but it's a start."

"Don't see why we have to listen to him," one of her maids said behind the screen—scrawny Pantisilea, who wasn't so improbably named as I'd thought. Penthesilea the Amazon queen had dragged all the men she met off to captivity; Pantisilea the maid dragged all the men she met off to her bed. "I've never had a dwarf," she'd told me cheerfully on first acquaintance. "Want to try me?" And we'd had a laugh or two between the sheets, but now she was looking at me over the screen with a dubious eye. "What does a bodyguard know about dresses?"

"We are in dire need of a man's opinion," Giulia informed her. "Oof, that's tight, loosen those laces—"

"He's not a man, *madonna*," one of the other maids objected.

"But at least he's impartial," I said from my wall. "What you need is a pair of eyes that does not notice your beauty."

"You don't think I'm beautiful, Leonello?" Giulia peeked over the top of the screen, giving me the benefit of her big wounded eyes before being yanked down again by the maids.

"Certainly you are." I turned a page absently. "But I have worked in your company near a year now, *madonna*, and no matter how beautiful the frescoes on one's wall, eventually one ceases to notice them."

"You're horrid," Giulia complained. "His Holiness says he's as struck as he was when he first laid eyes on me."

"Which is why you want my opinion instead of His Holiness the Pope's."

Giulia flew out behind the screen again, this time arrayed in embroidered yellow-green silk. "Well?"

"Better," I said. Not really—even unjeweled and swathed in a dress the color of cat vomit, Giulia Farnese would still draw all eyes. The virtuous women of Rome could be divided fairly evenly into two camps: those who drew their skirts aside from the Bride of Christ and her scandalous reputation, and those who fawned on her because their husbands hoped for some favor from His Holiness. But every woman in Rome, whether scornful or sycophantic, craned their necks to see every detail of what Giulia Farnese wore. If she appeared at Mass in the Basilica San Pietro in a blue velvet gown, every cloth merchant in the city began hawking "papal blue." If she wore a dashing little furred cap tilted over one eye when she went to confession, every woman in Rome with a claim to high fashion was sporting a "Farnese *biretta*" within a fortnight. Doubtless by tomorrow morning, there would be a storm of women racing off to their robe makers for dresses in cat-vomit silk.

"Better," I said again as my mistress twirled. "You'll be the least ostentatious woman at the Gilded Excrescence."

"I wish you wouldn't call Lucrezia's wedding that." Giulia made a face at me as her maids tied her sleeves. "It's sure to be a beautiful occasion."

"Certainly it will be a sumptuous one." His Holiness the Pope was sparing no expense in the wedding of his bastard daughter. I looked down into the cradle beside my wall bench at the bride's little sister.

"Will you be having a wedding like this in thirteen years or so, little one?"

The baby gnawed on her own fist in her nest of crested linens: the latest addition to the papal seraglio, born almost nine months to the week that Rodrigo Borgia became Pope Alexander VI, and there wasn't a soul in Rome who hadn't done their sums on hearing *that*.

"Why shouldn't Laura have a wedding like this someday?" Brushing the maids aside, Giulia came to lift her daughter out of the ornately carved cradle. The baby gurgled and spit up on her mother's shoulder, but Giulia dabbed at the silk unconcernedly. "A count or a duke is none too good for a pope's daughter."

"And by the time she grows old enough to think of marrying, His Holiness will be bankrupt from all the other weddings." Thirteen-year-old Lucrezia was the first of the Borgia bastards to marry (at least the first of the bastards he had here in Rome) but there was already talk of a Spanish bride for Juan and a Neapolitan princess for little Joffre. I wasn't supposed to know His Holiness's ruminations, but I still liked to keep my card-play sharp, and I often played *primiera* with the papal secretaries. They sometimes put papal secrets in the pot instead of coin. "His Holiness should just put her in a convent to save money," I advised.

"Nonsense; if she's anything like me *or* her father, she'd be a dreadful nun. Won't you, *Lauretta mia*—look, doesn't she have Rodrigo's nose?"

"She has exactly the same nose as any other baby."

Giulia ignored me, blowing loud kisses all over baby Laura and finally laying her back in the carved cradle. "Oh, dear, I'm late!"

"You're always late, *madonna*," one of the maids scolded, and La Bella flew like a yellow-green bird with her entourage behind her.

I slipped down from the wall bench, shooing the white goat as it moved on from a mostly consumed slipper to a pair of embroidered gloves, and I sauntered after my mistress. I paused a moment to lean over the cradle, partly to tickle little Laura until she giggled and partly to make the superstitious nursemaid fork the sign of the devil behind her back as she always did when the little fiend—that would be me—came too close to her charge.

The new Pope was not a man to waste time. Immediately after his ascension to the throne of San Pietro, he moved the papal seraglio containing Madonna Adriana and his daughter and his mistress to the exquisite Palazzo Santa Maria in Portico, a stone's throw from the Vatican itself. All Rome was abuzz at the scandal, and even I had raised an eyebrow; popes had kept mistresses and bastards before, and most cardinals maintained at least one unofficial household, but there was always the necessary shell of respectability: concubines passed off as cousins, illegitimate sons as nephews. But Pope Alexander VI cared not a fig for gossip and made no such pretense, moving his mistress openly to her new home, and I had been moved right along with the rest of her servants and belongings. We had all let out gasps and whistles at the sight of the Palazzo Santa Maria: the high-arched loggias framing the jewel-like gardens, the marble terraces and splashing fountains, the long flights of shallow steps leading to breathtaking vistas over Rome. An Eden fit for Dante's *Paradiso* . . .

And just now, it could have doubled for the *Inferno*. Perhaps one of the livelier rings of hell, with a few of the more energetic sins. Despair; yes, I saw plenty of that as I descended into a throng of servants wringing their hands and wild-eyed stewards perusing fistfuls of increasingly frayed lists. Vanity, certainly; I saw that too—the bride's attendants preening everywhere there was a reflective surface and trying to pretend they weren't counting the pearls on the bodice of the girl beside them. Wrath; plenty of that too as maids got their ears violently boxed for not being fast enough with a cup of wine, and pages shouted at each other with voices gone shrill from strain.

Dio. Weddings.

"Where are you going, dwarf?" a rude voice demanded as I made my way through the throng to a certain tapestry-covered archway. My eyes traveled up a pair of absurd cloth-of-silver pantaloons, a gold robe with a dagged edge that trailed the floor, and a broad collar of pearls and balas rubies.

"I see one of the Sultan's concubines has gone astray."

Juan Borgia flushed under his absurd turban with its ceiling-scraping plume and huge ruby. A suave Turkish prince had arrived in Rome as a hostage not long ago, and his flamboyant robes and pantaloons had been adopted by all the young fops in Rome. One could look out over a sea of turbans at Mass and not be sure whether one was in a church or a mosque.

"I wouldn't expect a dwarf to understand the fashions," he said, giving an eye to my ill-fitting Borgia livery. A year in the Pope's service and I still didn't have a doublet that fit around my oddly proportioned body.

"There's some advantage at least in being a dwarf," I answered the Duke of Gandia. "Even in a hat as silly as that one, I could still clear a doorway without ducking. Do try not to trip on those curly shoes, will you, and send the bride sprawling on her way to her husband?"

I swept a flourish of a bow and continued past him. Not wise, perhaps, to be rude to the Pope's favorite son, but my viper tongue still required a fool now and then on which to exercise its edges, and Juan Borgia served admirably in place of drunken innkeepers and tavern cheats.

Lucrezia Borgia would pass through the streets of Rome on her way to the Vatican, escorted in her bridal procession by her brother the faux Turk and Madonna Giulia and a full hundred and fifty additional Roman ladies arrayed in their finest. Crowds would gather to see them pass, commenting on the jewels and the gowns and the splendor of the occasion, craning their necks and hoping for largesse until the moment the Pope's daughter disappeared into the Vatican. I wondered idly what the crowds really thought of such pomp—a train of hundreds for the Borgia bride when most Roman girls went accompanied only by family and friends; diamonds and sables and pedigreed horses for wedding gifts when most girls got only embroidered belts or perhaps a length of cloth; a fifteen-thousand-ducat wedding dress when most fathers, on their yearly earnings of perhaps twenty-five ducats, could afford only a pair of new sleeves to dress up their daughter's best gown.

If I knew crowds, they would be pleased by the pomp, dazzled rather than offended. The Borgias, in the eyes of most of the world including themselves, had been put upon the earth by God to lead sumptuous lives on behalf of the masses. Their pomp was God's will.

I took the private route out of the *palazzo*, not caring to be crushed by eager crowds. A passage already existed between the Palazzo Santa Maria and the Vatican itself, by which the Pope could visit his mistress and family, and all Rome was abuzz with that bit of gossip too. At least three times a week the Holy Father quite openly dismissed his retinue and took the short walk from his papal apartments, and the satin-textured, intensely feminine world of the papal seraglio changed to an ordinary bustling Roman household as Giulia Farnese dispensed wifely kisses, Madonna Adriana called for another place at the table, and Lucrezia bounced for her share of fatherly hugs. The Holy Father could relax like any ordinary Roman merchant, sit down to a good *cena* with a pretty wife on one side and a capable mother-in-law on the other and a cherished daughter running to refill his wine cup. Common, happy domesticity: a drug even for Christendom's most powerful man.

The fact that the woman who served as the Pope's wife had a quite legal husband of her own stashed away in the countryside—well, that was a mere detail.

The passage was unlit, but tiled and well swept. I kept pace with one shoulder brushing the wall, counting steps as I took out my knives and flicked their edges in the dark. A new set of knives, presented to me by His Excellency Cesare Borgia on the day after the Pope's ascension, when I'd been offered a permanent position as Giulia Farnese's body-guard. "The charge of murder against you is gone," the young Bishop had deigned to tell me, cocked back at his desk with his auburn hair mussed around its very slight tonsure. "But the charge can be resurrected if any more recreational murders come from those stubby little hands of yours. Understood?"

"Recreational murders," I'd grinned. "I like that."

"See you don't get to like it too much. For murders in your daily line of work, perhaps you would care to have these." And he'd tossed a bundled set of new finger knives at me, crafted along the lines of my old ones but a set of ten rather than four, exquisitely balanced little blades ranging from a mere inch in length to a pig-sticker of half a foot. "Perhaps you will not turn up your nose at this Toledo steel?"

He wanted my Toledo steel at his sister's wedding today. "I'll have you up close," he said. "With the other guards beside His Holiness's throne."

I nodded. The cream of Roman nobility would be in attendance at the wedding of the Pope's daughter, and the cream of a dozen other cities as well—Ferrara and Milan and Mantua and Venice—and the Borgia enemies would be thick among them. Should any decide to melt from the throng with murderous intent during the wedding vows, the papal guard would spring around the Pope, but I had different targets to protect: Lucrezia and Giulia. "The twin stars of the Borgia firmament," I said in my most extravagant poet's drawl, and gave a bark of laughter at myself for flights of fancy. Too much poetry; too many late nights translating a volume of Provençal troubadour verses I'd recently found. "Back to the ancient Romans," I promised myself as I clambered up the final flight of shallow steps toward the private entrance into the Vatican. Caesar's commentaries on the Gallic wars; that simple straightforward Latin could knock the fancy language out of anyone, and the library at the Palazzo Santa Maria had a gorgeously engraved volume of the *Commentarii de Bello Gallico*. Even more than for the Toledo blades hidden in my belt and boot tops and wrist sheaths, I was growing spoiled for fine books.

"Oh, *Gott im Himmel*, save me from this day!" I heard a frantic mumble as I entered the new Borgia apartments the Pope had carved out for himself among the older, mustier chambers of the Vatican. "This is the end, this is the absolute *end*!"

"Messer Burchard." I greeted the Pope's master of ceremonies cheerfully. "What ails you today?"

The little German in his dusty black robe and his square cap crammed over a frizzing head of hair shook a fistful of lists at me. "Only the end of all order and sanity in God's good earth, that's all! *Gott im Himmel!*"

By which he could have meant the bridal attendants were late, the

Pope had worn the wrong color shoes, or the pages had attempted to make their entrance without gloves. I had grown to know Johann Burchard well in the past months, generally because he was always rushing about as though his head were on fire or the world about to end, or perhaps both, and was therefore usually in need of someone to wail at. He could certainly not wail at the Pope, and the other officials tended to find pressing duties whenever he collared them, but my legs were too short to carry me out of earshot of his complaints.

"The ladies," he began indignantly in his stiff German accents. "The ladies were first into the *sala*, just as arranged, and I'd planned the most *beautiful* little procession for them where they advanced by twos, and bowed to the Pope and kissed his shoe, and did any of them listen to me? No! They just rushed in any which way, like cattle released into a pen, and not *one* of them paused to bow! It's the end, Messer Leonello, it's the absolute end of the world!"

"That the Pope's shoe went unkissed?" I inquired.

"Moral decay! Tradition slips, propriety slips, then morality slips, and before you know it the end is nigh!" He ran through his lists again, wild-eyed. "Oh, why did I keep this position, *why*? I should have quit, that's what I should have done. Before this wedding, I should have quit. Because there is *no* proper way to host an official wedding of the Pope's daughter, attended by the Pope's sons and the Pope's concubine! None! Because by rights, none of them should exist in the first place!"

I looked at him with a certain degree of sympathy. I would not have wanted his job, that was certain: pasting papal legalities over the antics of the Borgia Pope and his offspring. It was certainly no job for a prim little German from Strasbourg who heard the hoofbeats of the Four Horsemen of the Apocalypse if the Pope's slipper went unkissed. "Cheer up, Burchard," I said with a thump to his arm. "Another twelve hours and you can go get drunk."

He regarded me with as much horror as though I'd suggested he attend the papal wedding in the nude. "Twelve hours? You think it will all end in twelve hours? Are you mad? The evening banquet and the subsequent dancing *alone* . . ."

I left Burchard to his Teutonic anguish and slipped into the crowds of silk-decked wedding guests already thronging the high-ceilinged chamber. The first of the private anterooms the Pope had staked out for himself, setting the great Pinturicchio to paint them with gorgeous new frescoes. Pinturicchio worked slowly, so the frescoes were not yet near done, but the walls had been hung for the time being with silken tapestries, the floors covered with Oriental carpets deep enough to cover my boot heels, every wall bracket gleamed with fresh gilt, the ceiling arched over the guests high-carved and corniced. The Pope's throne had been brought in to loom over the proceedings on its own dais, and he already sat ensconced: Rodrigo Borgia no more, but Pope Alexander VI. I wondered if anyone else besides myself had thought it significant that he chose not an apostle's name or a virtuous name—no Paul or John, no Innocent or Pius—but the name of a conqueror.

Even with the welcome refuge of his seraglio to relax him, a year on the papal throne had already worn grained circles under the eyes of Pope Alexander. But his heavy-lidded gaze was alert as ever as he looked out over the wedding guests, his heavy three-tiered papal tiara pushed back as nonchalantly as a cap on his black hair, and he lounged in his white and gold robes as Alexander the Great must have lounged as he contemplated Darius and the Persian hordes.

Until his daughter entered, flanked by his mistress. Then he had only the proudest and most tender of smiles.

The procession came with great pomp: a great fanfare of music, the Duke of Gandia in all his gaudy finery slipping back into place beside his father, Cesare Borgia coming behind almost unnoticed in his churchman's robes. Archbishop of Valencia now, not just Bishop of Pamplona, but he still looked more like a lazy leopard dozing in the sun than a churchman. The guests fluttered, craned their necks, chattered excitedly among themselves . . . and yet the moment when it came was almost quiet: a girl of thirteen, swamped in jewels, slipping through the door into the crowded *sala* and pausing for a moment out of sheer nerves.

From my position squashed among the papal guards I saw Lucrezia Borgia swallow, her slim throat moving behind a collar of pearls and emeralds—and I saw Giulia, standing just behind, touch a finger to her elbow and murmur something too quiet to be heard. "Chin up," I rather thought she would be saying. "You are the Pope's daughter, so head high! Don't worry about your dress; it has so many jewels it will fall into line all on its own." For days before the wedding, Giulia had coached Lucrezia in her fifteen-thousand-ducat wedding dress, around and around the garden. "Glide, don't struggle. Move *with* your skirts, not against them. That's it, look how beautiful you are!"

She wasn't beautiful, she was just young. Painfully young, and almost swamped under the weight of stiff jeweled brocade and ornate headdress and loops of pearls. But Giulia's coaching paid off, because Lucrezia Borgia lifted her head and glided into the *sala*, moving at the center of her jeweled skirts like a shackled young swan. A rustle of admiration crossed the throng, and Giulia gave a smile of pride as she followed.

Dio. So much fuss, so much anticipation, so much expense, and the wedding itself was over in no time at all. Lucrezia knelt before her father on a golden cushion, facing her bridegroom—Giovanni Sforza, Count of Pesaro, an agreeable-enough looking fellow of twenty-six with a long nose and a fashionable beard. He looked pleased enough as he listened to the notary drone, and I saw Lucrezia cast little sidelong peeping glances at her bridegroom.

"Illustrious Sir, are you prepared to pledge yourself to, and to receive pledges from, your lawful spouse, and to marry the Illustrious Donna Lucrezia Borgia, who is here present and promises to become your wife?"

"I do," Giovanni Sforza said, "most willingly."

Lucrezia Borgia repeated her vows in a firm voice (Giulia had coached her on that too); the rings were given; a naked sword was lowered ceremoniously over the heads of the bridal couple; a brisk homily on marriage was delivered . . . and the thing was done. Burchard sagged with relief; I rather wished there had been an assassin to liven things up.

The festivities moved out to the Sala Reale after that, a high-arched hall that had already been prepared with stools, padded benches, and liveried pages with trays of sweetmeats. The guests chattered and circulated, freed from the stifling confines of Burchard's propriety and the small *sala*. I obeyed my orders and drifted, keeping my charges in my sight. Lucrezia, stiff with the importance of the moment, sitting between her papal father and her new husband as the first dishes were presented . . . Giulia moving effortlessly through the crowd, laughing and easy, drawing every eye . . . little Joffre in a slashed-velvet doublet, pop-eyed with the effort to behave like a prince . . . Cesare, dark and loung-ing, lifting his cup across the room to his sister and winning from her the first effortless smile of the evening . . . Still no assassins, and a troupe of players came out, painted and masked, to launch into one of those mindless comedies that seem inevitable at all weddings, and I thought, *How Anna would have loved this.*

Had my friend been alive, I would have smuggled her in to watch this gathering of the greats. Gotten her a temporary job as serving maid, perhaps. But of course, Anna could not ever have been here to gape at the young bride's jeweled gown, or marvel as the Pope settled himself in his throne with all his Spanish arrogance. If Anna had not died, I would never have swum into the Borgia orbit at all.

The comedy was succeeded by a more classical offering; a Latin play by Plautus that the Pope silenced halfway through, bored and frowning. Giulia Farnese slid from her chair to curl on the step below his throne, her fingers stealing upward to twine with his inside his sleeve, and he smiled down at her as a poet hastened forward with a pastoral eclogue. Papal thunder, abated by a woman's slow-burning smile.

I could hear Anna's voice, but not remember her face. It had been a long time since I'd thought about the man who had escaped me: the one in the mask who had helped kill her. I'd done for the other two, after all. No need to look for the third. Especially not with Cesare Borgia warning me just what would happen if my knives stirred up any trouble, for any reason other than protecting his family. I was certainly no hero—bringing a murderer in a mask to justice wasn't worth having my own murder charges resurrected.

The eclogue concluded with a flourish, and a roll of laughter and applause crossed the vast *sala*. Women were squealing and fighting over the passed trays of sweets, and I recognized *Signorina Cuoca's* little fluted *tourtes* with the rosewater glaze, her stuffed and sugared figs, her colorfully dyed marzipan treats. I never understood how that unsmiling stalk of a woman with her fiery glares and dark Venetian curses could produce such airy delights in food. On the dais, Lucrezia looked far too excited to eat, but Giulia reach up to press a slice of candied pear into her papal lover's mouth, and he unhurriedly sucked the sugar from her fingertips.

What is wrong with me? I wondered in some irritation. Everything I had ever dreamed of—money in my purse that did not depend on the fickle luck of the cards; good food when I wanted it; a soft bed; books enough to drown in; and spectacles like this for marveling and mockery. But all I felt was discontent rising in a gray tide, and I couldn't shake the thought of Anna. I didn't miss her—I remembered how her giggle had sometimes grated on me, how her breath was stale and how her openmouthed awe at the doings of the great had brought cutting japes out of me until her eyes welled with hurt. I didn't miss her, not really . . . but maybe I missed the taut, focused fury of the chase I'd launched on her behalf. *Fool,* I mocked myself. *Fool to be dissatisfied just because you're bored.*

But perhaps the soft bed and the easy money and good food wasn't all I needed to be happy. "What is it you most wish for?" Cesare Borgia had asked me at our first interview.

Books. To be tall. To matter.

One of three, surely, was not at all bad in this unlucky world. The Borgia library *was* splendid. If I grew bored sometimes—and bodyguarding could be an idle, tedious business—then a good book did much to distract my restless brain.

"Little man!" The ambassador from Milan paused in a tipsy lurch across the *sala.* "Juggle for us, little man!"

"No."

The ribald comedies ended as the skies outside darkened, and one by one the guests began drifting for the doors, casting longing looks behind them to where the Pope had gathered his most intimate circle of allies and enemies. A private *cena*, I knew; perhaps twenty or thirty guests, and every ambassador present took note of those who stayed— those who mattered. Cardinal della Rovere, spouting hatred toward the rival who had beaten him for the papal throne; Cardinal Sforza, who oozed complacency for having sold his vote in the papal Conclave for this marriage of Lucrezia Borgia into the Sforza clan; Adriana da Mila, for once just beaming instead of counting her ducats . . .

Wedding gifts: a *credenza* service of solid silver; lengths of Milanese brocade; two massive rings from the Duke of Milan. Giovanni Sforza took the pearl ring and slipped it over his bride's finger, lifting her hand to show it off in a credible courtly gesture, and Lucrezia forgot her stiff dignity for a moment and giggled like the child she was. Giulia had slipped from her chair to sit openly on the Pope's knee, one affectionate hand toying with the black locks of his hair, and Rodrigo Borgia deliberately dropped a candied cherry between her breasts. Giulia gazed at him in mock outrage, but he bent his head and teased the cherry out between his teeth. She laughed a little, cheeks brightening, and every man in the room stared on in envy. I pushed off from my place against the tapestried wall and swung away for the stairs leading outside, craving fresh air. No assassins in this crowd, and if there were they would soon be too drunk to stab anyone.

The vast Piazza San Pietro outside was quite dark, but still busy enough with dawdling citizens. Women clustered, whispering and squealing, as wedding guests trailed out in their grand silks, some pausing to toss a few coins into the crowd, and children hopped and scrabbled under the brightly lit windows of the Vatican. I saw a tall figure standing in the shadows, a little distance from the papal guards who kept their vigilance by torchlight, and raised a hand to her. *"Signorina Cuoca!"* I felt a twinge of pain in my twisted thigh muscles as I crossed the stones toward her. It had been a very long day for my malformed legs. "Why aren't you eavesdropping on the festivities with the rest of the servants?"

She didn't answer me, just looked out over the *piazza* with a bitter twist to her mouth and her arms folded across her small breasts. "Look at that," she said, and jerked her chin.

I saw nothing but a shadowy expanse of stones thronged with beggars and idlers. "What?"

The cook took a few angry strides into the *piazza*, bent and retrieved something, then stamped back. "Look!" she exclaimed, and thrust her hand under my nose. I saw something small and flattened in her palm, and it took me a moment to recognize it: one of her tiny bite-size strawberry *tourtes*, the ones she had shaped into minuscule roses with thin sugared slices of strawberry curving and overlapping like rose petals about flower stamens fashioned of saffron threads. Half the petals were gone now, the *tourte* squashed almost flat and the saffron center missing.

"They threw my sweets out the windows," she growled. "Near half of them, judging from the mess stamped flat on these stones! Just ate their fill and tossed the rest away like trash!"

She flung the ruined *tourte* into the darkened *piazza* with one of her muttered Venetian oaths, and I watched a beggar hitch his crutch to scrabble it up. "Largesse to the crowds," I said. "Sugared *tourtes* instead of bread; well, the Borgias do like to be flamboyant. Even in their acts of charity."

"Everything could have been taken down in baskets for distribution!" She gave her hands an angry swipe across her apron. "Not just heaved out the window like scraps tossed for dogs. Three hundred pounds of sweets, and at least half are out here crushed into the ground! Weeks I spent working—you could recite two rosaries for how long each of those strawberry *tourtes* took. I didn't even sleep last night, I—"

Her angular shoulders sagged, and I wondered if she'd even registered whom she was talking to. Carmelina Mangano was usually careful to avoid my company. Probably because I could rarely dodge the temptation to ruffle her easily ruffled feathers. "Cheer up," I said, giving a deliberately familiar pat to her hip. "Surely you wouldn't grudge the beggars of Rome a taste of your confections. Or are the fruits of your labor reserved only for the great?"

"If the great bother to eat them!" A burst of music and laughter issued from the brightly lit windows above, and she glanced up. "I suppose the celebrations will go on till dawn."

"Till the bride goes to bed, at least."

"Such a little thing to be a wife."

"Oh, they won't bed her down with Lord Sforza yet. Consummation of the marriage, by the Pope's decree, is to wait at least another six months out of consideration for her tender youth."

"A kind father."

"A practical one. If the marriage goes unconsummated, he can annul it should a better match present itself."

"What, so all this was wasted? The fifteen-thousand-ducat dress, and the wedding banquet, and my sweets?" Another bitter glance out at the *piazza* of smashed pastries.

"What's a little waste to a pope?"

It was the most civil exchange we'd ever had, this lanky prickly cook and me. Weariness and darkness, I suppose, can turn any conversation cordial out of sheer exhaustion. Her voice was almost friendly . . . just as long as we were speaking of neutral things, anyway. Weddings and food and anything, really, except herself.

And I found that strange, because I've never known a woman who didn't like to talk about herself with an attentive man. Even a small man like me.

"I don't suppose you bothered to try any of my sweets." Carmelina slanted a glance at me, arms still folded across her breasts in challenge. The torchlight from the papal guards cut harsh shadows across her strong nose and long jaw. "You don't eat more than a bird, Messer Leonello!"

"I am forced to abstemiousness in food and drink." Gesturing down at my short trunk. "Dwarves, I fear, are prone to fat. Such is the effect of a grown man's appetite in a stunted body. But I confess I did try a few of those *tourtes*. The tiny blood-orange things with the honey glaze. Bitter to go with the sweet."

Like you, I almost said. *Signorina Cuoca* was all dark angles and lean corners in both face and body; nothing like the soft curves of figure and fair tints of skin that the world deemed beautiful. But she had a tang that prettier women lacked, a tang as tart and refreshing as a dash of lemon water on a hot day, and I wondered if her skin tasted like lemon on the tongue. But she grimaced before I could think of anything charming to say, and I cocked my head instead. "What is it?"

"Those blood-orange *tourtes* you liked?" Carmelina said. "The woman at market who sells me fruit every week; well, I bought six whole crates of blood oranges off her to make those. And I just heard a few days ago from the scullions that she's dead. Found with her throat slashed, and staked down right through the hands too." Carmelina crossed herself. "Spread out and left to die right in her own fruit stall, Santa Marta save her soul."

"Staked," I said. "Through the hands?"

"She was so pleased to sell me all those oranges. I was looking forward to telling her how well the pastries turned out . . ." Carmelina sighed. "Good night, Messer Leonello."

I stood looking out over the *piazza*, long after she had disappeared. One woman dead of a slashed throat, staked to a table. Now . . . two?

It means nothing, I told myself. Women died every night in Rome, their throats cut by jealous husbands or thieving footpads or angry debtors. Many women. In the great scheme of this violent city, it meant nothing.

And even if two died in what might be called a similar fashion— well, so what? One could draw similarities between any two deaths, if one tried hard enough. Two deaths; it was merely a coincidence. You would need at least three to call it a pattern.

But I couldn't help thinking of my third man, the man I'd never found. A man wearing a mask.

It wouldn't do any harm, I supposed, to ask a few questions about this woman Carmelina had known. The unfortunate orange seller.

I kicked one of Carmelina's flattened *tourtes* away into the shadows, not liking myself very much. Because a woman was dead, and yet the news made me feel suddenly, oddly cheerful. Refreshed, almost. Not bored at all.

At dawn I saw the wedding guests stumble tipsily into the dark. A bare-shouldered beauty whose companion was still fumbling candied cherries out of her bodice in imitation of the Pope . . . Madonna Adriana, asleep in a sedan chair with her mouth sagging open . . . and Cesare Borgia in his churchman's robes, his little jeweled bride of his sister fast asleep in his arms as he carried her back to her virgin bed.

CHAPTER EIGHT

✦

Rarely do great beauty and great virtue live together.

—PETRARCH

Giulia

I had the most perfect and beautiful baby in the world.

"She may be pretty, but she is far from perfect," Leonello commented when I said as much, on the long lazy afternoon the day after the wedding. Most of the household was still asleep, and those few who *were* awake lay around the *palazzo* like felled oxen, moaning gently from the results of too much wine. Weddings are exhausting, aren't they? "That baby yells louder than a Venetian fishwife when she's hungry, and she's usually hungry," Leonello continued. "Why couldn't you send her to live in the country with a wet nurse, like most mothers? The whole *palazzo* would get a good deal more sleep."

"Send Laura away? Never."

My daughter had just been a slimy collection of flailing limbs when they first laid her in my arms, a little red frog of a thing with one ear inexplicably folded down and stuck to itself. I'd been quite unreasonably worried about that ear. My daughter couldn't grow up with a bent ear! She wasn't one hour old before I was rocking her worriedly, loving her so much I could die and reassuring her that I'd fix her hair in knotted shell braids on each side of her head so no one would ever be able to laugh at her ear. I'd kill anybody who laughed at her; I already knew that before she was a day old. But the ear unfolded itself, the newborn redness gave way to poreless peach-soft skin, and she turned into the prettiest baby ever born. Not that it mattered to me because Laura was my daughter and I'd adore her whether she was pretty or plain.

Though I was glad about the ear. Those knotted shell braids on either side of the head don't really look well on anybody, do they?

"Her hair's growing," I said as I turned on my back in the grass and hoisted my bright-eyed baby into the air above my head. "I think she'll be as blond as me."

"She had better be, with a name like Laura. Did you really have to name her after the most famous blond bore in the world's history of bad poetry?" Leonello complained. "She'll go brunette as she gets older, you wait, and then she'll spend her life gritting her teeth when people ask why she isn't golden like Petrarch's Laura."

"Nonsense. She's going to have lovely fair hair just like mine, and I'll show her how to rinse it with a saffron cinnabar decoction." I drew Laura down on my breast, kissing her downy head and basking in the warmth of the sun. The grass of the *palazzo* garden was soft beneath me; the fountain splashed somewhere to my right; the sun was summer-warm above, and a breeze blew delightfully over my bare arms and bare neck and bare feet. I'd come downstairs in my sleeveless filmy shift without even a robe, reveling in the joy of free limbs after all those long hours at the wedding yesterday laced into a stiff bodice and tight sleeves.

"You'll get freckled," Leonello observed from his wall bench in the shade, his boots propped up on a padded stool and a book facedown in his lap. My pet goat lay asleep beside him, periodically stirring himself with a flap of silky ears to nibble the buds off the vines that flowered over the walls. "Freckled and sunburned, and you won't be anybody's mistress then."

"I don't care." All I cared about was that the wedding was *over*; all the frantic fuss and frenzy of it finally done. Madonna Adriana had yet to appear from her chamber though it was past noon, and of course dear Lucrezia had still been fast asleep when I poked my head in on rising from my own bed. I'd been the one to tuck her into her bed at dawn this morning, helping the maids unhook her sleepy body from the stiff jeweled dress and smooth her between the silk sheets. Until she was old enough to consummate her marriage, she would continue to reside with me at the Palazzo Santa Maria rather than with her new husband, and I was glad of it. "Beautiful," she'd whispered, sliding into sleep, and I loved her almost as much as Laura.

"She's exhausted," I'd whispered to Rodrigo, who had come through the passage to the Palazzo Santa Maria to see his daughter back safe to her bed after the last wedding festivities.

"I hope *you* aren't exhausted," he'd said with that glint in his black eyes that never failed to put a quiver in my knees, and, winding his hands deep into my hair, he'd dragged me back to my bed and made love to me with as much energy as though he hadn't been awake for the past day and night together. He was gone when I woke very late this morning, but then he could never stay. The Pope was always too busy to linger anywhere, even in my bed. But he'd left a new pearl bracelet on the pillow where the dent of his head had been.

"Did the Holy Father mean those pearls for the baby?" Leonello inquired as I unhooked the bracelet from my wrist and doubled it around Laura's plump little ankle instead. "I see the Dominicans are right when they thunder on about the extravagance of upstart Spanish popes and their debauched harems, where even the babies are bejeweled."

"I want Laura to grow up with beautiful things; she deserves it. Look at that skin, she's made for pearls! Yes, aren't you beautiful, *Lauretta mia*—" I blew kisses all over her neck, sitting up in the grass. "Do you want to hold her?"

"No."

"Here, just support her head."

"I don't want to hold her!"

"Careful, she kicks."

"*Dio.*" Leonello dropped his book as I deposited Laura into his stubby hands. He held her at arm's length, making a series of ghastly leering faces like a procession of devilish Carnival masks, and Laura stared in utter fascination.

I laughed. "See? She likes you."

"She shows a lamentable lapse of judgment." Leonello twisted his features into a horrible gargoyle's glower. Laura crowed, waving at him, and I smiled. You wouldn't think a dwarf would make a good midwife, but Leonello had been *such* a help during the birthing two months ago. Not that he did much more than sit in the corner ignoring the various attempts to evict him and remarking that childbirth was a disgusting business—but frankly, he was right. Childbirth *is* disgusting, and what's more it's boring, all the panting and the walking up and down and the midwives telling me to breathe or push or pray (as if I could remember any prayers around the pains!). What I'd needed was distractions, not prayers, and Leonello had ignored the shooing of the midwives and set himself to distracting me, telling a rapid series of obscene jokes in that expressionless monotone of his that seemed to make everything funnier. I'd laughed helplessly around the pains, and I swear the laughter made Laura come faster.

"You're very good with her." I turned on my side in the grass, propping my chin on my hand. "You should get married and have some babies of your own."

"I don't think so."

"Why not?"

"Is it not obvious?" His voice was very dry.

"You're learned and clever and you have a wonderful voice. If you'd just read poetry instead of mocking it, you'd have women positively swooning." I looked him over critically. "You could dress better, though. That Borgia mulberry color doesn't do anything for you. Green, perhaps, or black. You could look very sinister and dashing in black."

"Dashing," he said, making another horrible face at Laura.

"Maybe a turban in the Turkish style," I giggled. "You could hide a half-dozen more knives in a turban, I'm sure. And lace cuffs—"

"Lace? Lace? *Dio.* You have a baby and a goat to dress in frills, woman; leave me in peace!"

A frigid voice interrupted our laughter. "Is there no one awake in this *palazzo* except dwarves and goats and giggling maidservants?"

"No," said Leonello, looking up to our visitor. "We are all locked fast in enchanted slumber, like a princess in her thorn-bound tower. Victims not of a witch's enchantment, but of that gilded excrescence of a wedding. Welcome to the seraglio. Whom do you seek, fair lady?"

I followed his gaze to see a woman in the arches of the loggia just above me. Perhaps forty-five; auburn-haired, tall, and trim-waisted in russet velvet with a pair of plum silk sleeves; beautiful in her powdered and preserved fashion. I'd never met her before, but she gazed at me down the length of her high-bridged nose in a way that was acutely familiar.

"Ah," she said, scrutinizing me top to toe. "You are La Bella, I take it?"

"I am Giulia Farnese." I rose with as much poise as I could summon while brushing bits of grass from my crumpled shift. "And you are—?"

Of course I knew exactly who she was.

"Vannozza dei Cattanei." Her voice was cold. "Your predecessor."

"Indeed," I said, as though unimpressed, and repressed the urge to pat at my hair.

Rodrigo had told me something of his past mistresses, with a certain deprecating amusement—"Why is it women always have to *know*?" There had been a Valencian courtesan who had given him his first son, a son who had died in Spain along with the courtesan herself—there had been a complaisant vintner's wife in Madrid, who had given him two daughters. But most of all there had been the woman he had kept at his side for a decade; the woman by whom he had fathered Cesare, Juan, Lucrezia, and Joffre. "Though I always had my doubts about Joffre," Rodrigo had told me, circling the point of my bare shoulder with his thumb. "Vannozza was growing bored with me by then."

I'd laughed. "How could anyone get bored with you?" My Pope was exasperating at times, stubborn, self-willed, prone to the occasional rage, but boring? Never.

Still, he always chuckled when Vannozza's name was mentioned, shaking his head with unmistakable fondness, and it had made me wonder about my predecessor. I'd even been curious to meet her. Preferably *not* when I stood in nothing but a grass-stained shift with my hair hanging in a braid like a shepherdess.

She looked me up and down again, and I recognized the expression. Her eldest son Cesare had looked just the same upon meeting me for the first time. *Another of my father's whores*—the words might as well have been engraved across his forehead.

"Madonna," I said finally, repressing the urge to hide my bare arms behind my back. "May I offer you some lemon water? Or perhaps wine?"

"No, thank you, I am here to see my daughter."

"Lucrezia is still asleep." I smiled. "She made a beautiful bride yesterday, but I'm afraid all the excitement exhausted her terribly."

"I wouldn't know. I was not allowed to attend. But you know that."

Of course I'd known, and I'd raised an eyebrow too—a mother not attending her own daughter's wedding? I ask you. But Rodrigo had been quite casual about it all. "Those Sforza are prideful bastards. They don't consider Vannozza's bloodlines quite up to their standards! Mine either, but the papal tiara helps them overlook that. Vannozza understands these things; she won't mind keeping her distance."

Apparently not.

"I am sorry," I said finally. "I understand it was a matter of politics."

"Was it?" She raised her plucked brows. "I thought it was a matter of what suited Rodrigo. But of course, that *is* politics to him."

My cheeks heated. I was not used to anyone referring to my lover as Rodrigo but—well, me. To the world he was Pope Alexander VI. To his children he was Father—or now, teasingly, Holy Father. To his clerics he was Your Holiness. Only to me was he Rodrigo, the name I whispered in the soft fullness of night as he wrapped his hands through my hair and drew me close.

"It was a beautiful wedding," I said at last. "Lucrezia looked like a queen."

But Vannozza dei Cattanei had shifted her auburn eyes away from me, fastening them on Leonello and the bundle of blankets he still held. "Your daughter?" she asked, coming down from the loggia into the garden. "Lucrezia told me you'd finally birthed."

"Yes." I reached for my daughter, feeling a wave of protectiveness, and Laura waved her plump baby fist as Leonello surrendered her. He had shifted on his wall bench, fading somehow from an abrasive little presence to a colorless shadow against the wall.

Vannozza's eyes flicked over my child. "She's small," my predecessor said at last. "Lucrezia was much bigger at that age. Pinker, too—*she* was a beauty, even in the cradle."

I took a deep breath but let it out shallowly, forcing some warmth into my face and smiling instead. My mother had always said there was no defense against the rude like a good, sweet-toned courtesy. "Yes, Lucrezia is such a beauty," I cooed to Vannozza dei Cattanei. "A pity she doesn't look like you. I think she takes after Rodrigo . . . that warmth of his, you know, and the laughing voice." I gave a little shiver of pleasure. "*So* attractive."

Her eyes flared a little. Maybe sweet-toned courtesy *did* work against the rude. In my own experience, I found it worked better with a hint of vinegar under the honey.

"You had better hope your own daughter grows up as pretty as mine," Vannozza snapped. "She'll be a far more useful marriage pawn when Rodrigo starts shopping her around in a few years' time. I wonder if you'll be allowed to attend her wedding, Giulia la Bella? Perhaps Rodrigo's next concubine will be the one to walk your daughter to the altar. They'll probably be just the same age."

I molded my smile to an expression of sweet blandness. "Oh, Vannozza—may I call you Vannozza? Such venom, and I really don't see why. I didn't take His Holiness from you, after all. From what I understand, you were already long finished with each other."

"Yes, Rodrigo finished with me." The thin mask of courtesy had stripped from her face. Oh, good. "Just as he will finish someday with you. I wonder, my dear Giulia, if you'll last as long as I did—ten years and four children?" Her eyes swept me again. "I doubt it. One more baby, and you'll be stout as a barrel of cider."

"Better a plump juicy peach," I said, "than a dried-up old prune."

"Better a slim swan than a fat little capon." Vannozza smoothed her own waist, still narrow after four births, and I wondered if I could have Leonello stab her to death. One of those sharp little finger knives of his, planted right between those powdered breasts. Surely I could claim it was self-defense?

"Rodrigo *loves* me plump," I said instead, with all the innocence I could muster. "You should have seen him when I was carrying Laura. He never had his hands off my stomach." Or the rest of me—my Pope was not a man who believed in the cessation of nocturnal attentions during a woman's ripening months. Thank the Holy Virgin, because my pregnant passions for sweets had been thoroughly matched by passions of a different kind.

"Yes, Rodrigo does like a budding woman," Vannozza said, as though reading my mind. "It makes him feel young again. I suppose even old bulls find they can still kick up their heels when they see a young heifer."

"Moo," I said, putting Laura up to my shoulder and patting her small back. "Are you sure you won't go away and be snide to somebody else? Lucrezia really is very tired from the wedding. A *good* mother would let her sleep."

Vannozza's lips thinned. "And all mothers should be allowed to attend their daughter's wedding. I should have been there. I should have been the one to escort her. Not her father's whore, who spends the feast dropping cherries down her own bodice and giggling."

"You seem very well informed, considering you weren't there. Tell me, did you know I was the one to teach Lucrezia how to manage her train? There's a trick to it, making it flare without tripping, and that wedding dress was very heavy. We practiced for hours around this garden, so she would be ready on her wedding day." I lifted my chin. "Lucrezia visits you often enough. Do you spend all her visits dripping poison about her father and complaining? Why was I the one to teach her how to walk in a train, and not her mother?"

Vannozza's eyes dropped at that, down to the fountain in the center of the garden. My pet goat had wandered over to nibble at the moss growing along the lip, and she watched him as she turned a ring around and around one finger. A fine sapphire ring, I saw, in a heavy gold setting of carved acanthus leaves. I wondered if it had been a present from Rodrigo. "The Pope will tire of you," she said evenly, still looking at the ring. "Make sure you get something out of it besides jewelry. I got a house and three prosperous inns, a series of respectable husbands, and a steady income. That lasts longer than love. Or at least Rodrigo's love."

I felt a pang of reluctant pity for her. It could have been Laura's wedding, after all—someday it *would* be Laura's wedding. What if I'd been the one forbidden to see my own daughter married? I hesitated, but then Vannozza dei Cattanei looked up at me again, and I saw the spite in her gaze had redoubled.

"At least he won't take your daughter like he did mine," she said. "It's all about the Borgia blood for Rodrigo, you know. And that one you're holding isn't a Borgia."

"I don't know what you're talking about." I tossed my head, any pity for her evaporating on the spot. "All Rome knows who Laura's father is."

"Yes, Rome does love to gossip." She smiled. "But if that child were a Borgia, she'd never have been christened Laura Orsini. I take it back, what I said before—Rodrigo's next concubine won't be walking *your* daughter up the aisle at her wedding after all. Because your little Orsini will never be worth a Borgia alliance."

"Well, naturally she was *christened* Orsini. The law, you know." Rodrigo had explained it to me when I was pregnant—existing bastards were one thing, but no sitting pope could officially sire a newborn child. That hadn't precisely pleased me, but it was the *law*.

"You think Rodrigo Borgia would be stopped by a law?" Vannozza looked amused.

"The scandal—"

"He doesn't care about scandal, and never has. If he'd really sired that child, he'd have found a way around the law. He'd have been proud to do it." Vannozza smiled. "Rodrigo loves his children, you see. But he doesn't love that one. She's just a cuckoo in the nest."

I felt like I'd been stabbed. Laura began to fuss as she felt the sudden protective clutch of my arms around her little body. But I'd let the Holy Virgin herself take me off to heaven—or hell if my sins demanded it—before I'd let my wrinkled, spiteful cow of a predecessor see me flinch.

The truth was, my daughter had been born nine months after I'd first gone to Rodrigo's bed—and a week before that, to my husband's bed, if that awkward coupling against a wall counted as a bedding. Of course Laura's father had to be Rodrigo—how ridiculous, to think that Orsino's one clumsy fumble around the stiff barrier of my skirts had borne more fruit than all the languorous hours I'd spent in my Pope's arms. I'd never had a doubt who Laura's sire was.

Does Rodrigo . . . ?

"Why don't you concern yourself with your own daughter rather than mine?" I managed to say. "Lucrezia's chamber is at the top of the stairs on the east side of the *palazzo*, if you really do insist on waking her."

"Thank you." We exchanged a last long measuring look, and I refused to drop my eyes or smooth my hair or fiddle with my rings—refused to give her one solitary indication that she might have pierced my armor. I held her eyes, and finally she gave a flick of her brows that reminded me of Cesare and swept around me toward the stairs.

The click of Vannozza dei Cattanei's heels and the rustle of her plum and russet velvets retreated behind me. The goat bleated after her. I stared at the fountain, jogging Laura, who was fretting, and felt a small reassuring presence at my side.

"Shall I arrange a fatal accident for her?" Leonello suggested. "A swift blow over the head, perhaps, and then I'll bash away at the ceiling until a few stones come down and make the whole thing look like a tragic accident. A favorite assassination method, I'll have you know."

I hardly heard him, looking down at my beautiful daughter. Rodrigo rarely gave more than a passing smile into her cradle, but men don't really coo over babies, did they? It wasn't to be expected. But he did love her; he *did*. She'd have a wedding someday in the papal apartments, just like her sister Lucrezia; a wedding with a jeweled dress and a noble husband and a dowry fit for a pope's daughter. Because she *was* a pope's daughter. She had Rodrigo's *nose*!

But not his name. And I hated Vannozza dei Cattanei with a rush of sudden black bitterness for spoiling my happiness.

"If it's any consolation"—Leonello wound his small hands through his belt, tilting his head back at me—"you made her look stale, powdered, bitter, and old."

I rested my cheek against Laura's downy head. "I'm afraid it's no consolation at all."

Carmelina

I gave a final glance over the row of little corpses. "They'll do," I decreed, and turned to my obedient row of aproned apprentices. "Take each bird down, and stuff the cavities with fennel and nettle—"

"Why nettle?" piped a boy's voice, interrupting.

I turned a glare on a certain redheaded scullion named Bartolomeo, craning his freckled face over his shoulder at me when he should have been tackling the stack of oily pots at the cistern. "Nettle keeps the flies from settling," I said. "And get back to those pots!"

"Sorry, *signorina*." He sounded chastened, but he'd soon be asking questions again. He was quicker at his work than any of the other potboys, but oh, the questions! Why was chestnut flour sweeter than other flour? Why was there a hole bored in the bottom of the butter crock? Why did the best bacon come from male hogs fed in the woods rather than female hogs fed in farmyards? Questions that a pot-boy had no business asking in the first place. I was all in favor of a little enthusiasm for one's work, but I had a busy kitchen to run. I couldn't spend all day satisfying a pot-boy's idle curiosity. Santa Marta, grant me patience!

"Stuff the cavities with nettle," I continued in my lecture to the apprentices, whose business it very much was. "Then hang the birds to draw. And if I find you hanging them too close together, I'll stuff *you* lot with nettle."

My apprentices scattered, a flock of headless chickens but at least well-organized ones. From the kitchens inside I could hear the under-cooks calling out orders as they whipped together a midday *pranzo*—it was Marco's free afternoon, which meant he had taken himself off for a cool drink and a game of dice at the wine shop at the next *piazza*. A pity, because in this summer heat all the manservants were sweating and shirtless by the kitchen's fires, and no man looked better with his shirt off than a tall strapping cook.

Of course I knew better than to moon over men the way the maid-servants did in this weather—forever ogling and finding excuses to drop into the kitchens. That was all very well for a girl with nothing in her head but marriage, but a woman with a kitchen full of surly apprentices and insolent scullions to manage would have no authority at all if they thought they could get around her with a smile and a bit of a flirt.

I turned to survey the newest arrival of fresh-killed ducks and wild cranes, lying in a heap of beaks and limp webbed feet on a scrubbed trestle table. Empty feathered sacks just waiting to be transformed by the magic of spices and skill into plates of tastiness—there was no sight I liked better than a pile of dead birds! Perhaps a *cena* menu this evening of tiny game birds, roasted and gutless just like my apprentices . . .

Bartolomeo's voice piped up again as he staggered past Ottaviano with a load of clean pans. "Ottaviano—why fennel flowers inside the wild ducks instead of plain fennel like the hens?"

"Don't know," Ottaviano grunted, uninterested.

"No chatter!" I called, pulling a menu together for the evening. "All mouths are shut, and all hands are moving!"

"Sorry, *signorina*." A brief silence, and then I heard a loud whisper. "Ugo, why fennel flowers instead of—"

"No whispering either!" My hands were already flying, pulling ingredients. Spit-roasted pigeons with a salad of cold asparagus (page 22, Chapter: Salads); a dish of anchovies with oil and vinegar and oregano . . .

"*Signorina?*" Bartolomeo's voice came at my shoulder again. "Sorry to disturb you—"

"Not sorry enough, apparently." I recorked the olive oil with a slam of my palm.

"It's that last hen on the hook, *signorina*," he persisted. "It's not fresh."

"What is a pot-boy doing sniffing my birds?" I glared. "Besides, I checked every one myself when they arrived. Of course that last one on the hook is fresh."

He shifted from foot to foot, scrubbing his soapy hands on his grubby shirt. His head ducked, and his face flamed up the same color as his hair. "But it's not," he said softly.

I looked at him through narrowed eyes, aware that the apprentices and the other pot-boys had all stopped to gape pleasurably. Mutiny—as dangerous in a kitchen as on any ship.

"Well, let's see, pot-boy." I dried my hands on my apron, stalking over to the last hen hanging dead and nettle-stuffed on its hook, and gave a good sniff. "Smells fresh to me. Perhaps you'd care to explain why you think your nose is better than mine?"

He took the bird off the hook and turned it mutely, cavity up. I gave another sniff. Nettle, fennel, pepper, salt; all as it should be—

Or not?

I gave another lingering sniff. Under the spicy mix, like a thread of smoke from a fire just barely kindled: the faintest, faintest hint of rot.

"Hmph." I took the bird and tossed it to one of the other pot-boys. "Dispose of that. Bartolomeo, come with me."

"Sorry, *signorina*." He trotted to keep up with me as I stalked out of the cold room into the main kitchen. "It didn't smell right."

"Not too far gone, though. You could have kept quiet."

He shuffled, running a hand through his unruly hair. "But it didn't *smell* right."

"Mmm." I paused to cast an eagle eye around the heat-shimmering kitchens, but the undercooks were all working as they should be. I found a bowl of mixed spices someone had assembled for a sauce on the roast and thrust it under Bartolomeo's nose. "What do you smell?"

He gave an obliging whiff, screwing up his nose. "Sweet, mostly."

"Pick out the individual spices for me."

"Cinnamon," he said at once, and sniffed again. "Nutmeg . . . something that smells like nutmeg but a bit woodsier . . ."

"That's cloves. What else?"

"Ginger, sugar. That yellowy stuff that comes in flowers—saffron. Something else . . ." He gave another sniff, doubtful. "Something sort of peppery? But it's not pepper."

"You're sure?" I said ominously.

He looked scared, but shook his head. "Not pepper."

"Well, you're right. It's called grains of paradise, and it's a very expensive imported spice." I set the bowl aside, putting fists on hips. "Where did you come from, Bartolomeo?"

"Dumenza," the boy mumbled, shuffling. "A little place, up north in Lombardy. My father died last year; I went to live with my uncle in Rome. He's a tanner."

"So why aren't you working in his tanner's yard? Strong boy like you."

"Wasn't any good at it. He had to find me other work."

"Why?"

"The *smells*," Bartolomeo burst out. "I kept throwing up all over the tannery. Have you ever smelled a tanner's yard, *signorina*? Piss and dung and ox hides with bits of rotting flesh still sticking to them—the stench near killed me."

"Hmph." I drummed my fingers against my side for a moment, then made a decision. "Put this on," I ordered, and threw him a bundle.

He caught it with a start of surprise. A clean apron, exactly like those worn by the other apprentices. *"Signorina?"*

"You're years behind the other apprentices, and you'll find it hard to catch up," I warned. "They all started at nine or ten, as is proper." And how I was going to square this with Marco, I really didn't know.

Much less Madonna Adriana, who would certainly want to see an apprentice fee . . . but my red-haired pot-boy had that great rarity, a cook's nose. A better one even than mine, I would guess, and I wasn't about to let it go to waste.

"*Signorina*," he stammered, still gazing in shock at the apron.

"Don't stand there gawking, boy! Put that apron on. Those spices you sniffed out for me; I'll wager you don't know their uses *or* their proportions."

His face glowed like a torch. "No, *signorina*."

"Then get over here and let me teach you. Four and a half parts cinnamon to one part each of ginger and nutmeg, two parts cloves, and just a pinch of grains of paradise . . ."

CHAPTER NINE

❖

Either Caesar, or nothing.

—PERSONAL MOTTO OF CESARE BORGIA

Leonello

I heard the sharp call from the courtyard clear up in the loggia. *"Juan!"* But I didn't turn my head at the shout. I stood in my shirtsleeves, one hand poised at my side, eyes closed, breathing evenly. I could feel the tiles through my boots, baking reflected heat up at the top of the *palazzo*. The sun fell warm on my arm from the open arches of the loggia on my left, but the shade on the other arm was no cooler.

"Juan!" The voice came again, closer, followed by a rattle of Catalan. I ignored it, taking a breath instead and then letting it out halfway. I opened my eyes, flicked a Toledo blade from my cuff, and sent it winging down to its target: a side of beef ribs hanging from the open arch at the other end of the loggia.

I was smiling even before I'd trotted the length of the loggia to check my throw. The blade had sunk true, I could feel it—right between the third and fourth ribs, up to the hilt. On a man, it would have pierced something vital.

I heard the doors yank open behind me, followed by a furious *swish* of robes. "Little man," a clipped voice greeted me. "Have you seen my fool of a brother?"

"I fear I have not, Your Excellency." I turned to make a bow to Cesare Borgia, Archbishop of Valencia. "The Duke of Gandia travels in such a crowd, it is impossible to miss him." A pack of swaggering young men like himself, gaudily dressed, forever shoving and laughing like a pack of high-spirited, high-bred colts overdue for gelding. "He was sniffing about yesterday," I added. "There's a maid of Madonna Adriana's he fancies."

"He fancies anything female with a heart that beats," Cesare said shortly. "And no doubt if pressed he'd compromise on the heart. Nor would I rule out sheep."

"Perhaps." I studied the young Archbishop—still a few months from eighteen, but rumor around the wine shops and betting touts of Rome had it that he was poised for a cardinalate. Unlike his brother, Cesare Borgia did not surround himself with the retinue of servants, priests, hangers-on, and retainers normally due one of his rank. He was alone now save for his colorless and expressionless guardsman Michelotto, who had already faded back against the doors like a statue as his master came to my side in a restless movement. The young Archbishop's dark narrow face was stone-set above his purple robes, and his hands had stilled in a way I'd come to recognize. In the year I'd watched the Pope's children, I had come to observe that while they all might have the same charming smile in happiness, in anger they spanned all possible variations. Lucrezia never angered at anything, Juan raged and threw tantrums, Joffre wilted into sulkiness—and Cesare grew very, very still. "Some trouble, Your Excellency?" I said neutrally.

He ignored my question, folding his arms across his chest. "What's that?" He jerked his chin at the side of beef, swaying from side to side in the light summer breeze as it hung in the arch of the loggia.

"Practice." I stood on tiptoe to jerk out my knife from between the two ribs. "No killers have made any attempts on Madonna Giulia or Madonna Lucrezia as yet, but that doesn't mean one won't turn up tomorrow. I take an hour or two up here each day, practicing throws." Besides the practice, it was an hour or two of silence—precious in the ever-busy seraglio with its chattering servants, fluttery women, and giggling children.

Cesare Borgia assessed my hanging target, buzzing with flies in the heat and dripping old blood from a dozen previous hits. "You could not practice on a target board?"

"Target boards don't have ribs, Your Excellency. Blades glance off bone, so it's good to practice on something with a skeleton." Besides, I'd appropriated the side of beef from the kitchens behind that prickly cook's back (or rather, I'd suborned a burly manservant to appropriate it for me), and later when returning it I'd have the pleasure of watching her fly into a rage. She looked almost pretty when she yelled.

"Why such a short distance?" The Archbishop outpaced me as I turned for the other end of the loggia again—perhaps twenty steps. "Michelotto can put a knife through a man's eye at twice this range. Can't you, Michelotto?"

A grunt from the doors. For Michelotto, that was lengthy conversation.

"I don't need to put a knife through a man's eye at twice this range." Such a distance was also near impossible for my shorter arms, but I was damned if I'd say so. "Any assassin who gets past all the guards on his way to Madonna Giulia will have gotten very close indeed. My kills are far more likely to be made up close."

"An hour's practice every day for such a short distance?" Cesare Borgia sounded faintly scornful. "How hard could it be?"

I offered him the longest of my Toledo blades.

He hefted it a moment, giving an easy flip to test the balance, then squinted one eye shut as he measured the distance. He let fly, and swore as the knife glanced off at an angle and clattered to the tiles.

I tilted a shoulder at him. "Try again."

He waved my second blade off. "I see what you mean about ribs, little man." He watched instead with hands clasped behind him as I threw my remaining blades one by one, a rhythm I found as easy and soothing as my own heartbeat. "How much would I have to throw until I could match you?"

"Every day." The finger blade from my cuff went humming, then sank between the first and second ribs. "With large targets and small ones." The blade from my other cuff hit the space between the second and third ribs. "In the day, and in the dark." The blade from my boot top; third and fourth rib. "In quiet, and in noise." My last blade glanced off, and I grimaced. "Like any skill, one has to work at it."

"Practice on my brother," Cesare Borgia muttered. "I'll hang him upside down for you and you can prickle him all you like."

Muttered asides of a personal nature, when spoken from a nobleman to a dwarf, do not count as conversation and are best treated as though unheard. "I've not seen the Duke of Gandia since yesterday," I said instead. "I imagine you might find him in a brothel. Sowing his oats before the wedding." The Pope had not been content with one child illustriously settled in matrimony—Juan Borgia had been found a match of his own, a Spanish princess who was cousin to King Ferdinand himself, and the only good thing I could see about the whole business was that the Duke of Gandia would sail to Spain to claim both his bride and his duchy, and thus spare us another gilded excrescence of a wedding here in Rome.

"My brother had better stir himself from his whores, because I need the papal troops and my father will expect Juan to head them," the Archbishop of Valencia said shortly, and turned to go in a flutter of purple.

"Some trouble in the city, Your Excellency?"

He hesitated, but answered me. "Tell Madonna Adriana to keep my sister close inside today. There's a crowd of fools gathering in the Borgo—a girl staked out in a tavern like Christ on the cross, they say, and now everyone thinks the Jews are making devil sacrifices."

The day was hot, but I felt a small chill trace the length of my crooked back. "Staked?" I said, and was surprised at my voice's evenness.

"A tavern maid raped on a table, with her throat slit. Hands staked out wide, a knife through each palm." Cesare held his arms wide, a dark Christ in ecclesiastical robes. "It wouldn't matter, normally. Whores and tavern maids die every day. But now we have the Spanish Jews to blame, so suddenly it must be a pagan sacrifice."

"Not to mention that little fruit seller who died in the market not long ago," I added. "One hears she died the same way. Staked and throat-slit."

Cesare eyed me, dark eyes curious. "What's it to you, Messer Leonello?"

"Nothing at all." I began lacing up the front of my doublet. "Though I doubt it was the Jews. They're too grateful to be safe out of Spain to be stirring up trouble here."

"Of course it wasn't the Jews," Cesare snorted. "But you'll tell my sister and that golden-haired giggler of my father's to stay close to home. I won't have them running afoul of any uneasy crowds." He ran a hand over the dent in his auburn hair that was the faintest possible nod to a clerical tonsure. "If Juan can't be roused from his brothels, I'll take the papal troops, see the girl disposed of, and send any grumblers home with cracked skulls."

"That's what you intended to do all along, Your Excellency," I told him. "You'd rather disperse an incipient mob yourself and get the credit with His Holiness. You're only here looking for the Duke of Gandia so you can tell the Pope you did your best to find him."

Cesare Borgia gave a wintry half smile. "Clever little lion man," he said. "What other clever thoughts do you have in that oversized head of yours?"

I'm thinking your brother Juan might have murdered that girl in the Borgo, I almost said. *And before her a fruit-seller named Eleonora, and a girl named Anna.* Juan Borgia's name had come easily to mind once I began contemplating my masked murderer again, after Carmelina told me of her fruit-seller friend's death. After all, what did I know about the man I sought? I knew he was a young man from within the Borgia household, gone slumming in the common quarters and splashing money about, trailing a guardsman and a steward appointed to keep him out of trouble. That certainly fit the arrogant young Duke of

Gandia. But as neatly as it fit, I had my doubts. Whoever had staked those girls down was exercising a lust far darker and stranger than mere commonplace rape, and Juan Borgia's lusts were of the extremely ordinary variety. I didn't think he had the imagination for dark ritual murder. Or the patience, or the brains . . .

"You've gone a long way away, little lion man," Cesare Borgia observed.

If not Juan, who? One of his swaggering, violent young friends, perhaps—

A yell from the door interrupted my thoughts. *"Leonello!"* A furious female voice shattered the heat. *"What in the name of Santa Marta are you doing to my side of beef!"*

"Signorina Cuoca," I greeted the tall figure with the wrathful blackbrowed face. "How untimely."

"That was for tonight's *cena*!" Carmelina shouted, pointing at my large and fly-specked target. "It's supposed to be going on a *spit*!"

"Think of it as pre-spitted, for your convenience." I held up my hands, modest. "No need to thank me."

She muttered some Venetian curse and began to storm past, then noticed the lounging figure of Cesare Borgia and his guardsman. "Your Excellency," she muttered, and dropped a belated curtsy.

"Not at all." He waved her up with a rare grin. "Better than a play. Do you require rescuing, Messer Leonello?"

"I do apologize," she began, eyes lowered, but Cesare shrugged her apologies aside as well. One last lazy salute to me, and he was gone as though whisked from a stage by pulleys, Michelotto ghosting behind him.

Carmelina had already hastened to look at my makeshift target. "Mucked and torn to pieces, look at that hide! Pierced through a hundred times at least, it will never hold its juices now—" But I stood quite still now that Cesare was gone, tapping the toe of my boot against a crack in the tile. *Tap tap tap.*

Another woman found staked to a table, with two knives through her palms. Anna first. Then the fruit seller in the market, though I had been able to discover very little about her. And now this one.

One, I remembered thinking before, might be an accident. *Two* was a coincidence. But *three*?

Anna's masked killer flickered again before my eyes. Whoever he was.

I turned and made for the hanging carcass where Carmelina was fussing. The trips back and forth along the length of the loggia over my hour of practicing had made my cramped muscles ache. I longed to lapse into the rapid spraddle that saved my bones their pains, but not when there were any other eyes to see me. Besides, Carmelina Mangano had a tart prettiness when she was shouting at me like this, so for her I would walk tall.

Not to mention that I had one or two questions I wished to ask her. Better to sweeten her for once, rather than ruffle her feathers.

"I do apologize for spoiling your spit-roasted beef, *Signorina Cuoca*." Surveying the side of ox ribs. "But don't you have a word of praise for my skill? Eight of ten in a line up the ladder of ribs! You won't see that every day."

"And you won't see another day at all if you keep raiding my kitchens for targets." She began yanking the blades out from between the ox ribs and tossing them at me.

"So, another girl dead." I swiped the blades clean one at a time as she shoved them at me. "Like that fruit seller friend of yours. What was her name?" I knew her name perfectly well.

"Eleonora." Carmelina crossed herself. "She wasn't really a friend. We just traded the odd word or two at market. But she knew I'd toss out any peach that was even a little bruised, so she always saved the pick of the fruit for me . . ."

"And now another girl." I leaned against the balustrade. "Do you think the Jews are to blame?"

"More likely she took the wrong man home, whoever she was. That's why women die. Drunken men, not Jews." Carmelina yanked the last of my little knives free. "And I'll wager most of those Spanish Jews are too tired and dusty to spend much time on satanic sacrifices."

"You seem sympathetic to our newest batch of exiles, my dear lady."

A great many exiles; Jews fleeing Spain from the attentions of Torque-mada. What *Signorina Cuoca* was fleeing, I had no idea. Though I found that almost as interesting as the pattern I was starting to see around Anna and Eleonora and now this new girl. This dead girl.

"I had a friend who died last year much like your friend Eleonora." I laid all ten of my knives out on the stone balustrade, precisely arrayed from biggest to smallest. "I doubt anyone bothered to blame the Jews on her account. She was simply carted off and forgotten. Most whores like her and your Eleonora are."

"Who says she was a whore?" Carmelina waved flies away from the carcass with her apron. "Men are quick to throw that word about. A girl takes a man home now and then, and if he leaves her a coin or two . . ."

"Any family to mourn her?" I polished a speck of ox blood off my biggest knife. "A husband?"

"No."

Not for Anna either.

Patterns. Had Cesare Borgia brought this latest murder up to me deliberately, knowing as he did that Anna's murder had been the event that brought me into his orbit? But I'd never told him how Anna died, or even her name—not even in our first probing interview.

I hitched myself up to sit on the stone balustrade beside my knives, and Carmelina put an automatic hand to my arm. "Careful, Messer Leonello—that's a long drop." Casting her eyes the long five stories down behind me.

"Worrying for me?" I was nearly on an eye level with her now, which was precisely why I'd done it. "How kind."

"I could toss you off a loggia myself for what you did to my nice rack of beef," she retorted. "Now, if you will excuse me—"

I captured her fingers before she could take them from my arm. "It's you who should be careful, *Signorina Cuoca*. That's three women I know of now who died the same way. I would be wary of strange men, if I were a woman like you."

"What do you mean, a woman like me?" She cocked her head, not pulling her hand away from mine quite yet. She had a scatter of new summer freckles, and her wiry arms below their rolled-up sleeves were scarred and practical. Her fingers were callused in mine, and a black curl had worked itself determinedly out of her scarf to lie against her brown neck.

"A woman like you," I repeated, holding her in my eyes. "More precisely, you are a woman like *them*. Low women, if you will forgive me. Two tavern maidservants and one fruit seller—working women. None of them whores, precisely—"

"I am not a whore!" Tugging against my hand. "No woman in my position could afford to be. Do you know how kitchens talk when a woman gets a reputation for spreading her knees?"

"Calm your feathers, Carmelina, I've no intention of insulting you—or the women who died. As you say, *whore* is a word that comes quick to men's lips." I gave a squeeze of her hand in apology. "These are women, rather, who met a great many men in the course of their work. Women who would not be missed once they were dead. Women without families of note. Women like you."

Were there other women, dead the same way in the year between Anna and Eleonora the fruit seller? I had not heard of any such thing, but I had not been looking. Were there more than three?

Carmelina shivered a little, crossing herself. "God rest their souls," she said soberly, and seemed to have forgotten her other hand still lay in mine. Her wariness of me had abated—a trick I knew well how to play. Everyone finds it easy to forget that a dwarf can be a threat. Her fingers were warm and rough in mine; she smelled of the fresh bread they must have been baking in the kitchens this afternoon, and I thought of tugging her to sit beside me on the balustrade. I could make her forget her shivers for the dead fruit-seller, make her laugh, flatter her and flirt with her until the moment came when I could lean in and snatch a kiss. I did like tall women. They even liked me, when I made an effort. Carmelina might come to like me, too.

So, of course, I had to ruin it.

"There's one way you're different from those women who died," I said casually. "None of them seem to have had families. And you've got that wrathful father up in Venice, haven't you?"

Her head whipped around, and I saw her eyes snap wide and wary. "How—"

I smiled. "Your cousin Marco likes games of chance. Even more, he likes to talk. Especially when he's winning, which I grant you isn't often. But enough to piece together a few interesting things here and there. Tell me, is your father still working in Venice? Has he managed to wrangle himself that job cooking for the Doge yet, considering you stole all his recipes?"

"It's none of your business!"

"I don't suppose your father's forgiven you, even if he hasn't pursued you here," I continued as though she hadn't spoken. "What cook forgives another for making off with his life's work?"

She tried to yank her hand away from mine, but I tightened my grip, holding her fast. My arms were short, but I had strong hands and odd double-jointed fingers, and they made for a vise grip.

"Why so skittish, *Signorina Cuoca*?" I cocked my head, wondering even as I said it why I was provoking her with my viper tongue, why I wasn't kissing her instead. "Stealing recipes isn't much of a sin, after all. Nothing they can put you in the stocks for. Unless you have a few more sins on your conscience than recipe theft, of course. Something they *can* put you in the stocks for." I studied her, the white around her eyes, and smiled. "You have, haven't you? What did you do? Steal from a lord? Burn a storeroom down to sell the supplies? Murder an apprentice?"

She wrenched away. "Keep your nose out of my affairs, dwarf."

"Why should I? You interest me, Carmelina. People with secrets always interest me."

"I don't have any secrets."

"Oh, but you do."

She stalked away. "I'll be sending my scullions up for that carcass," she threw over her shoulder. "And if you ever steal from my kitchens again, I'll geld you!"

"Always a pleasure," I called after her, and laughed silently as the thud of a door was my only response. I hopped down from the balustrade, stretching my cramped legs for a moment.

A cook with a secret. A murderer in a mask.

"I wonder," I said aloud, and as I slipped my gleaming Toledo blades home to their hidden sheaths, I began to whistle.

Giulia

T hank you, Sandro," I whispered as my brother pressed a kerchief into my hand. I raised it to my face to dab away a tear.

"Faker," he whispered.

Thank the Holy Virgin for dead fish and stinking mud. Normally I wasn't quite so happy to have such smells clogging up my nose, but today I was grateful for the stench of refuse and dead cats that drifted perennially off the Tiber. Juan Borgia was taking sail for his Spanish duchy and his Spanish bride, and I'd be expected to shed a graceful tear or two at his departure along with the rest of the family. And I knew I'd never manage it without that river stench making my eyes water. Juan gone from Rome? It was all I could do to suppress a happy wave and a carol of joy.

I wasn't the only one rejoicing inside, but outwardly of course the whole party was Spanish gloom—gloom, and grandeur. I'd already watched Rodrigo bid Juan a private farewell among the half-finished frescoes of the private papal apartments, both of them getting very Catalan and emotional in their embracing and kissing of cheeks. There had been a good many final admonitions too, among the smells of wet plaster and paint. "You will write to Us often," the Pope had admonished, very much the grand Pope with the divine *We*. "Listen to Don Gines Fera and Mossen Jayme Pertusa, they'll not steer you wrong—pay Their Catholic Majesties all respect—"

"I will, Your Holiness." Juan bounced on his curly-slippered toes, impatient to be off.

"And tend to your bride! We wish a son from her as soon as possible; a Borgia sprig on the royal tree of Spain." Rodrigo cupped Juan's face in his hands, voice thick as he lapsed from Father of all Christendom to father of a more mortal variety. "A princess is none too good for my son!"

Maria Enriques of Spain. Did she have any idea what kind of man she was getting? Girls all dream of a handsome young husband, but there's more to husbands than a pretty face. Juan's auburn good looks didn't really make up for his more inexcusable habits: riding horses to death, harassing the maids, hanging about the Piazza degli Ebrei looking for Jews to taunt. Not to mention his habit of wearing lace *and* tassels on the same doublet. Still, maybe Maria Enriques of Spain would tame him. Or at least keep him in Spain a good long time.

"Your eyes are sparkling," Sandro whispered at me.

"They are not." I pressed the kerchief more firmly against my face.

"I won't miss him either." Sandro wrinkled his nose. "You know I've seen him go trooping around with his friends at night, getting drunk and killing cats in dark alleys?"

"And what are you doing in dark alleys, brother?"

"Taking the discreet route to visit my mistress, of course, and that's a perfectly legitimate reason to be strolling down any dark alley. 'Paolo goes to Francesca in the dead of the night—'"

"Shh!"

Private farewells were done now, and the Duke of Gandia had set out in state for the docks where four laden galleys waited to bear him off to Barcelona. Half of Rome had turned out to see him off this fine summer morning, clustering along the Campo dei Fiori and below the great crenellated pile of the Castel San Angelo. Rodrigo would be pleased by the crowds. He'd originally planned a more private family gathering for Juan's departure, but after all the grumbling through the city about that poor murdered girl who was found spread out as though on a crucifix—well, my Pope had seen the wisdom of giving his flock something else to marvel at. After today, the prevailing gossip in the city would all be of Juan's gold robe and the emerald in his hat that was the size of my eye, not satanic sacrifices and Jewish magic and the blood of innocent virgins spilled in the night. I'd had Masses said for the murdered girl's soul, poor savaged thing. Such a hideous death in what was supposed to be the Holy City.

I crossed myself and tried to put her from mind. Whoever had killed her, she was with God now. Cesare Borgia was leading the swarm of churchmen now, tallest of them all. What I would have given to hear what thoughts were going on behind *that* immobile face—he wasn't mourning his brother's departure, that was for certain! My mother-in-law bustled along with Lucrezia and a bouncing Joffre, I came next on Sandro's arm; then a crowd of Juan's cronies jockeying and pushing for precedence. Fortunately he was taking most of them to Spain with him, young louts . . . and there was Vannozza dei Cattanei, blowing Juan a farewell kiss. She must have bribed my robe makers to see what I was wearing, because she was decked out in the exact same shade of sunshine-yellow satin, only with a great deal more gold embroidery and silver embroidery and pearls. She looked like a lemon, and she might as well have been sucking on one too from the set of her mouth. She tossed her head as she caught my eye, and I sent her my sweetest, sweetest smile.

My Pope—oh dear, he looked very grand in all his papal finery, elaborate robes fluttering about his sedan chair, but his swarthy face was as immobile as Cesare's, and that meant he was fighting back tears. Rodrigo's favorite son (though only God Himself knew why!) was gone from the nest. Lucrezia would have to be released to join her husband soon—and after that, I supposed it would be Joffre's turn. Little Joffre, who stood hand in hand with Lucrezia at the dockside beside their papal father, both of them biting their lips. Just little lambs, really, but lambs grew up fast in the Borgia fold.

Juan Borgia dismounted his horse with a flamboyant toss of his dagged gold hem, holding his hand up to the crowd, who roared applause. He knelt, sweeping his cap from his head in a waft of plumes and pearls, and Cesare Borgia stepped forward, handsome face stony, to pronounce a blessing.

"I'll bet you an archbishopric that he's just mouthing that blessing," I whispered to Sandro. "They're not very fond of each other, those two."

"Cain and Abel," my brother said with one of his mountebank flourishes. "Joined by blood and bound by hatred—"

"I wouldn't go that far. Nobody's killed anybody yet. Though it did get close when Juan poached Cesare's favorite horse last year and ended up breaking its leg over a jump."

"—locked at each other's throats for all eternity—"

"Holy Virgin, Sandro!" I stifled a giggle, casting a guilty glance at my Pope, who didn't care what people said of him but took a very dim view indeed of any errant gossiping about his children. "I'll see you get made an archbishop if you just shut up."

"Don't you dare ask the Holy Father for any favors on my behalf!"

"Now it wasn't my idea, his making you part of the Roman Curia. He appointed you because he likes you, Sandro."

"How dare he like me. I don't like *him*—"

My big brother: making his way up the ladder of the Church with surprising speed—though he hadn't accepted the Curia position until I begged and cajoled him for a full fortnight.

"I didn't want to take it," Sandro scowled. "And I don't want anything else from His Holiness's hands, so don't you dare go asking."

He glowered at the white and gold figure of my Pope in his sedan chair, now raising a hand to sketch a cross over the crowd as the blessing concluded. My brother still wasn't very happy about my status. It's not really what any fond big brother wants to say, is it?—*My little sister, the Pope's concubine.* I counted it a miracle, really, that Sandro had come as far as grudging acceptance. All through the papal elections and the subsequent festivities, Sandro had been swearing vengeance up and down on "that Spanish whoremonger," threatening castration and decapitation and the *strappado*, despite all my insisting that I'd chosen my position in all contentment. I'd had to plead for days and days even to get him to *meet* with Rodrigo—and my wily Pope had been clever enough not to appear in full regalia, but in rumpled shirt and doublet like any Roman merchant, patting my hand like any fond husband, pouring wine for my stiff-faced brother like any charming host. My two favorite men in all the world, dining privately together that first time, some weeks after the election's frenzy had subsided. "Leave it to me," Rodrigo said blithely, and left me to my pacing up and down outside the room where they dined, biting my nails and wondering if my favorite brother was going to shun me forever as a harlot. Men! But then Sandro had reappeared, no longer purple-faced but puzzled and slightly glowering, to tell me, "I don't like this at all, *sorellina*. Not one bit. So I don't understand how I'm no longer furious. He's . . ."

"I know." I'd stood on tiptoe to kiss my brother. "Thank you, Sandro."

As for the rest of *la famiglia Farnese* . . . well. What exactly had they all done, learning I had skipped away from my husband's bed to the Holy Father's? *We should exile you from this family for the shame you've brought upon it*, my brother Angelo had written in more than one furious letter . . . until the Pope bestowed upon him an Orsini bride with a hefty dowry. *I would never have believed that any sister of mine could behave like a common flea-house trollop*, my second brother had written icily . . . and then finished his letter asking if I would ask the Pope to pay for repairs on our crumbling *castello* by the lake. *You were always flighty and vain, and now you're a common slut!* my sister Gerolama had written me . . . but now her letters begged favors for her stick-like Florentine husband.

I ask you. So much for the vaunted family morals. I hadn't gone home to Capodimonte once since my wedding, and I didn't think I'd be returning any time soon. My family didn't want to see me, after all; they just wanted to see the things I could get them, and those could be requested by letter without the inconvenience of my immoral self in their presence.

A great roar came up from the crowd then, yanking me from my thoughts. Juan Borgia had mounted his gilded-prow galley that would whisk him off to Barcelona, pausing to wave his emerald-studded cap at the docks again. Oh, would he just hurry up and be gone? I couldn't stand around faking tears much longer.

"Four galleys to see him to Barcelona?" Sandro scoffed as the oars shipped with a slow graceful motion, and the galley glided ponderously away from the dock like a fat dowager in huge skirts.

"Full of jewels, furs, brocades, carpets, tapestries, presents for his bride, more presents for King Ferdinand and Queen Isabella . . ." I stood on tiptoe to watch the galleys retreat, finally allowing myself a beam. "And they say women pack too heavily on journeys."

"How long do you wager it will take him to spend all four galleys' worth?"

"At least he's gone." I waved happily. "Gone for good, if I'm *very* well behaved and the Holy Virgin answers my prayers."

"Since when have you ever been well behaved?"

"Oh, you're one to lecture me, Alessandro Farnese. What's the name of your latest *amore*? Battestina, isn't it?"

"Silvia," my brother confessed. "Battestina got clingy."

"You should send your mistresses to me for advice. I'm never clingy."

The crowd was dispersing now, wandering off in search of a new diversion—but the Pope stayed, looking out over the gleaming river in his sedan chair, papal guard clustered about him. Sandro slipped away, murmuring of Curia duties—"Don't you mean duties to this new Silvia of yours?" I whispered—but the Borgias stayed until Juan's ship had disappeared from sight around the bend in the river. Then Rodrigo's gaze stirred as he found my face, dashing a heavy hand at his eyes, and I blew him a kiss.

N ow that I was officially a fallen woman, a woman of loose morals, a harlot, take your pick of titles, people liked to tell me about the weight of sin I carried on my shoulders. Mostly mendicant friars and virtuous women, who really got far more excited about this sort of thing than I did. I didn't have the heart to tell them that my shoulders felt quite unweighted. Rodrigo was right: Why *should* I be afraid of hellfire as a fornicator and an adulteress, when I could have my absolution straight from the Holy Father's own lips (between kisses)? Who was more qualified to forgive my sins than God's own chosen Vicar?

Mind you, being a mistress has its responsibilities. Wives can be capricious or bad-tempered sometimes, or prone to headaches—but a mistress must always be charming, sprightly, and ready to entertain. And wives only have to get dressed and ready to face the day, whereas I have to get dressed and ready to face the night as well.

If I'd been a proper wife, no doubt Orsino would be tired of me by now and trouble me only once a week or so when he'd come into my chamber, climb on for a quick poke under my nightdress, then roll off and start to snore. Everyone knew husbands got bored with their wives, who, properly speaking, weren't supposed to enjoy the nighttime side of things anyway. But Rodrigo, well . . . I gave a little involuntary laugh. The Holy Father was *different* when it came to passion, let us say. And furthermore, I never knew when he might take the passage from the Vatican to the Palazzo Santa Maria. Even if he couldn't come to spend *cena* with Lucrezia and me, sometimes he would steal an hour or two after midnight to come to my bed, so I always made sure to prepare myself: velvet dress changed for a filmy shift, a light combing of rosewater through my hair to keep it lying smooth instead of frizzing out from the day's plaits and pins, a scented apricot cream rubbed all over my skin (with special attention to heels and elbows), and only then would I tuck myself between the silk sheets of my huge curtained bed with no idea whether I'd be allowed to sleep the night through or not.

I knew I'd see my Pope tonight, however, so I hurried more than usual with the rosewater and creams, hesitating just a moment when Pantisilea handed me a sealed letter. "Another one, *madonna*. Tell me what's in this one?"

"Certainly not. You can go to bed now, Pantisilea."

"I've got a squire waiting for me." She winked and flitted off in high good humor. I waited till the heavy door shut before taking my letter out again. Pantisilea and I were quite fond of each other now that I'd suborned her loyalty from my mother-in-law's side to mine. She was the one to privately smuggle me the letters I sometimes got from my husband.

I broke the seal on the letter and made my way through the childlike scrawl. He wrote the letters with his own hand; that was clear enough from the spelling, which was even more appalling than Lucrezia's.

Orsino wrote to tell me that he was wel. He hoped I was wel. There was good hunting at Carbognano; yesterday he had bagged a stagge with a fine rakk of antlers. There was talk of the French invading . . .

Pages of awkward courtesies, hardly different from the last letter and the letter before that. I sighed, touching the page to a candle flame and letting it burn in the shallow dish where I kept a handful of Carmelina's honey-drenched *mostaccioli*, or would have kept a handful of her honey-drenched *mostaccioli* if I didn't keep eating them all in one sitting. The letter flared into ash, and I nibbled a thumbnail. Poor Orsino; why did he keep writing to me when we hadn't even seen each other since that awkward coupling in the stables? If he didn't want me enough to claim me for his own, or my daughter for that matter (and she wasn't his! *He* knew that, surely; he hadn't even come to Rome for her christening!), then why did he write? I wrote him back only because I still felt sorry for him, sorry and sometimes vaguely guilty. I kept my notes brief and formal, smuggled back to Orsino through Pantisilea so my mother-in-law wouldn't find out and tell my Pope. If Rodrigo knew, he'd have my young husband on the *strappado* and no mistake.

Or perhaps he'd just laugh derisively. Either way, I didn't really want to find out. I had no affection for Orsino, but I didn't want to see him hurt, either.

"Hello, *mi perla*."

I smiled, hearing the deep voice behind me. I had plenty of nicknames in Rome by now—"La Bella," which was really quite flattering, and "the Venus of the Vatican," which was somewhat flattering, and "the Bride of Christ," which I didn't find flattering at all, though Leonello found it so sidesplittingly funny that I had a dark suspicion he might have been the one to come up with it in the first place. Only Rodrigo, however, called me his pearl. "Your Holiness," I said softly, and blew out all the tapers but one. Padding across the woven carpet in my bare feet, I brought his hand up to my lips and kissed his ring. He nodded gravely, as he always did, then scooped me up in his burly arms and carried me to bed. He always did that too. There's something about being small—men always seemed to want to pick you up and carry you somewhere, didn't they? I was forever being toted about like a doll. "Oddly," Leonello had told me once when I said as much to him, "I find my experience of being small somewhat different."

Tonight, however, my Pope did not seem inclined for love. He put his head against my breast instead, absently kissing the base of my throat, and I leaned my cheek against his head and curled the locks of his black hair around my fingers. "You're thinking of Juan," I said at last.

"Juan." Rodrigo was just a somber profile in the flickering half-dark of the single candle: an eagle nose, a bulky chest, a sad voice. "Gone, like Pedro Luis. Pedro, he was so young when . . ." Rodrigo's voice trailed off, as it always did when he spoke of the firstborn son in Spain who had died after his first military command. "They said he was brave, very brave. I've told you that?"

"Many times."

"Juan, he's brave. Like Pedro Luis. He'll be a great *condottiere*."

I had my own doubts that a boy of seventeen who could hardly tear himself away from his hobbies of harassing the kitchen maids and killing cats in alleys was really poised to be the next Achilles, but I certainly wasn't fool enough to say so. "Juan is gone, but he's not dead, you know," I said instead, smoothing Rodrigo's hair. "He'll be back."

"I don't like him going at all! Any of them. I like my family *here*, with me."

"Says the man who wore my ear to a nub one night, telling me how his children were going to found a great web of interconnected dynasties throughout the world!" I bit Rodrigo's earlobe, playful. "How are they supposed to make a great web of anything if they all stay here?"

"I'm still working on that," he admitted.

I laughed. "So until you have the perfect solution, Your Holiness, leave Juan to Spain and Spain to Juan. Cesare—"

"The next Borgia Pope." Rodrigo nodded. "The only problem is, I won't be there to see him do it."

" 'We have for Pope Cesare Borgia, Pope Alexander VII.' " I sounded out the words. "Doesn't sound like him at all. He'd rather be the kind of Alexander who conquers the world."

"Juan can conquer the world. He's hot-blooded; made for the battle-field. Cesare, he's got a cooler head, and one needs that in the Church."

"I don't think he wants the Church."

"Someone in the Church doesn't want him, that's certain." Rodrigo gave a derisive chuckle. "Someone's made a nasty attempt to keep Cesare out of the College of Cardinals. That murdered girl in the Borgo, the one with her throat cut—I'll eat my throne if it was the Jews. Judging from what turned up on the girl's body, it was someone doing their best to smear Cesare's reputation. Cardinal della Rovere, perhaps? He's appalled enough at the idea of one Borgia Pope, let alone two . . ."

Rodrigo went on, half amused and half angry, and it was something faintly sinister about a dagger that had possibly belonged to Cesare, but I didn't want to hear the details. I had no desire think about women murdered in the night, not when I lay so cozy and safe in my Pope's arms. "So, if Cesare is to be the next Borgia Pope," I said instead, changing the subject, "and Juan is bound to lead the papal armies, what does that leave for Joffre?"

"Naples." Rodrigo frowned, fingers drumming against my arm as he looked up at the ceiling. He'd had it painted with a fresco of a golden-haired Europa being borne off by Jupiter in his form as a bull. Europa looked quite a lot like me, and the bull had a cloth of the Borgia mulberry and yellow across its broad back. "I shall have to do something about Naples."

"Now?" I poked his ribs until he squirmed. He was quite endearingly ticklish, my Pope. I aimed ruthlessly for the sensitive spot at his waist, and he caught my wrists together in one strong hand. He pinioned me against his broad chest, speaking in his most thunderous papal whisper.

"I shall excommunicate you, minx, if you make me squeal."

"And I shall beg my Holy Father for forgiveness. On my knees, of course."

"Then I may excommunicate you just for the pleasure of the sight." He kissed the tip of my nose, finally smiling, but his mind was still on

Naples. At least it was no longer gloomily fixed on Juan and poor dead Pedro Luis. "I think Joffre will rope Naples in for me. King Ferrente has a few spare princesses lying about—he'll give one to Joffre, if I support him against France and Spain too . . ."

"Don't tell me Spain wants Naples now." I made a face. "You just gave them a continent!" It had been all the talk that spring: the new Eden discovered by that Genoese sailor whose name I could never remember, an Eden Rodrigo had ceded mostly to Spain. I'd been less interested in the maps and treaties of it all than the strange things brought back from this new world: odd plants and dusky-skinned slaves in manacles, and strange bright-colored birds that were supposed to talk. Rodrigo had obtained one of the birds as a present for Lucrezia, but so far it refused to say anything, just sat sullenly on its perch and tried to take the fingers off anyone who fed it. Privately I'd named it *Vannozza*.

I dandled my fingers along Rodrigo's chest. "So, Joffre ropes in Naples, through a Neapolitan princess. Lucrezia ropes in Milan, through a Sforza husband. What fish are you going to catch with Laura?"

"I don't know. France, perhaps? They're starting to make trouble."

I smiled. Vannozza had been entirely wrong—Rodrigo was already making plans for Laura, plans every bit as grand as for any of *her* children. "A French duke," I began, envisioning my daughter's rosy future, but Rodrigo had already moved on.

"France will have to wait for the moment. Naples comes first." His fingers drummed mine decisively, all his pensive silence gone in the fire of decision making. I'd never yet seen my Pope tired. "And the College of Cardinals—it needs a batch of young blood to shake up those old ganders in their red hats. It's time Cesare was a cardinal, anyway. And what about your brother—does he fancy a red hat?"

I picked my head up off the papal shoulder. "Sandro?"

"Yes, why not? He's a jokester and he'll never amount to much, but he's amusing. Besides, I like offering him favors." Rodrigo grinned. "He rather likes me, you see, or he would if I weren't bedding his sister"—leaning down to lay kisses along the line of my shoulder—"so I get to watch him wishing he could hit me, and wishing he could accept whatever I'm offering, all as he's saying no with exquisite coldness. Refreshing, after all the slithering sycophants I usually deal with."

"If you really do want to offer him a red hat, I'll make him say yes." My brother had turned down several lucrative favors offered by my Pope, despite all my pleading and persuading. To be made *cardinal*, though ... it would be the making of my big brother. He'd be secure for life, a great man, and I wanted that for him: success, happiness, everything in the world. Maybe because he was the only one of my family who didn't hold out a greedy hand to me now that I was in a position to grant favors.

I didn't *like* asking for favors, really. Rodrigo might shower me with gifts in his easy, open-handed way, and my family too, but I never requested any of it. I wasn't a whore, no matter what the people of Rome called me—and they did call me that, alongside the prettier names like *the Venus of the Vatican*. It still distressed me sometimes. I was a girl of noble birth and good rearing, raised to adorn a man's household and bear his children, and sometimes I had to wonder just how I'd come so far from that.

And sometimes I wondered if I'd really come very far from it at all. I *did* adorn a man's household, after all, and I *had* borne his child, and all in all the days I spent tending my baby and getting fitted for dresses and going to Mass and presiding over the family *cena* in the evenings weren't so very different from the life I'd expected to have after marriage.

It had all gotten very muddled.

I sighed, and Rodrigo lifted my chin on the point of one finger. "Come to me," he whispered.

"Yes, Your Holiness," I whispered back, and he pulled me against him.

When Rodrigo had first made love to me, I had not the faintest idea what he was doing. From everything I'd heard whispered by my mother and her various pious, bawdy, or downright ghoulish maidservants, I knew the whole process of lovemaking was at first painful, and after that it could be either pleasant or boring, but it would be brief. Men took their pleasure, and it was a straightforward business. Rodrigo was neither straightforward nor brief. "What are you doing?" I'd asked, flushing pink and crossing my arms over my breasts as he gazed at me that first time.

"Appreciating," he said, taking my hands away. And not just appreciating the parts of me everyone seemed to notice—my hair and my breasts and the obvious bits. "The skin just inside your wrist is like satin," he might announce one night, and slowly thumb the pulse there until it was beating like a fall of fast spring rain. "And do you know you have dimples in your knees?" Tracing them all around. "And in your elbows?" His touch sliding up the line of my ribs, around the point of one shoulder and down to my elbows. "And one more dimple at the very base of your spine . . ." I'd feel his mouth there, moving my hair aside unhurriedly as he appreciated his way up the whole length of my back, and my entire body would be thrumming, happy to be appreciated all night long.

I still didn't know if Rodrigo was doing it all wrong, or everyone else was. But my swarthy, heavyset lover of sixty-two years could appreciate a patch of skin over my hip until it was leaping off my body in the effort to follow his hand, and in the end I decided I'd rather have that than a handsome profile or a youthful countenance. A great many young girls have to marry old men, after all—I was lucky enough to get one with power, presence, charm, and the most useful penchant for both gift giving and lovemaking; a man whose passion for me remained undimmed after a year.

Yes, I'd call that lucky indeed.

"My Papal Bull," I teased, my lips brushing his, and his burly chest rumbled laughter against my breasts. A blasphemy and a double entendre all in one; the kind of joke that he liked, and I slid myself down over him in a long candlelit shimmer of hair and apricot-scented skin. His eyes glittered dark in the shadows, still devouring me, until passion shuttered them and he groaned. "*Mi perla*," he whispered, one hand tracing the dimple at the base of my spine, the other cupping my neck and then roping my hair about his palm to pull me down against him.

Our mouths clashed, drank, clashed again. On my painted ceiling, Europa rode her bull. Down below, I rode mine.

"Rodrigo?" I said softly afterward. "Can I ask something of you?"

"You women, always picking at a man when his defenses are low!" Rodrigo's eyes were still closed, his voice drowsy now, though I could hear the smile in his words. "What is it you want, *mi perla*? Diamonds? You can have as many as you like."

"No." I rested the point of my chin on his shoulder. "I want our daughter to have the Borgia name instead of Orsini."

He was silent for a moment. "It's against all law, Giulia."

"You could change the law." I smiled, kissing the side of his throat. "You're the Holy Father, after all!"

"And *Laura Orsini* is a perfectly good name." His eyes opened in the dark. "So let us leave it there, Giulia."

"But everyone knows she's *your* daughter, not Orsino's. Why not make it official?" I could charm Rodrigo into anything; surely I could have my way in this. "'Laura Borgia,' just imagine—"

"No!"

I stared at him through the dark. Our limbs were still entwined so companionably, my pale skin pressed against his swarthy flesh beneath the sheet, my hair coiling over us both—but his voice had snapped out with the force of a lash. "Rodrigo, surely you can't doubt that Laura—"

"Why should I believe she's mine, Giulia? You were bedding down at the same time with that squinting sapling of a boy!"

I felt a sick swoop in my stomach. "I wasn't—"

His voice was curt. "Don't lie to me."

"I'm not lying," I said, bewildered. "I *told* you I bedded with my husband. I told you the day I came to you—I said I was no virgin anymore, and *you* said you didn't care!"

Rodrigo sat up in bed, a bulky shape in the dark, and his voice was cold. "I'd have cared a great deal more if you'd bothered to mention you were bedding your husband *and* me the same damned week. I had to hear *that* from Adriana, once she got it out of that little coward she calls a son."

Adriana. That rancid, tattling old trout. "I *told* you, it was only once with Orsino!" I said, and heard my voice scale up. How had this become a quarrel? My Pope and I had never fought before, not about anything. "Once!"

My Pope flung back the bedcovers in an angry motion and rose. "So you say."

"It *was*." I sat up, clutching the sheet to my breasts. "Adriana didn't tell you that too, when she was busy telling tales?"

"Adriana always has my interests at heart." Rodrigo reached for his robe in an angry swipe. "Clearly I can't say the same for you."

"You can't possibly think— How dare you—" Angry words choked in my throat like hot sparks, but my Pope cut me off before I could string any of them together.

"Who put this foolish notion about Laura's name into your head, anyway?"

"Vannozza," I threw back. "She said you'd find a way around the law, if you really wanted to. And she's right, you could!"

He let out a bark of laughter. "That wife of mine does like to meddle."

I erupted out of bed, pulling my hair around me instead of a robe. *"Wife?"*

"She was at my side for more than ten years, Giulia. She was wife in everything but name."

"And what does that make me?" I sputtered.

"Never mind." Rodrigo raked a hand through his hair. "The law is the law, Giulia, and I will not go bending it just to put my name on the result of your foolishness."

"She's not a result!" I cried. "She's a *Borgia*. One time with Orsino, just one time against all the times—"

"I don't want to hear about him," Rodrigo snarled, and I would have flinched at the rage in his voice except that suddenly I understood it.

"You think I would ever choose Orsino over you? Just because he's young and—" I'd been about to say *handsome*, but that didn't seem quite tactful. "Just because he's young? Is that why you never said anything to me, when Adriana first told you?"

He made a furious little chuff of denial, but his eyes slid away from me.

"Rodrigo." I took my Pope's big hand in both of mine, my sore heart softening just a little, though my pulse still pounded outrage. "Rodrigo, you know you have nothing to fear on that score, I—"

"We are Pope, Giulia Farnese, and We fear nothing." He jerked his hand from mine, turning in a quick whirl like a bull about to storm into the arena. And oh, Holy Virgin, but it was a bad sign when the papal *We* emerged. "It is late. There is work to be done. We shall bid you good night."

I felt like I'd been slapped. Hot tears sprang to my eyes and a tight misery clutched my chest, but I pushed it down. "And Laura?" I couldn't help whispering.

"Will remain an Orsini." Rodrigo looked at me over his shoulder, and I saw the glint of steel in his eyes. "Really, Giulia, you're very lucky she was born a girl. If you'd borne a son, I'd be far more angry with you!"

"Your Holiness," I managed to say, flat-voiced, trying to hide how very much that hurt me. He gave an angry jerk of his chin, not quite a farewell, certainly not the fond kiss with which he usually left me, and I stood clutching myself, cold and naked and miserable as the door banged behind him. I squeezed my eyes shut, feeling the tears burn my cheeks. My Pope gave me pearls and diamonds and velvet gowns; he gave me a silver teething ring for Laura and a cardinal's red hat for my favorite brother—but he wouldn't give a name to my daughter.

Not that.

Apparently even the Venus of the Vatican cannot have everything.

CHAPTER TEN

✦

It is better to be feared than loved.

—MACHIAVELLI

Carmelina

Y ou," I told Bartolomeo, "are a disgrace. You are unfit to do so much as sweep a floor in my kitchen. You bring shame to the skill of good cooks everywhere, and you will die a miserable failure unable to even boil an egg."

Needless to say, I was delighted with my new apprentice.

"What's wrong with it?" Bartolomeo stared crestfallen at the toughened egg lying before him like a little stone. "I've seen my mother do this—"

"Seeing and doing are far different things." Maybe little boys watched their mothers in the kitchen as they grew, but they didn't pay attention, and why should they? Most boys did not grow up to be cooks. When they came to me as apprentices, they had no store of basic knowledge such as a girl would, since any girl knew from infancy that the management of her future husband's kitchen would be her domain. I insisted all *my* apprentices start with the basics. Or rather, Marco's apprentices, but since I was the one who taught them while he took care of the household's menu planning, I could do it all my way. (Half the time I planned the menus too.) Young Bartolomeo looked mortified to be shown how to hold a knife or beat cream into peaks, especially with the other apprentices his age rolling out pastry dough and whipping up sauces and snickering at him, but a little mortification was good for the soul. I was sure Santa Marta would agree with me. She'd been reduced to a withered hand that lived in a spice box, and she didn't seem to mind her demotion at all.

"An egg should be boiled for as long as it takes to say the Credo, and no more." Straight from my father's book: page 303, Chapter: Lenten Dishes. I tossed Bartolomeo another egg, and he scrambled to catch it against his flour-grimed shirt. "Try again."

He blew out a breath and dropped the egg into the pot to boil. *"Credo in unum Deum—"* One of the other apprentices sniggered into a pan of bubbling orange sauce, and Bartolomeo faltered. He'd been bouncing and full of questions when he was just a pot-boy, but now that he was the lowest of all the apprentices, shyness had come with a rush. *"Credo in unum Deum—"*

"I can't hear you!" I thundered.

"Patrem omnipoténtem, factorem cæli et terræ—"

"Passable," I said as his next egg came off the fire soft and perfect. "Now do it again until you don't have to disrupt my kitchen by shouting a lot of prayers, you pottage-brained, boil-beaked lout."

"Why do you shout at me, *signorina*?" he burst out. "You don't shout at any of the others!"

Because none of the others showed his promise, that was why. By the end of Bartolomeo's first full day as kitchen apprentice, I went down on my knees before the severed hand of Santa Marta and thanked her for softening Marco's heart enough to let me keep Bartolomeo on. Not only did my former pot-boy have a cook's nose, he had a soft wrist that boded well for his future sauces and a natural eye for how long to sear a piece of meat. I would never, however, dream of telling him so.

"You question my methods?" I pointed at the door toward the

kitchen yard. "If so, you are free to leave now, Bartolomeo. Back to your uncle's tannery yard and the smell of piss. Is that what you want?"

He set his jaw at me in a resentful look. "No, *signorina*."

A little defiance—good. Cooks with pepper in the soul fared better than those without. "Boil another egg," I told him, "and kindly do not question my instructions again."

"Yes, *signorina*."

I gave his knuckles another whack and moved on, barely hiding my grin as I heard a steely, determined mutter of *"Credo in unum Deum"* start up again behind me. I do like breaking in a good apprentice! It cleanses the palate, like chewing mint leaves in between courses of a long banquet.

The kitchens hummed today at a lower key, half the volume of any normal afternoon. Madonna Adriana had announced last week that Rome was still far too sultry for October, and she intended to retire to take the waters in Viterbo for a few weeks until this unseasonable heat finally broke. Madonna Giulia had pouted her cherry mouth at the Pope until he agreed a week in the country at her side would be most agreeable, and the whole household had been thrown into a frenzy. Marco had already gone ahead to Viterbo with half the scullions, maidservants, and pastry cooks and the lightest of the essential cooking equipment: skillets and mortars and cauldrons loaded into wagons or lashed to mules as he called back at me to bring those copper oil bottles or the straining cloths. I was to follow with the rest when Madonna Giulia and her mother-in-law and young Lucrezia finally set out. I was already fantasizing about the cool green quietness of Viterbo: fresh breezes to wash away the city's stinking-summer smell of dead cats and baking bricks and sweating bodies. Lighter summer menus would be called on, to cool the blood and tempt heat-dulled appetites: snow-chilled wine and fresh-pressed infusions of mulberry or tart peach; salads of endives and caper flowers; chicken served cold with limes and just a splash of rose vinegar; featherlight omelets with goat's milk and chopped truffles . . .

"Signorina?" One of the stewards paused in the archway, not quite putting foot into my kitchens. I had them all well trained now, ever since an understeward had jostled me as I was shifting a kettle off the fire and spilled a very nice pottage all over the floor. I'd chased the man out, whacking him over the head with a salted tench at every step, and I hadn't had any trouble with the lot of them ever since. *"Signorina,* Madonna Giulia has sent down for you—she needs a packet of saffron for her hair rinse."

"Every time she washes her hair, there goes my saffron." But I didn't mind so much—I didn't have to pay for the saffron, after all, and besides, I was fond of Madonna Giulia. The way she consumed entire basketfuls of my *frittelle* in one sitting would have melted the heart of any cook on earth. "I'll take it to her myself," I called, stripping off my dirty apron and seizing an unopened packet of saffron.

The Pope's concubine lounged comfortably on a pile of velvet cushions in the grass of the central garden, wrapped in a series of towels with her little white feet bared under the sun. The top of her head protruded from a crownless straw hat the size of a wheel, her wet hair draped out over the vast brim to dry under the noon heat. Her face had been frozen into complete immobility behind a stiff white mask of some mysterious claylike substance, and she was buffing her nails with a piece of soft leather, occasionally leaning over to blow kisses at the baby who gurgled at her side in a little basket rigged with its own sunshade. Maidservants bustled back and forth, bees around their queen: one maid working at the soles of her mistress's little feet with a pumice stone, another maid plucking at her hairline with a pair of tweezers to heighten the smooth white forehead, a third maid hunching witchlike over a jar of bubbling hair potion and shooing away that wretched pet goat. *What a lot of bother it is to be a beauty,* I thought. Myself, I would rather devote the passing hours to a complex sauce than to my own hairline and cuticles.

"Carmelina!" Behind the stiff mask, Madonna Giulia's lively dark eyes lit up as though she'd been yearning all day to see me and only now could her life be called complete. I'd seen other women with that trick of worshipful welcome—my sister used to practice it before a mirror—but Giulia Farnese's was too spontaneous and all-encompassing to be anything but sincere. "Have you brought my saffron?" she asked. "You won't believe what it does for my hair—I put together a rinse of saffron, cinnabar, and sulfur, or rather Pia here does, and it gives me handfuls of pale gold streaks. Little red-gold ones too, which looks *very* well." She gave a little bounce of pleasure. "I'm sorry I keep using your supplies, though. It would be very sad if you had to stop making those little saffron *biscotti*. I adore those *biscotti*. Did you bring any?"

"I'm afraid not, Madonna Giulia."

"Good. I'm getting plump again. Sit down, sit down!"

"I should return to my kitchens, Madonna Giulia—"

"Oh, nonsense, you can take an hour." She passed the packet of saffron threads back to the maid with the pot of hair potion. "I always eat when I'm sunning my hair, after all, and since I can't eat until I take a bit of weight off, you might as well keep me company." She tilted her little head on one side, assessing me as I sat. "No sense putting saffron in beautiful dark hair like yours, though. What shall we try instead . . ."

"A tincture of quicklime and lead," the maid named Pia contributed, giving the hair rinse another good stir. "Good for dark hair, *madonna*."

"But I never like putting metal in my hair, do you? A rinse with rosemary and sage, that's what we used in Capodimonte." Madonna Giulia gestured at the maids, who bustled behind me with giggles and began unpinning my hair. "And you must have a mask—it feels very strange and stiff, but it whitens the skin no end."

"I don't need white skin," I protested, trying to swat away the maids. I'd never had a maid to do my hair in my life; my sister had always been the one to yank a comb through my curls and complain about the tangles. "I'm no fine lady, Madonna Giulia, I don't—"

"Here, hold still." With her own hands, the Pope's mistress began smoothing cream over my cheeks. "Don't screw up your nose like that; I know it smells, but it's just bean flour, egg white, goat's milk, and one or two other things. Some people like to add a dove's entrails to the mix, but I never like putting bird parts on my face, do you? Goodness, but beauty can be a disgusting business. Men think it's all Venus-in-her-bower, dabbing lotions and sprinkling perfumes, but they have no idea."

"Better to keep the masks and the smelly bits out of their sight, I always say," another of the maids agreed. Madonna Giulia sat back, tilting her head as a maid began combing the new saffron and cinnabar mix through her damp hair, and one of the other maids was working something herbal-smelling through mine. My wiry curls had grown out to my shoulders again, long enough to plait. Leonello still made a point of offering outlandish theories about it whenever he saw me. "Let me guess," he said yesterday when we crossed paths in the courtyard. "You're a runaway nun fleeing the cloister!" Two days before that his guess had been, "A singer of plainchant, passing herself off as a boy to continue singing in a boys' choir! You're certainly flat enough for it." A week before that: "Ah, I have it! You're a Venetian courtesan who titillates her clients by dressing up like a man! The things one hears about Venetians . . ."

"I traveled to Rome alone," I always replied coldly, "and to keep myself safe, I traveled in men's disguise. As you already know, because I've told you Santa Marta knows how many times!" But little Messer Leonello always gave me a knowing grin. Ever since he'd sniffed out the fact that I'd fled Venice with my father's recipes, he wanted the rest of my story. Santa Marta help me if he found out just what I was fleeing. He'd turn me in just for the pleasure of seeing if he was right, the horrid little man.

Well, serve *me* right for lowering my guard around him. Up in the loggia I'd been thinking he wasn't so bad at all. Perhaps even likeable. And then he'd struck, biting me like a snake lying in wait.

I wouldn't be so careless again. Madonna Giulia might like her body-guard, but I'd keep my lips sealed in his presence from now on. He was far too clever for his own good, and I didn't need his cleverness focused on me.

All the maids were settling down now, creamed and painted with pilfered cosmetics and looking ready for a good gossip. "Is this usual?" I whispered to scrawny Pantisilea as she plopped beside me, unashamedly scraping out the remains of her mistress's face mask from its pot and patting it over her own cheeks. I didn't know Madonna Giulia's maids near as well as I knew my kitchen girls and maidservants—in the strict hierarchy of servants in the *palazzo*, we inhabited an entirely different world than this perfumed and feminine one. But I'd never seen a noble-born lady of any household sharing her beauty supplies and her gossip with the maids before.

"You would not believe how the College of Cardinals is fussing," Giulia Farnese was chattering. "You'd think we were about to be invaded by devils . . ."

No, I decided as the whispers began to fly, this was *not* usual, at least outside this enclosed world Leonello called the papal seraglio. My father had served a great many highborn Venetian ladies, and some might be willing to confide in their maids on occasion, but they were far less willing to hear any confessions in return. *That* was only for equals.

Then again, perhaps the Pope's mistress didn't really have equals. Women of her own birth and station never came calling on her now that she was the most notorious woman in Rome—the only people who called on her were petty lords and suave churchmen and their various functionaries, people who wanted to wheedle favors from the Pope, and they certainly didn't bring their wives and daughters along. If she had been a courtesan she might have had friends among the other women of easy virtue, but such women would never be allowed into this house where the Pope's virgin daughter dwelled. Giulia Farnese occupied a gray territory, I realized: too sinful for ladies and too virtuous for whores. No wonder she befriended her maids and came tripping down into my kitchens for *tourtes* and cooking instruction. Were there any other women she could talk to?

"So poor Francesca's pregnant?" she was saying. The conversation had apparently moved from world gossip to household gossip. "I told her that guardsman was no good. I don't suppose he'll marry her?"

"No, and Madonna Adriana's turned her out," Pantisilea contributed, unashamedly rummaging among her mistress's perfume vials. "No one keeps a maid on when her belly's under her chin, we all know that."

"How you keep *yours* flat with all the rutting you do—!"

"I have my ways," Pantisilea said smugly. "You have to, if you want a man under the sheets *and* your post to go with it!"

Nods among the maids. They were a young and silly lot, most of them—Santa Marta forbid Madonna Adriana hire trained maidservants when she could get raw country girls so much cheaper!—and this batch of gigglers might not know that maidservants weren't really supposed to gossip with their mistress or help themselves to her perfumes . . . but even inexperienced girls like these knew that a maidservant kept her belly empty, or she lost her place.

"Francesca was taking a potion," Pia whispered. "She got it from an old crone who swore if she drank it every Sunday and sang a little charm, it would keep her from conceiving—"

"None of those potions work, do they?"

I glanced behind me involuntarily, and I wasn't the only one. If there's anything priests love to thunder about, it's the things women do to keep their bellies flat.

"Well, don't ask me how it's done," the Pope's mistress said. "I may be a wicked woman, but I don't know a thing about how to stop babies from coming, except to keep nursing the one you have as long as possible. That's what my mother-in-law says, anyway." Madonna Giulia lifted her baby out of the basket, settling little Laura's plump limbs into her own lap. "Of course the old trout had to tell me that the very first time I was *nursing* Laura. 'Nothing grinds away a woman's youth like a series of births, my dear, so you'd best avoid more babies if you want to keep your figure and your place.'"

We couldn't help laughing at her flawless mimicry, though there were more sidelong glances.

"It's a sin," one of the maids said firmly, crossing herself. "It's a sin, trying to limit the children you bear. You have to take what God sends!" But the other girls were already whispering. Maybe it was something about that stiff white mask most of us were wearing by now—we could hide our eagerness, hide our faces from the things we were saying. The things priests told us women were never supposed to say.

"If you can get your man not to seed you," one of the maids whispered, "when he *finishes*, that is—then you won't conceive. If he finishes elsewhere—"

"Oh, when can you ever get a man to do that!"

More giggles. I wondered if they were all blushing as hard as I was under the mask.

"It's all to do with the moon," Pantisilea said with authority. She was our resident harlot, after all, though a nicer harlot had never been born. "When we're ripe to breed, I mean. You watch the moon and you chart your courses with it—"

"There are more reliable ways than that," I heard myself saying. All those white-masked faces turned toward me, and I rubbed self-consciously at my cheek, which was beginning to flake. "Well, there are."

"How would you know?" Pantisilea asked, offended. She was the harlot, after all; she couldn't have a kitchen grubber like me infringing on her field of expertise.

"Venice is the city of courtesans," I said. "There was one called La Turca, she was shining black all over, the most expensive whore in La Serenissima—well, I knew one of the girls she hired as a maid. I learned a thing or two."

"Let's hear it, then!" Giulia bestowed a kiss on the dimpled fist Laura had wound around a lock of her mother's hair. "I love my baby, but I don't want eight more. Out with it!"

I hesitated, wondering just what kind of sin it was to be giving the most notorious woman in Rome advice about limiting the number of bastards she bore to a pope. "Take a lime and halve it," I said at last. "Then . . ." I mimed silently.

Noses wrinkled around our little circle. "Sounds uncomfortable," Pantisilea decreed.

"Neapolitan limes," I advised. "They're smaller. More expensive, of course, but you buy the good limes to stuff into a chicken's cavity, after all. No reason not to stuff your own with quality ingredients." I shrugged again. "It's not foolproof, La Turca's maid said, but I suppose nothing is."

"Except staying a virgin." My mistress smiled, cracking the mask still further about her eyes. Giulia Farnese could not go two sentences without smiling. "And who wants to do that?"

"Not me," about four maids said in unison, and everyone went off into gales of giggles.

Not me either, I thought. I'd not been virgin since I was seventeen and a handsome apprentice of my father's managed to addle my wits in a storeroom behind a stack of crated oranges. It had all been rather sweaty and rushed, but a few times later I was starting to see the point of it all. Unfortunately that was when the apprentice boasted to the wrong friend, who in turn let it slip to my father, and then there was a great deal of shouting, and benches were thrown, not to mention oranges. When all was settled and done, my foolish lover found himself dismissed and packed off home, and I got a sound lashing as my father roared on about how difficult it would be to find me a husband who would take a soiled bride. I'd castigated myself a good deal at the time for my shameful lusts, but now I just castigated myself for not choosing a more discreet lover. A busy kitchen was the worst place on earth to keep secrets, and a little pleasant rolling about behind a crate of oranges had been no trade for a lost reputation.

"So—" Madonna Giulia fixed me with a pointed finger, dark eyes merry. "Who gets the benefit of your experience with halved limes, Carmelina? Do you have a sweetheart?"

"Do tell, do tell!" the cry went up.

"Certainly not." I patted my stiff face. "Surely it's time to wash this mask off?"

"Don't be evasive!" Giulia uncurled her baby's little fist and waved it at me. "Wait, I've got it. It's Leonello, isn't it?"

I had been reaching for a towel to wipe my face, and I nearly dropped it. *"Leonello?"*

"He can't take his eyes off you, you know. Every time you come into a room, he stares and stares until you leave again."

Because he's trying to figure out all my secrets, that's why. "Not Leonello," I said instead, and began to scrub at my cheeks with the towel. "I can't stand the little wretch."

"He's *stunted*." One of the other maids wrinkled her nose. "Besides that, he's fair cruel. Said I had a nose like a hook, and made up jokes about it for days until all the stewards were laughing too. All because I asked if dwarves were really born with hair all over them like bear cubs—"

"And he's got all those knives. Stab you as soon as bed you, I should think."

"But he's clever," Giulia overrode them. "And funny; he can always make me laugh—"

"I've had him," said Pantisilea. "He's short, but that doesn't make such a difference, lying down . . ."

"Better you than me," I said. I wouldn't take Leonello in a thousand years.

"It's that good-looking cousin of yours, isn't it?" another maid grinned, cracking her own drying mask. "You're bedding Maestro Santini on the sly, admit it—"

"Certainly not." Tell these laughing maids anything, and even if they did inhabit a different world from the scullions and undercooks, there still wouldn't be a scullion or undercook who didn't know everything by next week. I wasn't about to tell a soul here that I'd begun keeping a prudent store of those Neapolitan limes on hand in my chamber, for those rare occasions when Marco won at the dicing table instead of losing, and came home victorious and amorous. Those were the nights he nuzzled at my ears and told me I was pretty even if I was as tall as a man, though I suspected most of my appeal came from the fact that I couldn't pester him for marriage as any of the other maids would have done. I'd been putting off his attentions since I came to Rome, as was prudent, but I'd needed a favor out of him if I wanted to keep Bartolomeo on as apprentice . . . and after Marco tumbled me back onto my bedclothes like an eager hound, beaming from a recent win at the *zara* board, it had been easy to pick my moment and murmur just how we could slide a new apprentice past Madonna Adriana without the fees. And after that, if Marco came prowling at my door every now and then when he felt like a bit of a romp, at least he understood the need to do it discreetly.

"No pinching my bum or sneaking a kiss where anyone can see us," I'd said sternly that first time, putting my nose right up against Marco's on the pillow. "I'll get nothing but snickers and sly jokes from the scullions if they think I'm giving it to the *maestro di cucina*. And if the maids find out, they'll think you're only keeping me on for a whore, and then won't I have a time getting any work out of them."

"Sworn to secrecy," my cousin grinned. There would be no such condemnation for him, of course, if he were to be caught bedding me—an unlimited supply of pretty maidservants was one of the great privileges of a *maestro di cucina*'s position. But that was the way of the world, and there was no sense wailing about it, so at that point I'd just yanked my shift over my head and enjoyed myself. It counted for sin, I suppose. Certainly the priests would all say so. But Marco had done me a favor in taking me in, not to mention fudging the kitchen accounts for Madonna Adriana so it looked like Bartolomeo's apprentice fees had been paid. It seemed wiser to keep him happy when he wanted a bedmate. Not to mention the fact that he was clean and sweet-smelling between the sheets, and more than pleasant to look on without his clothes.

That, I suppose, was the sinful part. Though when you've robbed a church, fornication seems like fairly small change as far as sins go.

One of the maids crowed, pouncing on my small involuntary smile. "It *is* Maestro Santini you're bedding, Carmelina, admit it! I don't blame you; he's near as handsome as Cesare Borgia—"

"I've had him," Pantisilea volunteered.

"Maestro Santini, or Cesare Borgia?" I asked. Anything to divert the subject away from me and my possible bedmates.

"Both. And I can tell you, Marco Santini's handsome, but the *Archbishop* . . ." Sighs all around from the maids. We were all mad for the young Archbishop of Valencia—I had to admit, even my sensible knees had buckled when he aimed that one passing grin at me, up on the loggia when I'd gone to shout at Leonello. I felt a moment's envy of Pantisilea, but Madonna Giulia was shaking her head.

"I don't see what all of you see in Cesare," she scolded us. "Really, all your heads turned by a handsome face! He's cold as a corpse, you know. After I saw how he reacted to that nasty business—"

"What nasty business?" I couldn't help asking.

"That poor girl in the Borgo who was found killed?" Madonna Giulia grimaced. "The one found staked down, with a blade through each hand."

We all shivered and crossed ourselves.

"Now, I heard this direct from the Holy Father—I wouldn't be telling you, but it's going to be all over the city in a week anyway." Madonna Giulia snuggled baby Laura closer, as though suddenly feeling a draft. "His Holiness had the papal guards clear that poor girl's body away, since there was so much uproar. And one of the blades through the girl's hand was just a common kitchen knife, but the other was a good dagger. Toledo steel, with a filigreed hilt and a sapphire the size of a pigeon's egg."

We looked at each other, blank. There wasn't a one of us who didn't know that dagger by sight. We'd all seen it with our own eyes, resting on Cesaer Borgia's hip whenever he abandoned his ecclesiastical robes.

The day was still warm, but suddenly I felt chilled.

Little Pia said what we were all thinking. "Well, surely it doesn't mean . . ."

"Of course not." Madonna Giulia waved the uneasy unspoken suggestion away. "Someone stole it to slander him; I don't doubt that. But it was his *reaction* to it all. Any man would be furious, wouldn't he, if he thought someone was spreading such foul implications? The Holy Father was certainly angry—he doesn't care if anyone starts nasty rumors about him, but let anyone make an attack against his children—" Giulia shook her head. "Even *Juan* was raging up and down, swearing vengeance on whoever had done it. But Cesare, he just smiled and put the dagger back at his belt. And when Juan asked him how he'd lost it, you know that snide way he likes jabbing people, Cesare just said, 'I didn't lose it.'"

We looked at each other again. The cold little chill spread to my stomach and sank in. I could just hear the young Archbishop's cool voice, the way it never held any emotion at all.

"So what kind of man doesn't care if the whole city thinks he's a murderer?" Madonna Giulia asked. "His Holiness wanted to cover everything up—as much as you can ever cover up something like this, anyway—and Cesare just said, 'Let them talk.' It'll be all over Rome in a week, the news about the dagger, and Cesare doesn't care. He's handsome," Giulia concluded, "but he's a *snake*."

"About as limber as one," Pantisilea agreed. "I don't mind telling you, he likes some *very* odd things. Between the sheets, I mean. Not that there were sheets involved, with me. It wasn't anything I'd really want to do again, truth be told. You can't imagine the places I got bruised—"

Giulia covered her ears. "No more details, please!"

"I wouldn't mind a few more," one of the other maids said, and the odd uneasy silence cracked. Guilty giggles rippled through our little circle as the chatter began to flow again. Madonna Giulia tilted her head back, damp blond hair sliding on its wide hat brim, and began wiping the flaking mask off her face with a damp cloth.

"Let's get ourselves prettified for Viterbo, shall we?" she suggested in a brighter voice. "It's just the place for a romantic tryst—love among the summer breezes, with the scent of flowers everywhere! Pia, you need a good thyme and fig mask to cool that sunburn you got at the market . . . Pantisilea, the mint and rosemary bleaching paste if you really want to whiten up those teeth against that lovely olive complexion . . . and Carmelina, cucumber-parsley milk with a hot towel compress, infallible for soft skin . . ."

My mistress sounded relieved to be moved on from the thought of grim things like daggers in the night. But I looked up then and I saw Leonello, standing halfway down the steps into the garden as though he'd frozen in place. He was not smiling.

"Taking up eavesdropping now?" I demanded, scraping the last of the mask off my face. But he looked at me expressionlessly, and then he turned and reversed out of the garden.

Leonello

T he masked man melted toward me from the vaulted shadows.
I jerked upright on my stone wall bench, breath freezing
behind my teeth. *He found out*, I thought inconsequentially. *He found
out I was asking questions, heard I was making inquiries about the women
who died staked to tables.* Curiosity was said to kill cats; what would it
do to dwarves? *Dio.*

I wondered if the masked man would pin my palms to the floor with
knives too, before he pulled my head back by the hair to bare my throat.

My thoughts might have frozen, but my hands did not. The finger
blade at my wrist cuff popped into one hand and the knife tucked into
my boot top leaped into the other as the man in black came padding
noiselessly toward me, eyes glittering behind the half mask.

"Don't kill me, little lion man," Cesare Borgia said from behind the
mask. "My father would not thank you for that."

The Pope's son tossed his mask aside, revealing the familiar lean
Borgia face. Even with the mask, I should have recognized the neatly
clipped auburn beard, the lithe serpentine grace, the ever-present shadow
behind him who was blank-eyed Michelotto. *Just Cesare Borgia*, I
thought, but my hands would not relinquish the Toledo blades. I had
to force the knife back into its boot sheath, and when I looked down I
saw my fingers were trembling.

"It is unwise to approach an armed man while wearing a mask, Your
Excellency," I said, and heard my voice come cool and remote into the
odd echoes of the arched windowless chamber. "Your Eminence, that
is. My apologies; I'm not yet used to the red hat." Nor was Rome. The
Pope had elevated a batch of his supporters to cardinals in order to
bolster his votes in the College; that was business as usual in papal
politics—but for one of those cardinals to be his own bastard son, and
a boy of a mere eighteen years . . .

And when there were such strange and violent rumors beginning to
circulate through the city about that same boy.

"I'm not used to the red hat myself, yet." The new Cardinal Borgia looked around the stone vaults, lit by long beeswax tapers and casting odd flickering shadows over the wall benches. "And I come masked because I like a long lone ride from time to time. Better if my father's enemies don't know they can find me unattended."

"What about your own enemies?" The question came unbidden.

He smiled. "I have no enemies."

Of course not. "You've just come from Rome, Your Eminence?"

"Yes. Some news for my father, from the French and Spanish ambassadors."

"Miles on a horse, just to give some news?"

"I did say I liked a long lone ride."

Yes, he did. He was frequently alone, Cesare Borgia, taking only Michelotto for a guard when he went out. Unlike his brother who had never gone anywhere without a pack of thugs and toadies, and young Lucrezia who was always surrounded by Giulia Farnese and Madonna Adriana and a half-dozen other giggling women in the papal seraglio. But the Pope's eldest son seemed to prefer his own company.

So did I, of course. But if there was anything I knew about the solitary men of the world, being one myself, it was that they kept their own company so they would not have to explain their actions to others.

What do you do in all those lone hours, Your Eminence?

He was stripping his riding gloves off now, tossing them down on the wall bench as he dismissed Michelotto. "Is His Holiness within?"

"With Madonna Giulia. He complained it was too hot, but she persuaded him to take the waters for his health, to ease his humours. They may be . . . some time."

My mistress's low rippling laugh bubbled from the other side of the door, and the sound of splashing. The hot springs of Viterbo were famous—the ancient Romans had bathed here, quipping in their clipped sonorous Latin instead of our lazy vulgar Italian as they soaked in the healing sulfur springs under the sky. Pope Nicholas V had ordered massive baths erected, and now instead of sunny skies and arching trees overhead we had a battlemented, crenellated pile of marble and stone.

Now the bathers tripped down shallow flights of stone steps and flitted along vaulted halls in their towels to reach the same steaming-hot springs. Giulia Farnese had tugged her papal lover through the arched doors with a wicked little laugh, flicking his entourage back with one small white hand, and the doors had closed on her shriek as the Holy Father tossed his shirt aside to reveal a swarthy bull's chest and tossed her bodily into the bubbling pool. There had been some quarrel between them after the Duke of Gandia's departure, but all appeared to be mended.

"Where are the others?" Cesare Borgia asked, looking around the vaulted antechamber. "The Holy Father's entourage?" Doublets and shirts, discarded shoes and belts, a stack of snowy towels, and a chessboard and a flagon of wine lay scattered along the wall benches. I sat alone on a folded cloak under a silver branch of candles, a book resting facedown over my knee.

"Taken themselves to the next set of springs, since His Holiness indicated he did not wish company in this one." Idly I moved a pawn on the chessboard beside me. The last players had abandoned their game partway through; black was eight moves from winning.

"You do not care for the baths, Messer Leonello?" Cesare Borgia discarded his cloak in a careless shrug, dropping it to the floor beside his mask.

"I killed my first man in a steam room," I found myself saying. "I've never cared for them since."

"Steam rooms, or killing?"

"Either."

He flopped to the wall bench beside me. I moved another pawn on the chessboard, and he studied the pieces. "Black is nine moves from winning."

"Eight."

"Play me."

It was not a request. "With pleasure, Your Eminence."

The bass rumble of the Pope's laughter sounded through the bolted doors to the bathing rooms, and I sat outside with the Pope's son as he swiftly reset the chessboard. "Black or white?" I asked, and found my mouth inexplicably dry.

The gleam of his teeth showed in the dim room. "Black."

I rotated the board. Carved ivory pieces standing in their ranks against carved ebony . . . but all I could see was blood welling in the dimple of a sweet, dead girl . . . and a black mask lying on a stone floor . . . and a dagger with a sapphire in its hilt.

I took a deep breath and moved my first pawn. "Go on," I said. "Ask."

"Ask what?"

"Did I truly kill my first man in a steam room?" Cesare Borgia was clever; I'd never get this conversation where I wanted it unless I made him curious.

"All right, Messer Leonello." Cesare Borgia moved a black pawn to meet mine. "Did you?"

"Yes," I said. "I was seventeen. He stalked me there after a card game. I'd won the last *scudi* out of his purse, and he was angered."

"You used a knife?" Another black pawn advanced.

"Poorly—the man slipped on the wet floor, down low enough for me to strike." I moved a knight out onto the checkered field of battle. "I stabbed until he looked like a cut of cheese."

"Sloppy," said Cesare. "Only a clean kill is a good kill."

"Surely any kill one can walk away from unscathed is a good kill?"

"No. Killing is a skill like any other. It should be practiced until it comes easily."

"And what was your first kill, Your Eminence?"

"I am a man of the cloth, not the knife." Cesare moved his bishop toward me, giving its little carved miter a caress.

"But you have killed." I kept my eyes from straying to the mask on the floor. But I could see it, oh yes, I could see it very clearly. "I know the look."

He looked at me across the board a moment, then shrugged. "A footpad. He wanted my purse."

"And did you use a knife too?"

"Poorly." The gleam of teeth again. "It took me four tries to cut his throat. But I was only sixteen."

"Young."

"We Borgias age quickly." He advanced his queen. "We have to. We all die young."

"Your father has not." Another rumble of laughter came from the bolted doors as if in answer, accompanied by Giulia's throaty murmur. Rodrigo Borgia sounded very vigorously alive indeed.

"The exception to the family rule." Cesare dismissed his father. "My older brother died young—Pedro Luis. And one of my halfsisters in Spain." He sounded remarkably unconcerned by their fates. "I imagine I'll be next."

"The thought doesn't seem to trouble you."

"Better to die young and in a saddle than in bed as an old man."

"Perhaps." I fingered my own queen; moved a bishop instead. "Tell me, why did you kill your footpad? Surely you could have chased him off."

"He angered me. Besides, I wanted to know what it was like."

"Killing?"

"Yes. I knew I would have to do it one day or another. And I thought, 'Why not now?'" He took one of my pawns.

I took one of his knights. "Do you remember his face?"

"No. Do you remember your bathhouse drunk?"

"I never remember the men I've killed." *True.* I gave a reminiscent whistle, tapping the carved crown of my white queen. "The one I remember is the woman." *False.*

"A woman?"

"A whore," I lied, making up the details haltingly as though made uneasy by a bad memory. "She tried to rob me, afterward. Everyone tries to rob a dwarf. I fought her; she pulled a little knife out. I got it from her . . ." A shrug. "Women die differently than men."

A black rook advanced, taking my knight. "Do they?"

I had no idea, and no intention of ever putting the theory to the test.

"They do," I lied, giving a bitter little laugh. "The bitch deserved it, but I still remember her face. Did you ever kill a woman, Your Eminence?"

The question fell into the vaulted room like a drop of water into a pool, spreading outward in silent ripples. There was a barely perceptible pause, and then—

"Careful," said Cesare Borgia pleasantly, moving his knight. "Your king is in danger."

I slid my king out of harm's way. "I take it that is a no?"

"Take it however you wish, little lion man. I will tell you this— women aren't worth the effort of killing."

"Some might disagree. Did you ever find that man who staked those whores to the table?"

"As long as the crowds are quiet and do no more muttering about sacrifice to devils, who cares if we find him?"

"I thought you might be burning to find him, Eminence. If only to discover how he came to use your dagger on the last girl." I had been turning that piece of information over in my mind since I'd first heard it, overheard from Giulia Farnese and her maids. Just a vicious bit of slander, I'd thought at first; no different from any other vicious slander that habitually circulated about the great. But then wildfire rumors overtook the city, and I found myself wondering.

"Ah." Cesare looked amused, sliding a bishop one square. "You think I did it?"

"No." I sacrificed a pawn. "You would never be so stupid as to leave your dagger behind to implicate you."

"Perhaps I was arrogant rather than stupid," he suggested. "Perhaps I wished to see how far I could go, and still get away with it."

"An interesting notion." My mouth was paper dry. "Did the first three girls not garner enough attention?"

"Three?" Bland. "I thought there were only two."

"Three." Anna, the first of them. She did appear to be the first, with her four-times-clumsily-slashed throat. No other girls had turned up on tables before her that I could find out. Another girl after that, one I had not even known about, killed a few months later. Then Carmelina's fruit-seller friend, and finally the girl in the Borgo. And each woman, according to the answers I'd ferreted out from a few quiet chats with the Borgia guards, the idle city constables, the tavernkeepers where the bodies had been found—each woman had died more neatly than the last. Their throats gaping in progressively tidier slashes.

Killing is a skill like any other. Cesare's words whispered in my ear. *It should be practiced until it comes easily.*

"On the other hand," Cesare Borgia said serenely, studying the chessboard, "perhaps my dagger was stolen by some enemy of my father's, and used to stir up ill feeling against me. Cardinal della Rovere would have sacrificed a whore's life in an eyeblink, if it would have kept me from getting my red hat."

"That does seem more likely," I agreed. It *was* more likely, so why was I sweating in this cool stone room?

"And either way, why should anyone care?" Cesare shrugged. "They were only whores."

"Only whores," I echoed. "What, indeed, does it matter?"

Cesare Borgia's black eyes found mine over the chessboard. I smiled back. "You aren't paying attention, little lion man," he said, and gave a wave of his elegant hand over the board. "I believe the win is mine in six moves."

"So it is." I tipped my king with a flick of the finger. "Another game, Your Eminence? And perhaps you will tell me your news from the French and Spanish ambassadors . . ."

We talked lightly, our voices even as I reset the board. Threats from France; apparently their king had threatened invasion to press his claim to Naples. "And from Spain more serious news—Juan has arrived in Barcelona and has already managed to offend everyone. Roaming about the city whoring and fighting and killing stray dogs. I imagine our Holy Father will write Juan an angry letter."

"Indeed."

I won the second game. Cesare Borgia rose, stretching lightly like a long-bodied cat. "You fight a good game of chess, Messer Leonello. You play like a Roman—encircling defenses and sudden piercing attacks from the rear guard."

"You play like a Spaniard, Your Eminence. No retreat, not ever."

He smiled. I smiled.

"It seems La Bella will not release my father from her clutches until nightfall," he observed. "How has she not killed him yet?"

The new Cardinal Borgia sauntered out without a further word. The black half mask swung easily from one hand.

I took the ebony-carved bishop from the chessboard, balancing it in my palm. And wondered, with that focused hunter's thrill I'd first felt in chasing down Anna's killers, if I had found my third killer after all.

The one in the mask.

CHAPTER ELEVEN

❖

From a tiny spark may burst a mighty flame.

—DANTE

Giulia

See?" I pressed my back against Lucrezia's, reaching up to level my hand over our heads. "You're taller than me. You've grown since the wedding."

"Really?" Lucrezia's narrow little face brightened as she looked down at herself. "I thought my dresses seemed shorter—"

"We'll add an embroidered band on all your hems," I promised. "It will give you a few inches to cover your slippers, *and* make the gowns feel like new." I turned to the pair of robe makers bustling about my chamber with cloth samples and mouthfuls of pins. "Be sure to refit her bodices too! Extra lacing and another dart under the bust—height isn't the only place you're growing," I told Lucrezia.

She looked down at her modest breasts, which had made a sudden appearance earlier this year and been greeted with rapture. "Not growing fast enough!" she accused them, but gave a happy sigh as the robe makers came forward with samples of figured velvet draped over their arms and began holding up swatches. I liked my chamber best when it was a lovely cozy mess like this: gowns here and gowns there, sewing girls and maidservants picking through the piles like chattering birds, Lucrezia twirling in the middle looking down at herself and dreaming, and of course Leonello carping about something. "I am not a cloak hook," my bodyguard's voice complained from his usual corner, flicking a discarded sleeve off his propped boots. "Will you ladies quit draping things on me? *Dio.*" But his dark looks were no match for all the bustle of needles and pins and silks, and I heard a muttered oath as he went back to his book.

We'd all returned from Viterbo to Rome at the beginning of November, a Rome gone autumn-cool at last so that the wind tugged at the mane of my pretty gray mare as I trotted through the city gates in my ring of guards. Even the *palazzo* was chilly now, despite the hot coals in the braziers and the heavy shutters over every window, and at night I abandoned my filmy shifts and snuggled into a sable-lined *zimarra*. Maybe it was just the emptiness of my big bed that made it seem cold. My Pope had sent us on to Rome, but departed himself in a whirl of energy to take care of some papal business in Pitigliano—though the letters he sent me were enough to warm my bones. Rodrigo was all passion and sweetness again, now that I'd given in on the subject of Laura's name—his way of apologizing for the quarrel we'd had on the subject. Not that he ever *would* apologize, but powerful men never do say they're sorry for anything, do they?

"I really am taller than you!" Lucrezia smiled at me as the robe makers began to measure her hem. "You think I'll be taller than Sancha of Aragon?"

"The Neapolitan ambassador described her as small-statured." Lucrezia and I had devoured every bit of news we could gather about Sancha of Aragon: sixteen-year-old bastard daughter to the would-be King of Naples, bride-to-be of little Joffre Borgia, and the marriage link my Pope had devised to bind Naples to his interests. The wedding wasn't to be announced until Christmas, but rumors flew.

"They say she's pretty, too . . ." Lucrezia frowned down at her bosom. "*And* curvaceous!"

"But she's dark." I slipped an arm about Lucrezia's waist, holding up a carved hand mirror to reflect both our faces. "So we two blond beauties can't possibly be outshone. You must have a new dress for Joffre's wedding—fresh hems on old gowns are very well for every day, but everyone who is anyone will be there to see Joffre and Sancha married. Pale green silk, I think, with silver brocade sleeves so you look like a mermaid . . ."

Lucrezia's face brightened in the mirror, but only for an instant. "You think my father will let my Lord Sforza accompany me to the wedding?" she ventured.

"Perhaps you can ask," I said lightly. "Now, let's try this gown here with a pair of yellow sleeves—"

"I *have* asked! He just says my husband is to keep his distance till I've properly grown. I *have* grown. I'm fourteen, and I'm taller than *you*!"

The maidservants looked at each other, and I shooed them back. Lucrezia made an angry swipe at her eyes with the back of her hand. Leonello turned a page, deaf in his corner, and I went on pulling a yellow silk sleeve over Lucrezia's arm. "Fathers aren't always the most keen-eyed when it comes to seeing that their daughters have turned into women," I murmured, soothing.

"I'm Countess of Pesaro, and I've never even shared a *roof* with my husband, much less a bed." Lucrezia's lower lip pushed out. "I'm a married woman, and I'm still living in my father's household learning French verbs and Greek translations and—and Machaut songs. Everyone laughs at me, I'm sure of it. They think Lord Sforza doesn't want me—they think he won't have me in Pesaro with him because I'm ugly, or because I'm bastard-born—"

"Nonsense." I began tying the silk laces of her sleeve, tugging puffs of gauzy shift out through the fashionable slashes. "I saw him at the wedding; he went round-eyed at the sight of you."

"Caterina Gonzaga said he was looking at you!"

"Caterina Gonzaga is a goose." I put a finger under her little chin, lifting it up. "Lord Sforza comes to visit us in a few weeks—then you'll see. He'll be too busy staring at you over the table to even know I'm there." And if he did stare at me, I thought privately, I'd catch myself a convenient cough and take to my chamber to allow the newlyweds a little private conversation over *cena*.

"He won't be allowed to stay the night when he visits, will he?" Lucrezia fiddled with her cuff. "With me, I mean."

"No," I admitted, picking up the other yellow sleeve and moving to her other side. I'd already had quite explicit orders from His Holiness on that point. *Keep that Sforza bravo out of my daughter's bed*, he'd written me from Pitigliano. *I want the marriage unconsummated a little longer—I don't care if he's hot for her; he can damned well wait.*

"Can't you ask Father for me?" Lucrezia pleaded. "Ask him to let me be a proper wife?"

"I'll ask," I promised, but I didn't hold out much hope that Rodrigo would listen. My Papal Bull was as stubborn as a bull too, sometimes.

On the other hand, so was his daughter. Her lower lip pushed out as she looked at herself in the hand mirror again. "I'll have a new dress for my husband's visit, too," she decided. "Something wicked— something *older*. I'll make him so mad for me that he'll carry me off to Pesaro on his horse the next morning, no matter what my father says."

"If he does, he'll be promptly stabbed by papal guards," Leonello said from behind his book.

"Then he'll die and I'll join a nunnery," Lucrezia said darkly. "I'd rather be a *nun* than have Sancha of Aragon laugh at me for being a virgin wife."

"She'll be the virgin wife," I said, making a warning face at my body-guard behind Lucrezia's back. "She'll be marrying Joffre, after all, and he's a dear boy but he's just a child and I doubt he'll be able to do much between the sheets when they're bedded down on their wedding night. And if she's a virgin wife too, then she won't dare laugh at you for anything."

"Really?" Lucrezia's little blond head twisted to look at me on her long neck—one of her best features. Her features were small, her eyes blue-gray rather than pure blue, and her skin prone to spots, but that swan neck made every turn of her head graceful.

"Really," I told her. "And if you really want to look older and a little wicked for Lord Sforza, I think we can manage that. Let's see . . ." I rummaged among the cloth samples. "Dark green silk . . . too sallow on you. Yellow velvet, no, too close a color to your hair. Pink figured brocade, definitely not. Too girlish . . ." I had an entire team of robe makers on hand now who did nothing but dress me, and enough cloth samples and embroidery patterns on hand for a hundred gowns. The respectable women of Rome didn't want to be seen talking with me, or even walking on the same side of the street as me, but they certainly took an interest in everything I wore. And if I was going to set the fashions I might as well do it right, so I put a great deal of thought these days into the design of each new dress—not like the days when I just threw on anything that was pretty. I could certainly put all that new expertise to Lucrezia's benefit. "We want a new image for you," I announced. "Something to show you've grown up. You're still too young for black, but perhaps a midnight blue . . ." I tossed a fine lightweight French silk over her shoulders. "Yes, that's it."

"Cut to here?" Lucrezia tugged down her neckline.

"Let's say here." I moved her bodice back up. "But with black French lace at the edge; that will make it *quite* wicked. I do hope the French won't invade; then we wouldn't be able to get any more of this lace . . ."

"God forbid you ladies be left without lace," Leonello said behind his book, but we paid him no mind. I sat Lucrezia down and spent an hour pampering her after the robe makers left, plucking her brows into perfect arches and showing her how a little discreet powder would help cover the red spots that sometimes appeared on her skin. "I think if you wear pale green to Joffre's wedding, I shall wear sea green. Nobody can compete with a pair of stunning blondes dressed to match!"

"I don't really want Sancha to be ugly," Lucrezia confessed, restored to her usual sunny good humor. "Joffre deserves a pretty wife."

"Of course he does," I agreed. "But she won't be prettier than you; it is simply not possible. Now, make a sort of fish expression—suck your cheeks in, that's it—and I'll show you how to rouge your face so your cheekbones look higher. Just a dab, mind you, we don't want His

Holiness noticing. He'll excommunicate me for painting his daughter up like a courtesan. No use telling a man that nice fair skin like ours needs a little color. Men don't know anything about these things, much less men of the cloth . . ."

"That was kindly done," Leonello told me when Lucrezia finally scampered off, rosy and glowing, to practice her dancing, since I'd pointed out that even her father wouldn't forbid her dancing with Lord Sforza.

"Was it kindly done?" I folded my arms along my chair's high carved back, gesturing the rest of the maidservants out. I was suddenly tired of feminine bustle. "I doubt it."

"That child's lived her life among all these overbearing Spanish brothers and an even more overbearing Spanish father. Not to mention that bitter old bitch of a mother, which is worse than no mother at all." Leonello looked up at my painted ceiling. "No sisters, no women in her circle except Madonna Adriana, who takes her father's side in every-thing. But now she has you, the most glamorous woman in Rome, and you could brush her away like a tiresome puppy. But you don't. Instead, you help her to be a woman."

"Not a real woman." I pillowed my cheek on my folded arms. "I can't help her be a wife, not a proper wife the way she wants to be. But then I'm hardly a proper wife myself, so how could I ever help her with that?"

"Beg His Holiness very prettily on those dimpled knees of yours?"

"How do you know my knees are dimpled?" I asked, momentarily distracted.

"I overheard one of the guardsmen paying your maid Taddea five *scudi* just to hear what you looked like in the bath."

"I'll have a word with Taddea," I said, but without much heat. My maids liked me, gossiped with me, even confided in me, but they all took shameless advantage of me: pilfering my cosmetics, stealing ker-chiefs and shoes and other small things from my wardrobe they thought I wouldn't miss, selling locks of my hair for love tokens. I pretended not to notice, most of the time. How could I blame them for making a bit of extra coin when they had the opportunity? I'd been born to a good family and a life of ease, but my maids had only their wages (and my mother-in-law paid the skimpiest wages in Rome). If Pantisilea stole a vial of my perfume to attract yet another lover, or if Taddea made a few extra coins from describing how I looked in the bath, they were welcome. "I'll have a word with the Pope too," I added. "I'll intervene for Lucrezia with him, not that it will do any good. His mind's made up. He doesn't want the marriage consummated."

"I suppose not." Leonello marked his place in his book, setting it aside. "If Lucrezia stays a virgin, he can always annul the marriage in favor of a better one."

"If Lucrezia stays a virgin she'll remain His Holiness's daughter, not Sforza's wife."

"So that pretty head of yours *is* good for something besides growing massive amounts of hair."

"You're horrid," I told him, but laughed. "Stand up, Leonello."

"Why?"

"Because I'm the mistress of the household, and I say so."

"I am paid to protect you, not obey you."

"I'll pout," I warned. "You don't want to see me pout. I could bring down a city's gates with my pout, the Holy Father says."

"Who am I to contradict the Holy Father?" Leonello rose, and I picked up the measuring cord one of my robe makers had left behind.

"Arms out," I ordered, and stretched the cord along the length of his arm.

"Am I being fitted for a rack?" he inquired as I measured his wrists, the width around his chest, the length of his back. "I assure you, it's quite unnecessary. If you wish to punish me for my rudeness, you have only to cut off my access to the library."

"I promised you a new set of livery," I retorted. "I know you refused to wear that mulberry and yellow uniform the other guardsmen wear, and I don't blame you because mulberry does nothing for your coloring. But you're a disgrace in those disreputable boots and that doublet that doesn't fit. I cut a very stylish appearance in Rome, and I'll not be dragged down by a shabby bodyguard."

"*Dio*, no one cares what I wear. My clothes will never be the first thing noticed about me."

"Nonsense; you could cut a very fine figure if you tried. Have all the maids swooning." I thought of Carmelina's uncomfortably shifting eyes as I pestered her about Leonello. "Perhaps there's an errand you can run for me when I'm done," I added innocently. "Go down to the kitchens and talk to Signorina Carmelina?"

"And just what do you wish me to speak with our ill-tempered cook about?" A flare of interest in his hazel eyes; oh yes—I saw that with great satisfaction. Well, Carmelina was handsome in her lanky way—not pretty, with her long thin face and near-constant scowl, but she had beautiful dark brown eyes that flashed with her every change of expression, and she always trailed some tantalizing whiff of cinnamon or honey or sage in her wake. And the rosemary herbal rinses I'd pressed on her had tamed the wildness of her curly hair. I'd given her an entire vial and made her swear on the soul of blessed Santa Marta to keep using it.

"You might tell Carmelina to come see me when she's got a lull between meals," I remarked, carefully casual as I took the measure of Leonello's left leg. "Have you seen what she's done with her hair, by the way? I don't suppose you noticed; men never do . . . Yes, tell her to come see me for a talk about the Sforza visit."

"The menu?" Leonello asked. "He's a hunting lord of a small provincial town. He'll eat anything that's been wounded badly enough not to limp off his plate."

"No, Carmelina can take care of the menu as she pleases. She just needs to know that Lord Sforza's dishes might require an extra spice or two." I dropped to my knees to get the circumference of Leonello's ankles. His legs looked twisted even inside their boots, and I wondered just how much it pained him to walk. I never saw him limp or heard him complain, but suddenly I was convinced he hurt a good deal of the time.

"What extra spice does the Lord of Pesaro need?" My bodyguard sounded amused. "Some salt, perhaps? He seemed a very bland fellow from what little I've seen of him. If you told little Lucrezia that her husband is a thoroughgoing bore, perhaps she wouldn't be so eager to become his bedded bride."

"It's his eagerness I'm worried about, not hers." I straightened from the last of my measurements. "I've already had a letter from His Holiness, you see—he's told me that if the Count of Pesaro exhibits too much ardor for Lucrezia during his visit, he is to become . . . indisposed."

Leonello stared. "The Holy Father wants you to poison his son-in-law?"

"No! What a mind you have. I'm merely to make sure that Lord Sforza is gripped by watery bowels if he seems in an amorous frame of mind."

Leonello threw back his dark head and laughed. "That's a clever pope we have," he appreciated. "If there's anything to keep a man from thoughts of love, it's a set of griping guts."

"Carmelina will know what to use, if it proves necessary." I stood up, folding the measuring cord away. "Do you still think I was kind to Lucrezia, Leonello? Her father means to keep her away from her husband forever, and I'm helping him do it."

My bodyguard's dark eyes studied me. "You could defy him, you know. He won't be here, after all, when Lord Sforza comes to call."

I thought of all the angry words Rodrigo and I had thrown at each other over Laura and Orsino. I'd cried for a fortnight's worth of icy silence after that, fearing I'd lost my Pope, and he'd probably consoled himself with some courtesan. "It's sweetness he wants, my dear, not rebellion," Madonna Adriana had told me, and I'd felt too low to lash back at her. Things were certainly all sweetness again now . . . but they wouldn't stay that way if I sided with the Pope's daughter against her Holy Father.

"I don't dare," I found myself telling Leonello as I put away the measuring cord. "I just don't. I'm just a silly girl, you see, and I'm not very brave. Now, there are at least eight people waiting in the *sala* to ask me for favors from His Holiness, and it's not polite to keep sycophants waiting, is it?"

Carmelina

W hat did you *feed* them?"

I glanced down at odious little Leonello on my elbow. I had positioned myself discreetly on a turn of the stairs, half blocked by liveried manservants as I stole a look at the exceedingly giddy party of guests who had just come from eating my dishes at *cena*. "Just food," I said vaguely.

"Did you drug it?" Leonello stood on tiptoe, craning for a look of his own past the manservants. "*Dio.* Look at them."

"They're enjoying themselves!"

"That's one way to put it."

Madonna Adriana had arranged for a choir of sweet-voiced singers from Ferrara to entertain Lord Sforza and his entourage after their evening meal—but somehow nobody looked interested in music. The party of guests were all too busy laughing, flirting, flitting into the large *sala* like tipsy butterflies, the ladies in their bright satins giving little impromptu twirls and declaring that they felt like dancing, the men putting hand to heart and vowing eternal devotion to everything female in sight. I saw one lady in pale blue lose a slipper, and as the man on her arm knelt to slide it back over her coyly proffered foot, she twined a finger around his ear and whispered something inaudible. Madonna Giulia had an admirer on each side, both of them reciting verses to her beauty and fighting to be first to pull out her chair. Cesare Borgia had no less than four women tossing their curls and pouting their lips at him as he sat loose and coiled in his unclerical dark velvets. As for Lord Sforza, the guest of honor, Adriana da Mila had positioned the solid bulk of her forest green velvets very squarely between him and his wife, but that did not stop them from stealing glances behind her head. "The singers," Madonna Adriana was saying loudly over the laughter and the whispered jests, "the singers have for your entertainment a very fine arrangement of love songs!"

"Bad choice," Leonello whistled. "Better stick to grim liturgical chants about hellfire."

No one was listening anyway, as far as I could tell. The whole party of guests floated on a tide of golden giggles and glances heavy with meaning, extravagant compliments and secret caresses, and Lucrezia and her lord sailed highest of all in a fragile glass bubble as they stared wordlessly at each other over Madonna Adriana's head. Even Cesare Borgia smiled when he saw the light in his sister's eyes.

"And the evening started so badly," I whispered under the first sweet harmonies of the singers. Like good bread, a good *cena* needs certain key ingredients if it's to rise in the oven—a dash of goodwill and a dash of humor, a good sprinkling of laughter and a pinch of romance. And I'd gotten one hurried look at Lord Sforza as he dismounted his horse in the courtyard that afternoon, and hadn't held out much hope that the evening would be any kind of success. He'd gone striding into the house with a black scowl, his provincial Pesarese captains flocking after him like unkempt roosters. He'd looked more the unshaven outcast than ever among Madonna Giulia and Madonna Lucrezia and their surrounding peacock pride of well-groomed ladies, and even from down in the kitchens I could hear Lord Sforza complaining in loud tones to Cesare Borgia, slapping his gloves against his hand and demanding to know when the Holy Father would be contracting the Sforza soldiers against the French. He hardly had a word for the bride he wasn't allowed to touch. I foresaw a sour, awkward evening, with the Count of Pesaro looking irritable and Lucrezia wilting from his lack of attention.

Instead . . .

"What *did* you put in the food?" Leonello asked again.

"Nothing special!" Just a simple *cena*, really. I'd gotten a bit creative, of course. Rather than simply flipping to page 11, Chapter: *Credenza*, I'd whipped up a sideboard arrangement all my own: sugared cedar flowers and candied orange peel instead of the usual cheeses and spiced fruits. Not to mention the roast peacock garnished with sweet candied pine nuts and cinnamon sticks instead of the usual tangy sauce, and swimming on a bed of rose petals . . . the fresh oysters sautéed in butter and arranged back in their shells with a squeeze of orange over top . . . the grilled sea bass with a simmered sauce I had improvised of rosy wine, salmon roe, and truffle shavings ... "Maestro Santini left the menu to me," I shrugged. "He often does, these days."

"What were you thinking? The idea is to keep Lord Sforza *out* of his wife's bed. Those oysters alone would have roused the cock on a statue." Leonello tilted his oversized head at me. "Perhaps you weren't thinking of our good Count of Pesaro at all, eh? Can our *Signorina Cuoca* possibly be mooning for a lover of her own?" Clapping a hand to his heart. "It's me, isn't it? Your abiding lust for my small self could no longer be contained, and so it made its way into the food."

"Don't be ridiculous," I told Leonello. But something *had* made its way into the food, because I'd seen the excitement rising among the guests with my own eyes when I crept up to the gallery to peep down on the small *sala* after the laughter began to escalate. The guests had been lolling about the table with its wreaths of ivy and winter lilies, every one of them tipsy and flirtatious among the picked fish bones and oyster shells, barely containing themselves under Madonna Adriana's censorious gaze. One of the Pesarese captains had an arm around a red-haired beauty as he fed her an oyster, and she closed her eyes and swallowed with something between a moan and a giggle. Cesare Borgia lounged with an eager woman on each side, alternating feeding him candied flowers. Another bearded Pesarese soldier had his arm about the back of Madonna Giulia's chair, begging to see her hair down. Madonna Adriana called for the steward to stop serving wine, and as soon as her back was turned, Lord Sforza had plucked a garnishing rosebud off the peacock platter and tossed it into Madonna Lucrezia's lap. And I'd seen her blush and throw him a ripening glance. The Count of Pesaro might have begun the meal full of irritable questions about the French and his papal contract, but he ended it staring at his young wife. He looked and looked again; I'd seen those eyes go soft from clear up in the gallery above, and she had glowed like a saint in a niche: very young and blooming in her dark blue silks.

And now the entire party had more or less contained itself under the sweet winding melodies from the Ferrarese singers, but I saw hands twining together under cover of skirts, lips whispering in ears, and the earthy musk of the truffles and roe I'd prepared seemed stronger than the sweet sounds of the Latin love songs. Lord Sforza touched Lucrezia's elbow, drawing her attention as a new song began, and I saw her catch her breath.

Oh, dear, I thought.

"What are you doing here, anyway?" Leonello looked up at me. "Shouldn't you be scrubbing a pot? Stuffing a chicken? Torturing a scullion?"

"The steward said they were swilling their way through all the wine, so I brought more," I said, hefting the flagon I'd brought with me when I mounted the stairs, as an excuse to catch myself another look. "If you'll excuse me, I forgot something."

Oil of dill, to be precise, for Lord Sforza's cup, because oil of dill would turn any man's guts inside out. And the only thing that would get the Count of Pesaro's eyes off his wife, I judged, would be a good long trip to the privy.

"What?" I put fists on hips, looking down at the withered hand of Santa Marta when I went downstairs and back to my chamber for the vial of dill oil I'd reluctantly set aside on my mistress's orders. Santa Marta's gold ring seemed to glint at me disapprovingly, and I could have sworn one of her curled dried fingers had uncurled slightly to *point* in my direction. "If Madonna Giulia orders me to give a guest a set of griping guts, I have no choice! And she wasn't pleased about it either, so don't blame me."

Santa Marta continued to disapprove, or at least her hand did. How a severed hand could look disapproving, I did not understand. But I snapped the spice box closed on its shelf with a glower and shoved it back behind my comb and the little vial of hair rinse Madonna Giulia had pressed on me. "I don't recall asking you for advice," I told my patron saint, stashing the vial of dill oil in my sleeve. "Or opening your box, for that matter, so just stay out of sight and out of my business!"

"So, did you get a look at him?" the maids all pestered me as I slipped back into the busy kitchens. "Lord Sforza! Is he handsome up close?"

"One swaggering provincial lord looks very much like another." I knotted a fresh apron about my waist with a snap.

"Signorina Carmelina never looks at men," one of the older maids laughed. "Don't you all know that by now? If you can't cook it in a pot or roast it on a spit, she doesn't think it exists!"

They laughed at me good-naturedly as I scowled. Really, that was an excellent reputation to have. Marco had held to his word and kept secret our occasional discreet tumbles after his *primiera* wins—as far as everyone else was concerned, I was the inviolable Madonna of the Kitchens who could never be distracted by a handsome face or a wheedling smile. Being inviolable and unromantic was a *good* thing, at least when it came to the hierarchy of the kitchens.

"Mouths shut, hands moving," I told them, clapping my own hands, and they scattered obediently. *Cena* was done, but we still had hours of labor before us: Marco and the undercooks were already busy with the trays of sweet nibbles that would be sent up as a digestive, and the apprentices and pot-boys had dived into the business of mopping, sweeping, cleaning, and scrubbing. I fished a leftover oyster from the dish and tipped it down my throat, watching Bartolomeo stagger past with an armload of dirty bowls, mopping his freckled brow from the heat of the fires. "Fill an earthenware pot with a good dollop of cream, and beat till it peaks," I said, snagging him by the sleeve as I ate another oyster. I really had surpassed myself on those, if I did say so myself. "We'll send up a dish of milk-snow to go with the *biscotti.*"

"Yes, *signorina.*"

"Ottaviano, supervise the pot-boys; I want those skillets clean and dry *now.* Tommaso, the peacock bones and scraps, get them into the pots and boiling for broth. Bruno, Ugo, the floors—" Scullions dived to and fro under my clapping hands like a general's aides, and I fell in beside Marco, fingers flying as we put together the plates of sugared *biscotti,* the candied nuts, the sliced and honeyed fruits.

"—we all know why the man's really here!" my cousin was arguing with three of his servers as they brought more majolica plates and cups for the trays. "Lord Sforza hasn't dropped in just to check on his papal contract; he means to bed his wife! Four to one he slips into her chamber tonight—"

"I'll lay down twenty *scudi* on those odds," one of the servers replied promptly. "Madonna Adriana's squatting on the pair of them upstairs like a guardian dragon!"

"Dragons can be slain." Marco crushed a handful of candied pine nuts, slapping the fragments into a soft spiced peach. "Love will out, it always does. Bid your twenty *scudi* good-bye."

I'd have to drop a word in Marco's ear later tonight to retract his bet, if I didn't want to see him even more out of purse than usual. *Pazzo,* I thought as I popped a slice of sweet peach into my mouth. *My cousin is a fool.* But I couldn't help my eyes lingering on his broad shoulders, muscles moving under the shirt as he hoisted the first of the heavy trays. And my maids thought I never looked at men.

"*Signorina?*" Bartolomeo called plaintively from the cold room. "Is the cream frothed enough now?" His arm hung dead at his side now, limp as a loose entrail just yanked from a pig.

"Skim the froth off the top, add more fine sugar and rosewater, and beat for the length of time it takes to say a rosary." I dipped a finger into the earthenware pot. Sweet, savory, creamy, but not quite light enough yet in the texture. "Then heap on a plate with sprigs of rosemary. Don't you wilt on me now, boy! You want to be just as strong as Maestro Santini someday?"

Bartolomeo eyed Marco's shoulders too, and began beating at that cream like it was his worst enemy on earth. I smiled, though it occurred to me that milk-snow wasn't such a good idea to serve the guests either. Another dish for lovers—the last time I'd sent milk-snow up to Madonna Giulia and her Pope, most of it had ended up dotted all over the sheets as if the Holy Father had used it to paint his mistress like a canvas. If I saved a bowl, maybe Marco would paint me like a canvas . . .

Never mind. I knew what I was supposed to do here, and it did not involve idle dreams about bed sport.

"Where's Lord Sforza's cup?" I asked Marco, and gave a last tweak to my arrangement of Corinthian raisins and sweet chestnut *frittelle*.

"There." He nodded to the silver goblet set out for the guest of honor. "Have the singers started yet?"

"If they can even be heard over all the giggling and flirting. Half the guests are planning trysts and the other half are drunk."

"Well, let the apprentices bolt off to hear the singers too," Marco said tolerantly as the rest of the sweets were carried out. "If they can find a crack in the doors to listen through."

The apprentices trooped upstairs with cheerful whoops, hushing quickly as they tiptoed past the kitchen doors up the marble steps of the *palazzo* in search of a vantage point for the music. The pot-boys had already finished sweeping up the inevitable scrapings of sugar and drippings of fat that always adorned the floor after a long busy night; the spit-boys were banking the fires; and Marco had disappeared to lock up the wine cellars. No one was paying attention to me, so I reached for the silver cup.

"Carmelina?"

I turned toward the door of the kitchens. Giulia Farnese stood with the train of her apricot silk dress thrown over one arm, tilting her golden head at me. I felt rather than heard the pot-boys behind me staring at her, the spit-boys gaping too at this fabulous golden phoenix so out of place among the mess of pans and bowls and dirty ladles.

"Lord Sforza's cup," the Pope's concubine said to me softly. "I'll take it now."

"Yes, *madonna*." I curtsied, offering the little vial of dill oil I'd been about to empty into the wine. "I know what you're going to say—I saw the mood he's in; I know what I'm supposed to do—"

"Never mind that." She took the heavy silver cup in both hands, smiling. "I think Lucrezia can entertain her husband however she pleases this evening, don't you?"

"But Madonna Adriana," I managed to say. "Won't she . . ."

Giulia looked over the array of goblets. "Which one is hers?"

I pointed. "I saw her upstairs—she'll be watching everyone like a hawk. Especially Lord Sforza."

Giulia took the little vial of oil from my hand and emptied it rather dreamily into the cup. "Maybe not."

I felt a ripple of laughter rising in me like a bubble. Maybe I'd put too much rose-tinted wine in that sauce of truffles and roe, but I couldn't suppress the giggle that burst out of me.

"What did you *feed* them?" my mistress whispered.

"Why does everyone keep saying that?"

"Because by the time the oysters were done, Lucrezia and Lord Sforza were trying to hold hands under the table. Which by that point was the most innocent thing going on under that table!"

I couldn't answer, just spluttered with laughter as she picked up the two cups of wine and tiptoed away again.

"What are you laughing at?" Marco cocked his head at me.

"Nothing. Try this." I popped the very last leftover oyster into his mouth, pressing my fingers to his lips to be sure he got the last tangy drop of sauce, and his eyebrows flew upward as he looked down at me.

"That's . . . good," he said, swallowing.

"I know."

The news soon drifted down that Madonna Adriana was feeling unwell and had retired early for the evening, and after that the rest of the guests seemed disinclined to linger. In fact the party in the *sala* broke up at once in stifled laughter and whispered asides and rustling skirts, and when I put my head around the turn of the stairs again I saw the lady in pale blue already entwined with the man who'd replaced her slipper for her, kissing and fumbling their way upstairs as another couple twined themselves together in the wide doors to the *sala*. Of Lord Sforza and Lucrezia Borgia, I saw no sign at all.

"Good," I said aloud, and went downstairs blithely to shove the last dirty pot into its tub and give an airy wave to the rest of the maids and pot-boys. "Carry on," I bubbled, and went skipping along the back passage. Was that bony Pantisilea entwined with not one but *two* guardsmen in the stairwell?! I sailed into my quiet little chamber that smelled of olive oil and was glad to see that Santa Marta's hand had not come out of its box to chide. In fact, I rather thought she was pleased with me. I gave her a pat and then reached for something else on the shelf behind her box. A lime.

"Maestro Santini?" A harried-looking scullion paused in his

sweeping to answer my question. "He went out for a breath of air and a piss, he said." A snort. "Which is why he stopped by his chamber first for his cloak, his purse, *and* his set of dice."

"Oh." My voice came out rather flat. The scullion looked at me, puzzled, and I made a little motion to keep sweeping. He was one of the last in the kitchens; most of the others were flitting off in giggling pairs to any dark corner they could find. I heard an ecstatic *miaow* from under the trestle table and saw the ragged-eared tomcat ecstatically pumping over the sleek little mouser from the wine cellars. "You too?" I hissed. I'd cooked the whole household into a frenzy of passion, even the damned *cat*, and none of it was for me?

I had some vague thought of going up to the roof for a good sulk and a gulp of night air, something to cool my blood, but I was just trudging up the stairs at the east side of the *palazzo* when I saw the flicker of a taper at the other end of the loggia. "*Shhh*," came a girl's soft giggle. "Not so loud, they'll hear us!" and the taper guttered and nearly went out as a taller darker shape pressed against her, lowering its head to hers. I held my breath, folding back into the shadows, and in another flash the Pope's daughter dashed past in a rustle of silk skirts, her rosy face alight, tugging her husband along behind her by the hand. The Count of Pesaro: twenty-seven years old, tall, dark-haired, sporting a trimmed beard and a fashionable mustache. He had a half-smile of eagerness on his face as he raced after his bride like a boy. They disappeared into Madonna Lucrezia's chamber with another spate of soft laughter, and I heard the door click closed.

My sourness couldn't help but abate a little, and I found myself smiling in the dark. Perhaps I'd creep back down to the kitchens instead of the roof, and make up a posset of hot spiced wine for the newlyweds. Only one cup, because lovers only ever need one cup.

"Are you spying on my sister, girl?"

I yelped, whirling around. Despite the words, I half expected to see Leonello, because he had a way of sliding up noiselessly behind me with his rakish grin just because he knew how much it unsettled me. But the eyes that glittered at me from the deeper shadows were on a level with my own, and Cesare Borgia looked at me with his face like a knife.

"Your Eminence." I curtsied hastily, heart still jumping. He had that frightening guardsman behind him, that Michelotto who had no color and hardly any voice either, and I didn't know which of them scared me more as they appeared from the shadows. "I beg your pardon, Eminence, I did not mean to intrude. Please excuse me—"

"I don't excuse you. Were you spying on my sister?"

"Erm—no. I was—going to get her a hot posset." His eyes made my pulse leap nervously. My eyes had adjusted to the dark; I could see his blade-lean figure in its dark velvets that made him just another shadow leaning up against the wall with folded arms and tumbled hair. "Warm spiced wine."

"I know what a posset is," Cesare Borgia said.

A little silence fell. I wondered if I should retreat to the kitchens, but he hadn't dismissed me, and I felt it wise not to move. It was like facing a coiled serpent as opposed to a snorting bull: Juan Borgia was the bull, and on seeing him you dodged out of sight as quickly as possible. But for the serpent you stayed very still and moved only as directed.

"The bride becomes a wife." He looked at the door where Madonna Lucrezia had tugged her husband. "The Holy Father will not be pleased with me."

Then why . . . ? I thought, but was not fool enough to offer the question. I had no idea why young Cardinal Borgia would bother ruminating to a servant girl—perhaps he felt melancholy, seeing his little sister enter her future as a woman grown. But just because an illustrious prince of the Church deigns to muse aloud in your presence, it does not mean you should ever think your response is required.

His eyes found me again, though, as though he had heard my silent question. "I find it difficult to deny my sister anything," he said. "Sforza is an ass, but if she wants him, she shall have him." A gleam of teeth as he smiled. "Of course, if I find he did not treat her gently tonight, I shall cut his throat."

I couldn't really think of anything to say to that. "The Holy Father will blame Madonna Giulia," I found myself saying instead. "He charged her with keeping everything proper tonight."

"You are fond of Madonna Giulia?" His eyes returned to me, idle.

"Yes."

"She'll bat her eyes at him. He'll forgive her." Cesare clearly had no interest in Giulia Farnese, and I remembered her remarking that he might be handsome, but he was cold as a corpse. "If the Holy Father had tasted the oysters and the peacock tonight, he'd know she didn't have a chance in the world of keeping anything proper."

I felt pride expand through me, a warm bubble. "*My* oysters and peacock," I couldn't help saying. "Perhaps the Holy Father should blame me, Your Eminence."

"You are the cook?"

"Yes." Normally I would have cast my eyes down, given the credit to Marco. But Cesare Borgia's eyes had a way of hooking the truth out of you.

He stepped forward, still just a shadow. His eyes went over me coolly, and I hoped he could not see the pulse fluttering madly at the base of my throat.

"The cook," he said, thoughtful. "Well. You're not ill-looking. And it seems fair that if you rouse blood, you should have the burden of quenching it."

"Madonna Lucrezia's posset," I managed to say, dry-mouthed.

His fingers linked around my wrist, overlapping like a steel cuff. "Forget the posset."

He did not ask my name when he dismissed that frightening guard of his and took me to the nearest chamber. I doubted he cared to know my name, and in truth I didn't care if he knew it either. The room had one guttering taper, there was a mahogany table inlaid with gold, and there were two bodies moving together toward it and no need for names.

He swept the table clear with one violent motion and had me up on it before I had even heard the crash of something fragile and costly against the floor. There was no passion in his mouth when he claimed mine, just cool curiosity as he tasted me, and I tasted him back as though he were a new sauce coating a spoon. I could taste the sharp sea tang of oysters, the heady musk of the truffles, the roe and the sparkling wine and the sugared flowers, and his lean body was hard against mine. I spent my days sweating over hot stoves and reaching into hot ovens, and I still felt so cold: the inviolable Madonna of the Kitchens who cared for nothing but work. Even when Marco reached for me, it was the win of a card game or the jingle of a lucky bet that put the fire in his loins, not me.

I was tired of being cold.

Cesare Borgia cupped the smooth skin at the point of my bare shoulder where my sleeve had already slid down, and my blood bubbled through my veins like hot wine. I closed my eyes, burying my nose in the dent at his collarbone, tangling my hands through his hair. His mouth trailed down to my breast and lingered there, teeth grazing my skin as his hand found my bare knee under my hem. He skimmed along the naked length of my thigh as he tossed my skirts out of the way; I pushed the doublet off his lean shoulders, and he seized my wrists, laying me back on the table. He spread my arms out straight, nailing them to the table with his full weight as he loomed over me. "Look at me," he ordered, but I was already looking at him. Why wouldn't I? The Pope's son was a thing of beauty, amber-skinned in the light of the taper, his eyes like pitch.

"Odd," he said. "Mostly they won't look at me. I frighten them."

I curled my legs up around his waist, locking him against me. "Because you're the Devil, Your Eminence?"

"Yes." He still leaned his weight on my wrists, hurting them. "I *should* frighten you."

"You don't." Lie, lie, lie—I was remembering the dagger with the sapphire in its hilt, the dagger and where it had been found and all the whispers through Rome about who might have used it. A week or a day or an hour ago I'd found the thought utterly ridiculous, those whispers about a Pope's son murdering a tavern girl in his idle hours. Now his eyes were burning into me, and maybe I did find them frightening—but I still wanted to look at him.

He gazed back, quite expressionless. His fingers tightened in an abrupt, violent squeeze, steel bands cutting my hands off, and I cried out in sudden pain.

Then he began.

Leonello

Passion can fill a house like smoke. I felt it every time the Pope came through the passage to visit his pearl: the glance he'd give her over the *cena* dishes as he talked with Adriana da Mila and little Lucrezia, a glance so heavy with meaning that Giulia's lashes dropped under the weight of it; the way his thumb caressed the inside of her wrist as he took her arm to escort her from the room, as though the lovemaking had already begun; the swift, teasing smile she'd give him as the door of her chamber swung shut. Later you might hear small sounds coming from under those bolted doors—a soft cry of passion or the low bubble of laughter, and those sounds seemed to drift through the *palazzo* like fire along the nerves. Those were the nights Lucrezia turned snappish and yearning, the nights Madonna Adriana tapped her foot to some unseen music and looked dreamy, as though reliving some memory from a time when she was young, heedless, and not at all concerned with how many ducats she had spent or saved that day. Those were the nights the maids giggled and flirted with the guardsmen; the nights when the solitary men took themselves in hand with a groan for the penances the priest would make them do in atonement.

But I'd never seen passion fill a house like this.

Lucrezia Borgia's kindling was a sweeter, softer thing, a candle flame rather than the heady firestorm the Pope and his Venus could ignite through the *palazzo*, but no less insidious for all that. Giddy, happy, laughing love—it expanded outward from her, truffle-scented and oyster-fueled, a river like sparkling wine that intoxicated first her husband and then the guests, then the whole house.

"Leonello!" My mistress smiled as she opened the door of her chamber in answer to my knock. La Bella's hair was still piled high in the intricate coils and braids she'd worn to entertain the Count of Pesaro and his entourage, but she'd discarded her tight-laced gown for a loose fur-lined Neapolitan robe, all the fashion since the recent alliance with Naples. "It's late," my mistress continued. "I dismissed you an hour ago—why haven't you gone to bed?"

Because if I went to bed now I'd lie restless under the perfume of the passion little Lucrezia and her husband were spreading through the house, the passion that had already overcome a half-dozen other shadowy pairs of lovers I'd seen entwined behind pillars and flitting into shadowed places in the garden. Everyone was in love tonight, everyone but me, and if I went to bed I'd fall asleep to uneasy dreams of women staked to tables and black-clad men hovering over me in smiling masks.

But I did not want to think of such things, so I gave my mistress a light shrug. "I could ask you the same question," I returned. "Why haven't *you* gone to bed, Madonna Giulia?"

"I was tending my dear mother-in-law," she said, a bit too wide-eyed and innocent. "Her guts are griping, poor thing. It came on very suddenly."

I snorted.

"And once I settled her, well, I found I couldn't sleep either." Giulia fiddled with her sleeve, tucked a stray hair behind one ear, nibbled on a thumbnail. "I miss His Holiness."

Perhaps I wasn't the only one in the *palazzo* confined to a restless, empty bed tonight. "Why did you do it?" I couldn't help asking. "Disobey the Pope just to aid Lucrezia?"

"Over the table tonight, she looked so . . ." Giulia's little face lapsed from its usual dancing merriment to a somber sadness. She'd been very quiet that night at the table, folding herself deliberately into the background to let Lucrezia blossom. "She looked so hopeful. Full of love, I suppose. I think I looked like that too, when I married Orsino, but it didn't end so well for me. Hopefully it will for Lucrezia—but either way, she deserves the chance. She *is* married, after all—it's no sin to keep her from her husband, if they both want each other . . ."

My mistress sounded as though she were already marshaling her arguments for future storms. "I believe you are braver than you think, Madonna Giulia."

"I think so too," she said, smiling again. "I'm quite delighted with myself, really. I shall try to hang on to the feeling later, when Rodrigo is storming at me and threatening excommunication." She couldn't resist a shiver at the thought, whether of excommunication or her Pope's anger, but then she brushed both aside. "Come into my *sala* a moment, Leonello—you aren't too tired? You don't look sleepy."

"I'd meant to find a book," I lied. What I hoped to do, once my mistress was safely tucked away for the night, was take myself downstairs and find a girl. A maidservant in the kitchens who hadn't yet sneaked off with some other lover, or even that long-legged sharp-tongued Venetian cook if I could get her not to hate me for an hour or two. Some girl, anyway, willing to share a flask of wine with me and perhaps something more. No one thinks a dwarf can get a woman without paying her, but if I wanted a woman I could usually find one. It wasn't passion that brought them to my bed; it was curiosity—but that could be as strong a force as passion, in my experience. Women looked at me and they couldn't help wondering how a dwarf played a man's role between the sheets. They wanted to know if I looked as odd without my doublet as I did with it. Besides, I was small and amusing and made them laugh, so where was the harm?

And as long as I left before morning, when laughter and curiosity turned to acute embarrassment—as long as we pretended it had never happened—we might have a good time of it.

"You might as well come in for a moment, since we're both awake." Madonna Giulia gave me a pleased look. "I've a present for you, and you may as well have it now."

"A present?" I blinked, following her into the warmth of her private *sala*. Two more of her maids waited up for her, one dozing on the wall bench where her mistress's night shift had been laid out in preparation for bed, the other yawning as she stirred up the brazier. They looked up with sleepy starts of surprise, but Madonna Giulia waved them back as they started to rise. "Take your ease," she scolded. "I can unpin my own hair!"

First, however, she padded to a wall bench where a bundle sat wrapped in the immaculate linen that usually shrouded her new gowns when they came from the robe makers. "I'd meant to have this for you sooner," she said, putting the bundle into my arms. "But the boots took longer than expected."

"Boots?" I said, startled.

"Your new livery." She gave me a little push toward a dressing screen at the other end of the *sala*, lushly painted with scenes from the Rape of the Sabines. The most beautiful of the Sabine women, as was common in this room which had been so lavishly painted and decorated specially for the Pope's mistress, looked like Giulia. "Try it all on, I can't wait to see how it came out."

Self-consciously I retreated behind the screen, untying the linen wrappings. *If she put me in some motley suit or belled cap* . . . On the other side of the screen I could hear her chattering to the maids, asking one how her lamed mother was faring, listening to the second confess her hopes of marriage to one of the Borgia guards. "I'll speak to Madonna Adriana about him; I'm sure we can manage something. Is he handsome?"

I swallowed as I edged around the screen again. My mouth had gone dry, and I couldn't stop looking down at myself. Madonna Giulia turned midchatter to look at me, the maids following her eyes, and I suddenly found my stomach fluttering. *Don't laugh*, I thought wretchedly. *Please don't laugh.* I had not been laughed at in so very long—I might still be a dwarf but I was respected in this household, my skills feared and whispered of, and if any guardsman or rude maidservant japed at me, I had the right to cut them down with my viper tongue with no fear of punishment because I was more valued here than they. No one had japed at me in so long. If La Bella looked down at me from the height of her beauty and gave one of her merry laughs—

She did laugh—she laughed and clapped her hands. "*Dio,*" she said softly, the sheer honest delight in her eyes stopping the sick swoop in my stomach, "Messer Leonello, I *knew* you were a handsome man!"

"Hardly." I found my tongue again somehow as I looked down at myself. "Velvet feathers do not turn a lame bird into a peacock."

"Hush." She prowled around me consideringly. "Let me adjust those ties for you at the shoulder—girls, hold up my glass!"

The two maids brought the mirror over, tilting it down at an angle so I could see, and I swallowed at the sight of my own reflection. The livery Madonna Giulia Farnese had chosen for me was stark unadorned black velvet, a severely plain doublet tailored like a glove to the contours of my odd torso. The tabs at the armholes were cunningly tailored, extending my silhouette to make my shoulders look broader, my head less oversized. The shirt was crisp snowy white, just a thread of black-work embroidery at the wrists—"No lace," Giulia said behind me. "I did promise. And see, there are *two* sheaths sewn inside each cuff for those little wrist knives of yours." I had warm black hose that fit my stunted legs without bunching, black boots to the knee, a belt of supple black leather with several more stitched sheaths for my Toledo blades. The household emblem of the Borgia bull and the papal keys was confined to a discreet badge on one sleeve.

"The boots were the hardest," Madonna Giulia said, retying the laces of my sleeves so that just a touch of the shirt's blinding white showed at my shoulder. "I had the boot maker copy them from your old pair, with a few improvements. The soles are reinforced with extra support under the arches, and there are struts to stiffen the inner seam up to your knee."

My feet, I could already feel, would have to walk a good many hours before they began to hurt in these supple boots.

"There, test the arm—too binding? I know you'll want full range of motion through the shoulder if you're to throw your knives." Madonna Giulia stepped back, nodding as I swung my arm. "I've had four doublets made for you. This black velvet for lavish occasions, a good stout black linen for everyday summer wear, black wool for everyday winter—and a black leather for travel, or times you want more protection. I remember you saying sturdy leather is a good ward against a blade."

My eyes stung, blurring the image in the mirror. That image showed a cool shadow of a man, stark and unsmiling, somber and dangerous, eyes shifting from their undistinguished hazel to a startling green when contrasted against so much black. I looked—I looked— *Dio.* " 'Handsome' seems a stretch of the truth," I managed to say.

"I don't think so." Giulia tilted her head in the mirror. "Your father must have been a good-looking fellow, I think."

"No, not really." My father had been far too worn and frayed about the edges, too battered by life for good looks.

"Your mother then—did she give you that dark hair?"

"I don't know. I never met her."

"I'm sorry." Giulia's voice was instantly contrite. "God rest her soul."

"She didn't die. She might live yet, for all I know." There were gloves to go with the rest of my outfit; softest leather embroidered again with the bull and keys. "My mother was a whore, you see, and normally she wouldn't know which of her clients put the baby in her belly. But by the time I was a few months old, she could see it must have been the dwarf, the one who juggled apples and walnuts in the mountebank show in the Borgo. He paid her double, see, to look past his deformities and give him the occasional tumble . . . She left the freakish baby with its freak father, and then she left altogether."

There was a little silence. I didn't meet my mistress's eyes in the mirror, just pulled on my new gloves one by one. They fit perfectly, sewn to configure with the odd tridentlike setting of my stubby fingers.

"Your father must have been a kind man," Giulia Farnese said at last, quietly.

"Why do you say that, *madonna*?"

"Because you have too much kindness to have been raised entirely without it, Leonello."

I gave a bark of laughter, flexing my fingers in the new gloves. Such soft leather; it wouldn't stiffen my fingers when I needed them nimble on a knife hilt. "No one has ever called me kind before, Madonna Giulia, but thank you. And yes, my father was a kind man."

Too kind for this world, really. I remember his eyes, worn blue unlike mine, sad and anxious under the belled cap he wore for performing. He drank too much, I suppose, and it made him drop his walnuts and balls when he juggled, but people laughed all the harder so it didn't matter. And he never raised a hand to me, even when he drank. He'd been the one to insist on schooling for me, though he could hardly manage to pay for it and I was an ungrateful little bastard who didn't want to go in the first place. "They'll torment me," I'd protested. "The other boys!"

"Boys will torment you anywhere you go," my father said, dragging me along. "And that brain of yours is too clever to waste, Leonello. You could be a tutor someday, or a clerk!"

I wondered if he would be proud of me today. On the whole, I thought not.

Madonna Giulia had dismissed the two maids—"Go see to Madonna Adriana, will you? Tend her if her guts are still grumbling." The door clicked behind them, and she knelt on the fine woven carpet, her furred gown pooling around her as she sorted through the discarded pile of my old clothes in search of my Toledo blades in their hidden sheaths. "Where is your father now?" she murmured, and began passing me the finger knives one by one.

"Dead." I slipped the shortest blade into its new home at my wrist cuff. "Some fifteen years dead."

"What happened?"

"What happens to many of us." I pushed another knife into its place in my new boot top. "Three drunks at a wine shop. They thought it amusing to kick him about . . . one of them must have kicked too hard. He was spitting blood from inside by the time I returned from my lessons."

"Did you ever find them? The men who . . ."

"I vowed to find them, certainly. Find them and wreak bloody vengeance, oh yes. But how could I find them when all I had for a clue was 'three drunks'? Not that it stopped me from trying." I stretched my lips in a smile. "I was a stupid boy." Silence stretched between us, then, and I did not want to look at Madonna Giulia. *If you say you are sorry for me, I will choke you*, I thought. *Wrap these new-gloved hands around your pretty throat and squeeze every drop of pity out of you.*

But La Bella didn't say anything. She only looked at me, still on her knees beside my pile of clothing so she had to tilt her head back at me as though I were a man of normal height. Her big dark eyes brimmed silence, looking not only at but through me as she passed me the last of my blades, and I still wanted to choke her. I wanted to be cruel, call her a brainless whore and make her weep. *How dare you understand me. How dare you wheedle my secrets out of me.* But wasn't that what the best whores did, the ones who understood men to the tips of their intuitive fingers? The best whores weren't brainless at all, and neither was she.

I swallowed my cruelty, settling my last dagger into its tab on my new belt, and looked into the mirror the maids had left propped up before me. I saw a dark man, a dangerous man, even a handsome man. A man at whom larger men would laugh at their peril.

"Better take the mirror away," I said. "I'm in danger of growing as vain as you, Madonna Giulia."

"I pray I have not offended you, Messer Leonello," she said quietly.

"On the contrary, my dear lady." I turned and gave a faultless, empty bow over her hand. "Thank you."

CHAPTER TWELVE

✦

Thankless and perfidious Giulia!

—EXCERPT OF A LETTER FROM RODRIGO
BORGIA TO GIULIA FARNESE

Giulia

I t was always a bad sign when Rodrigo lost his temper without dropping the papal *We.*

"All Christendom bows before Us, and We can't command obedi-
ence from one witless harlot?" he roared. "As if the French aren't enough
trouble!"

"I am sorry as always if I have offended Your Holiness," I murmured,
looking down at my folded hands.

"*Offended Us?*" he shouted, storming up and down as though the
rage were too great to be contained by stillness. "*You foolish, feckless,
half-witted girl, you've destroyed everything!*"

I hadn't waited this time for Madonna Adriana or some other
helpful informant to tell my Pope that his daughter and her husband
had consummated their marriage. I had gone direct from bidding
Lord Sforza good-bye, watching him give Lucrezia's hand a squeeze from
the height of his horse as she unashamedly held her face up in the courtyard for a farewell kiss, and sat down to write Rodrigo myself. And when

I had the news he had returned to Rome a week later, I oiled and scented every inch of my skin, looped my throat with the huge teardrop pearl that had been his first gift, laced myself into my new lavender silk with the silver brocade insets, left my hair loose and rolling to my feet the way he liked it, and waited. By the time His Holiness Pope Alexander VI came storming into my *sala* at the Palazzo Santa Maria, his face was so dark with fury against his white robes that he could have been a Moor. My maids were fleeing for the door before the first furious Spanish roars erupted all over me like a fountain of scalding hot water.

"Lucrezia is a woman grown," I said when my Pope paused for breath. "Old enough to take up her duties as a wife. As you yourself wrote, signed, and had witnessed in her marriage contract."

"Don't play notary, Giulia Farnese," he snapped, still pacing the length of my *sala*. One of the maids had dropped the shift she was mending as she fled the room; he kicked it furiously out of the way. "You knew Our wishes in the matter. She was to remain virgin, and that Sforza lout was to keep his hands off!"

"I thought of Your Holiness's alliance with the Sforza and Milan." I kept my tone to a submissive murmur; soothing, caressing. "Lord Sforza had begun to believe you meant to cast him off—"

"We were damned well considering it! Count of Pesaro, hah. He's a failed *condottiere* and a provincial puppet, and he thinks he's worthy of a pope's daughter?" Rodrigo's papal ring flashed as he drove one fist against his other palm. "I bought a royal match each for Juan and Joffre; Lucrezia deserves no less!"

". . . So Your Holiness *does* mean to annul the marriage?"

"We can hardly do so now," he snarled at me. "Not with the marriage consummated! You air-brained fool, meddling in Our politics—"

"Cesare was there as well," I couldn't help pointing out, trying not to sound exasperated. "He knew your wishes when it came to Lucrezia's marriage. Why aren't you shouting at *him* for not stopping Lord Sforza?" Really, men. Lucrezia's duenna and her big brother at hand to watch over her, and her misbehavior was still all *my* fault? I ask you.

"Cesare will always take Lucrezia's side over Ours," Rodrigo snapped. "We thought We could at least count on you to follow Our wishes!"

He went ranting at me again, and I cast my lashes down. A touch of the penitent wouldn't hurt: a repentant Magdalene ready to kneel at his feet and press her lips to the papal shoes.

"Lucrezia is happy, Your Holiness," I ventured as soon as he stopped for a wrathful breath. "So happy. Lord Sforza pleases her, and she pleases him."

"It is not her business to be happy! She is Our daughter; she will do as she is told!"

"Always." I cast a glance up through my lashes. "But surely His Holiness is pleased to see her so content in the marriage *you* made for her?"

Not just content, but glowing. Lucrezia had flung ecstatic arms about me the moment the Sforza entourage left the courtyard in its important clatter of hooves. "Thank you," she had whispered. "I can bear it now, if he has to be gone for a time. I'm not *useless* anymore!" She had spent the past weeks humming all over the *palazzo*, stitching with great wifely industry on an embroidered shirt that she meant to give her husband on his next visit. "Husbands like presents from their wife's own hands," she told me with a sage nod, and I'd been careful not to smile.

Lucrezia's father was not smiling either. His dusky face darkened even further, and his eyes narrowed to folds at the corners in a way that prickled me.

"You are Our concubine, Giulia Farnese." His voice dropped from its bull roar to a cold levy of sentence. "Not Our councilor, not Our ambassador, not Our adviser. And certainly not the mother of Our daughter Lucrezia. Or of any other child of Ours."

That stabbed me. Tears pricked my eyes, but I bit fiercely on the inside of my cheek. I would *not* cry before him; I would *not*.

"I am none of those things, Your Holiness," I managed to say, looking up at him with a steady gaze. "Unlike your ambassadors and your councilors and your advisers, I care only for your happiness. Your happiness, and that of your family."

"That is precious little consolation." He clipped off the words. "You disappoint me, Giulia."

At least I disappointed *him*, not Us. "It pains me to think so." I stretched out a hand, touching the back of his knuckles, but he brushed me aside.

"I have a great deal of business to attend to." Turning away. "Do not look for me tonight."

I was *not* going to stand by for a fortnight this time, waiting and hoping for him to get over his temper as I had when we quarreled over Laura and Orsino. I caught hold of his embroidered sleeve, halting him. "Surely it is part of the Holy Father's duties to punish transgressors?"

"Yes." Impatiently, he shook at my grip.

"Then punish me." I sank to my knees before him, allowing my skirts to pool around me. "I am in error, Your Holiness, and I require penance. Punish me for my wrongdoing."

He stopped, looking down at me. I released his sleeve and bowed my head until my hair flooded forward over his feet: a penitent Magdalene in truth, kneeling at the feet of Christ. All the Magdalenes ever depicted in paint have wonderful hair, don't they? Penitence just doesn't look as picturesque without a good flood of hair. "Forgive me, Father," I whispered. "For I have sinned."

He was silent. But he did not move either, and I reached slowly, oh so slowly, for his hand. I brought it to my lips, allowing my breath to whisper across his fingertips, and kissed his ring. "Punish me," I whispered, and through my veil of hair I cast him a slow, burning glance.

His hand descended on my head, the papal benediction I had seen him bestow hundreds of times. But his hand wound through my hair, jerking me to my feet with a painful yank. "You deserve it," he whispered.

"I do," I whispered back, and kissed him with my teeth. He caught me up in an embrace so hard it hurt, tossing me down on the satin-covered daybed, and so much for my new lavender gown with the silver brocade insets because it came off me with a great rip of expensive silk.

I wrapped my arms around him, my knees, and I gasped quietly as his mouth left rough marks on my shoulders.

"Minx," he muttered with an angry, unwilling chuff of laughter against my breast. "Meddling minx—"

"Then punish me for my meddling," I whispered, setting my teeth into the lobe of his ear, raking his back with my nails, and he filled me with a groan that was half need and half fury.

"Goodness," I said afterward, curling against him. "I should anger you more often, Your Holiness." He had bent his head to my breasts and used his teeth until I cried out, not precisely from pain. My skin still tingled. "I do believe I like your kind of punishment."

He gave a *hmph* at that, a glint still showing dangerous in his eye, but he pulled my head down against his shoulder. "You're more trouble than you're worth, Giulia Farnese."

"Then I shall endeavor to give you more for your trouble."

"More?" He cocked a heavy dark brow. "More what?"

"I don't know," I said demurely. "I shall have to put my mind to it."

He laughed again, his old laugh with its thread of amusement at the world's follies. "My Lucrezia," he asked, "is she truly so happy?"

"She is."

"She's Sforza's wife," he grumbled, "but she is my daughter first!"

"She'll always be your daughter first. She loves you. But she will come to love her husband, too—you will have to share her."

"I don't like to share, *mi perla*. You should know that." He tweaked my breast, more fiercely than usual, but my heart warmed. Lucrezia was happy, and I was still her father's pearl. As long as I was that, all was forgiven.

But was it?

M y father seems irritable," Lucrezia complained after the year turned. "Do you think he's irritable?"

"This business with the French has him worried," I said lightly.

"Oh, the French." Lucrezia dismissed the French with a toss of her head, holding up the shirt she was still embroidering for her lord of Pesaro. It would be done long before he came to collect it; he was still with his soldiers, scrambling to assemble their pay. At least he found time to write to his wife now. Lucrezia was forever rhapsodizing over the letters, reading bits aloud so I could marvel at her lord's perspicacity, his turn of phrase, his unsophisticated bluntness that was really so much more pleasing than the polished empty compliments of courtiers. "I don't *want* the French to invade. Giovanni will never be able to take me back to Pesaro if he has to fight instead!"

"Perhaps it won't come to that." Though most of us knew it would. Old King Ferrente of Naples had died, mourned by no one—he had a nasty habit of keeping his enemies in cages and strolling among them like exhibits at a menagerie, or so I heard, which was not precisely a reassuring habit in a king. But mourned or not, he was gone and his throne vacant; my Pope had passed a few weeks in restless indecision and then bestowed the Neapolitan crown not on the French king but on King Ferrente's son. France, we heard, was Not Pleased.

Still, I did not think it the only reason His Holiness was so irked lately. Or perhaps *irked* was not the word.

Distant? Well, no. Not with Lucrezia; he could never manage to stay angry with her for long. Not with Cesare, who brushed off his father's displeasure and went on filling his duties as the Pope's clerical deputy with panache. Not with Juan, who had begun sending petulant letters from Spain about when he would be allowed home; not to little Joffre . . .

Maybe just distant to me.

"If I can't go to Pesaro yet, then I wish Father would let me go to Joffre's wedding," Lucrezia fretted, yanking on her tangled embroidery thread. "Everyone will be there!" My Pope was to crown the new King of Naples in the Castel Nuovo, and in case the Neapolitans had any ideas about backing away from the papal alliance once they had what they wanted, the wedding of the Pope's son to the new King's bastard daughter was to commence immediately afterward.

"Your father doesn't want you traveling as far as Naples."

"You're going, *and* Madonna Adriana." Lucrezia pouted briefly.

"I'll tell you every last detail about Sancha of Aragon and the other Neapolitan ladies," I promised. "They'll know they have an impossible task ahead of them if they try to put the two of us in the shade."

Lucrezia's pout disappeared in a flash of dimples. "Well, even if Sancha is a beauty, her wedding can't possibly be as lovely as mine."

It wasn't.

Can it possibly be me?" I complained to Leonello. "Am I an utter blight on all weddings? Mine was farcical, Lucrezia's was exhausting, and this one is just dismal."

"It does seem to have begun under a cloud," my bodyguard agreed. From the hour my Pope had sent me ahead to Naples with the rest of the entourage, it had poured sheets of rain. Four days and nights traveling, locked in a coach with Leonello and Madonna Adriana and that fussy little German master of ceremonies named Burchard who had been sent to coach the Neapolitans on every nuance of the complicated dual coronation-and-wedding ceremonies. Burchard spent four days moaning that the new King of Naples would be sure to drop the crucifix during the oath or wear the wrong cap with his crown, and Leonello amused himself first by baiting Madonna Adriana until even she lost her placid temper, and then by torturing Burchard by helpfully pointing out all the possible disasters Burchard hadn't yet thought of. By the time we reached the Castel Nuovo in Naples, I was damp, sneezing, and ready to throttle them all. I'd looked forward to seeing the beauties of Naples— the famous shrines, the bustling harbor, the looming Castel Nuovo with its twin turrets linked by a white marble triumphal arch. But the city was still shrouded in gloom; the flowers in the niches of all those famous shrines had been sodden into gummy piles of stems, and the white marble arch was lost in the mist over my head as our coach rolled muddily into the Castel Nuovo on the fifth day. My Pope, when he arrived, had no time for me in the tense chaos of the approaching alliance against France; the coronation was endless; I could hardly understand the heavy

Neapolitan dialect; and poor Burchard was moaning "*Gott im Himmel*" more or less without pause and looking ready to collapse.

He wasn't the only one. By the time the wedding approached on leaden wings, my nose was huge and red and running. Even before the Bishop made us stand about outside in the rain while he droned a blessing and sprinkled us with holy water—as if there weren't enough water already!—I was sneezing more or less constantly into my brocade sleeve. *Giulia la Bella*, I thought morosely as the wedding guests trailed muddy-hemmed and determinedly cheerful into the barren chapel of the Castel Nuovo. I didn't feel at all like the Venus of the Vatican today. I felt damp, draggled, spotty, and sniveling; not at all at my best in a rose-pink dress whose hem I had *not* been able to keep out of the mud. And it was a morning I would have liked to shine, because Sancha of Aragon was undeniably a beauty.

She was also, unless I was very much mistaken, trouble. A dark-haired, olive-skinned, blue-eyed little thing of sixteen, buxom and sashaying in a blue brocade gown, and even the roar of the rain outside couldn't dampen the bright glances she was casting all through the chapel. She dimpled at the Bishop; she dropped her lashes at Cesare, who stood saturnine and silent in his cardinal reds; she flashed her pearly teeth at my Pope, who looked amused. She didn't have a glance for poor little Joffre, kneeling at her side before the altar on a golden cushion, pop-eyed and sincere and a good head shorter than she was. A well-behaved boy of twelve years old, good-looking enough with his auburn hair and doublet of slashed velvet, but he looked nervous and twitchy beside his self-possessed bride—beside his brothers and sister too, truth be told. Joffre somehow looked like he'd been made up out of all the leftover bits after inscrutable Cesare and swaggering Juan and charming Lucrezia were finished. Rodrigo wasn't as fond of Joffre as he was of the others—I remembered what he'd once said, that Joffre perhaps wasn't of his getting at all. As if it were Joffre's fault that snippy, long-nosed Vannozza dei Cattanei had a wandering eye!

"Poor Joffre," I couldn't help murmuring, and sneezed into my sleeve.

"Yes," Madonna Adriana agreed unexpectedly at my side, keeping her voice low. "That's a little harlot if I ever saw one. Let's hope the help she brings from Naples against the French is worth it."

Sancha of Aragon cast another sparkling glance up at my Pope as her new title of Princess of Squillace was read out, and bent her head ceremonially to kiss Rodrigo's shoe. "Leonello," I whispered to my bodyguard as he craned for a look at the bridal breasts. "No ogling!"

"Tell that to your Pope." Leonello gave me a grin of pure mockery, eyes bright as glass and just as hard. Leonello had been cooler in my company these past months, sharper-tongued and a little remote. I knew well enough why—he didn't like the moment of confession he'd let slip when I gave him his new doublet. I hadn't been fool enough to pity him for the past he'd recounted, but he still resented me. Somehow the secrets he'd let slip were all *my* doing, but wasn't that always the way of it? Men erred, or thought they erred, and it was always a woman's fault.

Sancha of Aragon gave a little flounce of her skirts and a few other things as she settled herself again on her golden cushion. The Pope certainly did seem to be appreciating the Neapolitan breasts on such generous display before him! Not just Sancha but all her ladies, and the Roman ladies too were beginning to preen. I gave another forlorn sniffle, wishing the rain hadn't damped my eyes to watery slits and my kerchief into a sodden ball. By the time the oaths had been recited, the ceremonial sword lowered over the heads of the bride and her little husband, and the guests escorted out of the chapel by spiral staircase into the *sala* above, I would have traded all the pearls in my hair and around my neck for a chance to collapse in a quiet bed and die, or at least let myself dribble and molder unseen. But the Pope's concubine must be poised and beautiful and sprightly whenever in the public eye, so I gave a valiant sniff of my running nose and bestowed a kiss on Joffre as he descended with his new wife.

He and Sancha trod a graceful *pavane* after the lengthy banquet, Joffre squiring her solemn-faced through the complex passes even though he wasn't tall enough to lift her in the turns of *la volta* that followed. Cesare Borgia came down to partner his new sister for that, her ladies descending like a swirl of bright blossoms to join them.

"You won't join in, Giulia?" Rodrigo asked me where I sat nestled in a lake of my own skirts on a stool at his side. "I do like to watch you dance."

I knew I should try, but I was getting a touch light-headed as well as runny-nosed, and all in all it would be better if the Pope's mistress didn't fall over in front of the whole Neapolitan court like a drunken milkmaid at a harvest dance. "I fear I'm not up to it, Your Holiness," I said in apology, and gave the best smile I had. But the best I had wasn't much under watery eyes and a nose red as a pomegranate. Rodrigo looked impatient for a moment—the man who was never ill and never short of energy!—and turned with a shrug to watch the ladies dip and twirl. And I saw how his eyes tracked the buxom figure of Sancha of Aragon, then the slimmer fair-haired figure of goose-necked Caterina Gonzaga, then a pair of dark Neapolitan beauties who giggled and fluttered like peahens in the papal presence . . . then back to Caterina: wife of Count Ottaviano da Montevegio and a noted beauty of the papal court. Pale, beautiful, taller than me and nearly as blond—carrying on like an empress, and giving herself as many airs as the bride. Caterina Gonzaga dipped her head for Rodrigo's gaze, spinning gracefully to show a flash of ankle, and he grinned.

I felt suddenly cold. Nearly two years now I had kept my Pope's love. Oh, I wasn't fool enough to think he was entirely faithful to me. Lusty men like that are never faithful, are they? My mother always said that a straying husband could always be endured with a little extra prayer and a great deal of patience. Although I doubt she had a pope in mind when she recited that particular homily . . . In any case, I knew better than to fuss when Rodrigo strayed now and then with some courtesan at a private party, or some eager beauty who came to his bed on the nights I was indisposed with my monthly courses. But however his flesh sometimes wandered, his eyes never did—his eyes were full of me alone. A year ago he'd have applauded only for me in the dancing, then pulled me onto his knee afterward and whispered that there was no woman in Naples who could match me. A year ago he would not have been watching Caterina Gonzaga incline her queenly head under his hunter's eye as he politicked with the Neapolitan King and only gave me an absent token smile.

But a year ago I had not yet given him the child he wasn't sure was his—had not defied him openly in the matter of his daughter's marriage—didn't have a red nose and squinchy little eyes . . . I sneezed helplessly into my sleeve again.

"Our Holy Father appears to be enjoying himself," Leonello observed at my side. I cast him a sharp look and his hazel eyes met mine, penetrating as any of his knives, slicing through to the thoughts I was trying to hide.

"Yes, very much," I said brightly. "And you, Leonello? Are you enjoying yourself?"

"Tolerably. No one has yet asked me to juggle anything."

"They wouldn't dare," I couldn't resist saying. "Not the way you look in your new livery."

He slanted me an irked glance, and I resisted the urge to tell him he should be proud and not irritated. From the embittered son of a harlot and a failed juggler to this cool, hard, handsome little presence in the heart of the papal entourage! But I held my tongue. Whether tall or short, men don't like getting advice, do they?

Was that how I'd lost Rodrigo? a little voice in my head wondered. *Telling him I knew better in the matter of Lucrezia's marriage?*

I hadn't lost Rodrigo. I couldn't have. Just because his eye was wandering a little tonight—well, why *shouldn't* it wander? I was hardly an appetizing distraction with my runny nose and watery eyes. Certainly no match for queenly Caterina Gonzaga. Why did she have to be not just taller than me but slimmer? *She* didn't look like she had to swear off sweets and cheese and wine just to get into her dresses. Oh, I couldn't bear these effortlessly wand-slim women! Just wait till *she* bore a child or two; then we'd see if she was still inviting Cesare to measure her waist with his hands and casting regal glances over her shoulder to make sure Rodrigo was watching! I sneezed four times in a row, groping blindly for a kerchief. *Ugh, why can't I just die?* I thought, and chewed morosely on a morsel of Ligurian cheese. I always eat when I'm sick.

More dancing, more music, more of the bawdy jokes that always cropped up at wedding celebrations, especially as the bedding drew closer. I didn't imagine it would be much of a bedding—Joffre was trying to look lordly, but he flushed redder with every shouted jest, and he looked so very, very young. "Madonna Giulia," he muttered, retreating from his father's lewd grin and casual muss of the hair. "What if I don't know what to do?"

I mopped my nose, looking at my lover's youngest son. I didn't know Joffre as I did Lucrezia. Rodrigo never had any time for him, but he had supplied an army of tutors to groom his youngest son for his future role as Borgia princeling and papal pawn, and so Joffre rarely crossed my path in the *palazzo*. But he'd always been a nice little fellow, trailing after Lucrezia and occasionally playing games with my pet goat, and the brown eyes now wide with pleading couldn't help but touch me. "What do I do?" he whispered again.

"Give her a kiss and tell her she's beautiful," I whispered back. "That will please her."

"Yes, but how else do I please her? Cesare offered to get me a whore first to teach me a few things, but I was too embarrassed to say yes. And Juan wrote me pages of advice all the way from Spain and I don't understand half of it—"

"Your brothers mean well, but they're idiots." Holy Virgin, who knew what ghastly information Juan had seen fit to pass on for the occasion of his little brother's wedding night? Who knew Juan could even *write*? I reached out and smoothed Joffre's hair. Lucrezia's youth might have spared her the bedding ceremony, but a boy would not be so lucky. Any Borgia son would be expected to prove his virility, regardless of age—no doubt Juan and Cesare had tumbled their first girls while still in the cradle!

"Don't listen to what anyone says," I told Joffre firmly. "I would advise that you and your wife just get a good night's sleep. It's been a long, trying day, after all"—I paused to sneeze twice—"and there's more than enough time in the future for all the rest of it."

"There is?"

"Madonna Giulia!" Caterina Gonzaga paused before me as Sancha of Aragon disappeared into the giggling throng of her Neapolitan ladies, and the Pope descended laughing from his ornate chair to escort her upstairs and give his blessing for the bedding. "Surely you will join us in disrobing the bride?" Caterina cooed in her Lombard accent, smoothing a hand over that little waist again.

Only if I could bed you down in a coffin afterward, I thought, and gave her my sweetest smile in demurral, somewhat offset by the sneezing fit that followed it. Even if Sancha of Aragon looked like a trollop, she didn't deserve me sneezing all over her on her wedding night. I was hoping Rodrigo would stay with me—surely he could see how wretched I was feeling?—but he and the King of Naples were already ascending the stairs behind the giggling ladies, heads together as they traded wolfish grins. I gave Joffre a reassuring little wave of my sodden kerchief, and he was borne off in a tide of lewd well-wishers.

"Here you are, my dear." I looked through my itchy, watering eyes at the square figure of Adriana da Mila, settling down beside me with, may the Holy Virgin love her forever, a *clean* kerchief in hand. "Give that nose a good blow before they get back."

I honked gratefully. Below our dais the *sala* had mostly emptied, the courtiers gone streaming upstairs to bed the bridal couple. Only a few remained behind: couples seizing the privacy for a little passionate kissing and groping in the corners, one or two younger men unconscious from too much wine and slumped over the tables with their heads resting in a plate of sliced melon or a stack of honeyed pastry twists. A sharp-eyed steward clapped his hands, evaluating the mess of discarded cups and picked-over platters, and servants began trooping in for a little hasty tidying before the wedding guests reappeared for the revelry, the dancing, the drinking that was sure to last until dawn. I didn't think I could make it till midnight, much less dawn.

"Perhaps a bit of powder for that nose, too." Madonna Adriana surveyed me. "To be blunt, child, you aren't looking your best."

"Try me tomorrow." I honked my nose again like a goose. "I'll be dead by then. You can lay me out all pale and pretty in my coffin, and powder my nose all you like."

"Perhaps a visit to the country would do you good. Get away from Rome for a few weeks; avoid the heat. And there's no doubt His Holiness can be exhausting to entertain. Perhaps a short break from his attentions as well?"

I looked up from the kerchief at my mother-in-law. She sat calm and ringletted in an emerald-green dress, be-ringed hands resting in her lap, a serene half smile on her face. I looked down, folding her scented kerchief into precise squares and motioning Leonello back out of earshot. I didn't want his caustic commentary on *this* conversation.

"Why, mother-in-law," I said at last. "Are you trying to get rid of me?"

"On the contrary." She tilted her head. "My cousin's eye is wandering, you know."

I averted my gaze, trying to look stony. It's difficult to look stony with watery eyes. "It is not. *He* is not."

"Yes, he is. I know the signs."

"And I suppose that makes you happy!"

"Why on earth would you think that, Giulia Farnese?"

I aped her tones. "Because you've never liked me, Adriana da Mila." We'd settled into a wary coexistence, my mother-in-law and I. She was too cushioned in complacency to quarrel with me, but I'd never exactly warmed to her for all our mundane household chatter over the past two years. I couldn't quite forget how she'd acted the pander for her son's bride the morning after the wedding.

"On the contrary, my dear, I like you very well," Madonna Adriana answered me with an unexpected smile. "Which is why I want to help you keep my cousin's attention. To that end, may I offer you some advice?"

I stared at her. Old people always want to offer the young advice, don't they? Below us, the servants were clearing away the dirtied platters of picked-over bones and crusts of bread and melted fruit ices. The feast hadn't been half as good as the food I was accustomed to from

Carmelina's talented hands. "Why would you be giving me advice?" I finally asked. "You're always on Rodrigo's side, even over your own son's! Why would you help me, if your precious cousin decided he didn't want me anymore?"

"Because I *am* on Rodrigo's side, my dear, and I can see that you're good for him." She patted my hand. "The greedy little trollops he's picked up for mistresses before your day—oh, I shudder at the memory. And I was never exactly fond of Vannozza, either. Jewelry wasn't enough for that woman; she had to have *property* too. A new villa every year!" A little tut-tut at that. "Whereas you, my dear Giulia, are clever and good-natured and discreet, and you haven't tried to wheedle every last jewel, favor, and benefice in Rome out of him for yourself and your family. You seem content merely to *be* with him."

"Of course I am!" I tried to look scornful, but I had to sneeze.

"If you let Rodrigo go now, he'll fall into the lap of some rapacious harlot like that Lombard slut Caterina Gonzaga," my mother-in-law continued. "And then she'll queen it about the Vatican in every jewel she can extract from him, and the Borgia name will be a laughingstock throughout Rome."

The thought of Caterina Gonzaga on Rodrigo's arm made me want to scratch and spit. "What do you want me to do about that?"

Adriana tilted her head to one side like an inquisitive mother hen. "I'm sure you've heard that absence can make the heart yearn?"

"I've heard that," I said warily, and we bent our heads together. Not that she wanted to get too close to my streaming nose, but . . .

My Pope swung back into the *sala* shortly after in high good humor, his swarthy face amused above the papal robes as he traded a private snicker with the half-drunk King of Naples. "—see that bold-eyed daughter of yours giving us the eye when they stripped her and put her in bed!"

I'll bet she did, I thought, but put on a great beam of a smile as I sailed down upon my bull. "Your Holiness!" I purred with what remained of my depleted sparkle. My red nose was hidden temporarily under a layer of powder—it wouldn't survive the next sneeze, but I didn't need it to. I just needed a moment's worth of charm. "Your Holiness, I've just *heard*!" I continued as my Pope turned toward me. "Madonna Adriana told me you had decided to allow Lord Sforza to take Lucrezia back to Pesaro to see her new home!"

"I was thinking of it," he began. "I had not decided—" But I was already nodding.

"Very wise, Your Holiness, very wise. You know there's always plague in Rome after spring, not to mention the heat. And if the French come, well, better to have her safe in the provinces. Though surely they won't dare invade with our new allies at our side!" I dimpled at the King of Naples, who looked magnanimous and then looked down my bodice before staggering off to find his own mistress. "Lucrezia will be so pleased to see Pesaro at last, and so will I!" I twined my fingers through Rodrigo's caressingly. "Though I will miss Your Holiness terribly, of course."

"Miss me?" He had been looking at goose-necked Caterina again as she came gliding down the stairs from the bridal chamber, giving her arrogant queenly stare all around her—but now he frowned and looked back at me.

"Dear Adriana and I wouldn't dream of sending your daughter off to her new home without a proper escort." I reached out, drawing my mother-in-law's arm through mine with a bit more goodwill than usual. "We'll see she's properly settled, never fear. It shouldn't take more than, oh, a few months?"

I felt a sneeze building and my nose beginning to run again, so I unleashed the last of my dazzle in a final smile, swept a curtsy toward my Pope, and strolled away with my head close to my mother-in-law's. "Adriana, we must take Carmelina Mangano with us to Pesaro—your assistant cook? I may have to go without my Papal Bull for a few months, but I cannot go without her honeyed *mostaccioli*!"

I could almost hear Rodrigo frown behind us, and that was when I added, in an artless voice designed to carry just far enough, "And of course I know you must be pining to see your son after so many months, Adriana. How *is* dear Orsino faring, anyway?"

Leonello's murmur followed me out. *"Dio."*

Leonello

God knows I am a man with sins on his soul. Blasphemy, fornication, theft. Avarice, when it came to things like good wine and engraved books. One or two of the milder forms of heresy. Murder, of course, and unrepentant murder at that. But surely, *surely*, my sins did not warrant the punishment of two days' close confinement in a rattling carriage with Madonna Adriana, the Countess of Pesaro, the Bride of Christ, and the Bride of Christ's baby (who cried considerably more than our Lord must have done)—as the three women discussed, for ten hours each on two consecutive days, the relative merits of fur versus velvet linings on Neapolitan overgowns and how the new slippers had a much more pointed toe.

"Blue Spanish brocade with embroidered panels," Giulia said, jogging her baby against one shoulder. "I saw one of the Moscari girls wearing a gown just like that at Mass last month, and now I want one too. Not with those dagged sleeves, though, I don't think you can get away with hanging sleeves like that unless you're *very* tall, else you're just dragging your cuffs on the ground—"

"No, it was one of the Mocenigo girls who had the dagged sleeves," Lucrezia disagreed. "Luciana Moscari was wearing rose pink satin with gold embroidery. Rosy girls like that should never wear pink; she looked like a raspberry. But I liked her little marten fur collar—"

"Benedetta Bellonci had the marten fur collar," Adriana da Mila corrected.

"No, Benedetta Bellonci had a sable hood with green velvet lining. And the most ridiculous stilt clogs you ever saw . . ."

"It's like the Homeric catalogue of ships," I said to one of Lord Sforza's escorting guards when they paused to water the horses. "Only it's dresses. And even when it's ships, it's still the most boring chapter in the Iliad!"

"Better than riding in the rain," the guard pointed out to me, his livery draggled and dripping. "Safe and dry with the most beautiful women in Rome—don't ask me to pity you, Messer Leonello! If it were me, I'd burrow into Madonna Giulia's lap and never come up for air . . ."

Perhaps it was my fervent prayers that made the difference, but the third day of our journey from Rome to Pesaro dawned sunny and fair. I have no love for horses, but I left the carriage in a desperate lunge for the clean fresh air, the clop of hooves in the new June sunshine, and above all, the silence. "We'll have to put you on a mule with the baggage," one of the drovers said dubiously. "You can't be riding, not with those short legs—horse'll jerk you right over its head."

"I will ride a goat," I vowed. "I will ride the Devil Himself, as long as there are no more discussions on netted snoods or dagged sleeves."

Madonna Adriana stayed in her carriage, but the other ladies took to the saddle: Lucrezia on a little white jennet, which she raced back and forth between the carriage and the head of the procession where her lord Count rode with his soldiers. Madonna Giulia ambled more slowly on her gray mare, stray bits of hair blowing about her face like golden ribbons in the warm breeze. I had my perch on a pack mule, jammed between the beast's panniers, looking ahead at a line of three more pack mules tied nose to tail and being driven along by a bored guardsman. The mules stank like rancid manure piles and the dust rose off the road to tickle my nose, but the sun was warm on my back, and if I lifted my eyes from the swaying procession of mule arses, I could see the long stretches of countryside rolling golden-green and endless around us.

"Why are you gaping, Leonello?" Giulia asked, slowing her mare from its trot. "It's just countryside, you know. Sheep and shepherds and shrubs. Surely you've been riding in the country before!"

I hesitated, keeping my eyes on the dusty horizon of grass and goats. I had not been entirely easy with La Bella these past few months, ever since the night I'd so stupidly told her the story of my birth and seen the pity in her eyes. I had no desire to be pitied, not by anyone, and I'd been pierced with resentment afterward every time I looked at her. But I felt strangely happy now in the warm June sunshine, my feet swinging freely on either side of the mule. A boy on holiday, even though I'd never been a boy on holiday in all my life. "I've never been so far from Rome before," I confessed, feeling oddly giddy. "This is all very strange to a city lad."

"I grew up not so far from here." Giulia pointed west, or what I thought was west. How did an urban sort like me tell direction, except by the nearest church or *piazza* or shrine? I didn't know how these country people did it. "In Capodimonte, that way. It's got more trees than here," she said a little wistfully. "And a huge lake, Lake Bolsena. It's beautiful." She wrinkled her nose up at the sky, heedless of the freckles she'd already collected in a scatter of gold flakes across her cheeks. "I didn't realize it, but I miss the country."

She already looked far less like a pope's pampered mistress: hair bundled carelessly into a net, dust across the skirts of her sensible split-layered riding dress, not a pearl in sight. But they still knew who she was, the villagers who came in their dusty smocks to gape at the side of the road as the procession passed. Women pointed and whispered; the men swung their barefoot children up to their shoulders to watch the glittering procession of horses, carriages, pack mules, and guardsmen in Lord Sforza's colors. "That's the Count of Pesaro," the whisper went, but the land was fully of petty lordlings like him and no one gave Lord Sforza a second glance no matter how he pranced his caparisoned horse at the head of the line. "That's the Pope's daughter," a far more excited whisper would follow, and the new Countess of Pesaro waved and bowed from her saddle, gracious but remote, very conscious of her dignity now that she was a wife and a great lady. "*That's* the Pope's concubine!" the last whisper would run, and men would crane their necks and gape for a look at the woman who'd tempted God's own vicar from his vows, and Giulia laughed and blew kisses like a girl at a fair. We would travel another few days before reaching Pesaro, but late that afternoon my mule threw a shoe.

"I can't stop and reload the other mules now just to make room for you," the guardsman apologized as I slid stiffly to the ground around the laden panniers. "I'm afraid it's back into the carriage with you, Messer Leonello."

"He can ride behind me," Madonna Giulia offered, halting her mare with a flash of scarlet saddle cloth and silver mane.

"Absolutely not," I said. "You will start talking poetry again, or dress materials, and then I shall murder you. And my orders from Cardinal Borgia were to keep you safe, not murder you, so all in all I think I should find a cart to ride upon."

Giulia laughed, gesturing one of the guards to find a cart that could squeeze me in. "I'm surprised Cesare cared enough to give you any orders regarding me. He usually looks right through me, like I'm a decorative glass vase."

"He doesn't care." I massaged my cramped legs, the muscles beginning to unknot. "He cares for nothing outside the family. But he will not get the Holy Father's full attention on the matter of the French unless you are looked after in all regards. Thus, my orders."

"The French again!" Madonna Giulia made a face. "You really think they'll invade?"

"Cleverer people than me seem to think so."

"There's no one cleverer than you, Leonello."

Normally I'd agree with her, but I was starting to think Cesare Borgia might have me beaten there. I had traded a few words with him that day when he came to bid his sister farewell—he had handed her up into the carriage with a great deal more affection than he had Giulia, kissing Lucrezia on both cheeks and whispering fondly in the Catalan they all kept for private moments—but after that he had turned aside to me. He wore a doublet and hose, black like my own, suiting him much better than his red ecclesiastical dress, and the dagger with the sapphire in its hilt rode at his hip as it always did.

"Keep my sister safe," he ordered me, looping his horse's reins tight about his fingers. "And my father's little giggler. He'll miss them both sorely, but he'll have time to focus now on more pressing matters."

"Is it true, Your Eminence?" I couldn't help asking. Rome was a sea of whispers, but the College of Cardinals had all the real news before any of Rome's commoners. "That the French are massing?"

"Not only are they massing, they are massing a great army." Cesare

Borgia made it sound of no great importance. "The King of France leads them, and he's the ugliest man in Christendom, but he is no fool when it comes to war. They say he will bring thirty thousand men to press his claim to Naples."

I gave a low whistle. We had been standing a little apart in the busy courtyard as Lord Sforza rode back and forth dispensing his soldiers first here and then there and the women hung out the window of their carriage, anxious to be gone. I could hear baby Laura crying and Giulia soothing her with a little fragment of song. "And who do we have to oppose them?"

"The papal forces," Cesare Borgia said. "Such as they are."

"And who will lead them, Your Eminence?"

I asked the question only to be polite, and he did not answer it. Not with words—but in his eyes I saw such a fire kindle that it startled me. That spark wasn't just fire, it was lust; a burning, ravenous hunger.

"Who will lead the command against the French?" I repeated.

Cesare Borgia shrugged, bland and remote again, his big black horse nibbling at his sleeve. "Should I suggest you, little lion man? That would be a sight for the French."

I wondered if I had imagined that clawing beast in his gaze, the thing whose name might be Ambition. I wouldn't have thought a boy who could call himself a cardinal by the age of eighteen, with more benefices and properties and pensions than he could ever count spilling their bounty at his feet, could be ambitious for anything. What else in the great world was there to want?

There is always something.

"I don't fancy commanding an army, Your Eminence," I said at last. "I don't like sitting at the back and letting others do my killing for me. If murder must be done, I do it myself."

"So do I."

And when was the last murder at your hands? I thought. The question that had taunted me on and off, all winter, all through the turn of the year and the warming of spring, ever since I had played chess in Viterbo with a man who had tossed a mask aside to reveal he was the

Pope's eldest son. *When did you last see life fading from a pair of eyes, Your Eminence? Might it have been a tavern girl staked to a table?*

If I had kept up my quest after killing Don Luis and the Borgia guardsman, hunted for the masked man with whom they had gone whoring . . . if I had found that man and pulled his mask aside . . . would that face too have been the Pope's eldest son? As if it were a question I could ever ask, or a murder I could ever avenge, even if I had the answer.

I still *wanted* the answer, all the same. Though part of me hoped it wouldn't be Cesare. I rather liked him, after all. I owed him my life, and my knives, and my current prosperity. And besides which, he made an excellent partner in chess.

Giulia was laughing again, and it jerked me out of my dark thoughts. "—what do you think, Leonello?"

I blinked, collecting myself. "What do I think about what, Madonna Giulia?"

"What do you think of Lord Sforza's new sonnet, of course! The one in Lucrezia's honor—"

Lucrezia preened. She must have doubled back to halt her little jennet beside Giulia's mare while I stood lost in my semiheretical speculations about her favorite brother. "My lord husband compares me to the goddess Primavera," the Pope's daughter sighed. "So *very* romantic—"

"If you will excuse me, *madonna*," I said hastily. Lord Sforza's leaden little verses had made their way all over the *palazzo*, at least to those not quick enough to flee when the love-struck little Countess came looking for an audience for her lord's latest ditty. I hunted about me for an escape and caught sight of a familiar black head at the front of another wagon rolling past. "Madonna Giulia, I think I shall ride with the cooking equipment. Better pans than poetry—"

Signorina Cuoca gave an inhospitable sniff as I was boosted up to the boards beside her. "Ride somewhere else, Messer Leonello. Somewhere you're wanted."

"When I can have the pleasure of annoying you?" I propped my boots up on the board beside hers as the wagon lurched into motion again. "Never. What's that?" I asked, as she buried her nose ostentatiously in a packet of scribbled pages. "Ciphered, I see. Witchcraft? That's why you fled Venice, isn't it! Falsely accused by a jealous lover, you escaped a charge of sorcery by bribing the jailor and found no option but to flee to the Holy City!"

She gazed at me, wide-eyed. "How did you know?"

My brows flew up. "Don't tell me I've guessed—" Pointing at the ciphered pages. "Truly?"

"No." Her too-round eyes relaxed into mockery at me. "They're just *recipes*, you dolt."

"Ah." I doffed my cap. "Well played, *signorina*. Pity, I liked that witchcraft theory. Fear not, I have plenty of others. Might you possibly be a Jew, fleeing Spain to escape the Inquisition?"

I chattered on, watching her her fingers drum along her thigh as she pretended to ignore me. We were passing a roadside tavern now; drinkers scrambled up hastily from their trestle tables at the sight of the glittering Sforza banners. One or two fell to their knees; the rest blinked drunkenly. I saw two tavern maids dipping curtsy after curtsy like a pair of apples bobbing in a tub, drinking in every detail of Lucrezia's dress, Giulia's hair, the ornate carriage with its matched Sicilian horses and its coat of arms. Not terribly pretty girls, those tavern maids, but all girls looked prettier after enough cups of wine. Like Anna, whose dimple only seemed to get deeper and sweeter the more one drank. Strange how I could barely remember Anna's face, and yet she burned in my thoughts so constantly . . .

I caught a drift ahead from Giulia and Lucrezia, who had turned their mounts into the grass alongside the road to avoid the dust kicked up by the cart horses. Still going on about the Count of Pesaro's wretched sonnet. "*Hail to thee, O springtime goddess fair—*"

You're going mad, dwarf, I sometimes told myself. Because I had no reason, none at all, to think my masked man was the Pope's eldest son. Staking a woman to a table had to be the hot-blooded act of a madman— it hardly suited the cool deliberation with which Cesare Borgia moved through life. And surely any murder he committed would be murder with a purpose; the murder of someone who threatened either him or his family or his ambitions. He was so far above Anna and her ilk, they might as well have been beetles under his feet.

But wasn't it the arrogant of the world who crushed the beetles— simply because they could? "Killing is a skill like any other," Cesare had told me over the chessboard, speaking of his first murder. "It should be practiced until it comes easily." Could Anna and her successors have merely been *practice*? Cesare would have been very young at the time of her death, but he claimed he had killed his first foot-pad at sixteen—and been dissatisfied at how clumsily he had done it. And each kill after Anna had been progressively cleaner.

Maybe they weren't such hot-blooded kills after all. There was a certain lust about them, a dark deliberation in making each kill exactly the same—but Cesare Borgia had dark lusts, that I knew. I had seen for myself the black flames in his eyes when he bid our party farewell, and spoke to me of leading the papal armies. Since he hadn't been allowed to lead the papal armies, perhaps that black lust had found a different outlet . . .

"Roses springing in your lissome wake—"

But if Anna and the others had merely been a cold slaking of frustrated ambition, a cool self-education in the niceties of murder—if the victims had been chosen precisely because they would never be missed— then why leave the dagger with the last body to stir up so much speculation? I did not for one moment believe Cesare would have done such a thing out of mere carelessness.

Maybe he got bored, I thought. Hadn't he said it himself, baiting me? *"Perhaps I was arrogant rather than stupid . . . Perhaps I wished to see how far I could go, and still get away with it."*

I suppose I should have wondered why he would ever say such a thing to me, but that was the one thing in all this murky mess that didn't puzzle me in the slightest. Cesare Borgia liked games, games of every kind. Games played with chess pieces, games played with live pieces. Baiting me, whether with truth or with lies, was just one more game to amuse him. Perhaps the final game to finish off the string of murders, because it seemed possible to me that there would *be* no more murders.

I had kept my ears open all this winter, dropping questions among the cards when I played *primiera* with Borgia guards, papal guards, municipal guards—I even tried prying my way into granite-eyed Michelotto's confidence, though he just stared at me like a blind statue. And no more women had been found throat-slit and table-staked. Not since late last summer, when I had played chess with Cesare Borgia among the vaults of Viterbo and asked him if he was a murderer of women, watched by his discarded mask on the floor.

A question he had very carefully not answered.

"*Soft your voice, as feathers from a dove—*"

Carmelina looked up from her ciphered pages of recipes, hearing the drift of verse from the little Countess of Pesaro. "What's that poetry Madonna Lucrezia keeps going on about?"

"Don't ask, or she'll recite the whole sonnet," I said absently. "Love has turned Lord Sforza into a poet to rival Dante, to hear his little wife tell it. I could write better verse hung up by my thumbs."

"Poetry." Carmelina snorted, turning another page in her packet of recipes. "Thanks be to Santa Marta that nobody writes verses to common girls."

"Poetry doesn't move your heart?" I made big eyes at her, distracted for a moment.

"I'd be more moved if a man made me *cena*," she said. "No one ever cooks for the cook."

I looked at her thoughtfully as the wagon jolted beneath us. I could hear the clatter of pots in the boxes and sacks in the wagon—the kitchen equipment needed for any journey—and Carmelina turned to secure a knot on a box piled inside the wagon that had not been tightened to her standards. She was frowning, the familiar line showing between her straight black brows, but I judged she was as pleased as I to be out under the sky on a journey to places unknown. "May I ask you a question?" I asked.

"I came to Rome for the *work*, Leonello. Not because I'm a witch or a Jew or an exiled courtesan!"

"No, not that." I tried a smile on her, but our spiky-natured cook just got suspicious whenever I started being charming. Caught on to that, had she? "The maids in the Palazzo Santa Maria—I know they've had their, ah, difficulties with the Duke of Gandia—"

"Not now that he's in Spain," Carmelina snorted. "Every maid in the *palazzo* went about singing for a week."

"I can imagine." Juan Borgia regarded the papal seraglio as very much his own personal harem when it came to the maids. I wondered from time to time if *he* might be my masked man; he certainly had a taste for both low women and unwilling women, and he was certainly hot-blooded. But he didn't have the patience to hunt, kill, and butcher a deer properly, much less a woman. Idly putting his sword through stray dogs in alleys; that was about as much effort as he was willing to expend on violence. And though he might rape a girl, I didn't see him cutting her throat afterward. He'd toss her a coin and think himself magnanimous for honoring her with his attentions. "Have the maids had difficulties with Cesare Borgia?" I asked instead.

If anything, Carmelina looked even more suspicious. "Why do you want to know?"

"No reason." If Cesare Borgia truly felt that dark unspeakable lust that had led to Anna's death and all the others, perhaps there were warning signs among the maids in the Borgia household. "Do they flee Cesare's attentions as they do Juan's?"

"No." Carmelina hesitated. "Yes."

"Which is it?"

"The Duke of Gandia, he's a lout, but he might give you a coin afterward if you pleased him." As I'd thought, yes. "And he's quick," Carmelina added with a snort. "Beatrice the laundry maid said it took longer to wring out a wet shirt."

I couldn't help a laugh. Definitely not the style of my painstaking, pain-taking murderer. "And Cesare?"

"He doesn't pay, not ever. And he's not quick."

"Is he rough?" A man who liked blood might also like bruised flesh, in his milder moments.

Carmelina's hand circled her own wrist unconsciously, rubbing it. "How would I know?"

I studied her. "Are you blushing?"

"Don't be ridiculous." She had the recipes up to her nose again, hiding her face. I nudged them down.

"You *are* blushing. Don't tell me you've had a roll in the hay with Cardinal Borgia, *Signorina Cuoca*."

"Why would he look at the *palazzo* cook when he has the most expensive courtesans in Rome?"

"Why are you dodging the question?" I grinned at her glower. "Besides, all highborn lordlings like a low woman now and then, young Cardinal Borgia included. A deliberate roll in the mud, such filthy pleasure to be found . . ."

I said it crudely, with a certain obscene gesture, and Carmelina's eyes flared again. "Is that what you're keen on, Messer Leonello? Hearing all the details?" A disgusted shake of her head. "Don't bother me with your perversions."

"I have a reason for asking," I said, and felt a pang of alarm that surprised me. No smiles now. "Did he hurt you?"

"No." She looked me right in the eye. "He was gentle as a lamb."

"You're lying." I felt the tautness in me again, the hunt. "What did he do? Hit you? Tie you?"

She smiled. "You know, I think I feel like walking for a while." With an arrogant flip of that pointed chin, she left me in possession of the field, sliding down the side of the wagon and marching ahead to join her red-haired apprentice where he was kicking a stone through the dust.

Gentle as a lamb, I thought, and kicked one boot against the boards underfoot. *Liar.* That gesture, circling her own wrist unconsciously. Marking a bruise that had long healed? The kind of bruise that would come, say, from having the arms pinned down.

What does it matter? I told myself. *Even if she told you Cesare Borgia likes to bruise his bedmates, it proves nothing. Even if he likes to wear a mask and take himself off alone on God knows what solitary adventures— even if his dagger was found slammed through the hand of the last girl, and he was the one to put it there—even if he confessed to you, what could you do? He is the Pope's son; he will never be brought to justice.*

But I wondered sometimes if I really gave a fig for justice either. It was knowledge I wanted: the answer to the puzzle that had filled my mind this winter. I wanted that masked man to take off his mask and show me his face, whatever face it might be, as he flicked his chessboard king on its side in defeat.

"Leonello!" Giulia had turned her little mare back to me again, trotting alongside the wagon. "Leonello, listen to this line the Count of Pesaro wrote. "*O Primavera bright and fair—*'"

"Please no more," I begged, wrenching my mind away from its useless whirlpool of speculations. *Dio*, no wonder the matter of murder had been weighing so heavily on my mind this winter—otherwise, it had been nothing but bad poetry.

"Caterina Gonzaga wants to visit us in Pesaro," Lucrezia was telling Giulia now, leaning over from her velvet saddle with a dark look. "We must be sure to have all new dresses; I will *not* be outshone in my own home—my new home, I mean—and you know she's always putting herself forward as though she were a queen! I'll bet her husband never wrote poetry to *her*—"

"Kill me," I pleaded. "Please, kill me at once before you begin talking about clothes again."

But no one ever listens to the dwarf.

CHAPTER THIRTEEN

❖

Beside you, she is a lantern compared to the sun.

—RODRIGO BORGIA, COMPARING CATERINA GONZAGA TO
GIULIA FARNESE

Carmelina

W here are we going, *signorina*?"

"The fish market. Hurry up, Bartolomeo!" I quickened my steps, tugging my cloak closer about me as my apprentice sped to a trot. All around us, Pesaro was just waking up to a pewter-colored dawn. Rome would have already been bustling: workers hurrying off to open their shops, drinkers staggering home from a night of revels, beggars staking out the likeliest corners to beg.

"Why are we going to the fish market, *signorina*?" Bartolomeo obediently toted the enormous basket I'd shoved at him as we left the *palazzo* kitchens. "The steward at the Palazzo Ducale said he'd order sturgeon for you, delivered fresh to the door—"

"That means the steward gets a bribe from the vendor who sells sturgeon. I'll see for myself what's on offer, thank you." Madonna Lucrezia was used to eating the best, and I'd make sure she kept getting it now that she was settling into her new home. A young bride should at least have a well-filled stomach as she learned how to manage her husband's household. Roast pigeon with blackberry sauce, perhaps, and flat crisp Roman *pizze* to remind her of home . . .

"It's a fine day, *signorina*." Bartolomeo ventured. He was fifteen now and had grown a good hand-span taller than he'd been when I first tossed him an apprentice's apron. He was still so milky pale that his freckles stood out across his face and neck like a dark sprinkle of cinnamon, but his arms had a layer of wiry muscle from so many hours of whipping egg whites and hefting sides of beef ribs. Ever since poor Eleonora the fruit seller had died so gruesomely in her own market stall, I'd seen the wisdom of taking a strong young apprentice with me to market when I did my shopping. Far better tall, alert Bartolomeo than the useless Sforza cook with his potbelly and his stale wine breath. "Looks like we'll have a sunny morning," my apprentice went on.

"Looks like fog to me." We had just passed the town's central *piazza*, where a few beggars and drunks huddled against buildings sleeping off a night's despair or drink. Not even a third the size of the Piazza Navona in Rome, but everything in Pesaro was small to a Roman's eyes. I'd seen Madonna Lucrezia's face fall just a little when she first laid eyes on her new home. "Oh!" she'd exclaimed. "It's very . . ." To a girl accustomed to all the glories of the Holy City, the clamor and the pomp and the spectacle, Pesaro might have seemed just a bit provincial. Nor did it help that we arrived in another storm of summer rain, winds buffeting flat both Madonna Lucrezia's careful confection of curls and all the banners that had been brought out to welcome her. Still, the skies cleared as the days passed, and Madonna Giulia waxed staunch enthusiasm in favor of Pesaro's beauties: the blue bay and winding river mouth, the heavy Romanesque cathedral with its altar dedicated to some gloomy and mustachioed saint, the Palazzo Ducale. *We'll see if their fish market measures up*, I thought, and quickened my steps through the *piazza*.

"They say the French will be invading soon," Bartolomeo volunteered, crossing himself. He had an easy, devout sort of soul; the kind of boy who makes cheerful confession to his priest every week and never has anything terribly sinful to confess, either; the kind who accepts the Borgia Pope and all his worldly sins as something far lofty and above him, and puts an easy faith in God the Father instead. The kind of untroubled, unstained conscience I'd long since left behind me. "That's what I hear from Lord Sforza's men, anyway, and they have all the news about the French, straight from Milan."

"Hmph." I was far less concerned about the French than my new kitchens. Lord Sforza's Palazzo Ducale was grand enough on the outside with its fountains and arcades and festooning coats of arms, but the kitchens were unspeakable. The apprentices were still banging into the low beams trying to find space for all the cauldrons and spits and ladles we had brought from Rome, and I had no idea how I was going to make milk-snow without a proper cold room to keep the cream from curdling. Still, Madonna Giulia had insisted on bringing us along, so we would all make do until we could get out of this backwater and back to Rome where the morals were depraved but I at least had space for my spoons.

My very first time as *maestra di cucina*—somehow I'd thought it would feel more momentous than this. Perhaps it would have in a kitchen with proper drainage. Still, these kitchens were mine to command until we returned to Rome; Adriana da Mila had not deemed it necessary to take two cooks to Pesaro, and Madonna Giulia had insisted it be me, so Marco had been left in Rome to mind the Palazzo Santa Maria while I accompanied the ladies to Pesaro. "Don't see why they passed me over," my cousin had humphed when he heard the news. "My *tourtes* are every bit as good as yours, little cousin!"

"You know I didn't ask for it," I pointed out. "Besides, now you'll have a summer free to dice as much as you like, without my nagging."

"There is that," he admitted, and felt sufficiently mollified to come knocking at my chamber that night for a last romp before I departed. "I'll miss you," he murmured afterward as he rolled away from me, just before falling asleep.

"You're just too lazy to find yourself another bedmate," I said tartly. Not that he couldn't find one, a man as handsome as Marco, but finding one who didn't start angling for marriage was another matter. Marco couldn't marry me, and we both knew that full well, so as a bedmate I was highly convenient.

"Do you think the French will invade, *signorina*?" Bartolomeo was saying. "They're savage, the French—they spit babies on pikes and desecrate churches, and salt the fields—"

"Salt," I mused as we wheeled the last turn around a gibbet where they'd hanged a local robber last week. His carcass still swayed from the noose, mostly picked clean by now, though a solitary crow still pecked at a thigh bone. I'd need to find a good salty cheese after visiting the fish market, and a wheel of Parmesan too. I could not live without Parmesan. My immortal soul, yes—that was probably lost to me, considering I desecrated churches just like the French. My morals, yes—those were certainly in tatters too after all the time Marco and I had spent under the blankets. Not to mention that dark and *very* strange hour I'd passed with Cesare Borgia . . . that had probably tacked a good century of hellfire onto my soul all by itself. But I'd far rather live without soul or morals than Parmesan.

I'd had no further visits from the Pope's eldest son, but I hadn't expected it. I was only a serving girl, after all; he had not bothered to learn my name at the time, and once he was done he'd left me with nothing more than a calm nod and a few bruises in odd places. I didn't even really want him back in my bed again, beautiful though he was. Coupling with Cesare Borgia had been an entirely different thing from Marco's friendly rumples under the sheets. More like coupling with a hurricane—something to leave you exhilarated and frightened, bruised and worn out. Something to remember with a certain private smile, but no particular desire to repeat the experience.

Cesare Borgia—now there was a man with no morals!

"*Signorina.*" Bartolomeo's voice cut off my inward smile. "What if the French—"

"Bartolomeo." I cut him off, brushing my thoughts away. "What do you plan to do if the French invade?"

"Um, well—"

"Nothing, that's what you'll do. Because it has nothing to do with either of us." I pulled my cloak closer around my shoulders as the breeze off the river began to nip. "If they invade, then they invade, and that's that. Personally I hope they keep themselves and their horrendous food on their side of the mountains. Baby-spitting French soldiers are bad enough, but they'll bring their rancid butter and their overdone roasts with them, and then Santa Marta help us all."

That stilled my apprentice's tongue, at least until we plunged into the tumult and noise of the fish market. "It's bigger than I thought." Bartolomeo blinked.

"Bigger," I agreed, "but fish markets all look the same the world over. Smell the same, too." The same reek of salt and rotting flounder, the same fish scales turning the ground iridescent in the gray dawn light, the same sights of live carp lashing away in buckets and dead ones hung up for display. A spicy mix of accents rose up from the fishermen who bickered and bargained in surly tones and the vendors who cried their wares like they were hawking pearls. "Oysters, fresh from the sea bed!" "Red mullet, first of the season!" "Sea bream, sea bream!" The sky was just starting to show pink along the edges, but the vendors were already in full cry.

"Pesaro has both a sea coast and a river mouth," I explained, looping my skirts up to keep my hem out of the fish scales. "Makes for a good fish market. Sea fish are better than freshwater fish, but sea fish that come into fresh water to feed make the most delicate eating."

"Why?"

"Because they do." Didn't everybody know that? "Bring that basket."

"Yes, *signorina*."

"And pay attention!" I added over my shoulder as we pushed our way into the throng of fishermen and vendors. "Every cook should inspect the markets himself, so he knows just what he's dealing with."

"Maestro Santini doesn't. I've never once seen him go to a butcher's yard or a fish market."

"He is *maestro di cucina*, so he can afford to send me in his stead." In truth, Marco never went to the fish market or the butcher's yard because he was lazy. My father had refused to give any fishmonger, cheese maker, or vintner his business until he vetted each premise himself, testing every single order to be sure it was the best, the freshest, the highest possible quality. Even after that, he'd make surprise inspections to be sure he wasn't being palmed off with second-best—and as my father did, so did I. But Marco would rather stay in a nice warm kitchen at dawn than go trudging down to a chilly, smelly dock to look at fish. Marco would have taken the steward's word that the sturgeon was the best on offer in Pesaro. The only times Marco stirred himself to make his own examination of a butcher's offal or a new pressing of olive oil, you could be sure there was a card game or a horse race somewhere nearby.

Just because I shared the man's bed from time to time didn't mean I couldn't see his faults.

"Sturgeon." I paused by the display of glassy-eyed fish, piled in a gleaming dark-green stack. I fixed the vendor with a scowl as he oozed toward me with a gap-toothed smile and a proffer of a hairy slablike hand covered in fish scales. "Caught yesterday or today, *signore*? Get a sturgeon fresh, Bartolomeo, and if you store it properly it will keep all year. No, I don't know why! Give a sniff, are they fresh?" That discerning nose of my apprentice's was very handy in a fish market, where the vendors were always trying to palm off dodgy fish under a layer of new-caught.

I gave the sturgeon a dismissive slap on Bartolomeo's recommendation, made an obscene gesture back at the vendor when he swore at me, and elbowed my way to the next set of buckets with my apprentice trailing behind. "Now, that's red mullet," I told him, pointing. "In Venice, they call red mullet *barbari*. No, I don't know why. You remember the recipe for grilling them? . . . Very good, but a mullet is left scaled, and *then* floured. That's turbot; excellent for making fish jellies. They don't have to be scaled either, but you do have to buy them live. I don't know; the jelly tastes better the more recently the turbot was killed. Horse mackerel—sniff it for me. Fresh? Good. These are too big. Of course fish can be too big; for grilling and frying they have to be smaller—ask *why* again, Bartolomeo, and I shall hit you!"

"Yes, *signorina*," he grunted, staggering along behind me with the now-heaping basket, the tips of his ears flushed red as his hair. I stopped abruptly and he fell over my foot.

"Pay attention. These are something special." I bent and gave a rapturous sniff to the display of tiny, tiny, nearly transparent fish. "Smelt, and good ones. Probably brought in from Lake Bolsena. We'll buy them for Madonna Giulia."

"Why?" Bartolomeo asked, and then hastily went on. "Why for Madonna Giulia, that is. She doesn't like red mullet? She eats everything."

"She was born at Lake Bolsena, and she'll have grown up eating smelt like this. She'll be reminded of home, and she'll smile, and those are the kinds of meals that get compliments sent down to the kitchens afterward." I paused, looking at my apprentice. He had a cook's nose; I'd known that almost at once. But there were other things a cook needed, and it was time to find out if he had them. "Do you want to be a cook, Bartolomeo?"

"Yes, *signorina*." No hesitation.

"Why?"

A third of my apprentices said their father would beat them if they failed this apprenticeship. Another third said it was better pay and better work than being a butcher or a candle maker. The final third said they wanted to cook for the Duke of Milan someday and be rich. Bartolomeo looked pinioned, shifting from one foot to another. "I want to live all my days with good smells," he said finally.

"Huh. And what do you think makes the best cooks? What skill, what quality?"

Most of my apprentices just mumbled something about knowing all the recipes by heart. Bartolomeo hesitated, then raked a hand through his hair and laughed. "I have no idea," he said. "I don't *know* enough yet to know."

I glowered, pleased. "Well, Bartolomeo, there's one thing that separates a great cook from a good one." Actually, there was far more than one, but apprentices could only handle information in small doses. "Above all else, you must know the natures of those you cook for: their histories, their tastes, their moods. It is not enough to serve just the same recipes from the book, the ones you've learned by rote one after the other. You serve them the food they don't even know they're craving."

He nodded. "Like the night when Lord Sforza came to dine, and you served sea bass in truffles and roe and everybody started making love." He grinned. "I kissed my first girl that night. Maria the laundry maid, in the stable yard."

I had a memory of steel-strong hands holding me utterly immobile as a cool mouth moved over me, and brushed it aside. "Immaterial. Just tell me—" I turned back to the bucket, stirring the smelt with my fingertips. "How would you prepare lake smelt like these?"

"Fried," he said promptly. "They're best when fried in butter."

"But how would you make lake smelt for Madonna Giulia?" I asked. "You've lived in her household for a year now; you know something of her tastes. What will appeal to her most?"

He hesitated, absently fingering the little wooden cruifix that always hung about his neck. He reached into the bucket, feeling the quality of the fish, leaning down for a sniff. "Still fried," he said slowly. "Because fried food makes people feel better—and Madonna Giulia is feeling sad lately, her maid says. Because the Holy Father's eye is wandering—"

"We don't need to know why she feels sad," I rapped out. "*That* would be prying, and a good cook never pries. So, fried smelt?"

"With a different sauce, though. You like sauces with a drizzle of orange, *signorina*, but that's too tangy for this." He frowned. "A green sauce. Parsley, burnet, sorrel, spinach tips, rocket—a little mint, maybe. Ground fine with almonds—"

"What kind of almonds?" I interrupted.

"Milanese almonds, they're the best."

"Why?" I challenged.

"They just are." His voice was absent, and I smothered a smile. "The green sauce, it should go over top; very simple, very fresh. It will remind Madonna Giulia of the country, when she was a girl—you said she grew up by Lake Bolsena? She'll think of being a girl again. It will make her . . ." he shrugged. "Happy."

"Then perhaps you'd care to prepare the dish for her tonight." I turned away from his stunned expression to rattle off my order to the fishmonger. He grunted assent and began scooping fresh smelt from the bucket for me. "I'll supervise, mind," I threatened, turning back to my apprentice. "One sign that you're mucking it up, and I take over. Understand?"

"Yes, *signorina*." He stood there clutching the basket, fighting off the grin that threatened to take over his entire face. He had a right to grin—he was a full year younger than any other apprentice I'd ever asked to prepare a dish for the high table. He was also, unless I was very much mistaken, the only one among them with the prospect for being a really *good* cook someday.

"A fish menu tonight, I think," I continued, allowing Bartolomeo to fall into step beside me as we proceeded to the next vendor. "And a good array of the local fruits." I was already pulling various dishes together. No Roman *pizze*, as I'd originally thought; that would just make Madonna Lucrezia homesick. She had to learn her new home, after all, and what better way than to give her that knowledge through food? A cold salad of spring onions and the local cucumbers; sturgeon from Pesaro's salt sea and trout from its freshwater river; grapes and peaches from its orchards and white melons from its vines; finished off with pastry diamonds stuffed with the ripe local apricots. A refreshing summer *cena* of all Pesaro had to offer, eaten in the *palazzo* garden and washed by the smell of the sea.

"No smelt for Madonna Adriana," I mused, pausing by a load of salted tench. "She thinks it's too expensive . . ."

"Lake trout," Bartolomeo said promptly. "She's an old trout herself; she'll love it."

I gave his shoulder a whack, suppressing a smile. "Never speak ill of an employer!"

"Well, trout's cheaper than smelt, and that will please her." He shifted the heaping basket to his other arm, undaunted. "If you don't mind, *signorina*—I heard a recipe from a cook to the German ambassador when he called on Madonna Giulia to ask favors of His Holiness. Trout simmered in a sort of sweet-and-bitter sauce with white wine and vinegar and a little butter, served over slices of toast . . . it's just the sort of cozy food Madonna Adriana likes."

"Never trust a German to get a sauce right," I sniffed. "Their solution to everything is just add more butter. Perhaps with a little pepper and cinnamon, though . . ."

Leonello

The little Countess of Pesaro rustled into place, arranging her arms carefully before her, tilting her head at just the right angle. "*Now* you may look!"

I had never bothered to close my eyes, but the rest of the company removed hands from faces and burst into applause. The Pope's daughter stood in a white gown painted all over with flowers upon the silk; her hair spilled loose down her back, a wreath of roses crowned her head, and she held more roses caught up in a fold of her skirt. She held her pose, lips parted, paused in the act of stepping forward. I had the feeling she was wishing for a breeze to rustle her hair upon command.

"Primavera!" Lord Sforza shouted. "From that painting, the fellow in Florence, or was it Mantua? You know the fellow I mean . . ."

"Botticelli," I murmured.

"Maestro Botticelli," the Count of Pesaro continued, not acknowledging me. "That's my dove, you're Botticelli's Primavera!"

"My lord husband is quite correct." Lucrezia broke her pose, curtsying prettily, and the company applauded again. Not a very lively company—Lord Sforza and several of his stolid-faced captains, Lucrezia and Madonna Adriana and their various favorite attendants, Giulia la Bella with her little pet goat in her lap—but a certain fair-haired Caterina Gonzaga and her husband, Count Ottaviano da Montevegio, had newly arrived on their northbound journey from Rome back to their estates in San Lorenzo, and that lent the evening's usual peaceful post-*cena* proceedings a certain edge.

"Caterina Gonzaga is a great beauty," Giulia explained to Lucrezia's new circle of ladies, who had been assembled for a council of war the instant the Countess's arrival was anticipated. "And what's more, she's a *very* ambitious one. Stalks about as though she's the queen of heaven, *and* she made eyes at His Holiness all through Joffre's wedding. With the cold I had then, I was hardly able to smack her down like the tart she is. I shall ransack Florence for brocade if necessary, but I will *not* be outshone this time."

I stood in the background in my perennial black and observed a great deal of kissing and cooing when all the ladies greeted Caterina Gonzaga. The degree to which women kiss and coo, I've found, is in direct proportion to the degree to which they dislike each other. Giulia and Lucrezia compared new rings and bracelets with the Countess before evening *cena*, gushed over new gowns as they settled to eat, and afterward rustled into the ill-painted and provincial little *sala* in a pretty trinity that did not turn its backs on each other for a moment. Lord Sforza and Caterina Gonzaga's paunchy Count and the other men sat in the candlelight talking grimly of the French campaign, the army that had just crossed south from France to Savoy, while the ladies made light conversation and planned campaigns of a different kind.

"Oh, the French," Lucrezia had finally exclaimed when the discussion turned ponderously to the matter of which cardinals had been suborned to the enemy's side. "Until the French actually land on my doorstep, I refuse to hear another word about them. I propose a game, instead—"

Each lady would present herself before the company as some famous work of art and be judged by the men to see who was fairest. "I haven't had time to prepare," Caterina Gonzaga said with a regal toss of her head, but that was brushed aside.

"*I* have," Lucrezia said smugly, dimpling at her husband again.

"Well, *that* isn't fair," the Countess said, outraged as any wronged queen, but Giulia came to Lucrezia's defense.

"We'll improvise! Isn't that half the fun?"

"Is a beauty contest between women ever a good idea?" I interjected into the commotion. "Doesn't anyone remember how the Trojan War began?"

"We're not going to war with the Trojans now too, are we?" one of Lord Sforza's loutish country captains wondered. "Trojans—are they from France?"

Dio. But my groan was lost in the rustle and bustle as the ladies prepared themselves. Lucrezia as hostess had presented her little tableau first, and the little Primavera now sat with a great satisfied rustle of her white skirts. Lord Sforza captured her hand in his rough one and brought it to his lips, still besotted, and she smiled back at him with her other hand grazing her belly. Botticelli's Primavera had been painted with a swelling belly beneath her flowery silks—I wondered if the Pope's daughter could possibly be breeding yet. *Quick work, my lord Sforza.* Though the Pope would be livid: Sforza had not acquitted himself well in his father-in-law's eyes of late. When *not* in bed with his new wife, the Count of Pesaro spent all his time vacillating between committing his soldiers with those of his French-allied family in Milan—or to the papal forces in Rome. Last I had heard, the Pope had got thoroughly tired of all the waffling and ordered him to do as he damned well pleased. Yes, the bloom had definitely gone from the Sforza alliance as far as His Holiness was concerned.

"My turn," Caterina Gonzaga said, rising proud as an empress. Whispers and giggles as her maids escorted her behind a screen to change her dress, and the men were furtively talking about the French again and Giulia fingering the great pearl at her throat as God knew what thoughts stole the smile from her face, and then we were bidden to close our eyes.

"Now!" the Countess's voice commanded. "Look at me now!"

I wondered if she had those words embroidered on all her sigils as a personal motto. I didn't care for our guest. Before *cena* she'd asked over my head if the dwarf juggled or tumbled, and then she'd spent the meal itself tossing me scraps from her plate as though I were a dog. Giulia had spent the meal requesting that she please desist, sweetness of tone decreasing markedly with each request.

Still, there could be no denying Caterina Gonzaga was a beauty. A very pale beauty: a great deal of white-blond hair and even whiter skin; pale gray eyes that gleamed like silver—and that, of course, was why she could be ill-tempered, capricious, and spiteful. Beauty excuses everything. Easy to forget that when living beside Giulia Farnese, who was certainly a beauty but who lost her temper at no one, offended nobody, made no demands, threw no tantrums. Far less regal than Caterina Gonzaga, but far easier to live with.

Count Ottaviano da Montevegio was already snoring at the back of the *sala* as his wife came out and struck her pose, and the audience burst into applause. More desultory applause this time, as the women clapped only the bare minimum they could get away with, and the men were too busy gawping to put their hands together. The Countess had not *quite* appeared before us naked, but she had stripped to the filmiest of shifts and loosened her pale hair to stream to her hips. One hand she held modestly across her breasts; the other brought a hank of her own hair around to cover the joining of her thighs, and she gazed out over our heads with all the splendid serenity of a goddess.

Madonna Adriana clicked her tongue in disapproval. The men shared lascivious grins, and Lucrezia jabbed an elbow into her husband's ribs. No one seemed inclined to make a guess, but the Countess did not seem to mind anyone taking their time.

"The Birth of Venus," I said at last into the small silence. "Also Botticelli. Though you are lacking a seashell to stand upon, Madonna Caterina, and you should have taken off that ruby on your hand. Venus came from the sea without the benefit of jewels."

"Oh, this?" the false Venus said artlessly, breaking her pose to display her hand (and as much as she could of her bosom), letting the ruby sparkle in the candlelight. "I couldn't bear to take it off, that's all. I treasure it—a present from His Holiness, you know. He was a *very* generous host when my husband and I were last in Rome."

Her eyes went to Madonna Giulia, alight with triumph, and I saw Lucrezia and Madonna Adriana give quick looks as well. My mistress never blinked; just lifted a hand from the pet goat sleeping in her lap and idly fingered the huge teardrop pearl about her neck. "I've never cared for rubies," she murmured. "So easy to fake these days, with all those clever glass copies coming in from Venice. Why, I've heard one can fake a good ruby for a handful of ducats, and no woman would be any the wiser! Pearls, now, those are far harder to palm off on the ignorant . . . Goodness, is it my turn already?"

That shut the Gonzaga bitch up, and she flounced off behind the screens to change back into her dress—making plans, I was sure, to present her ruby to the nearest jeweler for inspection. I thought I saw Giulia blink rather hard as she shifted the goat from her lap to rise, and wondered if she was fighting back tears. Letters from His Holiness, I knew, had been rather few.

"I'm afraid the best of Maestro Botticelli's work is taken already," she said. "A pity he doesn't seem to be painting anymore—I heard there was a mad monk preaching simplicity in Florence, and now half the artists in the city are renouncing paint as secular frivolity—"

"Fra Savonarola," I murmured from my obscure wall bench. The name gave me no disquiet at the time, though it should have.

"Seems a great waste of a painter like Maestro Botticelli," Giulia shrugged. "For tonight, anyway, I shall have to make do with Maestro Raphael."

She turned her back and dropped to her knees, the yellow light from the tapers gleaming on her coiled hair. With slow grace she reached up to unlace her dress, and I felt the men in the room stop breathing. La Bella slid one arm from her sleeve, tugging her dress down on one side to reveal a naked pearly shoulder, and lifted her bare arm in supplication. Her head turned to profile and she froze, lashes down.

No one made a guess. They all seemed content to stare—except the Countess, who suddenly looked more peevish than queenly . . . and Lucrezia, I noticed suddenly, who began fiddling with her flowered skirts with an almost inaudible sigh.

Giulia held her pose a moment longer and then lifted her lashes and looked back at us over her shoulder. Somehow with the one bare shoulder and naked arm and half-exposed back, she looked far more nude than the Gonzaga bitch had in her transparent shift.

"None of you will know the painting, I'm afraid." Giulia dropped her pose, sliding her naked arm back into its dangling sleeve. "I doubt it's even started yet. Maestro Raphael came to paint my portrait last year, but he persuaded me to sit for another sketch as well, posing just so. He wants to paint a *Transfiguration*, and he had me in mind for the beseeching mother. There will be angels and apostles and saints too, of course."

Giulia laced her dress back up and rose, returning to her chair. She picked up the slumbering goat, dropping a kiss on its nose, and looked up. The men were still staring, and Caterina Gonzaga looked as though she had eaten a lime.

"So which of us wins?" Caterina said rudely. I saw Madonna Adriana cast a disapproving glance from her embroidery. "Me, or Giulia Farnese?"

Lucrezia's face fell again, and I swung quickly off the wall bench.

"Perhaps the dwarf may prove the best judge of the contest?" I interjected quickly, striding to the front of the company. "Who, after all, can judge beauty better than one as ugly as myself?" I spread my arms at the little murmur of laughter. Lord Sforza guffawed. "I think, in all fairness to La Bella and to our beauteous visitor"—a bow in their direction—"we must award the crown to our fair Countess of Pesaro. Lovely as is the golden orb in its full glory, a dawning sun must always be counted the most beautiful."

"I think dawning suns are pale and scrawny," the Countess remarked *sotto voce*, but she was drowned in the prudent burst of applause led by Madonna Adriana. Lucrezia's face brightened a little, and I was glad to hear the subject of the French invasion raised again. Altogether a safer topic than the comparative beauty of women who are all present in the same room.

"Excellent, my dear," I heard Madonna Adriana murmur to Giulia as the men called for wine and maps and began loudly arguing over which route the King of France would choose in his march on Naples.

"You really think she got that ring from Rodrigo?" Giulia whispered back. "I saw how she made eyes at him at Joffre's wedding—"

"Maybe, but that ruby's nowhere near the value of your pearls. If he tumbled her, I assure you it was a tumble quickly forgotten . . ."

"And they say women know nothing of politics," I remarked as

Madonna Adriana patted Giulia's arm and bustled off. "Is it so important, keeping the Holy Father's favor?"

Giulia blinked. The other ladies were starting to yawn; any moment now they'd go trailing off to bed, leaving the men free to argue about the French until dawn. I took the stool at Giulia's feet, leaning back on my elbows, and she looked down at me, puzzled. "What do you mean, Leonello?"

"The Holy Father is more than forty years your elder. He has a short temper, an unfaithful heart, and a girth that will keep right on expanding until he looks like a sack of millet." I reached up to the goat in her lap and gave its silky ear a flick. "So why do you fight to keep him?"

She shrugged. "He's all I have."

"That's rot, my dear lady. You have a husband, you have a child, you have a family. You could let His Holiness's wandering eye wander off to someone new, and retire to that quiet married life you always told me you grew up wanting. But you sit here campaigning like a French general to get your papal lover back, and I wonder why." I cocked an eyebrow at her, wondering why I was talking like this, not caring enough to stop myself. "Is it the jewels? I doubt that young husband of yours could keep you in the kind of sparkly baubles you're used to. Can't bear the thought that another birthday might pass without a string of sapphires to mark the occasion? Or perhaps it's the Holy Father himself you'll miss—he may be aging and fattening, but that tongue of his must have some talent in it, judging from the sounds I hear you make behind your chamber doors. I assumed it was all performance and pretense, but perhaps not."

Two bright spots of color flared high in La Bella's cheeks, but I didn't let her speak.

"Or perhaps you just aren't suited for married life, even if you were raised to it." I gave her goat's ear another tweak. "The worst wives, one hears, make the best whores."

"Are you finished?" she said quietly.

"Oh, you know me. I can talk forever."

"You certainly can when it comes to being cruel. How good you are at it." She regarded me, giving a faint shake of her head. "Why, Leonello?"

"Because you're here," I said baldly. "And I'm bored, and I have to follow you about all day in this provincial mud hole when I'd rather be—"

Finding a murderer. Lately I'd begun to think it couldn't be Cesare Borgia at all. Surely a pope's son had better things to do than chase down low women to murder? If there was anyone in the Borgia service to suspect of dark deeds, blank-faced Michelotto was a far more likely candidate. From everything I'd heard, the man snuffed out human lives as casually as a cat killed mice. But Michelotto was his master's dog; he never said a word or made a move unless Cesare instructed it. Did he have the drive to commit murder at his own initiative rather than his master's? Perhaps not . . .

"When you'd rather be what?" Madonna Giulia asked.

"Nothing," I said, airy. "Twisted little men have twisted little souls, that's all. Didn't you know that, my lady whore?"

"I think I will go kiss Laura good night and then retire to bed." Giulia set down the goat and rose, smoothing stray white goat hairs off her velvet skirts. "I'll have no further need of you, Leonello."

"Tonight?" I challenged. "Or ever? I suppose you'll have me dismissed now. I must say, I shall miss your Pope's library."

"Why should I dismiss you?" She turned her head over one shoulder, the same angle of her bare-shouldered tableau of transfiguration. "Just because you're vindictive for no good reason doesn't mean I have to be. Thank you for awarding the crown of beauty to Lucrezia, by the way. It was kindly done."

"The least I could do," I said. "After that bare-armed simpering of yours made her husband hard as a pikestaff."

La Bella glanced toward Lucrezia, stricken, and it made me furious. All my insults just so many pebbles bouncing off her grave face, and the thing to pierce her was some hurt to Lucrezia.

My mistress glided off quietly, and I grimaced down at the goat. "Someone should have made you into pie long ago," I told it, and the wretched creature gave a *baaaa* and began nibbling my black velvet sleeve.

"Has Giulia gone to bed already?" I heard Lucrezia ask Madonna Adriana, rose-patterned skirts rustling.

"Yes, and in a very poor humor." Adriana glanced at me disapprovingly. "Leonello was rather unkind to her."

"It is not polite to eavesdrop," I remarked to the air, and Madonna Adriana sniffed and drew Lucrezia away from me toward the hearth.

"I didn't know any man in the world *could* be unkind to Giulia." Lucrezia ignored me, leaning her head in to Adriana's ringletted one. "Even my father—even when he's furious, all she has to do is wrinkle her nose at him, and he melts. It's not *fair*."

"Nothing's fair, my love." Adriana smoothed her former charge's hair.

The little Countess of Pesaro picked at a painted rose on her skirt. Her voice was very low, but I heard well enough as I took my deck of cards from my pouch and pretended to be absorbed in a complicated shuffle. It might not be polite to eavesdrop, but I was very good at it. "Hours I spent preparing this dress, and did anybody look at me?" Lucrezia demanded, and Adriana sighed. "No, they all looked at her. They always look at her. I'm taller than she is, and my eyes are blue which is much better than dark, and maybe my hair isn't as long but at least *I* don't get plump from eating too many *biscotti*—but she's still the one they look at. Even though I'm the Pope's daughter, and I'm the Countess of Pesaro, and this is *my* home."

"Of course it is," Madonna Adriana soothed. "And Giulia is your friend."

"I know." Lucrezia fiddled restlessly with a lock of her fair hair. "I'd never be here with my lord Sforza if not for her. But I wouldn't mind people looking at *me* now and then. Especially in *my* home." A resentful note entered her voice. "I'll write my father and tell him Caterina Gonzaga won our beauty contest. I'll tell him she's far taller and fairer than Giulia, too."

"And then maybe he'll take her for a mistress instead," Adriana said. "Do you really want to share his attention with that prancing Lombard instead of our Giulia, who is such delightful company over *pranzo*? Who lends you her jewelry whenever you ask? Who taught you how to manage the train on your wedding dress?"

The Countess of Pesaro sighed again, and Madonna Adriana put an arm about her shoulders. "To bed, my love," she said, and they rustled off without another word, leaving the men to the serious business of speculating on the French invasion. *Speculating* sounds so much more serious than *gossiping drunkenly*. Giulia's goat looked up at me, swallowing the tassel it had just eaten off a chair cushion, and gave another *baaa*.

"Don't you bleat at me," I told it. "I am not feeling guilty."

But maybe I was. Perhaps I *had* been rather hard on my poor giggly little mistress—who, quite truthfully, had never been cruel or dismissive or even thoughtless toward me in her life. Not even very giggly anymore; she'd turned quite quiet and introspective this summer in her worries over the Pope.

Twisted little men do indeed have twisted little souls.

CHAPTER FOURTEEN

✦

Where my treasure is, there is my heart.

—EXCERPT OF A LETTER FROM GIULIA FARNESE TO
RODRIGO BORGIA

Carmelina

Carmelina! Carmelina, listen to this." Water splashed from the huge blue-veined marble bath as Madonna Giulia beckoned me into the hot *bagno*. I set down the dish of *tourtes* I'd brought for the Pope's mistress to nibble as she had her hair washed. She sat alone in the enormous marble bath, half visible in the clouds of steam that filled the little blue-and-green marble chamber, wet tendrils of golden hair floating on the surface of the hot water like blond seaweed. Her naked shoulders gleamed pink above the water, and a maid stood behind with rolled-up sleeves, scrubbing at her scalp. I approached the bath carefully, watching my step on the steam-slick floor with its Roman-style mosaic of twining fish and mermaids, and Madonna Giulia beamed at me. "I've had a letter from His Holiness." Waving a very thick packet of pages. "Just listen to this!"

She cleared her throat, dropping her voice to an imposing bass and imitating the Pope's Spanish burr. " '*Everyone says that when you stood beside her*'—he means that nose-in-the-air tart Caterina Gonzaga—'*she was nothing but a lantern to your sun.*'"

"Very good," I approved, trading a grin with the maid massaging Madonna Giulia's hair. Podgy Count Ottaviano da Montevegio had offended nobody during his brief stay at the Palazzo Ducale, but his wife was another matter entirely. Madonna Caterina Gonzaga had turned up her nose at the *palazzo*, complained that my lemon-fried sardines were too salty, and left her chamber a sty. Had she not rustled north with her husband for their estates in San Lorenzo, the maids would have begun spitting in her wine. "I praised her to the skies when I wrote Rodrigo about her," Giulia said with relish. "It doesn't do to look too envious of other women. Men are already quite vain enough thinking we fight each other like cats for their attention, aren't they? Even if we *are* fighting like cats for their attention. Goodness, but love is complicated. If it weren't so enjoyable, no one would do it at all." Giulia kissed her letter, heedless of the water splashing from her bath to smear the ink. "I got a letter back, very next messenger. He calls himself '*the person who loves you more than anybody in the world.*' Isn't that lovely?"

"His Holiness turns a pretty phrase." A year or two ago I'd have been shocked to my bones at the thought of discussing the style and content of the Holy Father's love letters. Somehow, the shock had worn off. "He doesn't mince his affections, does he, Madonna Giulia?"

"He never minces anything he feels. And *some* people wonder why I want to keep him." Giulia la Bella gave a snort that was half anger, but her smile returned as she scanned the letter again. "He goes on to give me all the gossip from Rome. Juan is nagging to come home from Spain now that his wife is pregnant—can you imagine *Juan* a father? I ask you!—and the Tart of Aragon is making poor Joffre's life hell. She and Caterina Gonzaga would certainly get along . . ." Giulia rifled through more pages. "Here it is. My Pope accuses me of being heartless for enjoying myself without him." Her eyes glowed softly. "He misses me."

"I don't think anyone would miss me if I went absent," I said candidly, picking up the majolica plate of *tourtes* again and bringing it to the bath. "At least not until it came time to eat."

"What about that mysterious fellow of yours?" Madonna Giulia's eyes gleamed. "The one on whose behalf you learned about the many uses of limes? What was his name again?"

I suppressed a smile. "I never told you in the first place, Madonna Giulia."

"Well, tell me now. And do sit down, won't you, and eat some of those *tourtes* for me. I'm getting plump again, and I've got to take some of this fat off before I get back to Rome, so no sweets for me. Which is a shame, because I always eat when in the bath." Giulia looked envious, watching me help myself from the plate. Quince and ricotta *tourtes*—straight from page 412, Chapter: *Dolci*. "Why aren't you the one who's plump instead of me? Cooks are supposed to be fat!"

"They never are," I told her. "Real cooks are too busy running back and forth with kettles and spits and bread paddles to ever eat. We all survive on a taste of this and a spoonful of that and a nibble of something else. Never have anything to do with a fat cook, Madonna Giulia. Either he's too successful or too lazy to get off his rump."

"Good advice, I'm sure, but I want to hear more about this man of yours. Is he a cook? Is he handsome—"

"Under the water and rinse, Madonna Giulia," the maid ordered.

"No one say anything interesting until I'm rinsed," Madonna Giulia warned, setting her letter aside, and sank bubbling under the surface. She wriggled under the water, the occasional elbow or knee emerging as she swished the soap out of her hair, and surfaced like a mermaid. "If you won't tell me who your lover is, Carmelina, then listen to the letter I'm writing mine. He likes a good dramatic love letter, and I'm not sure I've got the tone quite right. '*My happiness depends upon Your Holiness, so I am unable to take delight in these pleasures of Pesaro—*'"

A gust of cool air blew into the clouds of steam before she could finish, and I looked over my shoulder to see the square velvet-skirted figure of Adriana da Mila coming into the scented heat of the *bagno*. I rose hastily from my stool—the Pope's mistress thought nothing of chattering with servants, but her mother-in-law did not care to see the time she paid for being wasted. But Madonna Adriana hardly spared a glance for me or the suddenly industrious maid who had wiped the grin from her face and busied herself hauling Giulia's mass of wet hair from the bathwater. Madonna Adriana looked at Giulia, and in her hand she held another letter.

"From His Holiness?" Giulia laughed. "I'll swear he's written every other day!"

"No, from Capodimonte. Your family." Madonna Adriana's face was unexpectedly grave. She looked at the maid and me and said, "Leave us."

I curtsied silently and retreated. "Let's listen," the maid whispered, and we both lingered beside the half-open door.

"It's bad news from your family, my dear," Madonna Adriana's voice continued. "I'm afraid it's your brother."

"Sandro?" Giulia whispered, so low I could hardly hear her. "Oh, no—"

"No, not Cardinal Farnese. Your older brother, Angelo. He's contracted a very bad fever. Your family thinks . . ."

I heard a great splash of water in the bath. "*Carmelina*," Giulia called. "*Pia!* Come back; I know you're both listening out there!"

I flew back inside with another curtsy, in time to see my mistress levering herself up out of the bath. Water shed in all directions, and the plate of ricotta *tourtes* flew with a *crack* to the marble floor. "Pia," she said to the maid, "fetch Laura's nurse and have them both readied."

"My dear, you can't think of going to Capodimonte," Madonna Adriana protested. "His Holiness will never allow it, not with the French army coming farther south every day—"

"This has nothing to do with Rodrigo."

"Of course it does. You think he will allow you to take a sudden journey unattended and without permission?"

"Carmelina, will you be good enough to find Leonello for me?" Madonna Giulia's eyes fell on me where I'd stooped to the floor to pick up the broken fragments of plate. "I know you can't stand the sight of him, and frankly right now I can't either, as nasty as he's been to me lately, but I'll want his protection on the journey. My usual guardsmen and grooms as well, of course; please tell the steward."

"Yes, Madonna Giulia," I said at once.

"You're coming too. I don't intend to stop at inns, so I'll need someone to cook on the road. Bring that apprentice of yours if you need someone to help with the heavy work."

"Giulia, please." Madonna Adriana's broad face had already begun to perspire in the steam still coming from the bath. "You really cannot—"

"—miss my own brother's deathbed?" Giulia flared at her, standing straight and naked on the mosaic floor, wet hair uncoiling in clinging strings over her back. "No, I quite agree. Please give Lucrezia my love, and tell her why I did not have time to thank Lord Sforza for his hospitality."

Madonna Giulia turned away, tugging her wet hair over one shoulder and beginning to weave it into a hasty plait as she called to the maid—"Just a riding dress and a few spares, Pia, nothing else!" But Madonna Adriana's hand fastened on her arm. She spoke in a low voice, one I shouldn't have heard, but I spent all my days tuning to the *sotto voce* mutters of my sulky scullions.

"Giulia, my dear, Rodrigo was very angry with you when you disobeyed him before, in the matter of Lucrezia's marriage. You think he will be forgiving again, when he's just gotten over his temper at your last disobedience? At least ask his permission first. Then you can go to your brother with a full papal guard."

Giulia took a deep breath, and I wondered if the flush from her cheeks came entirely from the bath's heat. "Carmelina," she said quietly, and I found myself hurrying to her side. "Go find Leonello now, and the stewards. We will all leave in one hour."

Giulia

I wasn't a half second out of my saddle before Sandro grabbed me up tight, lifting me clear off the courtyard's dusty stones. "*Sorellina*," he whispered. "I didn't think the Pope would allow you to make the journey, with the French—"

"The Pope does not own me." I felt my eyes prick and buried my face in my big brother's shoulder. "Angelo, is he—"

Sandro's lean handsome face was drawn tight about the eyes. "The fever took him this morning."

My heart squeezed. I'd half killed my poor gray mare on the ride to Lake Bolsena, I'd lashed at Carmelina and Leonello and the rest of my entourage whenever they proposed a stop for sleep or water or rest—and for what? My big brother was dead. I hadn't seen him since my wedding; I'd hardly given him a thought except to feel irritated when he wrote asking me to wheedle money or favors out of my Pope—but now he was gone, gone for good, and I'd never have a chance to mend things between us.

"Shhh, don't cry." Sandro ran a thumb under my welling eyes. "You came, and that's what matters."

So strange to be home—so very strange. Back in the drafty octagonal *castello* of my childhood, worn and just a little crumbling about the edges, washed by the lake on three sides so the sound of lapping water reached the ear from every room. The chilly chamber I had shared with Gerolama as a girl was the same: a curtained bed where I had wrestled her for my fair share of the blankets and dreamed about who my future husband would be. The smell of the lake was the same, and the dusty streets where old women in black gossiped on their steps and children ran shouting and clacking sticks together, and mules trudged past with loads of fish still flopping their death throes. An old dress I found in my girlhood clothes chest was the same, last worn when I was a virgin girl who had never even heard the names of Orsino Orsini or Rodrigo Borgia.

So strange.

"How long should we make preparations to stay?" Leonello asked me.

I looked at him oddly. He was foreign to me, a piece of one life entirely out of place among another very different existence. He stuck out like a harlot in a church, or an obscenity in a prayer, or a French army in Rome. "I don't know," I said in a blank voice, and moved to join my family.

I had never been close to Angelo, not as I was with Sandro. My older brother had been almost a man grown when I was born, too busy and important to take notice of another sister who would only have to be dowered and married off. He'd never had time for me, not until I became the Pope's mistress and thus a person to be asked for favors. I'd never quite forgiven him for that, and I hadn't wanted to come back to Capodimonte to visit him. Time enough to forgive him later, I'd thought— only now there wasn't.

He'd gotten fatter in the past two years; the folds of a premature double chin pressed stiff and waxy behind his collar as he lay on his bier surrounded by candles. His wife wept softly, clutching her two little girls. My sister, Gerolama, sat beside her, red-eyed and exhausted, and she rose to give me an unexpected hug instead of her usual scolding.

So strange.

I sat vigil beside my brother as Sandro and our other brother greeted the guests of Capodimonte who came to pay their respects. Familiar faces, faces I had known since childhood, so why did they look at me so avidly? "They've all heard of you, you know," Gerolama said with a touch of her old asperity.

Heard of me—of course. I was little Giulia Farnese, who had left home to be married, as all girls did, but then became the Pope's harlot. I was notorious. I'd been notorious for nearly two years, really, but I hadn't been home in all that time to see my neighbors gossiping and whispering as they looked at me. The following day during the funeral procession, more people looked at me than at Angelo's bier as it advanced slowly through the streets. I'd walked the Pope's daughter to her wedding in the Vatican, but I didn't walk behind my brother's body with Sandro—that wasn't how things were done here. I waited in the church in a borrowed black dress that didn't suit me, head decently covered, watching the priests and then the coffin and then my brothers trail past, and still people stared at me like I had two heads.

Sandro stood at my side during the requiem, splendid and remote in his scarlet regalia. Under cover of his red sleeve, his fingers twined with mine. "Cardinal Farnese," I heard someone snigger during the

Kyrie. "He's a petticoat cardinal if I ever saw one—only got the red hat for being the Borgia brother-in-law!"

Sandro whipped round with a black glare. "Hold your filthy tongue!" he snapped, and the priest broke off mid-word, and there was a moment of frozen silence in which people stared at us. I looked at the floor, but Sandro just leveled another glare. "*Kyrie eleison, Christe eleison . . .*" the priest resumed, but not before I heard soft giggles behind us.

The rest of the requiem was just a fog. I heard none of it, just stared at the altar. The church itself was the same as it ever was: the cross-eyed Madonna before whom I'd wriggled in childhood agonies of boredom during Mass; the steps I'd skipped up weekly to make confession; the shrine before which a half-drunk lay friar had tried to grope me when I was twelve. The churchyard was the same, the dry summer grass seeded with tiny yellow flowers. At Angelo's grave site, I stooped to pluck one of those flowers and stood twirling it between my fingers, watching dry-eyed as his coffin was lowered into the earth. His wife sobbed beside me—had she loved him so much? I'd had no idea. How strange, to have a husband you loved, who maybe even loved you in return.

"Whore," someone whispered in the crowd behind me.

"Will you go back to Rome?" Sandro asked me the day after we put our brother into the ground. He'd found me up on the tallest of the turrets, looking out over the rippling blue expanse of lake. I'd spent so many hours up here with my battered crownless straw hat, sunning my hair. I couldn't afford expensive saffron and cinnabar rinses back then. Sandro leaned an elbow on the stone parapet, looking down at me.

"I *should* go back to Rome." I'd already had a letter from Madonna Adriana, warning that Rodrigo was furious with me. Not that I'd flown to my brother's deathbed, but that I'd done so without permission and without considering the dangers of the advancing French army. I hadn't really given the French a thought. When you get news of a deathbed in the family, even the deathbed of a brother you've been on rather cold terms with, you *go*. Rodrigo wouldn't have given a thought to the French either, if he had gotten news that one of his precious children was deathly ill—yet he was angry with me for doing exactly the same thing! I ask you. "I don't want to go back to Rome just yet," I said.

"Good." Sandro ruffled my hair. "I hate seeing you hop just because that mitered old goat bleats."

I gave my brother a look. "I thought we agreed you wouldn't call the Holy Father names behind his back."

"I certainly can't say them to his *face*. I find I can't dislike him enough for that. *But*"—and a hint of relish entered Sandro's voice—"I quite enjoy the thought of our Holy Father fuming away like a spurned schoolboy as you skip off for a holiday."

"A family funeral? Hardly a holiday, Sandro!"

"—like Menelaus fuming as Helen skips off to Troy with Paris—"

I couldn't help but laugh. Sandro had been so drawn and sad since my arrival, and I was glad to see a little of his old sparkle returning. He wasn't meant for sadness.

"So you'll be staying awhile?" Sandro pressed. "I thought I'd stay myself; shirk my duties in Rome for a bit. Everyone thinks I'm a prancing clown as a cardinal anyway; might as well live up to the reputation."

"You *are* a prancing clown," I told my brother. "You're the worst cardinal in Christendom."

"I follow my Holy Father's example in all things," Sandro said piously. "Down to the fine *palazzo* and the bastard babies. You know Silvia's pregnant? My very first bastard; such a milestone!"

"Oh, Sandro."

"She craves oysters all the time," he said airily. "Did you crave oysters? They're very expensive. Maybe she just says she craves them, because she knows I'll buy her anything in this state. She wants a boy—she's already planning I'll be Pope someday; then she'll be La Bella of Rome and our son will marry a Spanish princess or a Neapolitan duchess just like the Borgia sons. I haven't the heart to tell her that your pet goat is more likely to be elected Pope than me."

"What you should tell her is that it's not all jewels and glamour being La Bella." I had found spittle on my hem after Angelo's funeral; men had leered at me while their wives dragged at their elbows to pull them away; and several friends I'd giggled with in childhood—girls I'd whispered and dreamed with, bouncing on the way to confession as we planned the dresses we would someday have and the handsome husbands we would marry—had looked right through me when I greeted them. In Rome I was a harlot, but I was at least an important one, someone of whom favors were begged and influence courted. Here in dusty little Capodimonte a straying wife was just a whore, no matter how powerful the man with whom she strayed. No wonder none of my now-respectably-married friends wanted to know me anymore.

"*Dio*," Leonello said dryly after a fortnight's stay. "I thought Pesaro was dull and backward. Now it seems a metropolis of enlightenment and culture." The servants all seemed to think my bodyguard was the Devil himself, from the way they forked their fingers in the sign of the evil eye every time he strode past. He didn't help matters by crossing his eyes at them and hissing like a serpent in response. My sister thought Leonello a freakish little man and far too rude, but Sandro liked him. They played *primiera* in the evenings, or they did before Sandro's duties as cardinal finally recalled him to Rome, and usually Leonello won.

I had letters. From Lucrezia, complaining that her father was blaming her for not keeping me in Pesaro, and really why did she deserve to be dragged into this? From Madonna Adriana, saying the usual, or so I assumed—I tore her letters up unread. From Orsino—he was hunting; he was wel; was I wel; and since I was so close by, would I consider visiting him in Basanelo before he had to leave with his troops to march against the Frenche? And of course, I had letters from my Pope.

"Not such a good letter as the last one, Madonna Giulia?" Carmelina asked me, bringing a plate of damson-stuffed *focaccia* roses to the rooftop where I sat looking out over the lake again and bouncing Laura in my lap, because I didn't feel like reading Rodrigo's furious scrawl.

"Not so good, no," I answered. "It's always a bad sign in his letters when he starts cursing in Spanish, Italian, *and* Latin."

Carmelina eyed me curiously. A month ago I'd have been frantic at the thought that Rodrigo was angry with me—I *had* been frantic. Now

I couldn't seem to care. I tossed the letter aside, holding Laura up so she could see the blue glitter of the lake below. "That's Lake Bolsena, *Lauretta mia*, isn't it beautiful? I'll take you swimming in it tomorrow—"

"How long will we be staying, Madonna Giulia?" Carmelina asked me, and I heard the real question. *Madonna Giulia, why are we staying?* In Pesaro, Leonello had asked me a question about my Pope. *Why do you fight to keep him?* I hadn't known how to answer that, but here I'd had time to think the matter through. "You know something, Carmelina?" I mused. "All my life, I've been trained to please. Please my mother; please the priests; please my husband." Only that hadn't worked out, so I'd set myself to pleasing Rodrigo Borgia instead. It had never even occurred to me to stop trying, when his eye began to wander. And where had all that eager-to-please anxiety gotten me? Holding my breath, worrying that I might anger him if I dared to side with his daughter or go to my own brother's funeral!

"I'm tired of trying to please everyone else," I announced. "I'm going to please myself for once, and I don't *care* if I anger His Holiness or my mother-in-law. I want some time to myself, time to play with Laura, and sit in the sun, and think and sleep and eat. So I'll take another plate of those *focaccia* things, Carmelina, and we're going to stay in Capodimonte until I feel like leaving."

She grinned at me. "As you please, Madonna Giulia."

A month—six weeks. Carmelina invaded the kitchens like a French army, and the food improved markedly. Pantisilea was so busy bed-hopping through the local farmers, she was looking quite hollow-eyed. Gerolama and her husband went back to Florence. "Not that Florence is a pleasant place these days," she sniffed. "That mad monk Savonarola has everyone stirred up! Not that he isn't right about most things, there's no doubting the world is a wicked greedy place, but now he wants us all to burn our good furniture and our nice clothes and live like mendicants!"

"Absurd," I agreed. But mad Dominican monks seemed as remote as anything else. I couldn't even get interested in the advancing French, though I'd heard dark whispers at Mass that they'd raped and murdered their way as far south as Parma, or maybe it was Bologna. Nothing would change Capodimonte, not even the French. Nothing ever changed here. Once I had found that maddening, but now I was not so sure.

I had another letter from my husband. I had another letter from my Pope, who must have heard about Orsino's letters, because Rodrigo went from irritated to enraged in one short page. He began *Thankless, treacherous Giulia!* and went swiftly downhill from there.

You'll lose him, warned the part of me that still worried about placating him. *You'll lose him, and then where will you be?*

Here, I thought. Because if Rodrigo tired of me, this life could be mine again, or one very much like it, with my husband in Carbognano or Bassanello. And even though I'd dreamed as a girl of a life of luxury in the Holy City, now I found I had been missing this old life. I liked eating quiet meals with my family rather than a *palazzo* full of ambitious courtiers and slippery ambassadors and scheming cardinals. I liked passing my visiting hours not with petitioners angling for favors, but with Angelo's widow, whom I was trying to dissuade from her notion of retiring to a nunnery; with Sandro and his pert little mistress Silvia, whom he had begun bringing with him on his visits from Rome whenever he felt like shirking his ecclesiastical duties. And more than anything, I liked spending my days with Laura. All day, every day; combing her hair and taking her swimming and teaching her her first prayers now that she was old enough to speak proper words. Mothering her myself, instead of passing her off to her nurse for hours because I was required for yet another banquet at the Vatican.

I liked being ordinary. Giulia Farnese again, not Giulia la Bella, not the Venus of the Vatican, not the Bride of Christ.

Summer fell toward autumn. My Pope was well beyond angry and approaching incensed—"He ordered me back here to retrieve you on pain of excommunication," Sandro said with a rueful wince on his next visit.

"Which of us is to be excommunicated?"

"Both, if we don't present ourselves to the Holy Father posthaste. I've been ordered to retrieve you." Sandro eyed me thoughtfully. "A little holiday is one thing, *sorellina*, but what are you up to?"

"I don't know," I confessed. I didn't seem to know much of anything anymore, except that I didn't feel like jumping to Rodrigo's side yet, just because he shouted. I did miss him—I ached sometimes at night for his warm arms around me in my big cold bed. But I still wanted time to *think*. I walked beside the lake with Laura, nodding to the fishermen, until they began to nod back shyly as they touched their caps. I took up my mother's old habit of collecting food and secondhand clothes and taking them for distribution to the beggars who huddled outside the church. The church itself was in bad need of repairs—"one more stormy season," the priest admitted, "and that tower will come through the roof!" I found myself looking at plans, speaking to stonemasons, scribbling estimates, browbeating the funds out of my brother for repairs. There was the yearly summer festival by the lake—our family had always presided over the festival, and I took my place to help bestow the prizes. When I gave out the purse for the largest catch of the season, one or two of the other women smiled at me.

"You can't keep lingering like this," Gerolama warned me on her next visit. "The Holy Father won't hang after you forever!"

"I thought you'd be pleased," I said tartly. "Aren't you the one who always said I was blotting the family honor by being the Pope's whore?"

Her eyes flickered.

"Besides," I added, "I want to see the church tower shored up. It's such a pleasure to have a project that isn't an altar cloth. Or achieving the perfectly sun-bleached head of hair." I felt . . . capable. Not just pretty. Good for something besides being decorative. Even more so the following day, when I heard a shriek and a string of Venetian curses from the kitchens, and ran in to find my imperturbable Carmelina crouched on top of the trestle table to get away from the serpent slithering idly over the flagstones. "It's just a water snake," I laughed. "They're always getting into the house from the lake. It's nothing to be afraid of!"

"Kill it, Bartolomeo!" Carmelina yelled, ignoring me.

"Are you insane?" Her red-haired apprentice scrambled right up onto the table beside her, clutching the little wooden cross around his neck. "I hate snakes!"

"It's harmless," I scolded. "You two! Not fazed at all when it comes to turning those disgusting Tiber eels into stew, but you're afraid of a *water snake*?" I forked the hissing thing up with a pair of Carmelina's tongs and tossed it out into the courtyard, only to find my cook staring at me.

"Santa Marta," she muttered, scrambling down. "Giulia *la Bella*? It should be Giulia *la Coraggiosa*."

Giulia the Brave? I liked that.

Perhaps it was brave of me to write to my papal lover and tell him I was thinking of paying a visit to Orsino before I came back to Rome. "He's written to request that I come see him before he departs Bassanello with his troops." Once such a letter would have taken me hours to write; I would have agonized over every word, and whether it would upset Rodrigo or not. Now I just wrote the bald truth, because I didn't feel like lying. Though I did feel a little guilty when I got his reply, because I think my honesty nearly killed my Pope. I could hear the apoplectic roar all the way from Rome.

We could not believe you would act with such ingratitude! he wrote in letters almost riven into the page of his next letter. *After all your repeated promises that you would be faithful to Our command, and not go near Orsino! But now you are doing the opposite! Risking your life going to Bassanello—and with the purpose, no doubt, of giving yourself to that stallion again!*

"Stallion." I ask you. I should have started trying to please myself instead of Rodrigo a long time ago. Even if he was angry, he was certainly a great deal more attentive now than he'd been when I was last in Rome!

In the end, I didn't go to Bassanello. Orsino came to me instead.

Leonello

C areful, now," I called after little Laura Orsini. Giulia Farnese's daughter flitted about the edge of Lake Bolsena, brown and naked as a tiny water nymph, her little shift lying in a discarded heap beside me where I sat under the shade of a tall oak keeping a vigilant eye on my small charge. It was November now, but the winter cold had yet to really settle in—still warm enough for naked frolicking by the lake, as far as Laura was concerned.

"You shouldn't let her run about like that," Madonna Giulia's sisters-in-law scolded, shocked. "It's not decent!"

"I swam naked in that lake too when I was her age," Giulia said. "And I didn't come to any harm. Let her run, there's plenty of time to teach her to be a lady."

"At least make her keep that shift on in front of the men!" A dark glance at me. But Giulia overrode them, and since she was off this afternoon on one of her surprisingly frequent mercy missions to Capodimonte's beggars, it fell to me and a few nursemaids to take her daughter along the winding path that descended from the *castello* like a stairway down to the lake that lapped below, where oaks had managed to sprout among the craggy rocks of the shore. I'd sent the nursemaids back to the *castello*, tired of their chattering, and the lake stretched blue and sparkling before me under an equally blue dome of sky; wood thrushes warbled overhead, and across the water church spires pierced up toward the sun. It might still be summer warm, but I could see leaves withering on the branches of the oak tree above me, feel their crunch beneath as I shifted on my spread-out cloak, and knew autumn was here.

Whether La Bella liked it or not, her summer idyll was over.

"Leo, Leo!" came Laura's shriek from the water. "*Tattels!*"

I was a fluent interpreter by now of Laura's eccentric eighteen-month-old vocabulary. *Tattels* were *turtles*. "Don't tell Signorina Carmelina when I take you back to the kitchens for your midday meal," I advised over the top of Marcus Aurelius's *Meditations*. "She'll tramp out here with a net and the next thing you know, that little baby turtle you're holding right now will turn up on your plate."

Laura giggled: a wriggling little imp of a girl, squatting on her small heels in the shallow rivulets of the water's edge, wiggling her toes in the soft lake mud as she carefully released the turtle back into the water. Half a summer spent learning to walk and run beside the lake had turned her brown all over, the fair soft rings of her hair bleached to pale gold. "No higher than your knees," I warned as she splashed deeper into the lake. "You know what your mother said."

"Iss, Leo." *Yes, Leo.* Laura liked me—I was clearly an Old Person, yet one built conveniently to her size, and it fascinated her. She had practiced her toddling baby steps clinging to my stubby fingers, and I didn't mind letting her. She was a fetching little thing, too young to know how to be cruel. I might as well enjoy that while it lasted.

"Leonello!"

Madonna Giulia's voice, and even before I lifted my eyes from my book, I thought she sounded strange. Oddly stifled, and as I found her approaching figure picking its way along the lapping edge of the lake, I saw another figure behind her. A young man of perhaps twenty-one, fair-haired, blue-eyed, his youthful skinniness not quite done filling out into a man's leanness. I fingered the little knife in my cuff, but more out of habit than fear. In my two years as bodyguard to La Bella, I'd never once been called upon to spring to her defense—and I didn't think that first time would come now, not against a man she was willingly bringing toward her daughter.

"Laura," she said, bending down, and the little girl hurled herself into her mother's arms like a small brown monkey. Giulia lifted her up, smoothing the fair curls, and turned toward the young man with a smile that was . . . nervous? "Laura, may I present you to Orsino Orsini."

Dio. I put my book down, looking at this unexpected guest with greater interest. I had never seen him either: the young husband who had been given cuckold's horns by the Pope himself.

"This is she?" The boy had a pleasant tenor voice, stiffer than a board from nerves.

"Yes. *Lauretta mia*, this is your—that is, he's my . . ."

It was a stopper as far as courtesies went. *Your father*; but Laura knew only the bluff merry-eyed figure of the Pope as far as fathers went. *My husband*; but Madonna Giulia had not to my knowledge laid eyes on him since before Laura was born. "Orsino Orsini," La Bella said at last, curtsying with the little girl in her arms and avoiding the whole tangled mess.

Orsino Orsini's blue eyes flicked over the little girl who bore his name. Looking, perhaps, for signs of his own face? *Useless*, I thought. One pretty little blond girl looked much like another—it's the vanity in men that makes them insist their children are their image. Laura was simply a happy-faced child in her mother's arms, nothing to declare her either an Orsini or a Borgia.

"She's beautiful," Orsino said at last. He reached a finger out toward Laura's cheek, but she retreated into her mother's neck, suddenly shy. Orsino looked shy too, looking at Giulia. "You're beautiful, too. Just as beautiful as I remembered."

"Thank you." If he was expecting her to blush like a girl, he did not know how much poise his wife had acquired over the past few years. "You look well, Orsino. You've grown."

"Yes. I'm a whole two inches taller." He squared his shoulders. "It's all the riding I do now, it's made me much stronger. You know I have a *condotta*? I ride everywhere with my soldiers—"

Giulia cocked her head, inspecting his profile. "Did you break your nose?"

"Yes." He coughed. "I, um. It was, well, it was a battle—my men against some of those Milanese thugs . . ."

I snorted, not very softly. Orsino looked down at me as though a bush had spoken. "What's that?" he asked Giulia.

"*That* is someone calling you a liar," I remarked before she could respond. "You didn't break that nose in any battle, my lord Orsini. Cardinal Farnese and I chat quite a bit, you know, when we play *primiera*, and it's not all gossip from the College of Cardinals. He's told me one or two other things closer to home . . ."

Giulia raised her eyebrows.

Orsino reddened, touching his crooked nose. "It was your brother," he admitted to her. "Sandro laid into me. After he, well . . ."

"After he found out you'd agreed to lend out your bride as a whore," I supplied helpfully, "Madonna Giulia's brother found you out hunting, dragged you off your horse, and broke your nose and two ribs."

"Really?" Giulia sounded rather pleased. "Sandro never told me.

What are you doing here, Orsino? You *are* supposed to be marching on the French with your men by now; I had your last letter."

So they wrote to each other? Interesting. I did not think the Pope would be pleased. On the other hand, very little about Giulia or her extended absence pleased him at the moment. And that did not seem to bother her one whit, which I found even more interesting.

"I sent the men on without me and went back to Bassanello. Then here." He looked down at his boots, toeing a mark in the lakeside mud and smudging it out with equal care. "I—wanted to see you."

Giulia looked at him steadily over Laura's curly head. Her smile had faded, along with the nervous flick of her eyes, and now she looked as bland and neutral as a marble goddess gazing out over the heads of her worshippers.

"You've never been to Bassanello, have you?" Orsino continued, still not meeting his wife's eyes. "It's not much—just little hills and a fortress, really. It's Carbognano that I want to show you someday—that's beautiful. We have a *castello* there; it may just look rough and square and crenellated on the outside, but it's beautiful inside. There's a *sala* with a painted ceiling."

"Goodness, the sophistication. Pack at once, *madonna*! This must be seen!"

"I've heard of Carbognano." Giulia looked around for Laura's discarded shift, stooping to retrieve it. "Is that the town you got lordship over from His Holiness, in exchange for the extended loan of your wife?" Her voice was level and fixed, not colored with anger, not colored with any emotion at all—but Orsino flushed.

"There's a lake nearby," he continued doggedly. "Lago di Vico. Not so big as this one"—waving an arm over the blue expanse of Lake Bolsena—"but pretty. The breeze comes right off the lake and cools us in summer. And we make a very good olive oil, not to mention our production of hazelnuts."

"Not just painted ceilings, but hazelnuts," I commented to the air. "How is such splendor to be imagined?"

Orsino looked at me, flushing. "Look here, you can leave now."

"Not on your orders," I replied. "*You* don't pay my wages. And if you try to force me, you'll find me much harder to move than my size would indicate." I hoped he'd try.

Orsino opened his mouth, but Giulia intervened. "Leonello, please don't. He is a guest here." She sent me a quelling look, then turned back at her husband. She looked almost encouraging. "You were saying? Lago di Vico, and Carbognano . . ."

But my scorn seemed to have taken whatever courage he had. He just gazed at her, pleading, and she gave a little sigh and dropped to her knees so she could tug the discarded shift over Laura's blond head.

Orsino shuffled. The silence grew. Giulia drew Laura's arms through the armholes of her shift; Laura struggled with her and scowled. "Don' like," she said mutinously. "Don' *like*."

"Doesn't like what?" Orsino asked.

"Clothes." Giulia at last wrestled her daughter's arms into their sleeves. "No matter what I put on her, she either takes it off at once or goes plunging into the lake, clothes and all. A shame, really, because half the fun of having a daughter is dressing her up in pretty gowns, isn't it?" Giulia straightened, taking Laura firmly by one hand.

"She'd like the lake in Carbognano," Orsino hedged. "If she were ever to see it, that is. Good swimming there."

"Is there?" Giulia's flat mask softened with the faintest of smiles. "Perhaps you'd care to walk with us, then, and tell me more about it."

He looked as though his breath had stopped in his chest.

Giulia looked back over her shoulder at me. She'd given up her elaborate coiffures here in the country; her hair was bundled at the back of her head in a net, and she had even more freckles across her nose and bosom like a dusting of gold sand. "Perhaps you could wait for us here, Leonello?"

"No," I said, tucking Marcus Aurelius into my doublet and rising. "It's Borgia coin that pays my wages, Madonna Giulia, and the Pope will not care to see his concubine stroll off into the sunset with her husband unchaperoned."

I spoke deliberately, looking at Orsino. He flushed, looking at the lake again. Giulia came closer to me in a rustle of dusty woolen skirts, lowering her voice.

"What harm will it really do, Leonello? He wants only to talk."

"He wants his wife back," I said. "Not that he'll do anything about it. It takes guts to go up against a Borgia, far less a pope, and that boy hasn't got the guts of a plucked chicken. I take it back, you know—what I said in Pesaro. I can see now why you abandoned the handsome lad for the aging cleric, and it wasn't for the jewels."

"Orsino Orsini is my husband." A spark of anger lit Giulia's eye as she looked down at me.

"But not Laura's father, I think, despite the Pope's doubts." I cocked an eyebrow, grinning. "If I were you, I'd be on my knees praying she turns out a bastard Borgia rather than a true-born Orsini. Bad enough having a gutless husband without getting saddled with his gutless offspring."

Giulia Farnese slapped me. Not one of those dainty slaps I'd seen women deal out to disobedient maids or pouting children either—she got her arm and all her weight behind it, and her hand crashed against my face like a clap of thunder. I staggered sideways and fell, barely catching myself on my elbows.

"Follow us or not, you twisted little bastard," she said. "As you like."

She turned and swept back to the puzzled Orsino, who had been crouching on his haunches to speak with a still-wary Laura. "There's a lovely view of the town a little way down the shore," Giulia announced, reaching to take Laura's hand. "Shall we?"

Orsino looked as though he wished he could take her hand too. But he took Laura's other palm instead.

I sat up slowly as they walked away, brushing off my muddy palms. I had lake slime on my fine black breeches. *Dio,* how I missed Rome. Give me stinking alleys and noisy wine shops and foul city smoke over the joys of the country any day.

Once I would have thought Giulia Farnese agreed with me—the Pope's elegant concubine in her velvets and jewels, dancing till dawn and reveling in parties and parades and masques. But after a summer spent in sleepy little Pesaro, sleepier little Capodimonte where the greatest event of the week was Sunday Mass . . .

Afternoon sun glinted off the trio of fair heads retreating down the shore of the lake. Young Orsini looked like he was describing something, waving his free hand. Giulia had her head tilted at the attentive angle all men seemed to find so flattering. Laura skipped between them, swinging on their hands. Husband, wife, child—a little trinity of family contentment.

If she decided to remain here, either in Capodimonte or in Carbognano, I might very well be unnecessary. No doubt she'd scrape up some consolation post for me, just to be kind. Which meant I would still be out of employment, because I wasn't going to rot in the country on Giulia Farnese's pity just for the sake of keeping my belly full.

"Here's a pretty mess," I said to no one in particular, and went inside to brush off the mud.

CHAPTER FIFTEEN

Fathers and other relations who violently
gag their daughters!

—SUORA ARCANGELA TARABOTTI, *"L'INFERNO MONACALE"*

Carmelina

"I miss Rome," I told the mummified hand crossly. "I miss the city, I miss proper kitchens with proper cold rooms for the cream and not just cramped little nooks with a freezing cold window slit, I miss that Sardinian dark-rinded cheese I can only get from that one-eyed cheese importer who won't ship all the way out here in the provinces. And if I have to cook up one more batch of that wretched lake smelt, I shall scream."

I could hear Santa Marta agreeing with me through the linen of the little drawstring bag. No more carrying her about beneath my overskirt; I'd hung her up on a rack with some rosemary I'd left to dry, so she could watch over the *cena* preparations. Santa Marta liked a vantage point, I'd found. I could swear that hand had a way of falling out of the pouch if I carried it too long out of sight beneath my skirt. It was a thought to make me cross myself and shiver, but there's nothing that doesn't stop being strange given enough time, and after a while I'd taken to hanging the little pouch up with the drying herbs where it had a nice view over the cramped little kitchens. I'd want a view too if I'd spent the last few centuries locked in a reliquary box with nothing edible in sight but the occasional holy wafer.

"I'm sure you miss the city, too," I told Santa Marta, reaching for a pile of garden greens. With so few luxuries on hand at the local markets, I'd been forced to do some experimenting with humbler ingredients than I was normally used to. Salads of simple dandelion leaves rather than the expensive lettuces I could get in Rome; little bite-sized cheese pillows flavored with mint and lemon from the gardens rather than costly spices imported from Venice; saddle of rabbit instead of breast of peacock. "Cooking for a provincial household is certainly good for one's creativity, but it's not the same as laying a table for a pope, is it?" I went on to Santa Marta. "Not to mention the difficulty of getting good saffron here. At least Madonna Giulia's left off stealing my supply to rinse her hair—"

"Who are you talking to, *signorina*?" Bartolomeo's voice sounded behind me as he reached for an apron. The rest of the household had gone brown under the blazing summer sun of Capodimonte, but Bartolomeo just pinkened and peeled and pinkened again even though it was now fall.

"No one. Start chopping those onions over there."

"You're talking to that little bag again, aren't you?" My apprentice grinned, testing the edge of his knife and then halving the first onion with an easy flourish. With so little to do out here in Capodimonte, we'd passed the summer days improving his knife skills. He had a way to go before he matched my speed, but his knife was a blur in his freckled hands as it reduced the onion to a minced heap. "What's *in* that bag, anyway? Ottaviano always swore it held the withered balls of all the apprentices you've killed and eaten."

"None of your business. And keep chopping," I added as Bartolomeo flipped his knife behind his back and gave another grin at me when he caught it. "Move the mouth less, please, and the hands more!" I reached for an apple that I began peeling in one long strip, just to show him he didn't know everything yet. "We'll prepare smoked onion bread, red mullet in a salt crust, and a good thick *zuppa* of asparagus in meat broth. That should do for *cena*."

"Yes, *signorina*." His eyes tracked the lengthening curl of apple peel ribboning evenly from my knife. "How many at table tonight?"

"Madonna Giulia, her sister, her brother and his wife—" The other brother, not Cardinal Farnese, who had gone back to Rome again what with the French approaching so near. I'd miss the young Cardinal, a jokester with a refined palate and as healthy an appreciation for my food as his sister. "I'm not too proud to have a woman managing my kitchens," he'd wheedled me last month with those dark eyes of his as merry as Madonna Giulia's. "Think about it, Signorina Carmelina!"

It was worth thinking about. Mistress of my own kitchens, and for a cardinal too! Even if he was only twenty-six and more jester than churchman, it would be a step up in the world for me, and no mistake. But I was all but mistress of the kitchens in the Palazzo Santa Maria, and I'd grown fond of them. The scullions who hopped like obedient frogs whenever I spoke, the unlimited papal budget for rare spices and imported cheeses and anything else I wanted for the storerooms, Madonna Giulia and her endless appetite for my *tourtes*. Not to mention Marco, and I wasn't at all sure Marco would let me leave Madonna Giulia's household. It wasn't my company in his bed that he couldn't do without—he could have any of the maids he chose, anytime he wanted a girl between his sheets. He probably *was* bedding one of the *palazzo* maids back in Rome, since I had been gone so long, and the thought did not make me jealous in the slightest.

No, Marco could get along well enough without me in his bed, but in his kitchens? That was a different matter. My cousin was a lazy soul, and my presence meant he didn't have to work near as hard. He wouldn't be happy if I moved on to greener fields and he had to do his own dawn shopping at the fish-market again. And I still owed him for taking me in when I first arrived in Rome.

I flicked the long ribbon of apple peel away with a final flourish, tossing the naked apple at Bartolomeo and rummaging for the tender shoots of asparagus I'd already set aside to blanch. If I were telling the truth (and *that* was something I kept strictly for Santa Marta and my own conscience), it wasn't Marco himself that I missed, but the presence of a man in my bed. Smooth male warmth stretched over me, kisses and laughter and the sharper smell of masculine sweat . . . One or two of the guardsmen here in Capodimonte had given me the eye, but I hadn't been tempted. I had *standards,* after all. Guardsmen stank of boiled leather and sour beer. The only two lovers I'd had since fleeing Venice had been a nobleman and a cook, and noblemen and cooks might not have a single other thing in common, but both kinds of men *smelled* wonderful. Sandalwood oil and leather and scent for Cesare Borgia; cloves and herbs and olive oil for Marco. I didn't see myself bedding any more noblemen, but I could at least look about for another cook rather than just fill my bed with guardsmen because I was lonely. Cooks not only smell lovely, they have dexterous fingers. If you can peel an apple in one long curl, the ties and laces of a woman's dress are nothing. Not to mention a cook's discerning tongue when it came to the tastes of the body: the salt of sweat, the fragrance of soap, the musk of desire rising hot in the blood like oil rising to the top of a sauce . . . My hands slowed on the chopping board.

"I'll bet I can peel an apple in one strip." Bartolomeo eyed the bowl of fruit. "Can I try?"

"No." I reached for more asparagus. "Keep chopping those onions for the bread. Then I'll show you how to cut out the dough in diamond patterns. Presentation is as important as flavor, you know."

"Yes, *signorina.*" He sounded faintly mutinous, but he obeyed me. "Is Madonna Giulia's husband staying for *cena* as well?"

I laid a double handful of slender green asparagus shoots in to cook with a few slices of prosciutto. "He is."

Bartolomeo let out a long whistle, and I slanted an eyebrow. "No gossiping about your employers, now!"

"I didn't say a word." But my apprentice shook his head, and truth be told the whole household was shaking its head ever since Orsino Orsini had arrived two days earlier. I think Madonna Giulia's brother was tempted to deny entrance at all, for fear he might just take his wife with him when he left. God forbid the Farnese family lose that stream of papal privileges from the sister they were so quick to call a harlot!

"I heard Orsini is going to drag her to Bassanello," one of the maids had confided. "By the hair!"

"You think His Holiness will stand for that?" the chief steward snorted. "He'll send troops against Orsino Orsini to fetch her back . . ."

"What *are* you going to do?" I'd heard Madonna Giulia's brother groan at her over the table. But the Bride of Christ, for once, didn't seem to be talking to anyone, and nobody knew anything.

"About Madonna Giulia," Bartolomeo began. "Do you think she'll really—"

"I don't think anything," I said, giving the asparagus a stir and adding half a jug of simmering beef broth. "Except that I wish Lord Orsini would be a little more specific when he sends down a compliment of 'lovely food' because how am I supposed to feed the man if I don't know what his tastes are. That, Bartolomeo, is our only concern."

"Yes, *signorina*."

"You might have more to concern you than Lord Orsini tonight," a voice full of sour amusement said at the entry to the kitchens. "His mother's just arrived."

I turned, still elbow-deep in asparagus, and saw Leonello leaning up against the doorjamb, arms folded across his chest. I wished Madonna Giulia hadn't given him that all-black livery—it became him well enough, no mistake, but he looked more like a devil than ever. Then his words sank in. "Madonna Adriana's here?"

"The lady herself, and a party of papal guards. Not to mention some stragglers they picked up on the road, some Venetian lords and an archbishop and their various entourages, getting out of the path of the French army and now begging hospitality for the night." Leonello shrugged. "You will have rather more mouths to feed this evening than anticipated, *Signorina Cuoca*."

"Why on earth is Madonna Adriana here?" I blinked, drying my hands on my apron. I could braise some fresh lake trout for her—trout for an old trout . . .

"I thought we weren't supposed to ask questions about our employers, *signorina*," Bartolomeo said innocently. I gave him a dirty look.

"Besides, why bother asking?" Leonello's voice was very dry. "Madonna Adriana is here to drag La Bella back to Rome, of course, and before the French can arrive."

Bartolomeo sealed his mixture of cheese and onions into its packet of enveloping pastry. "Are the French really almost here?"

"No more than two days' journey by the Montefiascone road, from what I hear."

I couldn't help a shiver. "So close?"

"Oh, I shouldn't worry, *Signorina Cuoca*. If you fall into French hands, you'll just be raped a few times. It's me and this apprentice lad of yours who have something to be afraid of. Him they'll kill, and me they'll dress in motley and set to dance for their king."

"Very funny." I dismembered a handful of asparagus spears in a violent yank.

"Don't prickle, my lady. I didn't have to give you advance warning of a dozen extra guests at your table, did I, but here I am. Out of kindness to you—and I might advise you begin packing up this sorry excuse for a kitchen with anything you brought from Rome, because I imagine a journey back to the city is imminent. Madonna Adriana is besieging the Bride of Christ in her bower as we speak, and she did not look at all willing to be fobbed off with excuses." Leonello tilted his head, hazel eyes glittering up at me. "There, doesn't that earn me a thank-you?"

"Thank you," I said, grudging. I still didn't like my mistress's little bodyguard with his probing eyes and his even more probing questions, but he seemed to have lost interest in tormenting me lately. Not a jibe for weeks—months, even—about what might possibly have brought me fleeing to Rome. Madonna Giulia was the target for his barbs these days, and I would never have wished her pain, but I was grateful to be left alone. I looked down at Leonello and felt almost friendly. "While you're feeling so helpful, Messer Leonello, perhaps you'll tell me how many guests will be sitting down to table tonight."

"I'd say twenty. That party from Venice is large, and they clearly think highly of themselves. Not much dignity in scuttling out of the path of the French like rats, but they're clinging to the shreds. There's an archbishop, by the way, who has brought his own cook—doesn't trust anything that doesn't come from his own fellow's hands, so I imagine you'll be sharing the kitchens this evening."

"Santa Marta bung me with a spoon," Bartolomeo groaned.

I whacked him on the shoulder. "No one swears in my kitchen but me. Now, we'll make a fricassee of those capons I was saving for *pranzo* tomorrow—go to the storeroom and get them for me. No, wait; first lay hold of that useless steward and tell him to round up any extra maids and servers and carvers and send them down." Bartolomeo had grown into a very capable assistant this summer, and with his help I could easily turn out a meal for five, but not for twenty. Extra hands would be needed.

I sent Bartolomeo on his way with another whack, and Leonello sauntered off whistling. I began whisking together the spices I'd need for the capons—perhaps a shoulder of wild boar too? No Venetian archbishop coming to *my* table would go away thinking the food provincial. Besides, if I had to share my kitchen with His Excellency's private cook, I meant to show him right away that he wasn't dealing with any jumped-up kitchen maid stirring a pot. Cooks sharing kitchens: never a good idea. You had to stake your territory right away or else they started laying claim to your spices. Or God forbid, touching your *knives*. Though there was always the possibility of sharing new recipes, once territory was staked and boundaries understood. A good heated argument on the Venetian versus the Roman sauce for a suckling pig was just the thing to liven up a long dull evening of chopping and stirring. Maybe this archbishop's cook was Milanese; I'd heard such interesting things about that leavened bread they made in Milan . . .

That was when I heard an autocratic voice in my doorway, sharp and pinging with a glass-clear Venetian accent just like my own. "Are you what passes for a cook in this household, girl? His Excellency my good master will require hot sops to soothe his stomach after a long journey, so you will fetch me muscatel pears, sugar, whole cinnamon, and as decent a red wine as you have in your cellars. And at once."

I put down the packet of cinnamon I had just been pinching closed. I put the bowl of mixed spices carefully to one side and automatically dusted a few grains of sugar from my fingertips. I turned slowly, sick in my soul, to face the man in the doorway. The man with a long face and a high-bridged nose like mine, imperious height and sharp all-seeing eyes to match mine. His arms in their rolled-up sleeves were singed smooth and hairless like mine, after so much reaching in and out of hot ovens. And his hands, like mine, were marked all over with the knife nicks and burn scars that told the world, *I am a cook.*

I stared at my father, and he gave a great start and stared at me.

I wondered if I looked so different after more than two years' absence. He looked the same, though he had grown a belly that overlapped his belt. Inanely I remembered telling Madonna Giulia that no great cook ever had the time to get fat. I suppose this meant my father was doing well—he'd never had the leisure before to get himself a belly.

"Last I'd heard," I found myself saying, "you were working for the Doge's great-nephew, Father. Not an archbishop."

"Carmelina," he said, still looking stunned.

"Is Mother with you?" I asked inanely. All my fears, working in Rome, that someday my father or someone else who knew me might cross my path—all the hiding I'd done in storerooms whenever there were Venetian visitors to the Palazzo Santa Maria—and now my father was here, not in the vast city of pilgrims where so many travelers passed, but in the backwaters of the provinces.

"Your mother's safe in Venice," my father replied automatically, still staring at me as though I were a resurrected corpse. "His Excellency took me with him to Florence on an advisory to Fra Savonarola. We were delayed returning, and now the French army..."

He trailed off. Maestro Paolo Mangano, the best cook in Venice, who had set me chopping my first onion at three years old, who had shouted at me for being slow to fetch olive oil and clouted me on the ear for dropping an egg and tanned my back with a ladle for arguing with him about the best way to make a royal sauce. Maestro Paolo Mangano, a right and proper bastard, may Santa Marta and all the saints forgive me for speaking so of my father. A right and proper bastard who had never had a fond word for me but still made me into a cook. For that at least I owed him, and I felt a child's urge to run to him, bow my head.

Instead, I picked up the nearest knife.

"Turn on your father now, girl?" His eyes narrowed, and I could see him collecting his thoughts. My father could be counted on never to be caught off guard for long. "I'd expect no less of a faithless, talentless slattern like you. I'd assumed you were dead in some whore's flophouse by now."

"I've missed you too, Father." He'd spoken in the crystal-sharp Venetian street patois he always used in the kitchens, if not to his distinguished clients, and unthinkingly I answered in the same dialect. Somewhere in the back of my head I was howling in panic, but my voice came out even. The days of hanging my head under the lash of my father's tongue were long done.

He took a step forward, unfolding his massive arms. "You're coming with me, girl."

"No." I took a step back, still holding the knife at my side. "Come any closer and I'll scream."

"Scream, then. And I'll tell this good household they're sheltering a runaway whore still wanted in Venice for the robbing of the church of the blessed Santa Marta." He took another step toward me, voice rising. "You're a sorry excuse for a daughter, but you're still mine. And if I say you're coming with me, then you'll obey. I'm your father—"

"And I'm cook to Madonna Giulia Farnese," I found myself shooting back. "The Holy Father's concubine herself. I have powerful friends—"

"The Pope's cunt?" For someone who could talk so smooth and pretty for the clients, he had a mouth like a gutter in the kitchen. His voice rose steadily toward the bellow I remembered so well. "I should have known you'd end up cooking for another whore. If you think she'll protect you, well, she'll be too busy flopping on her back for the French, once they finally arrive and turn this town into a sewer. We'll be well gone, and you'll be headed back to—"

"I'm not going back there!" I shouted back. "Not that place. Not ever!" The corner of the trestle table pressed into my hip, and I dodged around it.

"Oh, yes, you are." My father's voice dropped from a bellow to a silky whisper. One of his most effective tricks to terrify his apprentices, that sudden modulation from roar to murmur; I often used the same technique myself. "But I want my recipes back first, girl. Hand them over."

"I don't have them." My hand felt sweaty on the knife hilt.

"Lying bitch," he said almost fondly. "Hand them over and maybe I'll just turn turn a blind eye rather than report you to the Archbishop as a desecrator and a runaway—"

"I don't have your precious recipes!" I yelled. "I left them behind when Madonna Giulia took herself to the country, and you know why? Because I don't need them anymore, Father, because I make up my own recipes now and they're *better* than yours. Because I'm a better cook than you are now, and the Pope himself eats my food and—"

My father lunged at me across the trestle table then, giving a swipe of his massive cook's hand, and I dodged back. He missed the whipping end of my braid, but I stumbled on my own hem, and in a heartbeat he was on me, reeling me in by the knot of my apron. I hadn't known when I picked up the knife whether I could bear to threaten my own father with it—I'd never challenged him before when he gave me a beating, after all. Fathers hit their children, and cooks hit their scullions; it was the way of the world, and I'd never thought of fighting back, just taken my punishment like any other member of his kitchens and vowed to do it better next time, whatever *it* was: a curdled sauce or an overdone rack of lamb. But now I made a wild slash of the blade, scoring his arm deep, and felt a strange exhilaration as blood droplets sprayed in an arc across the floor. "Does it hurt?" I yelled, swinging the knife again and missing. "Or does it hurt worse that you're stuck cooking for an archbishop while your daughter serves the *Pope*!"

My father gave a roar and batted me across the side of my head with his hard open palm. A hot explosion of sparks filled the inside of my skull.

"Turning a blade on the man who sired you?" He flung me back against the wall, and I felt the drying racks press painfully into my shoulders. The knife flew out of my hand, skittering across the flagstones. "Whatever happened to 'Honor thy father,' Carmelina Mangano?"

"When you've robbed a church," I managed to say around the buzzing in my head, "a broken commandment or two doesn't seem like much, Father."

He swung a hand at me again, doubling up his fist this time, the kind of blow he dealt out to thieving fishmongers who tried to cheat him on a load of tench and lake carp; and I knew I'd have more than a buzz in my head to show for it. *No, no, he'll knock me unconscious and then cart me upstairs and lock me up.* The thoughts flitted by in utter panic, chasing each other through my head like frightened squirrels. *I'll wake up in chains, headed back to Venice—*

But the second blow never landed. My father gave another yell, this one of surprise, and batted at the back of his neck instead. A certain small linen bag had fallen from the drying rack overhead, jostled loose by all the struggling, and landed square between his shoulders—to be followed by a cascade of little earthenware spice jars as a whole shelf gave way. My father yelled again, swiping at a crock of dried rosemary as it came down on his head, and I twisted out of his grip, making a desperate lunge across the floor for my knife. I found the hilt, clutching with sweaty fingers and scrabbling backward as my father came toward me again, blotting out the light. I had enough time to think that I'd rather die here than be hauled back to Venice to face the fate that awaited me there. I'd rather take Leonello's option of being raped a few times by the French army.

"If you don't let me go, I'll spit you through the gut like a roast pig," I snarled, scrabbling to my feet, but I never had the chance. A great dull *clang* sounded like the echo of a church bell, and my father dropped at my feet like a hundredweight sack of flour. Standing behind him, cast-iron skillet still raised, was Bartolomeo.

We stared at each other, my apprentice and I, both of us panting hard.

"*Signorina*," he gulped, and dropped the skillet with a crash. "I heard the shouting—was he trying to force you?"

"In a manner of speaking." My apprentice blinked confusion, and I realized I was still speaking in the thick Venetian dialect of my childhood. Good; he wouldn't have understood much of what my father and I had been shouting at each other. I shook off my Venetian patois like an unwanted cloak, scrambling a story together. "He came down to make hot sops for the Archbishop, and then . . ." Dear God, how to explain it? I crossed myself shakily. "Never mind. None of it matters."

My head was still buzzing from the blow and the shock; I was trembling head to foot and my ears roared, but I forced my thoughts into some kind of working order as I threw a panicked look back at the half-open doors behind Bartolomeo. If he'd come running at the sound of all the crashing and shouting my father and I had done, others wouldn't be far behind. *Sweet Santa Marta, don't abandon me now*, I prayed, and reached down to seize one of my father's limp arms. "Bartolomeo, get his other side, quickly—help me get him out of the way!"

Bartolomeo never blinked, just reached down and hauled my father's massive arm over his shoulders. Between the two of us we dragged him on his knees to the farthest of the storerooms, where the Farnese steward stored the spare jars of olive oil and various other odds and ends. "What if he wakes up?" Bartolomeo ventured. "If he starts to shout—"

"Gag him." I twisted my apron into a rope, knotting it between my father's teeth. Was it more of a sin to gag your father than knock him unconscious? It felt sacrilegious, somehow, but that didn't stop me from tying up his hands and ankles too, with loops of the sturdy twine I used for tying up game birds. If you've trussed a chicken, you can truss your father.

"Leave him," I panted, and we left the greatest cook in Venice in an ignominious heap on the cold floor. A lump the size of a melon was already rising on the back of his head where Bartolomeo had whacked him, but his breathing was steady. It would take more than a skillet to kill my father.

"Shouldn't we report him to—" my apprentice began as we retreated from the storeroom.

"No time." I shot the bolt, dragged a barrel of salted herring in front of the door for good measure, and whirled back to the kitchen. "Help me clear up, quick!"

"But his archbishop will be expecting those hot sops from his own cook's hands—"

"I can make them. He'll never know the difference. Hurry!"

The steward arrived an instant later, followed by a trail of curious manservants and maids, but Bartolomeo was mopping up the very last of the blood drips from my father's arm, and I'd retrieved the fallen pouch with the hand of Santa Marta and begun sweeping up the spilled spice crocks. "Nothing, nothing," I said airily to the steward's suspicious look. "Just giving this disobedient apprentice of mine a good clout for knocking over the spices. We'll have everything ready in time. And," I added in a whisper to Bartolomeo as soon as the steward waddled away and the maids flitted into the kitchen to help, "I'm doubling your pay."

"I don't get any pay," he pointed out.

"That's about to change."

"No need, *signorina*." Bartolomeo grinned, stuffing the bloody cloth he'd used to wipe the floor into his sleeve before anyone could ask questions about it. "Anytime you need someone hit on the head with a skillet, I'm your man."

"Good boy." The hot shivers of fear and excitement that had kept me moving so fast were draining away now, replaced by a cold sickness. For the first time I felt pain in the side of my face, and winced as I touched my cheek where my father had backhanded me. It was swelling already—within a few hours I'd have a black bruise. I'd better have an explanation to go with it.

I'd have to explain more than a bruise if anyone found out I had my father locked up with the spare olive oil.

Tonight at least, I was surely safe. I could keep my own people out of that storeroom for an evening, and if my father woke up, the gag would keep him from shouting. The Archbishop wouldn't miss his cook as long as the food still arrived on time, and I'd wager the Archbishop's other servants wouldn't miss my father's presence either. They wouldn't be coming down to the kitchens, after all—my father never associated with a household's other servants; he held himself a cut above a mere manservant or guardsman, and thus strictly aloof from their company. No, no one would miss my father until tomorrow when the Venetian party prepared to leave.

Santa Marta, I prayed as I began numbly assembling the muscatel pears and red wine for that Venetian archbishop's damned hot sops. He couldn't have timed his return from Florence some other week? *Santa Marta, just get me out of this. You've already helped me once tonight*—really, I had to wonder just how the shelf of spice crocks had managed to tip over at such an opportune moment. *Now if you can, please* please *get me out of here before my father wakes up and tells them all who I am.*

Giulia

"Tell me about it again," I urged. "Carbognano."

Orsino's eyes crinkled at me in that nice way I liked. "I've told you half a dozen times."

"Again, please!" I smiled a little as my husband described his *castello* with its painted sala and long gallery, the quiet little surrounding town with its fields and hazelnut trees. His shyness had fallen away these past few days, especially in the quiet evenings like this when he would knock hesitantly at my chamber door before *cena*, and I would wave him in to sit with my maids and me as we sewed. Pantisilea would pour wine for us, her ears standing out like jug handles in her eagerness to hear anything juicy, and I'd stitch crooked seams across the altar cloth I was mangling, and Orsino and I would talk. Not of anything very important, really. Just ordinary talk, like any ordinary husband and wife.

I liked that.

"And there's a garden in the *castello* too, of course. Herbs for the kitchens, but I want to have it planted with flowers." My husband's blue eyes rested on me more easily now, and his voice was firmer than its previous nervous fits and starts. A young man now instead of a boy; handsome in his best doublet, which had just been brushed, and his boots, which had just been shined. A man come wooing, only Orsino was paying court to his own wife. That had touched me very much the past few days. "Do you like roses, Giulia?" he asked me, still enlarging on his plans for the *castello* garden.

"It is generally safe to assume that women like roses!" I teased him. I could see that little garden: just the kind of sunny place where the chatelaine of the *castello* might sit with her sun hat, reviewing the daily tasks with the steward and keeping watch over her children.

Orsino was talking about his horses now, and the good hunting to be had around the *castello*. Another night I would have been happy to listen as he rambled, but time was short this evening. *Cena* would be laid soon, and we would have an extra guest at table tonight: my mother-in-law had arrived by coach an hour ago. She'd been all correct courtesies in the hall, where I'd offered my greetings and escorted her to her own chamber to wash the travel dust away, but I didn't in the least imagine that she'd wait until *cena* was done to come chide me, or her son, or both.

"—herons and ducks in the lake for hawking," Orsino was saying. "I could get you a little merlin if you wanted to learn—"

"Husband," I interrupted gently. "Perhaps you should just say it."

He cleared his throat. "Say what?"

I set my own cup down, waving back Pantisilea and her pricked ears as she edged closer. "What you came to Capodimonte to ask me."

He rotated his goblet between his hands. "You know what I want . . ."

"Yes, but I want *you* to say it." Firmly. "Women are like that, I'm afraid."

He gulped and took the plunge. "I want you to come back with me to Carbognano." He even managed to look me in the eye. "It's a good place to live, Giulia. I'd have to rejoin my men at Bassanello first, but I'd come back to you once the fighting was done." A shy smile. "You know I want you there."

And oh, part of me wanted it too. Bring up my Laura by the lake, away from the serpentine politics of the Vatican that had governed Lucrezia's brief childhood. I could live quietly; not a harlot anymore,

not spat on in the streets. In time my notoriety would fade, and I'd just
be another young mother in the bosom of her family, taking her daughter to Mass and eating those little fried smelt that I liked so much. Eating
as many of them as I wanted because I wouldn't have to keep myself slim
anymore just to keep a man's passion stoked.

But—

"When the Pope orders you to send me back to Rome," I said, "what
will you do?"

His eyes flickered. "Maybe the Pope won't order you back. You said
his letters were angry—"

"But he still wants me." My long absence really had made his heart
grow fonder—which had been my aim, when I first departed Rome this
summer. Now it looked like I'd succeeded a little too well. "What will
you do if he comes for me himself, Orsino, instead of just sending your
mother?"

A long silence as my young husband bit his lip. And then a knock
sounded at the door, and before I could send Pantisilea to answer it, a
figure swept in: square-faced, sharp-eyed, powdered, and curled.

"Madonna Adriana da Mila," Leonello announced unnecessarily.

"Good evening, children," my mother-in-law beamed, and her eyes
did a fast relieved flick to see that we were well attended by maidservants.
Holy Virgin forbid I ever be alone with my own husband! "So lovely to
see you again, Orsino. Giulia, my dear, you've been too long gone from
Rome! I've missed you terribly, and I'm not the only one."

I didn't offer her either wine or a seat. She helped herself to both.

"Goodness, but I'm tired," she said, giving a wave of her hand to
dismiss my maids. I nodded Leonello out too, and he shut the door on
our little trio without comment. Normally, I'd have welcomed his presence here as a caustic-tongued shield against my mother-in-law, but I'd
hardly spoken to my little bodyguard since the day I'd slapped him
beside the shore. And I didn't really want his sharp eyes on the quarrel
I could already feel building in this room like storm clouds gathering
over the lake, hunching Orsino's shoulders and bringing my chin up at
a defiant angle, as Adriana settled herself like a cozy velvet-clad cat.

"His Holiness ordered the pace himself when I started out from Rome," she went on in her creamy voice, "and I must say it was a killing pace! Warm this wine for me over the brazier, won't you, Orsino? That's a dear boy. And then perhaps you'll run along and allow me a word with Giulia. I've one or two things to discuss with her in private."

"I think—" Orsino blushed as he took his mother's cup, but he looked at her squarely. "I think I should stay."

"Really, dear boy—"

"There is nothing you can say to me that you cannot say in front of my husband," I interrupted, and gave Orsino a quick smile.

Adriana looked at the pair of us and gave a shrug. "As you please. I've a letter for you, Giulia, from His Holiness. You really have made him very irate, you know."

"Yes. I know."

"You don't sound very bothered by that, my dear."

"I'm not." *Giulia la Coraggiosa*, I remembered Carmelina saying. "He doesn't own me, after all," I said, and gave another glance at Orsino where he stood warming his mother's wine over the brazier.

"Maybe not, but His Holiness is still frantic to have you back." Madonna Adriana gave a little smile. "Cardinals and ambassadors pressing him day and night about the French, and all he cares for is getting you safely back to Rome."

"Hmm." I picked up my mangled altar cloth again and began unpicking a crooked stitch. Orsino drew a deep breath. *Shout at her!* I winged the thought toward him, arrow-like. *Put her in her place!* But he crossed the room silently and gave his mother back her goblet.

"Thank you, dear." Adriana blew on the surface of the warmed wine. "Now, Giulia. Your return to Rome isn't just a matter of what the Holy Father wants anymore. It's a matter of safety. You really must not be here when the French army comes—have you heard what happened to the other towns they've passed through? Men murdered, women having their fingers sawed off for their rings, altar boys raped—you know the French. Babies no older than Laura having their heads dashed against the stones—"

I jabbed the needle into the ball of my thumb, and winced. I'd managed to put the French rather successfully out of my mind lately, what with everything else I had to worry about. "Is the army really so close?"

"No more than a few days north, my dear. The advance parties may be even closer."

"Then I'll prepare to leave tomorrow," I decided. Arranging my life to please myself instead of others was one thing, but there was no point in being foolhardy. One of my shutters had come loose in the night's breeze; I rose from the cushioned wall bench and crossed the room to close it. Capodimonte was unseasonably warm considering it was November, but the nights were winter cold again. I hoped the French froze in their camp.

"I'm glad you've seen sense, Giulia." My mother-in-law smiled. "I've already spoken with your sister downstairs; she's planning to leave tomorrow as well. We'll accompany her at first light, and strike out for Rome. Back and forth across the papal states at my age; goodness, but I feel like a message case sometimes—"

"Not to Rome." I turned and faced my husband and my mother-in-law. "Orsino was just inviting to take me to Carbognano."

"Was he?" Adriana looked at her son, who stood gazing at me with eyes suddenly alight. "Dear boy," she clucked. "You know that will never happen."

"Why not?" I challenged. "Even the Pope cannot excommunicate a man for taking back his lawful wife—"

"Excommunicate?" Orsino stammered.

"He's always threatening to excommunicate me." I brushed that aside. "It's not important."

"Some people would think it important," Adriana murmured.

"Stay out of this!" I felt anger rising in my throat, all the hot words I'd ever choked back at my mother-in-law, at my husband, at my family—at the whole lot of them who had connived to put me in the Pope's bed. Rodrigo's motive for wanting me there had at least been passion, straightforward as the sunlight. What was their excuse? Even if I had enjoyed my time in Rodrigo's bed, it did not excuse their greed.

Adriana ignored me, looking at her son. "I do hope you haven't bedded her during this unwise little visit, Orsino. The Holy Father took it very hard before—it was all I could do to keep him from taking Carbognano and Bassanello away from you in punishment. You aren't supposed to lay a finger on her; that's the arrangement, and you know it."

Orsino blushed. "I—that is, she's my wife, there's no wrong done if we—" He broke off, red as a sunset. "What I mean to say—"

"Oh good." She patted her son's arm. "You didn't."

"Either way, it is none of your business," I said crisply. Of course I'd wondered, when Orsino first arrived in Capodimonte, if he meant to demand his right to sleep in my bed. My family had stuck him firmly in the farthest possible chamber from mine, but he could have crept along the passage to my bed any night he liked. I thought of creeping along to his chamber myself, but I didn't think he'd like that—far too bold and unmannerly for a proper wife. I set myself to wait for him instead, and I couldn't help but remember another set of darkened stairs, another flickering taper, as Lucrezia sneaked her husband up into her chamber for the first time. Most women could bed openly with their husbands; Lucrezia and I had to visit ours in utter stealth . . .

But at least Lucrezia's husband had summoned the nerve to sneak into his wife's chamber. My husband hadn't. No more than he seemed able to summon the nerve now, to tell his mother what she could do with her meddling.

"Orsino," I said. "Look at me. Not at her, at *me*."

His blue eyes flickered as they met mine.

"Do you want me to come with you to Carbognano?"

"Yes," he whispered. "Jesu, yes."

"Dear boy," Adriana began.

"Be a dear, Adriana, and shut up," I told her without taking my eyes from Orsino. "This is a matter between husband and wife."

She pursed her lips tight, looking back to her wine. I reached for Orsino's hands, and I felt his pulse thrumming right through me. "I'll go with you," I said, and felt my own pulse speeding too. "We'll ride to Carbognano tomorrow, and I'll be your wife and keep your *castello* and bear you sons. But the question stands: When the Pope comes for me, what will you do?"

Another long silence. My husband bit his lip.

Say you'll bar the gates before you'll let him take me, Orsino, I found myself thinking. *Say you'd rather be excommunicated before you gave up your wife, Orsino. Say anything.*

I could face down my Pope—I knew that now. I could face him down, and I would. But not if my husband was not firmly allied behind me.

"If we sent him the child," Orsino blurted out. "If he had his own flesh and blood back, maybe he'd allow you to—"

"What?" I dropped his hands. Whatever I'd hoped he would say, it was not that. "I am not going to give away my daughter!"

"Giulia—" Orsino's eyes begged me. "I have to know. Is she his child? Or mine?"

"Oh, Holy Virgin!" I exploded, and found myself shouting. What a great relief it was, too. "We'll never know, Orsino, we'll never know and I'm sorry for that, but why does it *matter* by now? She's *Laura,* that's who she is. She's the loveliest girl any man could ever hope to have as a daughter, so what *is* it with you men? Why do you and Rodrigo refuse to have anything to do with her unless you can prove she has your blood? Why is any of that her fault? You don't *either* deserve to have fathered her!"

"I'm—I'm sorry—" Orsino stammered.

"You should be," Adriana commented. "Really, Orsino. Laura's a little love. And it's not as though she's your firstborn son and heir! There's plenty of time for that later."

I rounded on my mother-in-law. "So your plan is that I go back to the Pope until he's tired of me, and then I settle down with your son and start birthing plenty of legitimate little heirs?"

Adriana's voice was placid. "That seems entirely reasonable to me."

I nearly heaved the altar cloth at her head. "What kind of mother *are* you?"

"The practical kind." Her eyes met Orsino's, and I might as well not have been in the room at all. "My dear boy, I only want what's best for you. You're like your father—sweet as clover honey, but he had no notion at all how to forge a path in this world, and neither do you." Adriana looked momentarily sad, and Orsino reddened to the color of a pomegranate. "You'll need assistance in your career, Orsino, assistance and patronage, and how are you to get that if you anger the Holy Father?"

"So you'll just pack me off to the man who put horns on your son's head," I shouted, "and it's all for his own *good*?"

"A mother does what she must to make sure her children succeed."

"I'm sure you feel very proud of yourself!"

"Not very." She shook her graying head. "But the world is not a place of blacks and whites, Giulia Farnese. As I think you know by now."

I rounded away from her, toward Orsino, and took his hands in mine again. "You don't have to listen to her. She's wrong about you, she is. Tell her!"

His fingers were limp and cold in mine. He looked at me once, and then he stared at his boots. "Maybe she's right."

"What?"

A tentative voice sounded through the door just then. "Madonna Giulia?"

I whirled, tearing my hands away from Orsino's. *"What?"* I yelled all over again.

Carmelina Mangano's long face appeared cautiously around the door frame. "I'm sorry to interrupt, *madonna*—but do you wish me to postpone *cena*? The dishes have been ready an hour, if you wish to eat . . ."

"Thank you, Carmelina. We'll eat shortly." I smoothed the front of my loose Neapolitan overgown, trying to unclench my fingers, and motioned her in. "You might as well know," I said, struggling to keep my voice even. "I set off in the morning." I looked at Orsino. "For Rome."

"We do?" My cook blinked at that.

"Yes. Dawn if we can manage—" I broke off in surprise as Carmelina straightened, turning her face toward me full-on. "Holy Virgin," I said, distracted despite myself. "What's happened to you?" Her right cheek was one massive livid bruise.

She hesitated. Her eyes flickered as though she were thumbing through various stories, and she finally mumbled something about one of the travelers from Venice whom I had welcomed when they begged a night's hospitality. I didn't know whether to believe her, but she cut me off when I asked for the man's name. "Just one of the cooks, *madonna*. It doesn't matter if we're leaving tomorrow anyway." Carmelina hesitated, eyes flickering again. "Though if it's not too much to ask—could we leave by the Montefiascone road? The Venetians, they're setting out tomorrow too, and one of their guardsmen told me they meant to take the other road. If we were to leave by way of Montefiascone, we wouldn't have to travel with their party . . ."

"Of course."

She was gone with a swift bob of a curtsy, relief in every line of her body. I turned back to Orsino and Adriana, both still regarding me. "Enjoy *cena*, both of you," I said. "I have a great deal of packing to do."

Adriana's face had turned looked thoughtful. "You have gotten quite independent, haven't you, Giulia Farnese?"

"Perhaps," I said, and looked at Orsino. "I am twenty years old, after all—no longer quite such an ignorant little goose as I used to be."

My husband's whole body was hunched with misery. "Giulia—"

I looked at him, my husband in the blue doublet that matched his eyes. Eyes all soft with love, and full of tears. I'd been so touched, these days past when he was wooing me. Touched enough to imagine myself at his side, his wife in truth and not just in name.

"Giulia," he said again. "I'll take you back—when the Pope doesn't— I mean, when he's . . ." Orsino cleared his throat. "Our own life in Carbognano, and our own children—I'll grow all the roses you want in the garden—"

"I want you to grow a spine," I said, and slammed the door.

CHAPTER SIXTEEN

❖
---

*The French forced their way into houses, driving
out the inhabitants and then burning their firewood,
eating and drinking all they could find without
paying for anything.*

—JOHANN BURCHARD, "AT THE COURT OF THE BORGIA"

Carmelina

W e're safe!" Bartolomeo scrambled up into the wagon after me,
toting his bundle of clothes and a huge hamper. "He was starting to stir so I gave him another whack with the skillet."

"Tell me you didn't kill him!" I whimpered. My eventual berth in
hell was already probable; I had no desire to make it inevitable by adding my father's murder to the weight of my sins.

"Not dead, but he's down like an ox at the slaughter yard. He won't
stir for hours." Bartolomeo's eyes sparkled in the gray of dawn. "He
won't be found either, not with all this bustle of Madonna Giulia leaving. Everyone's far too busy to notice that some guest's private cook is
missing." My apprentice gave a flap of his hand at the throng in the
courtyard: thirty guardsmen clattering about on their horses, maids
carrying out one last bundle of clothing or casket of letters, Madonna
Adriana climbing wearily into the carriage that had brought her here
only yesterday afternoon. With all the racket my apprentice could have
shouted his words and not been overheard, but he kept his voice to a

dramatic whisper and leaned his head close to mine in the packed confines of the wagon. "By the time that Venetian whoreson wakes up or gets found, or someone goes looking for him, we'll be long gone, *signorina*. And in the opposite direction, too."

He grinned at me, alight with adventure, and I envied him his high spirits. I just felt ill. "Not a word about any of this," I warned him for at least the fourth time, settling my small bundle of clothes more firmly between the chests I'd loaded with the skillets, pots, spices, and other cooking essentials I'd brought for what had originally supposed to be a short summer trip away from Rome. "Not a word to Maestro Santini when we get back to Rome, or to Ottaviano or any of the other apprentices. Not to the fishmonger when I send you to the market for sturgeon, or your confessor when you go to Mass. I know it goes against the grain for a good, honest boy like you, not telling your priest something like this—"

"I'm up to my neck in this too, *signorina*," he cut me off. "I don't want trouble any more than you do. I won't be telling my confessor or anyone else."

"Swear it," I insisted.

"On Santa Marta's head."

"Swear on her hand." I produced the little bag from where it hung at my waist again. He peered inside and recoiled.

"That's what you've got in there, *signorina*? A saint's *hand*?"

"Likely it's a fake," I lied. "Swear on it anyway. She'll hear you."

He put a hand gingerly on the bag and swore.

"Good," I said, and barely managed to put the withered hand away again before I had to lean over the wagon's tailboard and void my empty, roiling stomach into the courtyard.

"That withered thing in the bag is enough to make anybody throw up." My apprentice sounded so cheerful I could have killed him. "A nice soothing meal, that's what you need, *signorina*. I packed us a hamper!" My apprentice patted the big basket he'd hauled in along with his clothes. He'd gotten very fond of packing meals for the outdoor repasts by the lake that the Farnese were so fond of here in Capodimonte. Myself, I preferred a good sturdy *credenza* rather than a picnic basket when it came to laying out food. My stomach churned, and I retched all over again.

"You're sure you don't want a little *zabaglione*?" Bartolomeo sounded hopeful. "I whipped it up this morning: good Milanese almonds through the strainer with some egg yolks and a little sweet white wine—"

"I hope you used the Trebbiano from Pistoia," I said, wiping my mouth. "That's the best vintage for *zabaglione*."

"Of course I used the Trebbiano from Pistoia! And a little cinnamon, fine sugar, a little rosewater—"

My apprentice was patting my back now as though I were a nervous horse. I should have brushed him away—a cook should never show weakness before underlings—but I felt too worn. My throbbing face was as swollen as a nut that had soaked in cold milk all night, and I'd slept sitting up at the trestle table outside the storeroom, straining my ears in my sleep for some sign my father was stirring. I kept waking up with the dream that he'd somehow unbolted the door from inside and was coming for me again. Coming to take me back to *that* place.

Even if you get away now, he could still come take you back, a little voice whispered in my head as Bartolomeo nattered on, listing ingredients like a demented auditory shopping list. *As soon as he's discovered in that storeroom, he'll report you. And he knows who you work for now. You could get back to Rome, and a month or two later you might find guards at the door waiting to arrest you for desecration.*

I'd worry about that later. I'd *have* to worry about that later—I had far too much to worry about right now to even think about adding anything else to the list.

Madonna Giulia appeared in the courtyard then: her breath misting white on the chill dawn air; Pantisilea tramping behind with the bundles; little Laura slumbering in her nurse's arms wrapped in a spare furred cloak; her sister, Gerolama, following behind in a long stream of complaints. Giulia ignored her, looking as drawn and tired as I did, worn under the eyes as she went to join Madonna Adriana in the carriage. Leonello followed, La Bella's eternal small shadow in black, and handed her in before scrambling up himself. As she disappeared inside I thought I saw the velvet gleam of the Pope's huge teardrop pearl about her neck again. She hadn't worn it all summer, but she wore it now. Somehow I didn't think Orsino Orsini would be accompanying his wife in that carriage. He was there in the courtyard, bareheaded despite the chill, and Giulia looked at him out the window of the carriage as though asking him a question. He opened his mouth, but just closed it again and looked wretched. Giulia pulled Laura into her lap and didn't look at her husband again.

The captain of the guards kicked his horse into a trot, spurring out of the courtyard toward the Montefiascone road. From the windows I thought I saw servants watching, and the rest of Madonna Giulia's family, but I didn't pay any attention to the faces. All I wanted to see was the road, the road, the road stretching ahead, leading me farther and farther away from the man locked in the storeroom.

By midmorning the roiling in my stomach had subsided almost entirely. The air was dry and cold, the sun shone overhead, and we rolled along briskly enough on the dusty road. Bartolomeo had grown restless and hopped out of the wagon to go loping alongside the wagons for a while, tossing a pebble up in the air and catching it again. The guards called back and forth to each other on their horses; Madonna Giulia sat gazing out the window of her carriage up ahead with her chin propped in her hand; I could hear the servants in the other wagon chattering. I could have ridden with them, but a good cook always rides with his equipment when traveling.

My father taught me that.

I leaned my head back against the wooden crate of skillets and plates and the good knives without which I never traveled. With every roll of the wheels taking me farther from my father, my fog of blind panic had started to clear. Surely my father wouldn't pursue me down into Rome? It must have stirred up talk when I ran away in the first place, especially when you considered just what I'd taken with me in the way of stolen goods, but the whispers would have blown over by now. Dragging me back to Venice as a desecrator of altars to be publicly punished before cheering crowds—*that* scandal would be enormous. What archbishop would keep my father on as cook then?

No. My father's first instinct when he laid eyes on me might have been to seize me, but when I was far away and no longer quite so easy to lay hold of . . . well, I thought it far more likely he'd swallow his rage and mumble some hasty excuse when he was found trussed in that storeroom. Who wanted to wreck a painstakingly built career as one of Venice's finest cooks, just to punish one disobedient daughter?

Not Paolo Mangano.

I couldn't help a smile. At least I'd had the chance to tell my father to his face that I was a better cook than he. Who cared if he'd never believe me? I knew it was true.

I was still smiling and dreaming, thinking that a dish of *zabaglione* with almond milk really sounded quite tasty after all, when the first screams sounded.

"Bartolomeo?" I poked my head over the wagon tailboard, looking for my apprentice. "Did a horse fall, or—"

Bartolomeo stood rigid, eyes stretched wide. I followed his gaze and saw something I hardly understood: two of the guards at the head of our small column, slumped and bloody in their saddles. Another clutched at his shoulder, screaming—and a wolf pack of soldiers in dirtied armor was leaping down upon us from all directions, spurring their horses with shrill cries.

I saw the captain of the guard where he had been riding alongside the carriage, bending down in his saddle as he attempted to flirt with Madonna Giulia—he jerked upright, head twisting wildly in all directions. He began to shout orders, but two more men were already toppling from their saddles in the rear, and inside the carriage I heard Madonna Giulia's sister begin to shriek. The maids were shrieking too in the wagon behind, and I saw a foreign sergeant with a grizzled face and a missing ear reach grinning into the wagon and drag one of Giulia's maids out by the hair. Her scream spiked my ears, and then I was knocked back into the wagon as Bartolomeo vaulted up, pushing me out of sight. Not before I'd seen the banners, though; banners flapping on the morning breeze as the soldiers closed around us like a vise. Banners flying the lilies of France.

"Stay down," Bartolomeo shouted, "stay down, *signorina*, stay out of sight!" But he was ripping the nearest crate open, pawing for the knives we'd packed away so carefully, and I clawed right along with him. I could hear more women screaming, and French voices cawing in that revolting flat language of theirs that grated the ear like a wire, and I wanted a knife in my hand. I heard the captain of Madonna Giulia's guard still shouting orders, and then his voice choked off in a rattle and I didn't know if it was a blade or a blow that had silenced him, but without seeing I knew he was choking on his own blood. "*Get down!*" Bartolomeo shouted again, shoving at me, but the wagon darkened suddenly and I saw a French soldier clambering over the tailboard like an ape.

He grinned, seeing me, saying something in that horrible French tongue, his own tongue lolling like a serpent, and all the panicked voices outside were shrieking in my head now, mixed up with all the rumors I'd ever heard of the French army. How they burned churches full of praying nuns, how they dashed the infant brains of babies out on altars, how they raped women and then cut off their fingers to pry the rings away from their hands—

Bartolomeo made a desperate empty-handed lunge, but the French soldier backhanded him almost casually out of the wagon. I saw the glint of armor outside, soldiers dismounting, soldiers everywhere, and I made a last frantic fumble in the crate, but my knives, my cleavers, my sharpened spits and basting needles all slid through my sweating fingers. I lunged with my nails instead, but the Frenchman backhanded me too, on my already swollen and black-bruised face, and the blow made the inside of my head light up with sparks. Dimly I felt a rough hand seize my hair, then collapsed as he dragged me forward, felt the tailboard at my knees, and collapsed again into the dust of the road as he shoved me out of the wagon to the ground.

Half the maids had tried to flee the cart ahead, and a trio of French soldiers hemmed them in like dogs herding sheep, pricking them with pike points and laughing as they screamed. The other soldiers were picking more professionally through the wagons or herding back the guards they'd subdued, directed by what I assumed was a captain in blue plumes and mirror-bright helmet. Three or four of our guards still fought in a ragged line before Madonna Giulia's carriage, but her horses had already been slashed loose from the harness and goaded away, leaving the carriage stranded like a ship run aground on a rock. The captain of our guard lay crumpled by one canted wheel, blood still pulsing slowly from the great slash in his throat. Bartolomeo lay facedown in the dust not an arm's length from me.

The soldier who had shoved me out of the wagon gave me one cursory glance but just spat in the dust and went back to rummaging among the crates. *Perhaps I should thank my father for hitting me*, I thought idiotically, feeling the throb of my swollen face. *He's made me so ugly even the French don't want to rape me.* So much for Leonello's prediction.

Leonello had made other predictions, too. That the French were close, only a short distance away on the Montefiascone road. The road we'd taken only because I'd talked Madonna Giulia into traveling a different way from my father's party. *My fault, all of this, God forgive me, it's my fault, it—*

"Bartolomeo?" I crawled to my apprentice where he lay still, his hair almost as bright against the white road as the trickle of blood from our fallen guardsmen. "Bartolomeo, sit up. Sit *up*, I did *not* spend a year teaching you to cook only to have the French murder you in a road! Sit up and tell me what goes in a *zabaglione*, sit up, *please*—"

He was so still. Behind me a woman screamed on a rising note, underlaid by that snickering French laughter. *My fault, my fault.*

"Ho, what have we here?" The French captain broke into heavily accented Italian, leaning one elbow on the pommel of his saddle and looking down at the carriage. The last of our guards had thrown down their weapons, and now at a gesture from the captain, a sergeant jerked open the carriage door. "*Viens ici!*" he snapped.

There was a pause, and then Madonna Adriana stumbled down. My employer no longer looked like the Pope's most trusted cousin, the complacent sharp-eyed dowager who combed my storeroom lists to point out any place where I might save ducats. She looked old, old and terrified as she stared up at the French captain. Madonna Giulia's salt-and-vinegar sister stumbled out next, no longer full of vinegar but terror as she sobbed and clung to Pantisilea, and then little Laura's nurse, who was babbling prayers. Madonna Giulia came last, clinging tight to her daughter and burying her beautiful face in the little girl's furs.

"Very nice," the French captain said in his repellent heavy-accented Italian, looking at the fine cloaks, the tooled leather slippers, the furred hems arrayed before him. "Very nice indeed. Don't you rich ladies know better than to travel at times like these?"

Adriana da Mila drew herself up. "My cousin is His Holiness the Pope, and I will thank you—"

The captain guffawed, and his ring of soldiers were quick to guffaw with him. "And I'm the King of France!"

"How dare you treat—"

He lashed out casually with one boot, still in its stirrup, and caught Madonna Adriana in the jaw. She collapsed gagging, and one of the maids gave a short scream, and the French captain laughed. His men laughed too, and the hulking sergeant with a spray of blood on his arm reached for Madonna Giulia. "Not just rich, Captain, but pretty too! Look at this one—"

Madonna Giulia jerked away, but the sergeant's hand had already fallen from her arm. He was staring down at the knife in his throat.

It appeared as suddenly as though it had grown there, a damascened hilt showing over the top edge of his rusted breastplate, its Toledo steel blade splitting the Frenchman's throat as neatly as an apple. The sight of it seemed to freeze everyone—the laughing captain, his ring of men, the little huddle of women, all staring as the French sergeant gave a slow gurgle and toppled into the dust. And a small figure in black stepped calmly down from the carriage with a knife in each hand.

Leonello took another man down before they even registered him as Death in their midst, a tiny finger blade evaporating from his stubby fingers and reappearing in the soft gullet of the soldier beside the fallen sergeant. The dwarf's face was emptily, terrifyingly calm as he advanced from the carriage, his hazel eyes flicking to a new target even as he pulled another knife from his boot top. The blade winged like a tiny angel; a man screamed as much in surprise as fear, but Leonello had already dismissed him and looked to the next man, and the impassive, inexorable slowness of his march never stopped. He reached Madonna Giulia and swept her behind him with one arm, even as he sent one of his dark Toledo blades flying at the French captain.

It clanged off the man's helmet, and the sound seemed to galvanize everyone into motion. The captain's horse reared, the captain himself began shouting in French, the soldiers lunged forward, but Leonello's face never moved. A man seized Madonna Giulia's arm but got too close; he screamed as a knife made a lightning double-slash across groin and thigh. Leonello whirled and flung the same blade as another soldier grabbed Adriana da Mila by the hair and jerked her to her feet, but the knife missed the man by a whisper and went spinning into the dust. The French captain roared something else then, and Leonello fired off one more blade before they converged on him. The little man went down in a welter of furious French soldiers, and even so I saw him draw the dagger at his waist and slam it through a man's knee before they brought him down.

Then he was gone.

Bartolomeo gave a groan, stirring on the ground. I dropped over him instinctively, keeping us both from view if God and Santa Marta were good, but I couldn't tear my horrified eyes away from the storm around the carriage. Madonna Giulia's sister was being dragged off by another French soldier, shrieking. Laura was crying in thin baby wails. Leonello was nothing but a huddled mass in a circle of boots and pikestaffs. The French captain was swearing and urging them on, and how her silver bell of a voice pierced the din I did not know.

"WHAT IS THE MEANING OF THIS?"

I had seen Giulia Farnese as the Venus of the Vatican, jeweled and poised in a throng of cardinals. I had seen her as passionate lover, naked in her bath, rosy and ripe for eating as a peach. I had seen her as doting mother frolicking with her baby; as everybody's friend who always had time for a joke and a gossip. I had never before seen her as a cold and furious queen.

No, more than a queen. Queens had only their birth to give them arrogance, but La Bella was loved by God Himself.

She had passed her little wailing Laura to the whimpering nursemaid without a glance and tossed aside her cloak to show the rich dress underneath. She threw her head back in stark cold fury, golden hair shining like a coin under the morning sun. The huge pearl at her throat gleamed like a chain of office. Her eyes went sword-straight to the French captain and she advanced on him in icy majesty: a lethally offended goddess ready to hurl thunderbolts at any mortal who dared rouse her rage.

"I am Giulia Farnese," she spat at him, her words slicing like another fistful of flying knives. "You have all heard of me. I am Giulia la Bella, the Venus of the Vatican, the Bride of Christ. I am the Pope's mistress. Lay one dirty finger on me or mine and it will be cut from your body. The rest of you will follow in small screaming pieces and then your soul will scream in hell for all eternity, cut off from God's grace when my Pope excommunicates you for daring to touch what he loves best in all the world."

"*Madame—*" The French captain's eyes flicked from her pearls to the white breasts underneath them, then hurriedly to her famous golden hair. *Please let him have heard of the hair*, I found myself praying, still hunched over Bartolomeo on the ground. *Please let him have heard of the Pope's golden mistress.* Or they would strip Madonna Giulia naked and pass her between them just like the rest of us. "*Madame*," the French captain began warily, "if you might prove—"

"Is that how you address a woman of my rank?" she interrupted icily. "So much for French manners."

The captain fumbled off his helmet. He had looked huge and imposing with his loud accented voice and extravagant plumes and big horse. Now he hardly looked older than Bartolomeo. "*Madame*, I do apologize—"

"And so you should. Is it the custom in France, boy, to make war upon defenseless women?" Giulia turned a slow circle, allowing her furious eyes to pass from the captain to his men, and her nostrils flared in freezing contempt. "You there, release my maid at once. It is quite impossible that I be left to wait upon myself. Release my bodyguard as well."

"*Madame*, he has killed three of my—"

"He has his orders direct from His Holiness Himself to kill anyone who threatens my person. Your men, rest assured, are already writhing in hell for daring to offer me offense." Her fine brows drew together. "Release him."

The soldiers were already moving before the French captain rapped out the command. My heart squeezed as I saw the still figure of Leonello on the ground, curled into a ball in a fruitless effort to protect his face and innards. I saw the bright ooze of blood coming from somewhere beneath him and my heart squeezed again, but then I saw his broken fingers twitch. At least he was alive.

"Carmelina?" Bartolomeo whispered muzzily.

"Shh," I hissed.

Giulia's eyes did not change as they swept over her bodyguard. She twitched her hem away from his small crumpled form and looked back up at the French captain. "Since you have incapacitated my bodyguard and guardsmen, I require an escort," she announced. "I suppose these ungroomed louts you call soldiers will have to do."

"Madame Farnese," the French captain began.

Giulia simply ignored him, tugging a pair of embroidered gloves from her belt and putting them on finger by finger. "Since my carriage has been ruined, I will need a horse." She nodded at the captain's gray gelding. "That one will do."

I heard the soldier who had hauled me from the wagon whisper to another, "That's the Pope's whore?"

"Acts like she's protected by God Himself," another grumbled, but his eyes dropped when Giulia's gaze fell on him. Her eyes regarded him like a louse, then traveled to me. I thought I saw a flash of relief, or maybe it was fear, but her cool arrogance never faltered as she found her servants one by one. The French captain tried to say something, but she rode over him with the same lordly impatience the Pope used when he rode over interrupting cardinals. "You may all take your places," she said, waving a hand to us all from the maids to the few remaining guards to her terrified sister and frozen mother-in-law. "No one will touch you. We are guests of the French King now, and we all know the French do not wage war upon women." She turned and raised an eyebrow to the captain until he flushed and scrambled off his horse. She stared at him again until he cupped his hands to receive her foot and boost her up into the saddle. "A litter for my bodyguard at once, and whatever sawbones hack of a surgeon you have on hand. I want him bandaged and tended before he is moved an inch. I assume we will be taken to see your general?" she said disinterestedly, arranging her skirts. "If I am to be taken captive, I must at least be captured by a man of suitable rank. Rest assured I shall have words for him about your conduct in this matter, *capitano*."

"*Madame—*"

"Do send ahead and be sure there are suitable amenities awaiting me. After such a trying journey I will require a rosewater bath and a good meal. None of that swill you French call wine, either, I drink only sweet whites from Ischia. See that your general is informed." She looked down at the young captain in faint surprise. "You may go."

Still looking flummoxed, he turned and rattled off orders in French to his men. They began to collect themselves, their dead, our dead. I saw Madonna Adriana take Laura in her arms and soothe her, turning to climb into the wagon with the servant girls now that the carriage was useless. The soldier who had begun dragging off Madonna Giulia's sister looked faintly sheepish and handed her up after Madonna Adriana with a placating smile. Leonello still lay in a crumpled heap, Pantisilea gingerly straightening his limbs as two soldiers began to improvise a litter. The Pope's concubine spurred her horse ahead, looking neither left nor right.

"Get up," I muttered to Bartolomeo, hauling on his arm. "Get up, and don't so much as look crosswise at any of these damned French soldiers."

"What?" He looked around him, still dazed from the blow that had tossed him out of the wagon. He'd have a bruise on the side of his face to match mine by tomorrow. *At least there will* be *a tomorrow*, I thought. "Wha's happened?" my apprentice slurred.

"We're prisoners of the French army," I told him grimly, helping boost him back to the wagon. "But on a happier note, we're not dead. La Bella, if I'm not mistaken, has just saved all our lives."

Giulia

It was a fair distance to Montefiascone where the French army was currently quartered, and I spent the long ride that day putting myself together. A recipe all my own, and not one to be found in any of Carmelina's recipe collections, either. Stir together Juan Borgia's arrogance with Vannozza dei Cattanei's malice, toss in my sister Gerolama's sharp tongue (when she wasn't paralyzed by terror, that is), add a good dollop of Caterina Gonzaga's regal self-importance, and season with the temper of a fishwife: clop after clop of my horse's hooves, I choked down the fright that gibbered in my throat and made myself into a haughty, highborn bitch.

I complained that my borrowed horse's gaits were too rough. I browbeat the French captain into stopping for half an hour just so I could get a pebble out of my shoe. I sneered at the French soldiers for being unshaved and unwashed. I turned up my nose at the bread and cheese I was offered at midday, then whined of my empty stomach for the next three hours. I pouted and bit my lip and pushed my breasts out, flashed my pearls and dropped my Pope's name every third sentence, and all the while I was aware, so terribly aware, of my sobbing sister and bruised mother-in-law and beaten guards, of my huddled maids and my terrified daughter and my poor, valiant, bloodied little bodyguard. All of us contained by that ominous ring of French soldiers who could turn on us at any moment, rob us or rape us or cut our throats, if they ceased believing that I was a prisoner of great value who must be handled with velvet gloves.

But all my manufactured complaints dried in my mouth when we came over the hill approaching Montefiascone and I saw the French army spread out before me. A vast lake of filthy doublets, of horses and pikes and tents and wagons, flapping with French lilies and stinking of blood. For months I had been hearing talk of the French army, of the havoc they had wreaked as they crossed Savoy in their inexorable march south—but it had only been idle talk over the table, far less real than the wine in my cup and the silk on my back; far less interesting than the question of what delicacy Carmelina would be providing next on my plate. Now I was in the thick of it, swallowed up by that lake of filthy swearing men as the young captain led our party down into the camp's outskirts. I was close enough to smell onions and rotten teeth on the breath of those thousands of soldiers, to see the fires and the horse manure and the mud, to feel the weight of so many leering, curious eyes as I trotted past, bracketed by my guards. I took in the sight of those lethal horse-drawn bronze cannons that flung iron shot at such a ferocious rate that a town's fortifications could be reduced to rubble within hours; saw those fearsome French pikes that had spitted babies all across Savoy, the savage destriers who could stove in a man's skull with one hoof, and it was now so horribly real.

"The might of the French army, *madame*," the French captain ventured, noting my silence—the first silence I had allowed to fall for hours. "I'll wager you've seen nothing like it before."

"The papal army is far more impressive," I said, bored. "What are mere gendarmes against the holy warriors of the Pope?"

"This is only the advance portion of our army, *madame*."

I swallowed.

The French captain gave a smirk at my silence, spurring ahead. I could do nothing but spur after him. A French sergeant came to the doorway of a wine shop on the outskirts of Montefiascone, giving a salacious whistle as I passed. My skin crawled, but I straightened in my saddle and pushed my hood back to show my high-piled hair. The more men who saw me, the faster the news would spread that the Pope's beloved had been captured. The faster the news spread, the sooner it would get to Rodrigo. And then I had better pray he was not too busy or too angry to save me.

First, however, I'd better pray that the French general proved more a *chevalier* than the men who had torn my traveling party apart like wolves.

"The Basilica of Santa Margherita," I announced as we made our way from the sprawling French camp into Montefiascone itself, and I saw the enormous half-completed dome of the famous cathedral rising over the homely tiled roofs around it. "I wish to pause there, to offer my prayers."

"*Madame*, General d'Allegre will wish to see you—"

"He may come to greet me here if he wishes," I sniffed. "Giulia la Bella does not present herself for inspection like some erring servant girl."

"The general is a busy man!"

I paid no attention whatsoever. When our party made its way through the narrow twisting streets into an open *piazza* and I saw the shallow steps rising to the basilica, I halted my horse unbidden and slid from the saddle. I had no idea if the guards in their ring around me would part when I swept toward them.

But they did.

"Bring my maids," I called without looking back, snapping my fingers over one shoulder. "And my bodyguard. We will lay him before the altar of Santa Margherita and pray for his swift recovery."

"Captain?" one of the sergeants protested.

"Let the bitch hole herself up in the church if she likes," the captain said in French, and I whirled on him cat-quick.

"Perhaps, *mon capitaine*, you should ensure that your captives speak no French before you insult them so coarsely." My French was scant, mostly culled from Lucrezia, who labored diligently at her languages with a variety of tutors, but my range of insults was impressive in any language, and I let the young captain have it in French, Italian, Latin, and Catalan. After I was done deriding his manners, his appearance, his ancestry, his manhood, and his competency, and loud enough so all his men could hear, he looked like a deflated bladder with two scarlet ears.

"*Madame* is more than welcome to wait in the cathedral," he mumbled, and I heaved a silent breath as my bedraggled entourage was allowed to disembark from their wagons. By the time they were pushed and prodded into the cathedral and the other worshippers ordered out, I was already on my knees at the altar, crossing myself ostentatiously and including loud references to the blessings and favor of the Holy Father in Rome. The French lost no time in banging the doors shut and posting a handful of muttering sentries outside.

The instant they were gone I flung myself off my knees and flew to my daughter. "*Lauretta mia*—" I squeezed her so hard I felt her little bones creak. She uttered no word of protest, just buried her face in my neck, and tears sprang to my eyes as I kissed her golden head over and over. "I won't let anything happen to you," I whispered. "I swear it, I swear it—"

"You brave girl," Madonna Adriana quavered, and hugged me for the first time in all our long acquaintance. "You dear brave girl, I won't forget what you've done today—"

"No time for that." I dashed at my eyes, looking about the cathedral. It was open to the elements, the nave littered with a handful of dead leaves like paper scraps, the scaffolding of the half-completed dome backed by a hard blue winter sky above. My people huddled shivering in the pews or on the steps of the altar, half of them muttering prayers, the other half whispering among each other with horrified faces. Laura's nursemaid burst into tears. Carmelina sat beside a cross-eyed statue of Santa Margherita, head buried in her hands, the redheaded kitchen boy at her side fruitlessly trying to press food on her out of a hamper. The guards had dumped Leonello in a makeshift litter before the altar of Santa Lucia. I hoisted Laura to my hip and flew to him, dropping to my knees. "Holy Virgin, let him be all right. Leonello—"

My little lion was an unconscious mess of wounds. His nose was smashed to a bloody smear, his face was puffed and purpled by fists, and all the fingers on one hand were broken and distended. He curled in on himself, breathing harshly through his open mouth, and from beneath him I saw a slow trickle of blood creeping from who knew what wound. I crossed myself. "Leonello?"

He looked so small, curled in on himself like a sick child. No bigger than a child, and yet he'd still sprung to my defense. Shoved me behind him and taken on the entire French army with nothing but a handful of knives. "Idiot," I told his unconscious ears, touching his bloody forehead. "You should have just let them take me."

But if he had, would we be here now? He'd bought me time, a moment to collect myself, to announce my name and my status before the chaos and the madness drove the French beyond listening.

"I tended him in the wagon as best I could." Madonna Adriana dropped to her knees beside me. "He was stabbed at least twice—if he doesn't get a surgeon . . ."

"Oh, he'll get one," I said grimly, settling beside him. I was not going to let my bodyguard die, not after what he'd done. "In the meantime, Adriana, go soak a kerchief in that baptismal font over there for me, and wash his face. Pia, unpack one of my shifts and rip it up for bandaging. Carmelina, surely we have some wine in that hamper—"

We waited two hours before the French general came to call on me. General Yves d'Allegre: grave, bearded, iron-haired, moving with a horseman's long stride at the head of a phalanx of officers. I felt a flutter at my stomach but lifted my chin and stared at them coolly from the top of the altar steps, where I had arranged myself for the advantage of a little more height. Adriana had chivvied the others into rows behind me: a phalanx of my own.

"A *general*?" I said before he had even finished introducing his officers. I wrinkled my nose as though he'd told me he was a stable boy. "Why am I not being received by King Charles himself? This is an insult to one of my rank, and I will not—"

"His Majesty is not here, *madame*." General d'Allegre spoke in a grave and modulated bass, his Italian far better than the young captain's. He looked far more imperturbable than the young captain, too. "King Charles marches with the bulk of our army, leaving the advance guard to me."

I breathed a little easier at that. Everyone had heard the rumors of

King Charles: his voracious appetite for women, willing or unwilling, and how he wrote them up in a book afterward with notes on their appearance and ratings of their skill between the sheets. I had no intention of being written up in a poxy Frenchman's book of conquests.

"I have heard much of the beauty of Giulia la Bella," General d'Allegre continued. His eyes went over me, slowly. "And I see nothing has been exaggerated."

Behind him, two of his officers snickered. My pulse leaped, but I kept my cold expression. "Is it your custom to mix compliments with assaults, General? To attack helpless female travelers? Three of my guards were slain, my maids accosted, my mother-in-law and sister abused, and my bodyguard all but butchered! Not to mention the loss of my horses and anything else in my baggage your men decided to steal for themselves—"

"My apologies, *madame*." He offered a smile with no apology at all behind it. "Had you been recognized, my men would have evinced more gentleness in making your acquaintance. I assure you that in France it is not the custom to make war upon women."

"Then you will let me return to Rome at once." I drummed my fingers, making sure my rings sparkled. The more expensive I looked in the finery Rodrigo had given me, the better. "*Such* an inconvenience; the Holy Father will be so annoyed—"

"I fear I cannot return you to Rome yet, *madame*."

I tasted fear in my mouth, sour and rancid, but I pushed my lip out in a pout. "And you consider yourself a gentleman, *mon general*?"

"I do as my King commands." General d'Allegre spread his hands in graceful apology, but his eyes were hard and cool. "It is possible His Majesty will wish to make your acquaintance before making further decisions as to your return. He has a great admiration for beautiful women, after all . . . and he would not wish to leave you with a poor opinion of French hospitality."

Oh, how very polite we were all being. I could already see my entry in the royal book of conquests: *Number ninety-six, fair-haired everywhere, skillful hands.* Holy Virgin, save me.

"Or perhaps His Majesty will give me leave to return you to Rome at once. Who knows, *madame*?" General d'Allegre noted my silence, and his lips curved. "For the meantime, I am honored to act as your host. You will dine with me tonight."

I didn't think it was an invitation. "My good mother-in-law Adriana da Mila and I will be delighted to join you." I felt Adriana lift her chin bravely at my side.

"I would not dream of parting your *belle-mere* from her duties to your traveling party," the general said smoothly, not even giving her a glance. "My officers and I will be honored to take the task of entertaining *La Belle Farnese* alone this evening."

More snickers from the officers behind him. One young man with a violently fashionable mustache bent to whisper to the other, neither bothering to hide the way their eyes went over me. Over the maids arrayed behind me, too: white-faced Carmelina and Laura's buxom nursemaid and poor Pantisilea, who for once had no flirtatious winks to give back.

"If I am to be your guest this evening, then I wish comfortable lodgings for my traveling party," I snapped. "Proper beds and food, and sentries posted to keep them safe."

"Of course, *madame*."

"And I want a good surgeon for my bodyguard," I added imperiously. "His wounds must be tended at once."

"That may be more difficult to provide." General d'Allegre was bland. "Your little man inflicted serious injuries upon several of my soldiers. My surgeons, I'm afraid, are all occupied tending *their* wounds."

I saw the sour looks the other French were casting Leonello and gave silent thanks to the Holy Virgin that he was unconscious. If he'd begun lacing into them with his sharp tongue, they looked only too happy to finish him off on his makeshift litter right now, holy ground or not. *No man likes to look foolish*, I remembered my bodyguard telling me once. *And that goes double when it's a dwarf making him look the fool.*

If Leonello didn't get a surgeon for his wounds, the French wouldn't need to finish him off with their swords.

"You *will* find a surgeon," I informed the French general, letting my voice scale up to queenly outrage. "I *will* have my guard looked after at once. If you think the Holy Father will be pleased to hear how you have treated us—"

I went on in that vein awhile, striding up and down and jabbing my jeweled finger toward heaven and all in all throwing a marvelous tantrum. The young French captain had wilted when I raged, but General d'Allegre stood imperturbably, watching my breasts heave and not listening to my words at all. I remembered the way my Pope could play affable patriarch or wily diplomat or majestic fisher of men, switching from one role to the next as determined by his audience. *Change your tactics,* mi perla, I could hear him say in his Spanish bass, and I halted mid-tantrum. I fluttered my fingers at the base of my throat as though overcome, dashing at my eyes with a well-jeweled hand before I looked back at General d'Allegre. "Forgive me," I said with a watery little sigh that was not faked in the slightest. My whole stomach was a mass of trembling knots. "This is all very upsetting. I'm sure you understand."

"Of course, *madame.*" Another French bow. "We will talk more tonight."

"*Oui, mon general.*" I lowered my lashes with the barest beginning of a flutter. "Tonight."

Tongues flickered behind thin lips as the French general and his officers looked at me, and for a panicky instant I thought I was surrounded by snakes.

CHAPTER SEVENTEEN

※

No one thinks how much blood it costs.

—DANTE

Leonello

A ceiling. Stone arches. Cobwebs. I concentrated on them.
Warmth, coming from somewhere. A glow. I blinked till the
glow turned into a brazier, shimmering with heat and giving a little
warmth to the sullen cold.

Softness. Blankets, heaped over me.

Pain. The less said about that, the better.

I closed my eyes, swallowing once or twice around the woolly dry-
ness of my tongue. "Not to belabor the cliché," I said, and was surprised
how weakly my voice came out, "but where am I?"

"Montefiascone. The vestry of the Basilica of Santa Margherita." A
bright jeweled blur moved to my side, and I blinked again, trying to
dispel the clouds. Eyes, eyes, what was wrong with my eyes? I'd been
stabbed in the chest and side and the hip, maybe the shoulder too, but
not the eyes, so what was wrong with them?

"General d'Allegre offered to move us to warmer quarters, but I
thought we might be safer on holy ground," the voice went on. "I had

blankets and braziers and fuel brought here, and moved us all into the vestry and the smaller chapels to get us out from under those open rafters." Giulia Farnese's face came slowly into focus. "How is the pain, Leonello?"

"Some moments are more agonizing than others." There was pain in my shoulder, pain in my side, pain in my hip; dull pain that chewed at my bones like a patient beast, and I could feel the stab of broken ribs with every breath. There was a rustling feeling in my chest as though my lungs were filled with parchment, and when I spat to one side I saw blood. *That is not at all good*, I thought distantly, but it was my hand that hurt the worst. I lifted it up for closer examination, and it hardly even looked like a hand anymore. The French had stamped on it, trying to get me to let go of my knives, and every finger was broken. The littlest finger skewed off at an angle so strange it hurt my eyes just to look on it: purple and mottled and queerly flattened. "How fortunate that I don't need a little finger to throw knives," I managed to remark. "The others might survive with a little splinting, but not that one."

"I'm trying to get you a surgeon," my mistress said. "The French have refused—it's all excuses; they're just humiliated you took down so many of their men." She let out a flat obscenity better suited to a stable boy than a pope's mistress, and I would have laughed but it hurt too much. *Dio*, but it hurt. "Can I make you more comfortable?" La Bella went on. "A cup of wine, another blanket—"

"No, I'm quite comfortable," I lied. The mists had cleared from my eyes a little and I could see Pantisilea sitting against the far wall tearing up a gauze shift to make bandages. Through the vestry door I could see movement: Madonna Adriana slumped in a chair with Laura in her lap and the nursemaid fussing. I twisted my head to where my mistress sat beside my pallet and looked her over. "Are you going to a party?" She wore her finest gown, heavy cloth-of-silver girdled with a sapphire-studded chain, and every jewel she owned had been latched around throat, wrists, fingers, waist. She looked expensive and gaudy, over-dressed and vain, and it didn't suit her.

"I've been invited to dine." Her smile was a twisted, tilted thing. "With the French officers."

"They'll strip those jewels right off you."

"They're welcome to the lot." Madonna Giulia looked down at herself. "I want them to see just how much the Pope has spent on me. What he'll be willing to spend to get me back, if they'll just agree to ransom me."

We hadn't spoken so cordially in weeks, my mistress and I—not since she'd slapped me for insulting Orsino Orsini, and before that when I'd been cruel to her in Pesaro for no particular reason other than the fact that I felt like it.

"I haven't had a chance to thank you," Giulia said, "for defending me."

A tongue of flame flared up in the brazier, and I focused on it. "Don't thank me, Madonna Giulia."

"I will," she said fiercely. "All your injuries—why did you do it, Leonello? You couldn't have beaten them, there were too many and you had only so many knives. Why?"

"I was hired to protect you. So I tried." I shrugged as best I could while lying flat on my back and piled with blankets that were beginning to weigh on my chest like stones. "Besides, I don't like the French. They're rude, they stink, and if one small man can make a few of them wish they'd stayed on their own side of the mountains, then so much the better. Well worth a few shattered ribs."

She looked at me. "That's truly why you did it?"

"Perhaps I was also making amends." I gazed up at the arched ceiling of the vestry again. A spider was spinning a web there, not caring about the little man lying below and possibly dying. "I am sorry I called you a whore, Madonna Giulia. In Pesaro." I hate making apologies, and I fumbled the words. I hate fumbling, too. "When I get in a temper—I need to cut someone, even if only with my tongue. You were there."

"And you were right." She was quite calm. "I am a whore. I used to pretend I wasn't, because I never asked for presents or payments, and I never asked to be anybody's mistress in the first place. But after a while it doesn't matter what you *ask*, does it?" She looked down at herself, all the gaudy jewels and the low-cut silver gown. "Don't I look like the most expensive harlot in Rome?"

"Never," I said.

"No need to defend my honor, Leonello." Her tone was light, social. Talking of anything, I suppose, as long as she could distract me from the pain in my body. "I'm a whore now, and I'll play the part for the French. But I won't always be one. This summer with my family . . . it showed me something."

"Which is?" I raised an eyebrow. Even that hurt. "The idyllic pleasures of Carbognano, as painted by your good lord husband?"

"Yes." Giulia reached to a table behind the brazier and uncorked a flask of wine. "Someday I'll have that. An ordinary life again."

"Do you want such a life?"

"Someday. Even if it comes with Orsino."

"He's not so terrible," I found myself saying.

"No," Giulia acknowledged. "But he's gutless. You were right about that."

"He loves you," I found myself saying. How had I found myself speaking of love with the most expensive harlot in Rome? *Dio*, but I wanted a drink.

"Orsino doesn't love me." She poured me a cup as though she had read my mind, helping lift my head so I could sip without spilling. "If he did, he'd spit in Rodrigo's eye and say he'd rather be excommunicated and damned than give me up. He'd hear I was being held captive by the French, and he'd come riding to rescue me." Giulia shook her head. "I don't think I inspire much love in men. Just passion, and the passion isn't really for *me*." She made a matter-of-fact gesture at her own face, her golden hair, her perfumed breasts. "The passion is for this."

"The Pope will harrow heaven and hell to get you back safely," I said. "Isn't that love?"

"More passion." She held the cup to my lips again; rearranged my blankets. "One day it will fade, and he'll tire of me, and I'll go back to my gutless husband. I'm not so afraid of that happening as I used to be, oddly." A shrug. "You know why silly women moon over Petrarch and Dante, Leonello?"

"Why?"

"Because we like to pretend that we're Laura or Beatrice. Women who inspire both passion *and* love, and in verse too." Giulia's tone turned wry. "But women like me aren't idols for poets. Laura and Beatrice were both chaste—no one writes poetry to harlots."

"Count yourself fortunate," I said. "Great love makes for terrible poetry. Remember Lord Sforza's unspeakable little sonnets about Lucrezia? '*Hail to thee, O springtime goddess fair—*'"

Giulia let out a laugh, and I thought a genuine one. It did my heart good to hear it. "Don't think I'm complaining too much about this life of mine, Leonello. Passion is more than most women get, after all. And His Holiness is burning hot enough for me right now to challenge all France, and that's more than Orsino would ever do."

I had no answer to that.

My mistress arranged the blankets closer around me and rose. "Until His Holiness sends an offer of ransom, however, I'd better go dine with General d'Allegre and do my best to keep us all safe and sound." A sigh as she gave a pat to her hair and her gleaming skirts, and arranged her huge pearl more prominently between her breasts. "Holy Virgin, but it's bound to be unpleasant."

I felt cold despite the blankets and the brazier. "Surely the general wouldn't lay a finger on a prisoner." Leaving me to die of my wounds was one thing; a dwarf guard was nothing. But the Pope's darling—

"I'll encourage him to lay a finger on me, Leonello," Giulia said quietly. "The whole hand, if he wants. If it will keep my daughter safe and my maids unraped, and get a surgeon in here to keep you from bleeding to death, I'll let that French general lift my skirts and ride me like a mare."

She glided from the vestry like an actress making her way onto the stage.

I heard Pantisilea's voice from the corner, cautious. "She told me to look after you, Leonello. I could get you some food—"

I shut my eyes. "Get out."

The vestry door thudded again, leaving me in the silence. I took a ragged bubbling breath and spat blood again. My hand throbbed like it was being crushed in a vise, and the wound in my hip had broken open under the bandages and soaked the bedclothes beneath me. At least I hoped it was blood. From the smell, I was very much afraid I had pissed myself. Piss and blood and rage; the room stank of it—and for what? I'd been hired to keep the Pope's mistress safe from danger, and I'd given my pathetic stunted body over to do it, and I'd still failed. She'd go play whore to the French and I'd lie here and die, and none of it mattered at all.

Failed. Failed.

Since I was alone, I let out one gasping sob between clenched teeth, cradling my maimed hand against my chest. *Dio*, but it hurt. I'd never known anything could hurt so much.

"Leonello, let me help—"

Carmelina Mangano's Venetian accents came from the door as it creaked open again. Quick footsteps sounded, and then I felt her wiry arm sliding under my head, raising me up so I could breathe easier. I hurt too badly to refuse the help, and resentment stung my mouth. How dare she offer it when I couldn't fling it in her face?

"Here, take some wine." She propped me up halfway so I was almost sitting, then went racing about the vestry poking up the brazier and uncorking the flask again. How she had so much energy at the end of the day we'd just endured, I didn't know. It was all I could do to take a few shallow breaths around my bubbling lungs and get my face under control again. My flattened little finger had begun to throb on an entirely different level from the rest of my mangled hand, pain sinking in like a ring of teeth.

"I think I'll have some wine too," Carmelina said over her bony shoulder, rummaging for another cup. "Madonna Giulia told us all to try to sleep while she was gone wining and dining the French officers. But I don't think any of us maidservants can even close our eyes, not after the things we've heard the French sentries call in at us." A shudder.

I looked up at her as she passed me a wine cup. "Thank you."

Her eyes flicked away. That bruise along the side of her face was nearly as spectacular as mine. On top of the bruising she had shadows of exhaustion under her eyes, and her wiry black curls had escaped their plait and bobbed at the middle of her back. Grown out to a respectable length now, that hair.

"Do you want something to eat?" She tugged at a straying thread on her sleeve. "The French gave us some provisions, and I've still got the remains of a nice *zabaglione* from Bartolomeo's hamper—"

"I'm not hungry." I managed to wrap my broken fingers around the cup, feeling the joints grind as though filled with molten-hot sand. "Besides, I don't think I'll live long enough to digest your *zabaglione*."

She winced, looking at the bulky lumps of my bandages under the blankets. "Is it so bad?"

"No, it's marvelous." I made a flamboyant gesture at my bruises, my bandages, the air around me that smelled so rank. I had definitely pissed myself. "Better than a massage, a hot bath, and a soft bed with Giulia Farnese in it, all rolled into one." I drained half the cup of wine. I drank sparingly most nights, but a dying man has his privileges. "Good vintage. That pale wine from Chiarello?"

"Yes, I uncorked the best wine we had before the French found it and stole it." She tossed down a great gulp. "I'd say we've earned it."

"I have, anyway." I managed to lift the flagon, topping up my cup. I felt rage kindling deep in my torn chest, and I nurtured it like a small flame. Rage felt much better than pain. "You, *Signorina Cuoca*, have much to answer for."

Her voice was wary. "What do you mean?"

"I mean, it's your fault we traveled the Montefiascone road into the hands of the French. I was standing guard outside Madonna Giulia's chamber the night before we left Capodimonte. You brought her a plate of *biscotti*, and you trotted out some pretty story about a man giving you that bruise on your face"—I gestured—"and asked if we couldn't travel a different way, just to avoid him and his party."

"It's true. I *was* attacked." Her voice rose. "I didn't know the French would be along the other road. How could I?"

"Oh, I believe that. Just not the part about you being attacked. Madonna Giulia, she's a trusting soul, so perhaps she swallowed that story, but not me. I've seen you handle a cleaver, Carmelina. If a man tried to pry those long legs of yours apart without your permission, you'd run him off with a knife and then spit on him the next morning. Not go fleeing up the opposite road in a panic." I contemplated the ceiling and whistled. "I like that about you, really. If I were in any condition for it, I'd challenge you to a knife-throwing contest, get you drunk, and try to coax those legs apart myself. There's a certain height difference, but it's surprising how that goes away once one is lying down."

"You're drunk," Carmelina snapped. But her eyes were wide in that thin bruised face, and I felt a vicious satisfaction.

"It was that party of Venetians who stopped for the night, wasn't it? I suppose you ran into someone who knew you. Cousin, brother. Maybe the Archbishop himself—tell me, did he know you from your convent?"

She went perfectly still then. The flickering light from the brazier threw a shadow off her high-bridged nose. Somewhere outside the vestry I heard a maidservant weeping, and Madonna Adriana hushing her.

"You're wrong," Carmelina Mangano said at last. Her voice had a rusty scrape like an old wheel. "You're wrong, I never—"

"Spare me," I said contemptuously. "The chopped hair? The way you avoid churches? The way you have no proper education but know all the prayers whenever any visiting cardinal starts spouting in Latin? You might call yourself a cook, but you swapped that cook's apron with a nun's veil. Some convent in Venice, I suppose, where your family disposed of their spare daughter. The one too plain and sharp-tongued to get a husband even if she does cook like an angel." I stared her down. "You're a nun, Carmelina. You ran away, and if you're caught you'll be hauled back and subjected to the bread-and-water penance by your abbess, and never allowed to cook anything again but watery communal stews."

"No." She shook her head, a frantic little jerk back and forth, back and forth. "No, I—"

"I've known for months. Why do you think I stopped baiting you? There wasn't any point; I'd already figured it out. I wouldn't have bothered to say anything, except that it's your fault I hurt like this." I threw the empty cup at her, with a gasp of pain for the stab that shot through my side. "You were so petrified of being hauled back to your convent that you threw us all into the hands of the French. Three guards murdered, half the bones in my body cracked like green sticks, and Giulia spreading her legs for the French general right now, just to keep us all safe. Congratulations on your fine escape."

"I didn't know the French army was on that road! I didn't *know*!"

"Perhaps not, but I don't feel very forgiving at the moment. I'm still lying here dying, you see." Getting drunk had lost its appeal. I shoved at my pillows, struggling to lie flat again. "So now I know your secret, *Signorina Cuoca*. Or shall I call you Suora Carmelina?"

She gasped, and I felt a surge of savage satisfaction. I raised an eyebrow at her as I drew my blankets up to my chest. "Think on this," I said. "I'm probably going to die in this bed. But if I don't, and if we get back to Rome, I will turn you in and happily watch you get hauled off in chains back to your convent."

She stared at me.

I saluted her with my right hand, the one with the broken fingers. "Good night."

Carmelina

*S*ignorina?" Bartolomeo's head jerked up as I stumbled out of the vestry. He had been praying with that quiet surety of his, lips moving soundlessly as he gripped the little wooden crucifix about his neck in one freckled fist, but now he stared at me. "What's wrong, *signorina*?"

"What's wrong?" I looked around our huddled little party of maidservants and guardsmen, slumped in shock and exhaustion against the stone walls. "What's *right*, Bartolomeo? Tell me that!"

"Eat something," my apprentice said helplessly. "You should eat, *signorina*."

"That's your solution? Food?" All the strength had left my legs; I melted down to sit beside him on the floor. "You really are a cook, Bartolomeo."

His freckled face glowed. At least someone could find a ray of light in this black hell we were trapped in.

Because of me.

My hands doubled into fists, but they still shook. My head was one great mindless yammer of words; two words over and over. *He knows. He knows, he knows, he knows.* That malicious little man dying in the next room. Torn half to pieces, but still tearing *me* to pieces.

Suora Carmelina. Only half right, really. Suora Serafina was the name I'd been given, when I knelt on a stone floor in smoldering resentment and took my vows in the Convent of Santa Marta as a nun.

He knows, he knows, he knows. Though he didn't know how truly he had the power to destroy me. He'd report me only as a runaway nun, and for the most part runaway nuns were simply handed back to their convents for whatever private punishment their superiors deemed fit. But if I was exposed as a nun run from her convent, it would soon be known *what* convent—because if inquiries were made around Venice, the story would surely surface of the lay sister who had robbed her order of a relic, not just any relic but their patron saint's hand, and then fled. Desecrators faced a gruesome enough punishment: hanging upside-down on a public gallows as the crowds jeered and threw stones. But as a desecrator who was also a nun, I'd be returned to Venice to face a far worse fate.

"*Signorina?*" Bartolomeo ventured at my side.

I turned and buried my face in my apprentice's shoulder, winding my cold hand into his sleeve. A *maestro di cucina* should never show weakness before underlings, but I wasn't a *maestro di cucina.* I was a fraud. They called Giulia Farnese the Bride of Christ, but I was a true Bride of Christ, and there would be no forgiveness for any of my sins. Nuns were never forgiven; their misdeeds were counted twice as black because their souls belonged to God and must therefore be stainless. If a nun turned her back on her convent, she turned her back on God Himself. If a nun took a man to her bed, she committed adultery against God Himself. The punishment for a nun's sins would always be crueler—and my spiteful prioress from the Convent of Santa Marta, with her velvety voice and her highborn connections into all the powerful families of Venice, would see to it I suffered the worst possible punishment offered for altar desecration.

She'd make sure I had my hands and my nose chopped off.

Maybe after that I'd be strung upside-down on a gallows to die, or maybe I'd simply be returned to my convent, but it wouldn't matter. If I had no hands to stir and chop, no nose to smell, I'd never cook again. I'd had a long time to consider that fate, after I fled my veil and my convent walls. Maybe it was foolish of me to think so, but I knew I'd rather be dead than a noseless, stump-fisted horror.

My eyes stung; I was shaking all over, and I didn't protest when my apprentice put a hesitant arm about my shoulders.

"We'll be all right, Carmelina," Bartolomeo said, and I didn't protest when he called me by name, either.

Pantisilea had gone into the vestry with a tray, and now she came back out shaking her head over the untouched food. "Leonello won't eat," she said. "And he's spitting up blood again—I've got his wounds bandaged, but it's inside where he's bleeding."

One of the guards said it, brutally. "He's dying."

Not fast enough, I thought. I'd never in my life prayed for a man to die, but I was praying now. *Die, you spiteful little bastard. Just die and take my secret with you.*

"If Madonna Giulia can just get him a surgeon—" Pantisilea gnawed her lip. "Do you really think she'll have to—that nasty French general . . ."

Adriana da Mila spoke bleakly into little Laura's curls. "If she does, the Pope will never hear about it from me."

I flinched. The yammer of words in my head changed, from *He knows* to *My fault. My fault, my fault, my fault.*

"She'd better get that surgeon soon." Pantisilea dashed at her eyes. "He's trying so hard not to cry at the pain, he's got *me* crying. That much pain for such a little man, it's like to kill him."

I hoped it did kill him. It was him or me—perhaps it had always been him or me, since the day we met.

We all lapsed into silence again. Bartolomeo's arm still circled my shoulders, but I felt too frightened and exhausted to shrug it away. I wanted to howl and scream and hide, like a child afraid of the dark, but there was no hiding from this. *He knows, he knows, he knows.*

Bartolomeo kept trying to press food on me, rummaging in the hamper. Napkins piled up, cheeses and bread loaves, cold sliced meats, spoons, twists of dried herbs, the little stoppered vial of hemlock tincture that I kept to kill rats. My eyes fell on the vial.

"Have you got more wine, Bartolomeo?" Pantisilea joined my apprentice, rummaging in the hamper. "If we haven't got a surgeon yet for poor Leonello, at least I can get him drunk and numb the pain a little."

I knew something else that would numb the pain altogether. I stared at the little vial of hemlock tincture until it twinned itself, dancing in the haze around my vision. I could feel Santa Marta clicking her tongue at me in disapproval, if a severed hand in a pouch really had a tongue to click.

It's him or me. I could smell old blood and splinters; the smell of the executioner's block. I'd smell it when they forced my head down on it, right before they chopped off my nose. The last thing I'd ever smell, all thanks to a dwarf's malice.

Panic rose sour and nauseating in my throat, and I palmed the little vial into my sweaty hand.

EPILOGUE

Fear is the daughter of death.

—OLD ITALIAN PROVERB

Rome

The girl is terrified. Michelotto can see it, hear it, feel it, smell it, and if he puts his lips to her skin he knows he will be able to taste it. Fear in all five senses; it's always been his gift. He puts a gloved hand on her throat, stroking it. "I'm not going to hurt you," he promises, and he speaks truth. He would hurt her if he was ordered to, but he wasn't ordered to.

"Kill this one quickly," Cesare Borgia had told him. "She's just a whore from the Borgo, after all—she doesn't deserve this."

Michelotto shrugs as he takes the girl's wrists one at a time, roping them down wide and spread-eagled on the battered table. He doesn't bother thinking about the ones he kills, whether they deserve it or not. He is Cesare Borgia's dog, and like a good dog, he does what he is told. No more, no less.

"The dwarf's been asking questions."

"I know." Cesare Borgia had been amused.

"He won't stop."

"No." And when Michelotto had suggested throwing the little man off the scent, the Pope's son had seen the sense of it.

"You may kill this one, then," Cesare had said. "I shall be occupied elsewhere, with many witnesses. Not that there isn't enough to do," he added. "It seems La Bella has gotten herself captured by the French. If I'm not there to stop him, the Holy Father will end up declaring war on France."

The girl whimpers. Michelotto surveys the room: the details. Yes, it looks right. The little man won't know. Michelotto had offered to kill the little man—it would be simpler—but Cesare Borgia likes him.

"I'm sorry," Michelotto tells the girl. "This is unfair, I know." He puts his hand over her eyes so she won't see. A moment or two later he is gone, adjusting his borrowed mask and flicking drops of blood from his gloves as he disappears into the Holy City.

HISTORICAL NOTE

❖

The Borgias dominate the Renaissance, fascinating across time with their power, their charm, and their unsavory reputations. They have inspired countless books, movies, scholarly works, and rumors, and the one thing everyone can agree on is just how difficult they are to pin down: corrupt churchman and his incestuous brood, or loving paterfamilias and his misunderstood offspring? The truth is probably somewhere in the middle—and pure gold to a historical novelist.

It's fashionable to blame the Borgias for corrupting the Church, but the institution was already corrupted long before Rodrigo Borgia took the throne of St. Peter as Alexander VI. Benefices, pardons, and indulgences were openly bought and sold; vows of chastity and poverty among the clergy were blatantly ignored, and the Pope was politician and king over his unruly papal states just as much as he was Father of Christendom. Priests like Savonarola preached of the dangers of sin and hellfire, but it was understood by even the lowest on the social scale that there was no sin that could not be pardoned with the appropriate penance or payoff. The Borgias have become the poster children for this cynical system, but their real sin appears to be their lack of hypocrisy: Rodrigo Borgia was hardly the first Pope to aggrandize his family, keep a mistress, or sire illegitimate children; he simply refused to hide any of it under the usual cloak of lies. Such honesty about his various sins might be rather refreshing to a modern perspective—not so to his contemporaries.

Giulia Farnese was one of the great beauties of the Renaissance, already famous for her vivacity and her floor-length hair by the time she married wealthy young Orsino Orsini. It isn't known precisely when Giulia caught the eye of the womanizing Rodrigo Borgia, or if her marriage to Orsino was arranged from the beginning as a cover for an illicit affair—Rodrigo arranged several such compliant husbands for his previous mistress, Vannozza dei Cattanei. But by the time Cardinal Borgia was elected Pope, Giulia Farnese was his official mistress, installed in a cheerful domestic arrangement with her apparently compliant mother-in-law, Adriana da Mila, and the young Lucrezia Borgia. The deftness with which Giulia handled her volatile Pope throughout their long and evidently passion-filled affair indicates that the woman nicknamed the Bride of Christ had some brains under all that hair.

Giulia's daughter Laura has no certain birthdate or father. Gossip of the day believed her to be the Pope's child, but she was christened under the name Orsini. Giulia's husband was well rewarded for the loan of his wife, but he was never as compliant about the arrangement as were Vannozza dei Cattanei's husbands. Giulia nearly did rejoin Orsino once, after her flight to her family in Capodimonte to attend her brother's deathbed, but the Pope's furious letters (quoted in the book) soon sapped Orsino's resolve to reclaim his wife. All the delay caused Giulia and her traveling party to fall into the hands of the invading French army—and the French salivated at the power they had gained over the frantic Pope.

Carmelina is a fictional character. Most of the professional cooks in illustrious houses would have been male, but cooks of the day were trained without the strict oversight of a formal guild—a cook's daughter with talent might well have trained under her father. The Renaissance was a golden age for food as well as art; the recipes from this book have been taken almost exclusively from surviving Renaissance cookbooks. There was a convent of Santa Marta in Venice that boasted the reliquary hand of Santa Marta, the patron saint of cooks—but we have no record that the relic was ever stolen. Desecration of a church or altar was one of the more severe crimes of the day, punishable by such tortures as throttling, upside-down hanging, or the chopping of hands and ears. But justice in the Renaissance was always an arbitrary thing, punishments being handed out according to the social status or financial contributions of the offender.

Leonello is also a fictional character. Dwarves were hugely popular among Renaissance nobles as entertainers, jugglers, and companions; they were even bred like pets. Conversely they could be feared and abhorred by the ignorant as demons, changelings, or simply as cursed by God.

I have taken some liberties with the facts in order to serve the story. Giulia's marriage to Orsino occurred somewhat earlier, at the respective ages of fifteen and sixteen; I moved the occasion up to coincide with the papal election. I altered traveling plans so that Cesare could be present for Carmelina's aphrodisiac banquet, so the Pope could stand witness at his son Joffre's wedding in Naples, and so Orsino Orsini could visit Giulia at Capodimonte rather than merely writing her letters. Several unconfirmed portraits of Giulia exist, including the *Portrait of a Young Woman with Unicorn* by Raphael which hangs today in Rome's Galleria Borghese (the blond beauty in the picture not only sports a huge teardrop pearl necklace but has a baby goat in her lap painted as a miniature unicorn). Raphael's unfinished *Transfiguration*, currently hanging in the Vatican Museum, also supposedly features Giulia as the kneeling blond figure, in the same scene described in Pesaro's beauty contest. Both paintings, however, would have been painted much later, since Raphael was still very young during the events of this book.

The adventures of the Borgia family have only begun with the French invasion. Giulia and her friends will face many dangers to come, as the saga continues.

CHARACTERS

*denotes historical figures

THE BORGIA FAMILY

*RODRIGO BORGIA, Cardinal of Valencia, later Pope Alexander VI

    *CESARE BORGIA, his eldest son, Bishop of Pamplona, later Archbishop of Valencia and Cardinal Borgia

    *JUAN BORGIA, his second son, Duke of Gandia

    *LUCREZIA BORGIA, his daughter, later Countess of Pesaro

    *JOFFRE BORGIA, his youngest son, later Prince of Squillace

*VANNOZZA DEI CATTANEI, Rodrigo's former mistress, mother of his children

*ADRIANA DA MILA, a cousin

*ORSINO ORSINI, her son

THE FARNESE FAMILY

*GIULIA FARNESE

    *LAURA, her daughter

*ALESSANDRO FARNESE, called SANDRO, Giulia's brother; later Cardinal Farnese

*ANGELO FARNESE, Giulia's brother

*BARTOLOMEO FARNESE, Giulia's brother

*GEROLAMA FARNESE, Giulia's sister

*PUCCIO PUCCI, Gerolama's husband

IN ROME:

MARCO SANTINI, *maestro di cucina* for Adriana da Mila

CARMELINA MANGANO, his cousin from Venice

*PANTISILEA, PIA, TADDEA: household maidservants

LEONELLO, cardsharp and bodyguard

*MICHELOTTO CORELLA, Cesare Borgia's private assassin

*BARTOLOMEO, kitchen apprentice

PIERO, OTTAVIANO, GIULIANO, UGO, TOMMASO, BRUNO: other kitchen apprentices

*JOHANN BURCHARD, papal master of ceremonies

*MAESTRO PINTURICCHIO, an artist

*CATERINA GONZAGA, Countess of Montevegio

*COUNT OTTAVIANO DA MONTEVEGIO, her husband

ANNA, a tavern maid

SANTA MARTA, a holy relic

IN ITALY:

*GIOVANNI SFORZA, Count of Pesaro

PAOLO MANGANO, Carmelina's father, *maestro di cucina* in Venice

IN SPAIN:

*KING FERDINAND and *Queen Isabella

*MARIA ENRIQUES, a royal cousin, later Duchess of Gandia

IN NAPLES:

*Alfonso II, King of Naples

*Sancha of Aragon, his illegitimate daughter, later Princess of Squillace

IN FLORENCE:

*Fra Girolamo Savonarola, Dominican friar

IN FRANCE:

*Charles VIII of France, claimant to the throne of Naples

*General Yves d'Allegre, leader of the French armies

READERS GUIDE

The
SERPENT
and the PEARL

DISCUSSION QUESTIONS

———— ❖ ————

1. Which character most suitably earns the title of Serpent? The Pearl? Why?

2. Carmelina Mangano opens the novel. Already in the opening pages, it is noted that Carmelina possesses a cook's nose. How does her talent as a cook change her character? Her life?

3. Many characters in the book are based on real people involved with the Borgias. Did you have any preconceptions of the Borgia family that shaped your expectations of the story?

4. How does the relationship between Giulia and Lucrezia grow or change throughout the book? Do you have any sympathy for Vannozza dei Cattanei? Why or why not?

5. At one point, Madonna Adriana explains, "My boy [Orsino] will need help if he's to get on as he should," in response to Giulia's accusation that she is a terrible mother. Do you understand her choices or do you find them inexcusable?

6. Giulia's mother told her that a woman has three possible fates: "Wife, nun—or whore. And once you've chosen, there's no changing it." Carmelina disagrees. Discuss the female characters and assign each the label of "wife," "nun," or "whore." Why did you choose what you did? Do you agree with Giulia's mother or Carmelina? Why?

7. How is Madonna Adriana's relationship with Rodrigo Borgia (her cousin) similar to Giulia's with Sandro or Carmelina's with Marco? How do the three women manage the men who control their lives, when it comes to getting their own way?

8. Once Leonello was named Giulia's bodyguard, all three narrators had a chance to meet for the first time in Carmelina's kitchen. What did you

suspect would become of them? How did you think they would interact?

9. During Lucrezia's bridal processional to the Vatican, Leonello reflects on the crowd: "They would be pleased by the pomp, dazzled rather than offended. The Borgias, in the eyes of most of the world including themselves, had been put upon the earth by God to lead sumptuous lives on behalf of the masses. Their pomp was God's will." How is this similar to the way our modern culture idolizes celebrities?

10. Leonello is ashamed of himself when he finds cheer in the fact that the fruit vendor, Eleonora, was also staked. Were you happy that this storyline was continued? Did you suspect Cesare?

11. Leonello observes that "the degree to which women kiss and coo, I've found, is in direct proportion to the degree in which they dislike each other." Do you agree? How do Giulia and Carmelina relate differently to other women, from their very different stations in life? How do they relate to each other?

12. Giulia doesn't walk in her brother's funeral procession in Capodimonte because, "that wasn't how things were done here." Would you prefer Giulia live in the country where she's vilified or in the city where her relationship with the Pope removes her from judgment? How do these distinctions affect the story?

13. Do you suspect that Rodrigo cares to save Giulia once she's captured by the French? Why or why not?

14. Giulia reflects on the difference between passion and love, declaring that Rodrigo and Orsino both feel passion for her but not love. Do you agree? Are any of the female characters capable of inspiring love?

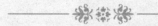

TURN THE PAGE FOR A SPECIAL PREVIEW
OF THE NEXT NOVEL OF THE BORGIAS,

The LION *and the* ROSE

AVAILABLE JANUARY 2014
FROM BERKLEY BOOKS

Giulia

You'd think that the Holy Father would have an all-seeing gaze, wouldn't you? Being God's Vicar here upon earth, surely he would be granted divine sight into the hearts and souls of men as soon as that silly papal hat everyone insisted on calling a tiara was lowered onto his brow. The truth is, most popes don't have divine insight into much of anything. If they did, they'd get on with the business of making saints and saving souls rather than pronouncing velvet gowns as impious, or persecuting the poor Jews. Blasphemy it may be, but most popes have no more insight into the minds of humanity than does any carter or candlestick-maker walking the streets of Rome in wooden clogs.

And my Pope was no exception. He was the cleverest man I knew in some ways—those black eyes of his had only to pass benignly over his bowing cardinals to know exactly which ones were scheming against him, and certainly that despicable French King had learned not to cross wits *or* swords with Rodrigo Borgia over the past year and a half since

I'd been ransomed. But when it came to his family, His Holiness Pope Alexander VI was as dense as a plank.

At least at the moment he was a very happy plank.

"*Mi familia,*" he said thickly, and began to raise his goblet but put it down again to dash a heavy hand at the water standing in his eyes. "My children all together again. Cesare, Lucrezia, Joffre—Juan—"

The loathsome young Duke of Gandia preened, sitting at his father's right where Rodrigo could easily reach out to touch his favorite son's shoulder. Juan Borgia, twenty years old now and returned from his lands in Spain. Although he was a duke, a husband, even a *father* (Holy Virgin, fetch me a basin!)—that auburn-haired young lout looked no different to me, lolling in his chair fiddling with his dagger hilt, already halfway through his cup of wine and giving me the occasional leer over the rim. I'd heaved a great sigh that afternoon, watching him strike a pose before the cheering crowd as he disembarked his Spanish ship. My lover's second son had been wearing silly stockings embroidered in rays and crowns, and I'd realized just how much I'd been hoping never to see Juan or his ridiculous clothes or his leer again. As soon as I heard Rodrigo had summoned Juan from Spain to take command of the papal forces against the French, I prayed so devoutly for a shipwreck. You'd think someone nicknamed the Bride of Christ could get the occasional prayer answered, wouldn't you?

But if I wasn't exactly thrilled to see Juan or his silly stockings again, my Pope was—he had rushed from his elaborate sedan chair across the docks to embrace his son in a great sweep of embroidered papal robes, kissing both his cheeks and uttering a great many ecstatic things in the Catalan Spanish he saved for moments of high emotion. Nobody else had missed Juan, when he departed Rome for Barcelona to take possession of the Spanish duchy and the Spanish bride my Pope had inveigled for his favorite son—but my Pope certainly had. And nothing would do but to gather the whole family together for an intimate evening *cena* in the Holy Father's private apartments at the Vatican.

And what apartments! Just a modest little nest of rooms in the Vatican where the Holy Father could remove his jeweled cope (along with the weight of all Christendom), and relax at the end of the evening like any ordinary man. But Rodrigo Borgia would have nothing ordinary. He had declared he would have the papal apartments new-made, stamped and decorated with a flair that said nothing but "Borgia." It had taken two years, but that little painter Maestro Pinturicchio had finally finished the frescoes that had been designed especially for the Holy Father's personal rooms, and the resulting splendor left all Rome gasping. Our small *cena* tonight had been set in the *Sala dei Santi*; the long table draped with sumptuous brocades and set with solid silver dishes and fragile Murano glass; the ceiling arched overhead painted in double crowns and the Borgia bull; the frescoes were framed with geometric Moorish patterns in a blaze of colors, imported straight from Spain.

Pinturicchio had used us all as models for his various scenes—Lucrezia dimpled and tossed her blond head under the beseeching figure of herself on the wall as Santa Caterina; inscrutable Cesare lounged under his own image as inscrutable Emperor Maximilian in a massive throne; fourteen-year-old Joffre pranced in the painted crowd as one of the background figures; and Juan cut a ridiculous figure on the wall in a silly Turkish mantle as a turbaned heathen. I was a Madonna in one of the other chambers, with my Laura on my lap for the Christ child. "Surely it's blasphemous to have a *girl* sit as model for our Lord!" Maestro Pinturicchio had protested.

"Any more blasphemous than to have a harlot sit for the Madonna?" I'd countered, the Holy Virgin's blue veil swinging about my face like a joke. I'd never *asked* to be a notorious woman; I'd been raised for a husband and children like any other girl of noble birth, but here I was. I'd made my own choices, and I made no bones either about what it made me—but I'd been determined to have my Laura in the frescoes along with all the other Borgia children. Maestro Pinturicchio had taken one look at the set of my chin, and begun sketching. A nice little man, ugly as the day was long, but skilled. His wife was the most notorious harpy in Rome, and I gave him a rose-quartz and crystal bracelet to give her in the hopes it would sweeten her temper. It hadn't, but he thanked me anyway, and he made Laura look very pretty indeed in our

Madonna-and-Child fresco. Though the halo certainly didn't suit her; she was a full three years old now and a proper little imp!

Rodrigo was still looking about the table with misty eyes, and I ceased my musing. "It's not just Our own children here tonight," he continued, beaming like any proud father despite the regal papal *We*. "Our new children as well. Sancha—"

Young Joffre's Neapolitan wife, Sancha of Aragon, was making doe eyes at Cesare through the candlelight, but she dropped her lashes demurely at her father-in-law.

"—and of course Lucrezia's Giovanni Sforza is here in our thoughts, if not the flesh. A pity he could not join Us—"

Lucrezia giggled behind her hand, not looking very put out about that. My Pope had called her back from her husband's home in Pesaro last winter for a long visit, declaring he could not do without his dear daughter any longer, and certainly I'd been delighted to see Lucrezia again, both of us chattering and gossiping in the Palazzo Santa Maria just like the old days when she'd been a little girl dreaming of marriage—but she had certainly not seemed inclined to go back to her new home now that she *was* married. I suppose Pesaro's provincial pleasures had worn rather thin after two years of marriage. Lord Sforza had stamped off home this spring, muttering of duties that could not be put off, and he'd stamped off alone.

"And a pity your beautiful Maria Enriques could not travel with you from Spain," Rodrigo continued, giving Juan's arm another pat. "We would have liked to see Our new daughter."

"She begged to come, but she's breeding again." Juan shrugged, rotating the silver stem of his wine goblet between restless fingers. "I'm happy enough to leave her behind. The cow is always weeping and praying."

"Now, now," Rodrigo chuckled. "She'll be mother to another Borgia prince soon!" He gave an indulgent shake of his head, and raised his goblet. "No matter. All of us are together again. As it should be."

His children raised their goblets too, but I couldn't help noticing that not everybody looked entirely pleased to see *la familia Borgia* reunited. Joffre was sulking, squashed in beside Juan and ignored by Sancha, and as for Cesare . . .

"*La familia,*" said the Holy Father.

"*La familia,*" everyone echoed, and the look Cesare sent his brother across the table could have kindled the napkins.

"So," I said brightly as a stream of papal servants entered with massive silver dishes, "how was the crossing from Spain? Did the waves stay smooth for the Duke of Gandia?"

"Smooth enough," Juan said, eyes flickering to my breasts.

"I suppose your Duchess will be very much distressed to have you gone." Myself, I'd have thrown a ball in celebration.

Juan shrugged again, clearly not interested in his wife. His eyes went to Cesare as the first dishes were laid before us on the *cena* table. "So, brother. Hostage to the French, were you? I hear you ran away."

"Escaped," said Cesare. He was a dark shadow among the candles—in his plain black velvets he seemed to eat the light and refuse to give it back again. "The Holy Father and I arranged it all. I escaped as a groom shortly after we set out from Rome."

"Ran." Juan grinned.

"He was ever so brave," Sancha cooed in her milky-sweet voice, tossing her gleaming dark head. She and Joffre had been recalled from their official seat in Naples to Rome that May, and it hadn't taken me more than a week to start despising that velvety purr of hers. I'd only met Sancha once, at her wedding to little Joffre when he was twelve and Sancha four years older, and that occasion had been quite enough to make me think we weren't destined to be the best of friends. And when Sancha took an idle look at my companion and bodyguard Leonello the first time she laid eyes on him, and told me, "Your dwarf is a fine specimen; have you ever considered breeding him? I have the most cunning little juggling woman—" Well, after that I'd started calling her the Tart of Aragon, and I knew I'd happily watch her choke to death on a fish bone. "Try the carp, Sancha," I suggested, but she was talking over me and toying with the pearl pendant about her neck to draw attention to her breasts.

"Cesare left all his baggage behind, you know." She left off the pendant long enough to hold her wine-cup to be refilled again—she certainly could put it away! "And when King Charles went to look he saw that all those chests that were supposed to be filled with coin and silver plate had nothing but stones under a top layer of ducats! You could hear the scream all the way in Rome."

Juan gave Sancha's breasts an automatic glance, but his attention was all for his brother. "I expect I'll do better than run when I see the French, brother."

Cesare toyed with his table knife.

"You'll send the French packing, boy!" my Pope said warmly. He'd left off his ecclesiastical robes, and in his embroidered doublet and linen shirt-sleeves he could have been any merchant father or ducal *pater-familias:* the proud and swarthy Spaniard surrounded by children who all looked like him. "We taught them a lesson at Fornovo; now you'll finish them off."

Really, after all that fuss the French had made declaring they would annex all Naples and the Papal territories too before they were done, everything had petered out so embarrassingly. Well, embarrassing if you were French. After they got their poxy noses bloodied at Fornovo and had to flee back north, my Pope made me a present straight from the French king's own abandoned baggage: a certain diary in execrable handwriting, detailing the ladies who had shared the royal bed on campaign, with descriptions of their skills. "No, thank you," I'd said, wrinkling my nose.

"Are you sure?" Rodrigo had turned the pages with great interest. "There are a few ideas here. Requiring a bit more flexibility than I'm capable of at my age, to be sure . . ."

"Really, Rodrigo," I'd scolded. "Dirty stories? Whatever happened to giving a woman flowers?"

"Then flowers you shall have." And I'd acquired a nice set of diamond roses to clip into my braided hair. Every time the Tart of Aragon looked at them I could see her little nose twitch with lust. Her little nose was usually twitching with lust of one kind or another. For the past two months it had been twitching for Cesare, in whose lap she appeared to be dandling her hand under cover of the damask tablecloth. She didn't have a glance for poor little Joffre—he'd grown to a tall gangly youth, but he still seemed like a child to me, sulking in the shadow of his voluptuous wife and his taller, handsomer brothers. I tried to engage him in the conversation—"You'll be next on the battlefield after your brothers, Joffre!"—but he pushed his lip out in sullen silence and I finally gave up and stabbed at my roast capon, which had been taken off the spit too soon and was now oozing red juice all over my plate like it had been wounded rather than cooked. You'd think the Pope would eat better than anyone else in the Holy City, but you'd be wrong. It wasn't fair, this reputation he'd acquired for dissipation and luxury—my Pope was so indifferent to what he ate, he didn't care if the Vatican cooks fed him or his guests on bread and water. Anyone who wanted a decent meal at the Pope's table had better hope they were eating at the Palazzo Santa Maria, where I presided over the table.

I pushed my plate away. All this *la familia* tension was giving me a headache, and I always eat when I have a headache, but this food was past enjoying. Besides, I was starting to get just a bit plump again—some women might be able to stay wand-slim no matter what they ate, but my dresses got tight if I even *looked* at a plate of *tourtes*. So very unfair. At least food like this was easy to push away.

"So you're to be *Gonfalonier*?" Sancha was bubbling now at Juan. "Our bold leader against the French! I see bravery in the Borgias isn't limited to just one brother!"

"One might doubt that," Cesare murmured.

"My husband wanted to lead the papal forces, you know." Lucrezia laughed. "Can you imagine? He has trouble enough with those Pesarese captains of his, and now he wants papal soldiers! He thinks he's Alexander the Great, you know; too ridiculous—"

Sancha tittered and Juan guffawed; even Rodrigo had a chuckle at his son-in-law's expense and I couldn't blame him either because Lord Sforza had gotten very sour this past year and spent most of his last visit pestering my Pope for money. But I couldn't help looking at Lucrezia—sixteen years old now but as poised as a woman of twice as many years, wearing a purple-and-crimson gown cut as low as Sancha's, rubies in her ears and rouge patted on her cheeks and a ring on every finger. She looked eager and glittering, greedy for every eye to be on her, and I thought back to the gently glowing girl who had first blushed at her new husband over my *cena* table.

Well, such girls grew up. And Lucrezia had acted alongside me as her father's hostess this past winter, finally old enough to take her place as the star of the papal court—perhaps it had gone to her head just a little. It certainly would have gone to mine at her age. I had only twenty-two years to my name, but sometimes I felt distinctly world-weary.

They were talking of that mad priest Fra Savonarola now, the one preaching and frothing at the mouth in Florence and getting everyone to give up their cards and their fine clothes and all their other luxuries. "Only in Florence," Juan snickered. "That would never work in Rome!"

"My Giulia might give up cards," Rodrigo said, giving my cheek an affectionate tweak. "But never her pearls!"

"As if anyone would go about in sackcloth just because one sour old man said puffed sleeves were heretical!" Lucrezia laughed.

"I don't know about heretical," I said, sipping my sour wine. "But puffed sleeves are certainly unflattering. And really, what's more heretical than that?"

Sancha plucked at her puffed sleeves, shooting me a nasty look.

"You'd be the only one safe under Savonarola, eh, brother?" Juan cast an eye over the unadorned black Cesare usually wore instead of his red cardinal's robes. "Maybe you should have been a Dominican! I'll fight the French and you'll preach hellfire."

"Careful, brother," said Cesare. "Or you might taste it."

Juan just beckoned in invitation, laughing. The two brothers should have looked alike—both tall and lean, both auburn-haired, both handsome—but they didn't. Not at all, and Juan's jittering overbright eyes met Cesare's still, black-steel gaze like a cross of swords. Sancha looked between them with parted lips, and Lucrezia cast her eyes up to the ceiling and said, "Really, you're both such *children*!" But I felt a twinge of disquiet.

"You'll have seen the new frescoes, Juan," I jumped in brightly. "But surely not examined them yet? Perhaps we can take a closer look, before the *biscotti* are brought in. Your figure shows to great advantage . . ."

I took my wine-cup in one hand, tucking the other into Rodrigo's broad arm, and we all rose from the *cena* table and flocked to the walls. "I *love* me as Santa Caterina," Lucrezia sighed over her own beseeching golden-haired figure. "I still have that dress . . ."

"I don't see why Joffre and I were just figures in the crowd," Sancha pouted. "I could have been a saint too, you know!"

"Or Salome," Juan leered. "The Dance of the Seven Veils—we'd get to see what you look like under the last one, new sister—"

"*Juan!*" Joffre burst out, flushing, but Sancha laughed and struck Juan a playful blow with her fan. One of those tiresome girls who is always doing something flirtatious with her fan. How I longed to smack her with it.

"My likeness is to be in the Resurrection fresco," my Pope was saying, oblivious. "When I have time to sit for it, that is—"

"And you really should *make* the time," I scolded. "Poor Maestro Pinturicchio has already finished everything else!"

"I don't like being painted," Rodrigo complained. "An utter waste of time!"

"But part of a pope's duty is to be preserved for posterity. You'll look magnificent, just wait and see." My Pope was sixty-five now, and he had put on weight now that he had no more time for the hunting and riding that had long kept him lean. But his massive shoulders were imposing as ever, his swarthy hawk-nosed profile just as confident, his vigorous dark hair only threaded with gray. The papal bull at the height of his powers.

"This marks the beginning of everything." My Pope beamed all about him: his children painted on the wall, his children clustered around him. "*La familia* reunited! Let's drink to it again."

His eyes were once more full of emotion, but I saw Cesare still glaring at Juan, saw Lucrezia biting her lips to make them redder, saw Sancha aiming hot looks at both her brothers-in-law, and Joffre stare vengefully at Sancha. I saw it all, and all I could think was a horribly, woefully inadequate *Oh, dear.*

But Rodrigo was looking at me expectantly, so I raised my goblet.

"*La familia* reunited," I echoed and drank in a prayer along with the wine.

S uch gloom, Giulia!" Rodrigo leaned back on his elbows against the pillows with their papal crest embroidered in gold. "When did you turn doom-cryer?"

"I'm only saying that it's vastly overrated, having all one's family together." I plucked the diamond roses out of my hair and began unlacing my moss-green velvet sleeves. "Holy Virgin knows, it's a disaster whenever my family are all in the same room. In no time my older brother is telling Sandro he's a prancing lightweight even if he is Cardinal Farnese now, and my sister is telling me I'm a harlot. And your children are even worse! Juan and Cesare looked ready to draw daggers over the *biscotti.*"

"Brothers compete. It's what they do." My Pope waved a hand, dismissive, and his massive papal ring glinted in the soft light from the tapers. "It brings out the best in both of them."

"I'll remind you of those words when the blood hits the walls," I said tartly, letting both my sleeves drop. "Why ever did you settle on Cesare for the church? Anyone can see he's born to lead armies and swing swords—"

"But he's cunning, and one needs that in the church." Rodrigo poured out a cup of wine for the two of us to share. "To survive in the College of Cardinals, you have to be able to outplot a spider."

"But he's not suited for priestly vows. Not in the slightest!"

Rodrigo laughed, gesturing around him. "Are any of us?" His private chamber was dim and rich, the walls hung in painted canvas that had been laid over in elaborate gilt designs, the bed elaborately curtained in crimson velvet embroidered with the papal crest again, silver brackets everywhere lighting the room with sweet-smelling beeswax tapers. My Pope used to visit me in my official domicile at the Palazzo Santa Maria, by way of a certain passage so very private that all Rome knew about it. But his wave of protectiveness after my return from the French army still hadn't abated, and now I slept more than half my nights at the papal apartments here in the Vatican, where Rodrigo had the sheets scattered with petals from my favorite yellow climbing roses, which he claimed looked like me. I looked around at the silks, the rose petals, the gilt and the glass and the velvet, all overlaid by that somber papal crest, and had to concede that it was not really very papal at all.

"Is your conscience bothering you?" Rodrigo made the sign of the cross over my forehead with his thumb. "*Ego te absolvo a peccatis tuis in nomine Patris, et Filii, et Spiritus Sancti.* There, you are washed clean of all your sins. Come kiss me."

I smiled and kissed him. The state of my soul had bothered me a great deal when I first became a harlot, a fallen woman, a foul adulteress, take your choice of epithets. But it's difficult to worry about the fires of hell when I get my divine forgiveness expressly from the Holy Father whenever I want it. I kissed him again, and then turned my back so he could unlace my moss-green velvet gown with the gold vines embroidered about the bosom and hem. "So you chose Cesare for the church—"

Rodrigo groaned, his fingers deft on the laces down my back. "Let it be, Giulia!"

I persisted. "—but why ever did you choose *Juan* for the military life?"

"Because that's how it always is." Rodrigo tickled the back of my neck with one of my golden bodice ribbons, making me squeal. "One son for the church, one for the battlefield."

"You men!" I couldn't help saying. "Slotting your children into various spaces the moment they're born, as if they were vases to be put into a niche! Just because you have two sons doesn't make them automatically fit for the Church *or* the battlefield, you know."

"Juan's full of fire. He'll make a fine Gonfalonier."

"Juan is interested in nothing but carousing, drinking, and chasing after women. I know how you've missed him while he was in Spain, but I have to say I have *not* missed the way he ogles me."

Or the way Juan teased Lucrezia for the spot on her chin she had tried to cover up with powder, or jeered at Joffre for padding the shoulders of his doublet in an effort to look more the man for Sancha. Or aimed a kick at my little pet goat who trailed me on a gilt leather leash. I loved that goat, had loved him since I'd rescued him from ending up in a *tourte* when he was just a floppy-eared baby kid, and Juan had put him bleating into the wall with one boot!

"Juan's just a boy," my Pope was saying with all his usual tolerance, unknotting a tangled ribbon at my back. "Perhaps he ogles you, but he ogles every beautiful woman he sees! He doesn't mean anything by it."

He'd cuckold you in a heartbeat, I thought, but didn't say it. To some things Rodrigo was entirely blind, and when it came to his favorite son . . . he hadn't even noticed this evening after *cena* when Juan flung an arm about my waist, looking at my likeness in Pinturicchio's fresco. "Our family harlot as the Madonna," he breathed hotly into my ear, and his fingers stole down to cup my hip. "How's that for irony, eh?"

I'd just smiled, giving his hand a good covert smack. "And this harlot will knock your ears around the back of your head if you touch her again, Juan Borgia."

I'd been able to intimidate him when he was sixteen, but not now. He'd just given me another lingering up-and-down look, and swaggered ahead to join Lucrezia and Sancha as they studied the Annunciation fresco with its angels and arabesques.

"Did you see Juan slavering over Sancha?" I said over my shoulder to Rodrigo, feeling the last of my tight laces come loose. "I thought poor Joffre was going to pop with outrage."

"She's a flirt, that one." Rodrigo chuckled, sliding the gown off my shoulders.

"And now all *three* of your sons are competing for her!" I stepped out of the circle of my gown on the floor. "If that's not a recipe for disaster—"

"Bah," Rodrigo dismissed, and pressed his lips to my shoulder above the edge of my filmy shift. "Take your hair down, *mi perla*. It's a sight I never tire of seeing—one of the great wonders of the world, your hair."

I attacked my pins, and he fell back on his elbows again, happily watching the first of my coiled plaits slither loose over my shoulder. My

Pope clearly had no interest in hearing any more about the shortcomings of his sons. He had lost his eldest son Pedro Luis many years ago in Spain; a memory that still veiled his eyes in grief whenever he spoke of it, and after that old loss I suppose his indulgence to his surviving children was understandable. "A pity Lord Sforza couldn't join us," I said by way of changing the subject. "I know he misses Lucrezia in Pesaro."

"Let him miss her. He's a waffling fool, and more than that, he's turned out to be a mediocre *condottiere* who does nothing but ask me for money. I wish I'd known *that* when I was considering his offer for her hand!" My Pope reached out to catch a lock of my loosened hair and bring it to his nose, inhaling deeply. I had expensive perfumes by the dozen in glass vials, but part of me was still a country girl, the girl who grew up in a tiny town beside Lake Bolsena and boiled flowers to make perfume, and I still preferred my old homemade scents of honeysuckle and gillyflower to all those expensive mixtures of frankincense and bergamot. "I heard from another mediocre *condottiere* today, you know," my Pope went on, inhaling my hair again.

"Who?"

"Monoculus."

"That's a cruel nickname, Rodrigo. He is not one-eyed; it's just a tiny squint." But I couldn't help a faint smile as I unraveled the last of my plaits. At least my Pope could joke now about my husband. Rodrigo was not jealous when other men looked at me—he just chuckled when envious archbishops ogled my bosom, or florid young lords paid me honeyed compliments. He liked being envied. But Orsino still worried my Pope sometimes. Orsino was my wedded husband; a man with the legal right to demand I return to his side, if he ever grew a spine and chose to exercise that right. Even the Holy Father could not really excommunicate a man for demanding that his wife cease committing adultery.

"That chinless little snip can't even scrape up the courage to ask me himself when he wants money," Rodrigo continued with a snort. "Instead he applies to his mother and gets her to ask me. This time, it's to pay his soldiers. They don't listen to him unless their pay is current. Or even when it *is* current. There's one son who should *not* have been slated for the battlefield!" My husband's family the Orsini had been among those to side with the French upon their march south—at least, the more illustrious and prosperous branches of the Orsini. Not Orsino, however, whose mother was cousin and firm friend to Rodrigo. Where his mother led, Orsino followed.

"We don't need to discuss Orsino, do we?" I shook my hair down, rippling clear to the floor, and Rodrigo clapped a hand to his chest as though pierced through the heart by the sight. I climbed onto the vast bed, sitting cross-legged like a tailor, and pulled his feet into my lap. People think it's all jewels and gowns and keeping yourself pretty, being a mistress, but I've found it's a good deal more about peace. Powerful men, whether kings of vast nations or lords of uncounted wealth or fathers of the world's souls, are *tired* men. A thousand voices clamor every moment for their attention, their time, their favors; everyone wants something and they all want it now. When my Pope came to me at the end of the day, he could at least relax with the knowledge that I wanted nothing but him. "Your feet are hurting you again, aren't they?" I scolded softly, rubbing his toes. "Why can't you sit still when you're dictating letters to your secretaries, instead of pacing like a madman . . ."

He gave a groan of pleasure, but his eyes were serious as they looked at me. "Does Orsino still write to you, Giulia?"

"He does," I said.

"What does he write?"

Still a note of anxiety in my Pope's deep voice. "Nothing very much," I said, kneading my thumbs into the arch of his right foot. "Read the letters anytime you wish."

"Oh, I trust *you*. It's Monoculus I don't trust. He wants you back."

"Always," I admitted. It had been a bargain my husband had made, or his mother Adriana da Mila had advised him to make: take little Giulia Farnese for a wife, let Rodrigo Borgia have her for a concubine, and he will advance your career, my dear boy! Orsino had regretted that bargain since the day he saw me at our wedding, but he still took the rewards, didn't he? A *condotta* to hire soldiers, a hefty annuity, a *castello* in Carbognano and governorship over the town to go with it . . .

My husband had been everything a girl could dream of: handsome, young, and he even said he loved me. I didn't know if I believed that, really—he didn't even know me. But he said he'd loved me since the moment he'd laid eyes on me, and he certainly had his heart in his eyes whenever he looked at me, and that would be enough for most girls. But it *wasn't* enough. What no one bothers to tell dreaming girls is that a handsome and adoring young husband isn't any use if he's gutless.

Still, a gutless husband is better than a brutal one. I'd have to go back to him someday, when either my Pope died or his passion for me did, and I gave a little sigh at the thought. Hopefully the first of those fates wouldn't happen for many, many years—and maybe the second wouldn't happen at all. Rodrigo had no cause to be anxious about Orsino—my husband would never muster up the courage to demand me back, no matter how many laws he had on his side.

"That's enough about Monoculus, eh?" Rodrigo ran a hand over my shoulder, the edge of my shift sliding down my arm. "My children too. It's making you morose."

"That batch of quarreling pups you fathered would make anybody morose!" I said lightly, and Rodrigo brightened just as I'd intended.

"I'll have you know my children are perfect." He pulled me up into his arms. "Shall we make another? A Borgia prince this time, a brother for Laura . . ."

"Juan won't be very happy about that," I murmured between kisses. "He went into such a sulk when I was carrying Laura . . ." Worried any child of mine would supplant him as the Pope's favorite. In truth Rodrigo had always been just a trifle veiled in his affection for Laura. She *was* his daughter, of that I was perfectly certain—you had only to look at the nose (though I did hope she wouldn't grow up with his bull shoulders). But she'd been christened under my husband's name, and in truth when I counted backward from nine months there *had* been a time when I was trying to persuade Orsino to show just a little courage, enough to fight for his wife if he truly wanted to keep her . . .

But I couldn't think of Orsino, not with Rodrigo bending his dark head to plant unhurried kisses across my naked shoulders. "Come to me," he whispered in his Catalan Spanish, and I threaded my arms around his neck and slid myself over him, making my hair into a candlelit curtain shutting out the world.

When I was a foolish virgin girl, I'd prayed very earnestly not to be married off to an old man as so many of my friends were. I dreamed of lean cavaliers and dashing poets, and what girl doesn't? But girls are fools. Poets aren't much good when it comes to love play, when you really think about it—all Dante ever managed to do after years of mooning after Beatrice was fantasize that she might one day give him a guided tour of Paradise. And as for lean cavaliers, well, Orsino had been the picture of a dashing young suitor, and our coupling had been awkward, clumsy, embarrassing, and brief. And afterward, he had stood back and given me away.

My Pope *savored* me every time he took me in his arms, tasted my skin and inhaled my hair, kissed me and cradled me and found something new in me every time to caress. "The curve of your spine is like a string of pearls," he would muse, and trace his lips over my back until I was vibrating down to my toes. Or he would drop slow tantalizing kisses over every part of my face from my ears to my chin, everywhere but my lips, until I dragged his mouth down against mine. He liked me bold and never accused me of being wanton; he tossed me and teased me, made me laugh and made me cry out—and my husband might have given me to Rodrigo, but Rodrigo had never forced me. "I've never had a woman by force, and I don't intend to start now," he'd told me on our first meeting, and then stood back in utter confidence to let *me* choose. It's not often a woman has a chance to choose, let me tell you. And I'd considered my options: the handsome young husband with the clumsy hands, or the ecclesiastical lover of more than sixty years who could curl my whole body up in shudders of pleasure?

Well.

"My papal bull," I whispered, and felt the rumble of laughter deep in his chest above me.

He slept afterward, his head heavy on my breast, my arms showing pale about his swarthy shoulders in the flickering candlelight, my hair coiling over us both. "Everything will be perfect now," he murmured, half-asleep. "You at my side, Juan returned, *la familia* reunited . . . the French defeated . . ." A yawn. "God has been kind, *mi perla.*"

Unease twinged at me again, and I didn't know why. Not until I rose and dressed and tiptoed out, back to the Palazzo Santa Maria so the Pope would be found alone in his bed in the morning by his entourage, as was proper (even if they all knew I'd been keeping him company there). I yawned as I trailed through the darkened papal apartments, and my feet slowed in the Sala dei Santi as I looked again at the finished frescoes all the Borgia family had admired last night at *cena*. I looked past the frescoes this time, Juan as proud Turk and Cesare as merciless emperor and Lucrezia as pleading saint, to the Borgia bull motif repeated over and over in the floors and the walls. Not the placid grazing ox that had been the family emblem when they were merely the lowly *Borja* of Spain, but a massive defiant beast gazing about with arrogant eyes. In public appearances Rodrigo displayed his papal emblem of the crossed keys, the keys to the kingdom of Heaven. But here there were no keys and no Heaven either. There were saints on every wall, but it was the Borgias who dominated—the Borgias and their pagan bull.

"God has been kind," Rodrigo had said. *La familia* united again, as they had not been for years, and the French had been swindled and outplayed by my wily Pope who had played that spotty French King like a harp, vowing eternal friendship and whispering confidential promises, and all the while he had been piecing together a Holy League to oppose them. Rome, Spain, Milan, Venice, even the Holy Roman Emperor; all allied against the French who had found themselves outnumbered and surrounded in Naples. What a victory—and with the French fleeing their shattered campaign, what enemy was there to oppose my Pope and his family?

And last night they had celebrated in these rooms, which might have an Annunciation and a Nativity and a Resurrection painted on the walls . . . but which glorified not God, but Borgia.